# Golden Girl

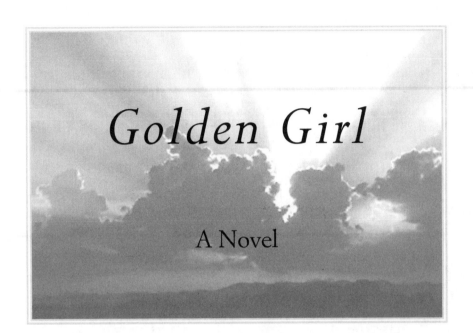

# Golden Girl

## A Novel

# Elin Hilderbrand

Little, Brown and Company

*New York   Boston   London*

Little, Brown and Company
Hachette Book Group
1290 Avenue of the Americas, New York, NY 10104
littlebrown.com

First Edition: June 2021

Little, Brown and Company is a division of Hachette Book Group, Inc. The Little, Brown name and logo are trademarks of Hachette Book Group, Inc.

The publisher is not responsible for websites (or their content) that are not owned by the publisher.

The Hachette Speakers Bureau provides a wide range of authors for speaking events. To find out more, go to hachettespeakersbureau.com or call (866) 376-6591.

ISBN 978-0-316-42008-2 (hardcover) / 978-0-316-27863-8 (large print) / 978-0-316-29449-2 (Canadian) / 978-0-316-26957-5 (signed) / 978-0-316-26967-4 (Barnes & Noble signed) / 978-0-316-32398-7 (Barnes & Noble) / 978-0-316-29557-4 (Target)

LCCN 2020951492

Printing 1, 2021

LSC-W

Printed in the United States of America

*To my children, Maxwell, Dawson, and Shelby*
*I will never leave you*

# Martha

She receives a message from the front office: a new soul is about to join them, and this soul has been assigned to Martha.

Martha puts on her reading glasses and finds her clipboard. The soul is arriving from...Nantucket Island.

Martha is both surprised and delighted. Surprised because Nantucket Harbor is where Martha met her own fateful end two summers ago and she'd thought the front office was intentionally keeping her away from coastal areas so she didn't become (as Gen Z said) "triggered."

And Martha is delighted because...well, who doesn't love Nantucket?

Martha swoops down from the northeast so that her first glimpse of the island is the lighthouse that stands sentry at the end of the slender golden arm of Great Point. Martha spies seals frolicking just off the coast (and sharks stalking them a little farther out). She continues over Polpis Harbor, where the twelve-year-old class of Nantucket Community Sailing are taking their lessons in Optimists. One boat keels *way* over and comes dangerously close to capsizing. Martha blows a little puff of air—and the boat rights itself.

Martha dips over the moors, dotted with ponds and crisscrossed with sandy roads. She sees deer hiding deep in the woods. A Jeep is stuck in the soft sand by Jewel Pond; next to the Jeep, a young man lets a stream of swears fly (*My oh my,* Martha thinks) while his girlfriend tries to get a cell signal. She's sorry, she says, she just really wanted the early-morning light for her Instagram photos.

Martha chooses the scenic coastal route along the uninterrupted stretch of the south shore. Despite the early hour, there are plenty of people out and about. A woman-of-a-certain-age throws a tennis ball into the rolling waves for a chocolate-Lab-of-a-certain-age. (Martha misses dogs! She's far too busy to ever make it over to the Pet Division.) A white haired gentleman charges into the water for his morning swim. There are a handful of fishermen out on Smith's Point, a cadre of young (and *very* attractive) surfers at Cisco, and a foursome teeing off—*thwack!*—from the first hole at the Miacomet Golf Course.

As Martha floats over Nobadeer Beach, she sees the town lifeguards gathering in the parking lot. Their conditioning session starts at a quarter past seven and it's nearly that time now. Martha has to hurry.

She has one more minute to appreciate the island on this clear, blue morning of Saturday, June 19—the sun glints off the gold cupola atop the Unitarian church; a line chef at Black-Eyed Susan's runs full speed down India Street, late for his shift. Across most of the island, irrigation systems switch on, sprinkling lawns and flower boxes, but not out in Sconset, where residents like to do things the old-fashioned way: they put on gardening clogs and grab watering cans. People are pouring their first cups of coffee, reading the front page of the *Nantucket Standard*. The thirty-five women who will be getting married today open their eyes and experience varying degrees of anticipation and anxiety. Contractors pull into Marine Home Center because they have punch lists that need to be completed *yesterday;* the summer people are arriving, they want their homes up and running. Charter fishing boats motor out of the harbor; the first batch of sugar doughnuts is pulled from the oven at the Downyflake—and oh, the scent!

Martha sighs. Nantucket isn't heaven, but it is heaven on Earth.

However, she isn't here to sightsee. She's here to collect a soul.

The pinned location on Martha's map is Kingsley Road, almost at the intersection of Madaket but not quite.

Martha arrives with a full thirty seconds to spare, giving her a chance to inhale the heady fragrance of the lilacs that are in full bloom below. There's a dark-haired woman with fantastic legs jogging down the road, singing along to her music, but the rest of Kingsley is quite sleepy.

Fifteen seconds, ten seconds, five seconds. Martha double-checks her coordinates; it says she's in the right place...

In the time that Martha takes her gaze off the road, tragedy strikes. It happens quickly, the literal blink of an eye. Martha winces. *What a pity!*

*All right,* Martha thinks. *Time to get to work.*

# Vivi

It's a beautiful June day, the kind that Vivi writes about. In fact, all thirteen of Vivian Howe's novels—beach reads set on Nantucket—start in June. Vivi has never considered changing this habit because June on Nantucket is when things *begin.* The summer is a newborn; it's still innocent, pristine, a blank page.

At a few minutes past seven, Vivi is ready for her run. She takes the same route she's taken ever since she moved into Money Pit ten years ago, after her divorce: down her dirt road, Kingsley, to the Madaket Road bike path. The path goes all the way to the beach, though Vivi hasn't made it that far in years. Her hips. Also, she doesn't have time.

Vivi is agitated despite the sunshine, the bluebird sky, and the luscious bloom of the peonies in her cutting garden. The night before, Vivi's daughter Willa called to say that she's pregnant again. This marks Willa's fourth pregnancy since last June, which was when she and Rip got married.

"Oh, Willie!" Vivi said. "Yay, hurray—good, good news! How far along are you?"

"Six weeks," Willa said.

*Still very, very early,* Vivi thinks. Willa basically *just* missed her period. "You took a test?"

"Yes, Mother."

"More than one?"

"Two," Willa said. "The first was inconclusive. The second had two lines."

What Vivi did *not* say was *Don't get your hopes up.* Willa had miscarried three times. The first pregnancy had progressed to fifteen weeks. Willa started bleeding while she was giving a tour of the Hadwen House to a group of VIPs from the governor's office. She ran out on the tour and drove herself to the hospital. It was a horrible day, the most physically painful and difficult of the three miscarriages, though after the third, Willa became convinced there was a problem.

A thorough examination at the Brigham and Women's fertility clinic in Boston, however, showed nothing wrong. Willa was a healthy twenty-four-year-old. She had no problem getting pregnant. If Rip even looked at her, she conceived.

Privately, Vivi suspected the miscarriages had something to do with Willa's type A personality, which Vivi and her ex-husband, JP, used to call her "type A-plus personality," because regular As were never good enough for Willa.

"If this doesn't work out, why don't you and Rip take a break? You're so young. You have years and years, decades even, to conceive. What's the *rush?*"

Predictably, Willa had become defensive. "What makes you think this won't work out? Do you think I'm a failure?"

"You succeed at everything you do," Vivi said. "I just think your body might benefit from a reset—"

"I'm *pregnant,* Mama," Willa said. "I will give birth to a perfectly healthy baby." She sounded like she was trying to convince herself.

"You *will* give birth to a perfectly healthy baby, Willie. I can't wait to hold her." Though Vivi didn't feel quite old enough to be a grandmother. She was only fifty-one and in terrific shape, if she did say so herself. Her dark hair, which she wore in a pixie cut, didn't have one strand of gray (Vivi checked every morning). She might occasionally be mistaken for the child's mother. (Well, she could hope.)

The conversation had ended there but an unsettled feeling had lingered in Vivi through the night. Are children ever punished for the mistakes of their parents, she wondered, or was that just her novelist's mind at work?

Vivi had woken up at five thirty, not only because it was June and sunlight streamed in through the windows like it was high noon, but also because she heard a noise. When she crept out into the hallway, she saw her daughter Carson stumbling up the stairs, smelling distinctly of marijuana.

Vivi had last seen Carson the afternoon before, dressed for work in cutoff jeans and her marigold-yellow Oystercatcher T-shirt, her dark hair still a little damp, neat in two French braids. Carson was the most attractive of Vivi's three children, though of course Vivi wasn't supposed to think that. Carson alone favored JP—the dark hair, the clear, glass-green eyes, the fine pointed nose, and teeth that came in white, straight, and even. She was a Quinboro through and through, whereas both Willa and Leo favored the Howes. They'd inherited Vivi's overbite and crowded lowers and spent years in braces.

Carson was still in her cutoffs, but she had downgraded her T-shirt to something that looked like a silver-mesh handkerchief that only just covered her breasts and left her midriff and back bare except for one slender chain. She had no shoes on; her hair was out of its braids but held kinky waves. When she saw her mother standing at the top of the stairs, her eyebrows shot up.

"Madre," she said. "What's good?"

"Are you just getting home?" Vivi asked, though the answer was obvious. Carson was walking in at five thirty in the morning when her shift had ended at eleven. She was twenty-one, fine, so she'd had a drink at work and she probably went to the Chicken Box to catch the band's last set, then she either went to the beach with friends or hooked up with a random stranger.

"Yes, ma'am." Carson sounded sober, but that only served to make Vivi angrier.

"The summer isn't going to be like this, Carson," Vivi said.

"I hope you're right," Carson said. "Work was slow, my tips were trash, the guys at the Box all looked like they were on the junior-high fencing team."

"You can't stay out all night then come home reeking of marijuana—"

*"Reeking of marijuana,"* Carson mimicked.

Vivi searched for extra patience, which was like trying to find a lost shoe in the depths of her maternal closet. *This is Carson.* Ten years earlier, when Vivi learned that her husband, JP, had fallen in love with his employee Amy, Vivi had moved out. All three kids took it hard, but especially Carson. Carson had been almost eleven years old and unusually attached to Vivi. Vivian's novel that year, *Along the South Shore,* had been something of a breakout book, and Vivi, wanting to escape the inevitable divorce fallout—people asking what happened, people asking was she okay, people telling her she was brave—had gone on a twenty-nine-stop book tour that kept her away for seven weeks (she'd missed the first day of school and Carson's birthday). By the time Vivi got back, Carson had changed from the funny little spitfire of the family to a "troubled child" who threw tantrums, swore, picked fights with her siblings, and generally did everything in her power to get attention. Vivi blamed the transformation on JP's affair (which their therapist had insisted they not disclose to the children), and JP blamed it on what he called Vivi's "abandonment."

Ten years had passed. Carson was no longer a little girl but she still had her challenging moments.

"This is my house," Vivi said. "I pay the mortgage, the taxes, the insurance, the electric bill, the heating bill, the cable bill. I do the shopping and make the meals. While you're sleeping under this roof, I don't want you out all night drinking, smoking, and having sex with complete strangers. Do you know how that *looks?*" Vivi stopped just short of reminding Carson that she'd already had chlamydia once, the previous summer. "You're setting a rotten example for your brother."

"He doesn't need me to set an example," Carson said. "He has Willa. I'm the screwup. It's my job to be a hideous disappointment."

"No one said you were a hideous disappointment, sweetheart."

"I'm twenty-one," Carson said. "I can drink legally. I can smoke pot legally."

"Since you're so grown up," Vivi said, "you can move out on your own."

"That's the plan," Carson said. "I'm saving."

*You're* not *saving,* Vivi wanted to say. Carson made good tips at the Oystercatcher but she spent them—on drinks, on weed, on clothes from Erica Wilson, Milly and Grace, the Lovely. Carson had finally dropped out of UVM after struggling through five semesters—her cumulative GPA was a 1.6—and although Vivi was initially aghast (an education makes you good company for yourself!), she knew college wasn't for everyone.

"I'm not giving you a curfew," Vivi said. "But this behavior won't be tolerated."

*"This behavior won't be tolerated,"* Carson mimicked. It was the response of a seven-year-old, and yet it brought the reaction Carson wanted. Vivi took a step toward her, arm tensed. "Are you going to spank me?" Carson asked.

"Of course not," Vivi said, though she kind of wanted to. "But you have to clean up your act, babe, or I'll ask you to leave."

"Fine," Carson said. "I'll go to Dad's."

"I'm sure Amy would take *very kindly* to you coming home like this."

"She's not as bad as you think," Carson said. "When you demonize her, you show how insecure you are."

Vivi stared at her child, but before she could come up with a response, she smelled something. "Did you...cook?" Vivi asked.

Carson stepped into the bedroom and slammed the door behind her.

Vivi flew down the stairs to the kitchen, which was filling with black smoke. The leftover sausage and basil pasta from last night's dinner was in Vivi's brand-new All-Clad three-quart sauté pan on a lit burner. The inside of the pan was charred black. Vivi turned the burner off, grabbed a towel, carried the smoldering pan outside, and set it on the flagstone path. It was so hot, it would have scorched the deck or the lawn.

Brand-new pan, ruined.

The sausage and basil pasta in a luscious mustard cream sauce, which Vivi had been thinking of taking over to Willa's as a peace offering, ruined.

And what if Vivi hadn't gotten out of bed? What if the kitchen had caught fire; what if flames had engulfed Money Pit while Vivi— and Leo—were sleeping? They would all be dead!

Back in the kitchen, Vivi caught sight of her bottle of Casa Dragones tequila on the side counter next to a shot glass. She felt a formidable strain of fury brewing inside her. That tequila was *hers;* she wouldn't even let her (almost-ex-) boyfriend, Dennis, make margaritas with it. Carson had come home, put the pasta on a burner, done two—or three?—shots of *Vivi's* tequila, which Carson knew was *not for public consumption,* and then left the pasta to burn on the stove.

Vivi marched back up the stairs and pounded on Carson's locked door.

"You left the pan on an open flame!" Vivi said. Leo would definitely be awake now, which Vivi felt bad about because it was Saturday morning, but oh, well. "What is *wrong* with you, Carson? Do you honestly not think about *anyone* but yourself? Do you not think, period?" There was no response. Vivi kicked the door.

"Please go away" came the response from inside. "I'm trying to sleep."

"And you drank my tequila!" Vivi said. "Which you know is off-limits."

"I didn't drink the tequila," Carson said. "I haven't had a drink since I left the Chicken Box and that was hours ago."

Vivi blinked. Carson sounded like she was telling the truth and she had seemed sober. "Who drank it, then?"

There was a pause before Carson said, "Well, who else lives here?"

*Leo?* Vivi thought. She looked at Leo's bedroom door, which was shut tight. Leo had been going to high-school parties since he was a sophomore, but a run-in with Jägermeister had propelled him away from the hard stuff. He drank Bud Light and the occasional White Claw.

Vivi turned back to Carson's door. "You are scrubbing that pot, young lady," she said. "Or buying me a new one."

After Vivi poured herself some coffee, opened all the windows, turned both sailcloth ceiling fans to high, washed the shot glass, and hid what remained of the Casa Dragones in the laundry room (her kids would never find it there), she calmed down a bit. She was the mother of three *very young adults* and parenting very young adults required just as much patience as parenting very young children. No one ever talked about this; it felt like a dirty little secret. Vivi had always imagined that by the time her kids were twenty-four, twenty-one, and eighteen, they'd all be drinking wine together around the outdoor table by the pool, and the kids would be cooking, clearing, and giving Vivi sage investment advice. Ha.

Vivi ties up her running shoes and stretches her hamstrings, using the bumper of her Jeep—then she clicks on her iTunes on her phone and takes off.

Carson makes Vivi's running playlists, which she has named Nine-Pound Hammer, Strawberry Cough, and White Fire OG. (It took Vivi a while to figure out that these were all strains of marijuana, probably the ones that Carson was smoking when she made the respective playlists.)

Today, Vivi listens to Nine-Pound Hammer. Shuffle.

The first song is "All That and More," by Rainbow Kitten Surprise. The best thing about Carson as DJ is that Vivi is exposed to music she never would have heard otherwise. Over the past few months Vivi has become an avid fan of this song; it's both folksy and bouncy. *All I ever wanted was to make you happy . . .*

Just as Vivi turns the volume up, her phone whistles with a text from Dennis, her (almost-ex-) boyfriend, who is out deep-sea fishing. The text is a picture of Dennis in his wraparound sunglasses smiling, revealing the gap between his two front teeth. He's holding up a striped bass. The caption says *Dinner!*

Vivi doesn't answer. A week or so earlier, she told Dennis that she needed some space, and she asked him not to spend the night at her house anymore. Predictably, this resulted in Dennis giving Vivi even less space than usual. He texts and calls and "checks in" and assumes Vivi will want to grill up the striped bass he's caught. Poor Dennis. Vivi met him three years ago when he came to Money

Pit to give her an estimate for central air. (Dennis owns a small HVAC company.) The AC was beyond Vivi's budget, but there had been chemistry between them and they started dating. Dennis works hard, plays hard, lives in the moment—fishing whenever he gets a chance in the summer, hunting in the fall, and he's the first person to get his scalloping license every year. He loves to drive his truck onto the beach and out into the moors; he showed Vivi hidden ponds and secret coves on the island that she'd never seen before, and she has lived on Nantucket three times as long as he has. JP once called Dennis "simple," but Vivi thinks of him as unencumbered. It was refreshing to date a man who could be happy with a good strong cup of coffee, an honest day's work, a swim in the ocean, a craft beer, and the sunset. He made Vivi laugh, he was her fierce champion, he was terrific in bed—and for a long while, this was all she needed or wanted.

She's not sure what happened; honestly, it was like God snapped Her fingers and all Vivi could see in Dennis was what he lacked, and everything he said and did started to chafe her. The magic is gone for Vivi and she suspects there will be no getting it back. She's ready to be a free woman again.

The lilacs along Kingsley Road are fragrant and full; they're peaking *today* and Vivi reminds herself to come back later and cut some for her bedside table. Next month, July, will be all about hydrangeas. Is another flower even photographed on Nantucket in July? Instagram would tell you no. Vivi inhales the scent of the lilacs and this improves her mood. When she gets home from her run, she will fix Carson some avocado toast with a slice of ripe hothouse tomato, a perfectly poached egg, and flaky sea salt on the excellent sourdough from Born and Bread. Food is Vivi's love language. Carson will know she's forgiven.

This summer, Carson is working as the head bartender at the Oystercatcher, a big old wooden shambles of a place, beat up in the best way, that sits right on Jetties Beach. There are low-slung chairs in the sand where people can have drinks while they wait to sit at one of the brightly painted picnic tables in the spacious open-air dining area. Up a few steps is the hostess station and a small stage that fits exactly one guitar player, one amp, and one mic. Up a few more steps there's the bar, the raw bar, the kitchen, and a retail shop that sells inflatable rafts, beach toys, T-shirts, sunscreen, and candy.

Vivi went to visit Carson at the Oystercatcher for the first time in mid-May, just after it opened for the season. There were a lot of familiar faces; Vivi and Dennis stopped to talk here and there before they took seats at the bar. Carson approached, seeming uncharacteristically shy.

"Can I get you two started with something to drink?"

She was already so professional and smooth! She recited the specials rapturously, like she was reading poetry. "The chef has prepared a shellfish pizza tonight, featuring..." Yes, yes, they definitely wanted the lobster and scallop pizza and they would start with a dozen oysters, a chopped salad, and the smoked blue-fish pâté.

Carson took their order without writing anything down. She looked adorable—the cutoffs, the T-shirt, a short black canvas apron tied around her waist that held her corkscrew and her bottle opener.

Carson busied herself polishing glasses, leaving Vivi to her sauvignon blanc and Dennis to his Bell's Two Hearted IPA. The guitar player started up, singing "Wonderwall," by Oasis. The sun was going down and it was getting chilly. Vivi considered asking Carson if she wanted her to grab her a cardigan from the car but she knew Carson would decline and, perhaps, tell her to stop acting like a mom, it was embarrassing.

Just then, Zach and Pamela Bridgeman took seats at the end of the bar. Vivi waved and Dennis raised his beer in their direction, but no words were exchanged. Pamela was the (much) older sister of Rip Bonham, Willa's husband, so they were, sort of, family. Pamela worked with Rip in the family's insurance agency and her husband, Zach, was an air traffic controller at Nantucket Memorial. Zach and Pamela had a son, Peter, who was in Leo's class, though the two boys weren't friends. At the beginning of their senior year, Peter and Leo had gotten into a fistfight at one of the Whaler football games. Peter had said something crass and pushed Leo, Leo pushed back, Peter swung, and a brawl ensued. Vivi blamed Peter—he had always been an odd, aggressive kid, and Leo was a sweetheart, a peacemaker who got along with everyone. What had Peter said to start the fight?

"Something stupid," Leo told Vivi. "He's a bully."

The stench of this incident had never really gone away; hence, conversation with the Bridgemans was a challenge. Vivi used to talk to Zach about books—they went through a simultaneous obsession with Greg Iles, then with Attica Locke—but at some point, Pamela made a snarky comment and Vivi realized that Pamela found the book conversations tiresome. If they didn't talk about books or about the boys, there was little to say.

What captured Vivi's attention was the way the Bridgemans' presence seemed to fluster Carson. She tripped on the rubber mat beneath her feet, tried to right herself, and crashed into a row of glassware.

"Oh, shi…zzle," she said, then clapped a hand over her mouth. "Hey, guys. What can I get you? To drink?"

"Hey." Pamela offered Carson a nonsmile smile. "May we see a menu?"

"I'll have a Maker's Mark over ice, please," Zach said.

"One Maker's on the rocks," Carson said. "And what about you, Pamela?"

"Menu?" Pamela said.

"Of course!" Carson said. She pulled a menu out of a slot and a couple of them fell to the floor, which she ignored.

"I didn't realize you were still working here," Pamela said. "I thought maybe you'd moved on to bigger and better things."

Vivi nearly choked on her wine. Who *said* things like that? Well, Pamela Bonham Bridgeman did.

Carson withdrew a couple of inches. "I used to be a barback. Now I'm...head bartender!"

"Good for you," Zach said.

"I'll have a Diet Coke," Pamela said.

"Coming right up," Carson said. "Will you two be having dinner?"

Pamela laughed. "I didn't come here just for a Diet Coke."

Vivi wanted to pipe up and say, *Can you please be nice? We're all family here.*

"Right, of course not," Carson said. "Let me get your drinks and then I'll take your order."

Carson's hands shook as she poured the bourbon; some spilled over the side of the glass, but she wiped the glass down with a bar towel and handed the glass to Zach, saying, "Oh, you need a menu too."

Pamela put on her reading glasses. Pamela's most distinctive feature was her hair. It was an unusual shade of dark red with an iconic stripe of white-blond in the front. She never wore makeup, and her skin still looked pretty good. (It was a pathetic habit of Vivi's to evaluate the appearance of other women to see if they were faring better or worse than Vivi herself. She had thought that by fifty, she would no longer care how she looked, but she'd been wrong. When *did* that happen? Sixty-five? Seventy-five? *Eighty*-five?)

Pamela leaned into her husband. "We'll share."

Dennis, perhaps noticing the Bridgemans' intimacy, bumped shoulders with Vivi and whispered, "She's doing real good."

*No*—well. *She's doing* really well, Vivi thought. But she had stopped correcting Dennis's grammar long ago. It would have been a full-time job.

"Yes!" Vivi said, too brightly. "She is." She eased away from Dennis and admitted to herself that the relationship was on its last, very weary pair of legs. She flagged down Carson. "Excuse me, most outstanding barkeep, may I please have another glass of wine?"

---

The second time Vivi visited Carson at the Oystercatcher was three days ago, right after Vivi had gotten two pieces of extraordinary news. She had received her first ever starred *McQuaid* review for her forthcoming novel, *Golden Girl*. And, as if that weren't enough, Tanya Price of *Great Morning USA* had liked the book so much that she wanted to interview Vivi on *national television*.

*I need a drink!* Vivi thought. She was elated that the book was getting this kind of major attention, but she was anxious as well. The book had...baggage.

Vivi overheard the Oystercatcher's manager, Nikki, say there was a two-hour wait for a table. The bar was three-deep; Vivi hadn't a prayer of getting a seat. She hung back and watched her daughter. What a difference a few weeks hado made. Carson was the leading lady in the night's production—taking drink orders, shaking up cocktails over her shoulder like she was playing a percussion instrument, setting out platters of oysters and cherrystones on crushed ice, calling back to the kitchen for extra horseradish, high-fiving her customers, ringing the bell every time someone threw a tip in the bucket on the bar. The live music hadn't yet started, but there was a 1980s playlist going—"Tainted Love" segued into "Don't You Want Me." People called out, "Carson, over here!" "Carson!"

Vivi eventually wiggled her way through to the bar, where she was wedged so tightly between two parties, she could practically read their minds. Then the party stuck to Vivi's backside left, and voilà! A seat opened up. Once Vivi had real estate, and a drink was becoming less of a faraway dream, she relaxed a bit.

The *McQuaid* review had been *glowing*. Vivi had legions of loyal readers, but she'd never quite captured the interest of the serious reviewers. The *McQuaid* reviews of her past books had been decidedly mediocre. They had called her first novel, *The Dune Daughters,* "three hundred pages of word salad," and because Vivi wasn't used to anyone (aside from the ruthless people at the Bread Loaf Conference) criticizing her writing, the review had come as an icy shock. She'd thought it was difficult enough getting a book *published,* but that was just the beginning. Bringing her book out into the world was like setting her heart on a platter and allowing the public to poke, prod, scrutinize, or—worst of all—ignore it.

Well, Vivian Howe was word salad no more!

Her first *McQuaid* starred review on her thirteenth try!

And *Great Morning USA*! National television coverage had eluded Vivi until now. Vivi wished her mother were still alive. Her mother had adored *Great Morning USA* and would have invited half of Parma, Ohio, over to watch.

Every indicator pointed to this book being *the big one.* Apparently, all Vivi had to do for this unprecedented attention…was write about the one thing she'd sworn to herself she'd keep secret.

Vivi snuffed this thought out just as Carson noticed her sitting at the bar and broke into a genuine smile.

*Ha!* Vivi thought. *Caught her by surprise.*

"Mama!" Carson said. "What can I get you?"

As Vivi jogs down Kingsley Road, she assures herself, as she does every morning, that her kids are fine. They're *fine!* Willa has a good job at the Nantucket Historical Association, and her husband, Rip, just inherited a summer cottage at the entrance of Smith's Point. Willa and Rip's life has become a dream—they now own a house in town *and* one at the beach. More important, Willa is pregnant again. Can Vivi let herself feel optimistic about this? Yes. Willa will be fine! The baby will be fine!

Carson will be a huge success at the Oystercatcher; she's on her way to becoming a Nantucket celebrity. She'll make money, garner attention, meet people, and take the next step: food and beverage director at a hotel or club. Or maybe she'll even start her own restaurant. Carson will be fine!

What about Leo? (He must have been the one who drank the tequila, Vivi thinks, but why? That was so unlike him.) When Leo was little, he was as sweet as dessert, but with every year that passed, he grew into more of a mystery to Vivi. He got good grades and played varsity football and lacrosse, he was well liked at school—but is he happy? Vivi can't quite say. *Still waters run deep* is the phrase that comes to mind when she thinks about her son. Who knows what's really going on in that mind of his, that heart? Leo's best friend is Cruz DeSantis. As far as Vivi's concerned, Cruz is family; he has his own place at the dining table, he knows where everything goes when he unloads the dishwasher, and Vivi has been listed as one of Cruz's emergency contacts since the kids were in kindergarten. All these years, Leo and Cruz have been insepa-rable—*Frick and freaking Frack,* Vivi calls them. When the boys got to high school, they discovered girls. Cruz started dating Jasmine Kelly in tenth grade, and in eleventh grade, Leo succumbed to the charms of Marissa Lopresti, who had been in hot pursuit of him since middle school.

Marissa is a *beautiful* girl—but like a bird or insect with brightly colored markings, she's dangerous. Vivi once overheard Marissa ridiculing one of her classmates' social media posts ("Look at Lindsay in this pic, she's such a cow, she needs to lose a hundred pounds and she should get a nose job while she's at it"), and Leo, to his credit, told her to ease up or go home. Marissa has no close girlfriends other than her older sister, Alexis—and for this reason, Marissa resents Leo's friendship with Cruz. She throws a tantrum any time Leo and Cruz have plans to hang out—go to breakfast, golf, sit in Leo's room and play Fortnite—and more than once, Marissa has invented family drama (a fight with her mother) or a health crisis (a supposed meningitis scare) to reclaim Leo's attention. It has been agonizing for Vivi to watch.

Vivi can only hope that Leo will break up with Marissa before he leaves for college in Boulder. He'll find another girlfriend; anyone would be an improvement.

Leo will be fine!

Another text comes in to her phone. *Oh, please,* she thinks, *not Dennis.*

No; the text is from Carson. Sorry about the pan, Mama, and the tequila wasn't me. I love you.

The tension in Vivi's neck and jaw releases. Her kids are fine.

The song changes to opening guitar chords that seize Vivi's attention. It's "Stone in Love," by Journey. Vivi almost trips over her own shoes. She stops and stares at her phone's screen. What is *this* song doing on the Nine-Pound Hammer playlist? Did Carson add it? But Carson *hates* classic rock; she calls it "music from beyond the grave."

Vivi is spooked. This song brings back such intense memories of high school that she feels if she turns her head, she'll see Brett Caspian standing in the middle of Kingsley Road. She nearly pushes the skip button, but she does love the song, despite her complicated history with it, and it's been so long since she's heard it. When she starts running again, she sings along, *Burning love comes once in a lifetime!*

Her eyes are closed and by the time she realizes something is wrong, it's too late—Vivi's neck snaps; her heart feels like a stick of dynamite exploding. Vivi is airborne, she's *flying*—until her head slams against the ground. Her leg. Something is wrong with her leg.

A tinny, faraway voice sings, *Golden girl, I'll keep you forever.*

Then the music stops. The dark turns to a velvety black. The quiet becomes silence.

# The Chief

Nantucket chief of police Ed Kapenash is on his way to work when he hears the call for an ambulance over the scanner. A woman's been found unresponsive near the Madaket bike path.

By the time he gets to the station, he has the low-down: A driver turning onto Kingsley Road from the Madaket Road noticed a woman lying on the ground. The driver pulled over and called 911. The woman's body was twisted and she was bleeding from the mouth and had a gash on her leg. The driver said he felt a faint pulse, but when the ambulance got her to Nantucket Cottage Hospital, she was pronounced dead.

Ed, sitting at his desk, bows his head. It's not even the summer solstice and they already have what sounds like a hit-and-run on their hands.

"Are you ready for the details you don't want to hear?" Sergeant Dixon asks. Dixon always seems to be the one who delivers the bad news.

"Yes," the Chief says, meaning no.

"The deceased is Vivian Howe, the writer. You know her, right?"

*Right,* Ed thinks. Andrea reads each new book of hers the day it comes out. He's learned that on the second Tuesday in July, he shouldn't say so much as a word to his wife. She reads those novels—all of which are set on Nantucket and have plots about one scandal or another (as if the poor island didn't have enough troubles without making more up!)—straight through the day and into the night. She hates to be interrupted.

The Chief and Andrea don't know the Howe woman personally, but they're all locals, so the Chief knows *of* her. Vivian Howe used to be married to JP Quinboro, who owns an ice cream parlor called the Cone on Old South Wharf. The Chief knows that Vivian Howe and JP Quinboro have three children. Their son just graduated from the high school; he played attack on the lacrosse team, and Ed used to see him written up in the newspaper. There are daughters too; one of them has been brought into the station a couple of times for minor infractions.

It's life on an island. The Chief doesn't—didn't—*know* Vivian Howe, but he knows a lot about her. And she probably knew just as much, if not more, about him. Andrea said that one year, the plot of Ms. Howe's novel came perilously close to the events of the summer when Andrea's cousin Tess and her husband, Greg, were killed in a sailing accident. Andrea had read Ed a passage while he was falling asleep.

"Do you think she heard about Tess and Greg and used it in this book?" Andrea had asked. She'd sounded excited about the prospect rather than angry.

"Who called it in?" the Chief asks Dixon now.

"Cruz DeSantis," Dixon says.

The Chief frowns. "How did he get involved?"

"He's friends with the son of the deceased," Dixon says. "He was on his way over to their house when he found Ms. Howe. He said at first he thought she'd twisted her ankle. He's pretty shaken up."

"Did he see anything?"

"They're bringing him in for questioning," Dixon says. "Falco was the responding. And here's where things get uncomfortable, Chief. Falco says he saw DeSantis run the stop sign at the end of Hooper Farm Road and take off down Surfside going way too fast less than five minutes before the call came in. Falco said he nearly pulled DeSantis over, but he recognized the kid and decided to let him go."

"So Falco thinks DeSantis hit the woman?" The Chief has known Cruz DeSantis since he was a toddler. Cruz's father, Joe DeSantis, owns the Nickel, a sandwich shop that the Chief patronizes three (meaning four and sometimes five) days a week. Cruz is going to Dartmouth in the fall on an academic scholarship. The Chief stands up. "I'll talk to him."

"What?"

"I'll do the questioning," the Chief says. "Let me know as soon as we hear from the ME. I assume Falco secured the scene?"

"Yes," Dixon says. "Forensics is on their way from the Cape."

"Any other witnesses? Any joggers? Dog walkers? Cars driving by?"

"A couple pulled over after DeSantis stopped," Dixon says. "But they weren't there at the time of impact."

"Neighbors?"

"Falco knocked on doors. Nobody saw anything."

"Great," the Chief says, meaning not great. "I'll talk to the kid."

Cruz DeSantis is tall, lanky, and Black; he wears his hair in a military-tight buzz cut. Joe, Cruz's father, flew with the Eighty-Second Airborne in the second Persian Gulf War. Less than a year after Joe got home from Iraq, Joe's wife was diagnosed with a rare, aggressive type of cancer, and she died shortly after, leaving Joe with a three-year-old to raise on his own. Joe has done a fine job with the young man, an extraordinary job, though when the Chief walks into the interview room, Cruz looks nothing like his usual self. He's wearing jeans and a rumpled T-shirt that says VIRGINITY ROCKS—maybe ironic, maybe not; Joe runs a pretty tight ship. Cruz's expression is 90 percent devastation and 10 percent *I don't want to be here.* Behind his glasses, his eyes are watering.

"Chief?" Cruz says, getting to his feet.

The kid looks so shook up that the Chief wants to give him a hug but instead he indicates that Cruz should sit. "Did anyone offer you something to drink? Water? Coffee?"

"I can't. I don't want..." Cruz collapses in the chair and clutches his head. "Vivi is *dead*. She's..." He swallows. "She's dead."

"Okay, okay," the Chief says. He wonders if he made a mistake deciding to do this interview himself. He's never had a problem separating his personal and professional lives, but the Chief holds Joe in very high esteem and he has grown fond of this kid and rooted for him to succeed. "Just take a couple deep breaths. I know you're upset. A lot of people are going to be sad when this news gets out. It's my responsibility to try and figure out what happened." The Chief eases into the seat across the table from Cruz. "Let's start with what you remember about finding Ms. Howe."

"Vivi," Cruz says. "She's like my second mom. Leo and I are...well, we've been best friends since preschool. And Vivi...she jokes that I'm her favorite child. I have, like, my own seat at their dinner table. And Vivi bought a Christmas stocking with my name on it that she hangs on the mantel." Cruz chokes up. "I feel like I *belong* at that house. Like I'm part of the family. Not because I'm some motherless kid she feels sorry for but because she...*loves* me."

"I'm sorry, son." The Chief picks up his pen. "You were headed to the Howe residence when you found her? At seven fifteen in the morning?"

"Yes, sir."

"Early visit for a Saturday," the Chief says.

Cruz drops his head onto the table and starts crying. The Chief gives him a minute, then says, "Where were you exactly when you first saw Ms. Howe? Walk me through it."

"I was coming from my house so I took that soft left onto Kingsley and I saw...a person, Vivi, lying on the ground. She was almost to the bike path but not quite. I thought she'd hurt herself,"

Cruz says. "I knew right away it was her. She runs that road every single morning. I thought she'd sprained her ankle so I pulled over and hopped out. And when I reached her, I saw...it was bad. I called 911."

"Wait," the Chief says. "Let's go back. You were coming from *your* house? You're sure about that?"

Cruz nods, but he's staring at his hands.

If Falco saw Cruz run a stop sign at the end of Hooper Farm Road, then Cruz is lying. Joe and Cruz live over on Delaney, just off Cliff. It's possible, he supposes, that Falco was mistaken. Or maybe Cruz was coming from someplace he wasn't supposed to be. His girlfriend's house, for example. If the Chief has seen it once, he's seen it a thousand times: when you investigate one crime, you often uncover a bunch of unrelated things that people are hiding.

"Cruz," the Chief says, and the kid looks up. Behind his glasses, his eyes are terrified. The Chief reminds himself that even good kids, even *great* kids, make mistakes. "Did any cars pass you on Madaket Road before you noticed Ms. Howe?"

"I don't think so," Cruz says. "Not that I remember."

"Did you pass any pedestrians on Madaket Road?"

"No."

"Did anyone other than you see what happened? Were there any bikers or joggers out?"

"If they saw what happened, wouldn't they have stopped?" Cruz says.

"Did you notice anyone on the bike path, Cruz?"

"No!" Cruz says. "I didn't notice anything except Vivi lying on the ground! I called 911, I waited for the ambulance to get there, and then I ran to the house to tell Leo what happened."

"But you didn't call him from the scene?"

"No."

"You didn't call your best friend to tell him his mother was hurt?"

Cruz removes his glasses and sets them down on the table, and it's only then that the Chief notices one of the lenses has a crack in it and there's the start of a bruise under Cruz's left eye.

"Leo and I got into a fight last night," Cruz says. "I didn't think he'd answer if I called."

*A fight,* the Chief thinks. That could explain the glasses, the eye, Cruz racing over to the Howe residence at seven in the morning.

"Did you see anyone in front of you on Madaket Road?" the Chief asks. "Maybe a car that pulled over?"

"No," Cruz says.

The Chief will need to look at the scene himself, but if he's understanding it correctly, whoever hit Vivian Howe would have been turning onto Kingsley, as Cruz would have done. There's no chance that a car driving on the Madaket Road would have hit someone who wasn't even on the bike path yet. But if a driver took the soft left onto Kingsley going too fast and not paying attention, he could have hit a pedestrian. Then, if he knew Kingsley was a dead end and he wanted to get away cleanly, he most likely would have backed up and continued down Madaket Road.

*It must have been a local,* the Chief thinks. And his day gets even worse. "So you called 911 and then what happened?"

"I waited with Vivi," Cruz says. "I held her hand and tried talking to her in case she could hear me. A couple of cars stopped; one woman asked if I was the one who'd hit her…"

"But you weren't?" the Chief asks gently. He knows that frequently in hit-and-runs, the person who did the hit is the one who calls it in, pretending to be a bystander. Is that what happened here? Did Cruz turn onto Kingsley too fast, did Vivian Howe appear in his path so suddenly that he couldn't react, was the sun in his eyes, was he upset about the fight with the son, was he, maybe, going over to apologize? The Chief had raised his own two kids and then he'd raised Tess and Greg's kids, Chloe and Finn. He has experienced enough teenage drama to write a six-season Netflix series. Any one of his kids could have taken an eye off the road to text or change the radio station—and unintentionally mowed someone down. "You weren't the one who hit her? If you did or you think you might have and not realized it, now is the time to tell me. I know you have a bright future ahead of you and you want to preserve that—"

"Chief Kapenash," Cruz says, and suddenly the kid is clear-eyed and earnest. "I didn't hit Vivi. I didn't see who did. I didn't see anyone until after I called 911. Vivi was on the ground when I found her." Cruz closes his eyes, and tears stream down his face.

The Chief sighs. He knows he shouldn't necessarily believe the kid, but he does. "We'll need to impound your Jeep until forensics can check it out, son, I'm sorry." He stands up. "Call your dad, have him come get you. I'm sorry this happened. I know you lost someone important to you in a tragic way. I've been there myself."

The boy is crying so hard now it sounds like he's choking. "She was like a mother to me," he says. "I was her favorite child."

# Vivi

She rises, higher and higher. She supposes this is a good thing— up and not down—but she feels like she's heading to the grocery store without her wallet. Which is to say, she's not prepared. She has unattended business, big and small, back on the ground, in her life.

Small: Her new All-Clad three-quart sauté pan is still sitting on the walk and she knows that Leo and Carson will never notice it. They'll step over it, and it will fill with rain and insects; maybe one of the field mice that have been infesting Money Pit since Vivi bought it will drown in it, or an unsuspecting blue jay will dip its beak into the acrid black water, mistaking the pan for a birdbath. It will fill with snow; it will become fused with the slate of the walk before anyone thinks to pick it up, take it inside, and scour it.

Willa will do it when she comes over, Vivi supposes. Or Vivi's landscaper, Anastasia—a woman whose photo is in the dictionary next to *perfectionist*—will handle it.

Small: Vivi has an outstanding invoice from Anastasia for twenty-one hundred dollars; that needs to be paid.

Bigger: Who will pay her bills, settle her affairs, make sure the kids are provided for? She doesn't have a will. Why would she need a will? She's fifty-one years old and has no medical problems. Vivi's father died when Vivi was seventeen, in a car in the garage, and Vivi's mother died five years later, at the age of forty-six, but she was a smoker and obese. Vivi ran every day, she was trim, she hadn't taken so much as a drag off a cigarette since leaving Ohio—she was the picture of good health. Why would she need a will?

She should have had a will. She should have named an executor, someone to handle things. Vivi's best friend in the life she's leaving behind, Savannah Hamilton, is coping with her two aging parents who are in an assisted-living facility in Weymouth; her mother has Alzheimer's, her father has regular dementia, and Savannah's overwhelmed. But the kids aren't quite capable yet, not even Willa, and so Savannah will have to handle it.

Bigger: Vivi's novel *Golden Girl* is coming out on July 13. Vivi can recite the (starred!) *McQuaid* review by heart.

*Howe digs deeper than usual in this shimmering tale of one young woman's quest to escape her past. Alison Revere grows up in a Cleveland suburb yearning to become a writer. Alison's high-school boyfriend, Stott Macklemore, sings in a garage band and dreams of making it big. After Alison's father kills himself, the two grow even closer and talk of getting married after they graduate. Stott writes a song for Alison called "Golden Girl" and is courted by a major recording label. Stott heads out to California, and Alison, devastated at losing another person so close to her, is determined to get him back to Cleveland, no matter what she has to do or say. In the second half of the novel, Alison finds herself summering with her college room-mate's family on Nantucket. She moves to the island year-round, meets and marries a local boy, and publishes her first novel, en-titled* Golden Girl. *Alison's life appears to be... golden... until Stott Macklemore reappears and forces her to reckon with the secrets of her past.* Golden Girl *is filled with Howe's signature summery scenes but it's her larger message about the irrevocable decision Alison made as a troubled teenager that will stay with the reader.*

The question Vivi was asked most often at her events and in interviews was *Do you base your characters on real people? Do you write about events from your own life?* Vivi often felt like her readers wanted the answer to be yes; they yearned for the fiction to be *true*. Vivi explained that she used *details* from her real life: Her white pitcher with the bisque scallop shell that she bought at Weeds on Centre Street appears in three of her novels. Vivi wears Jessica Hicks jewelry and so do all of her characters. Vivi's best friend, Savannah, is known for her witticisms, and Vivi borrowed (stole) them on a regular basis. But this wasn't the same as writing about people she knew or about her own life.

Until this year. The plot of *Golden Girl* recounts the dramatic events of Vivi's senior year in high school—but the only person who would know this was her high-school boyfriend, Brett Caspian, whom Vivi has not seen or spoken to in over thirty years. Before writing *Golden Girl*, Vivi had scoured the internet for any sign of Brett. He wasn't on Facebook or Twitter or Instagram or Snapchat or TikTok. He wasn't on LinkedIn. Vivi had checked the white pages, but there were no Caspians listed in the greater Cleveland area. A casual e-mail sent to the only two high-school friends Vivi remained in contact with—Stephanie Simon and Gina Mariani—confirmed that Brett had never been to a class reunion (neither had Vivi because her parents were both dead and the house in Parma sold). Though Vivi wondered what had become of him, she'd reached the conclusion that Brett Caspian didn't "do" social media; wherever he was, he had no idea she was a novelist and would never, ever realize that *Golden Girl* was about him. Them. With a few minor changes.

Concerns about Brett Caspian (somewhat) quelled, Vivi was excited about her new book. This was Vivi's best shot at finally hitting the top spot on the *New York Times* bestseller list. Number one. It sparkled for Vivi like the star on top of a Christmas tree. Her last book, *Main Street Gossip,* debuted at number three on the hardcover list and number two on the combined list. So close! She was poised—maybe?—to get to number one this time.

Vivi realizes that the powers that be aren't likely to let her return to her life on Earth so that she can move the All-Clad pan off the walk, pay her landscaper, or even promote her new novel.

But what about her most important responsibility?

Biggest: Caring for her children. Leo is eighteen, technically an adult, but he's still a mama's boy. He loves Vivi's cooking and often wakes up asking what she's making for dinner; he let Vivi take him to Murray's to buy clothes for his senior banquet and graduation (and he trusted her opinion, which both the girls summarily ignored). The winter before, when Vivi was knocked flat with a sinus infection, Leo binged the first three seasons of *The Crown* with her, and hadn't that been the thing that made her feel better—her big, strong son snuggled up at her side?

Earlier this spring, when Leo said he couldn't decide between the

College of Charleston and the University of Colorado, he and Vivi made a list of pros and cons that was evenly split. He asked Vivi what she thought he should do. Selfishly, Vivi wanted Charleston (there was a direct flight from Boston and, hello, it was Charleston) but her gut told her Charleston might not be *that* different from Nantucket and she thought Leo would thrive someplace completely new—like a big school in the Rocky Mountains.

"Boulder," she said.

He'd exhaled and said, "That's my choice too, but I thought you'd be sad if I was so far away."

"Oh, honey," she said. "I will be sad, you're my baby. But part of being a parent is wanting what's best for *you*."

Vivi had planned to drive Leo out to Colorado herself. It was going to be a proper road trip with carefully curated stops at diners and kitschy motels, scenic overlooks, and historical monuments. She was going to let Leo play his music no matter how badly it hurt her ears and she was hoping that when it was just the two of them in the car with nothing but open road ahead, they could really talk. And then, once Vivi had dropped him off (with the laminated card she'd make of laundry instructions), she would climb back in her car and have a good, loud cry. Her last child, her baby boy, launched.

Vivi *can't* miss taking Leo to college. And she has a grandchild on the way. Everyone would agree it's patently unfair for her to die without ever holding her first grandchild. Then there's Carson, who seems to need a mother now more than ever. Vivi can't leave her kids down there by themselves. They're her *kids*. She's their *mother*.

Dying isn't an option, sorry.

Vivi is up in the clouds now, though she can still make out her body lying on Kingsley. There's a white Jeep next to her. It's *Cruz's* Jeep; he bolts out and runs to her. "Vivi!" He whips out his phone, and she hears him saying he needs an ambulance at Kingsley and Madaket. "My mom is hurt, it looks like she was hit, she's on the ground. She needs help!"

Cruz crouches beside her, his shoulders heaving. He takes her hand. "Stay with me, Vivi, you're not going anywhere. I need you. We all need you."

*They all need me!* she thinks. Then she thinks, *He called me his mom.*

Vivi hears a siren in the distance. She can't look; her poor body, and poor Cruz! Vivi turns her head away—and comes face to face with a middle-aged woman with sensibly cut ash-blond hair wearing a flowing white muumuu and a silk scarf expertly knotted around her neck.

"Hello?" Vivi says. The woman standing before her appears to be flesh and blood, and she's holding a clipboard, like someone organizing a literary luncheon. Vivi feels like she's about to be given her table number.

The woman is wearing reading glasses perched on the end of her nose. Whereas the scarf is elegant and looks expensive—Vivi studies the elaborate animal print in the signature shade of orange and determines it's (excuse me!) an *Hermès* scarf—the glasses are of the drugstore variety. "Hello, Vivian," the woman says. "Welcome to the Beyond. I'm Martha."

Martha looks familiar. She reminds Vivi vaguely of...

"Of your first reader, Maribeth," Martha says. "Yes, she's my younger sister."

"You have *got* to be joking! You're Maribeth Schumacher's *sister?*" When Vivi's first novel, *The Dune Daughters,* came out, Maribeth Schumacher bought twenty copies and gave them to all her influential friends. These friends then told their friends and neighbors and sisters-in-law and so on and so on and so on—just like the infamous Fabergé shampoo commercial. In this way, Vivi's devoted readership was born.

"I *was*," Martha says. "She sent me all your books right up until I died, two summers ago. I lived in Memphis, so it was nice to read about the beach."

Memphis; Vivi went there on tour, but she stayed out by the University of Memphis and all she remembers is Central BBQ and the gated community where she went running. She didn't make it downtown to see Beale Street or the ducks at the Peabody Hotel. She'd told herself she'd do that next time.

Now there won't be a next time!

"But that's not why they assigned me to you," Martha says. "It's just a coincidental aside."

"Assigned you to me?"

"I'm your Person," Martha says. "I'm here to help you transition."

"I think there's been a mistake."

"Everyone says that," Martha says.

Vivi points to the ground where her body lies. The ambulance has arrived and Cruz is sprinting down Kingsley toward Money Pit. He's going to tell the kids. Vivi needs to do something. Can Martha help her walk this back somehow?

She tries to peek at Martha's clipboard. "Is there a place on your form, a box you can check, so that they save me at the hospital?"

"It's too late," Martha says. "You're dead."

"I'm dead," Vivi says. "But I didn't do anything wrong. How can I be *dead*?" She doesn't want to sound *too* indignant; if there's one thing Vivi has learned in her fifty-one years, it's that you should always be polite to the people who can help you, such as flight attendants and anyone who works at the DMV. "Martha, can you explain, please? Am I being…punished?"

"Don't be silly," Martha says.

"So then why…"

"You got hit by a car," Martha says. "It was an accident. Random bad luck."

"But that's not fair."

Martha purses her lips.

"Are you about to tell me that life isn't fair?" Vivi asks.

"Your death *was* particularly sudden," Martha says. Her tone suggests there might be some wiggle room. She scans the form on her clipboard and checks a box. "And for that reason, Vivian, I'm going to grant you a seventy-five VW and a three-N."

"Does that mean they'll save me at the hospital?"

"No," Martha says. "The seventy-five VW means a seventy-five-day viewing window. I'll let you watch what happens down on Earth between now and Labor Day. And"—Martha holds up a finger—"the three-N provision gives you the use of three nudges."

"Three nudges?"

"You can influence outcomes three times down below," Martha says. "But you should be judicious."

"This feels like some kind of fairy tale," Vivi says. "Am I really dead?"

"Yes, dear."

Vivi takes in the expert tying of Martha's Hermès scarf. "That looks so effortless, I would have guessed you were French."

"Well, thank you. I'm not."

"What did you do when you were alive?"

"I was a senior vice president at FedEx."

"Go, Martha!" Vivi says. "Lady boss!"

Martha says, "I can't be flattered, Vivian. You will not be revived at the hospital. You're dead. I'm granting you the summer to watch over your children and three nudges because you met such a random and sudden end. And because I like your books. You have a lot of fans up here." Now it sounds like Martha is the one trying to do the flattering.

"Who hit me?" Vivi asks. "It wasn't Cruz, was it?" This is too awful to even contemplate. He's such a good kid, so brilliant, going to Dartmouth on a full ride. He's good at everything—science, math, English. Instead of writing an essay for his college application, he wrote a poem called "Sacrifice," about his father, Joe. Vivi's feelings for Cruz DeSantis are just as tender and protective as they are for her own kids.

Martha shakes her head. "That, I can't tell you."

Martha can't tell her because it's not allowed or because she doesn't know? But whatever the answer, Vivi has a more pressing question. "What happens when the summer is over?"

"You join the choir," Martha says.

"The choir?"

"Of angels."

"But I can't sing," Vivi says.

Martha releases a belly laugh. "Don't worry," she says. "You'll learn. Now, come along. It's time to go."

"Go where?"

"To the greenroom. Please close your eyes."

Vivi regards Martha with suspicion. "I'd rather not."

"You're going to have to learn to trust me," Martha says. "I'm your Person."

Vivi waits a beat. What choice does she have? She closes her eyes.

When she opens them, she's in a room with one wall missing; it feels like the kind of shoebox diorama that kids make in school. Vivi blinks as she looks around; there's a lot to take in.

The crown molding and all the trim in the room is painted green, and the wallpaper is printed with eye-popping green and white vertical stripes. There are layered rugs on the floor—a neutral sisal underneath and a gorgeous silk Persian on top. A Moroccan lantern shaped like a genie's bottle hangs from the ceiling; it's polished brass and punctured with tiny holes that cast an intricate lacy pattern of light on the ceiling. This might be—no, it definitely is the coolest, most eclectic room Vivi has ever been in. There's a long green velvet chaise, two peach silk soufflé chairs, a coffee table that looks like a giant white enamel bean, leather pouf ottomans, two dwarf orange trees in copper pots, and a huge black-and-white photograph on the wall that Vivi identifies as a David Yarrow Western scene.

"This is the boho-chic room of my dreams," Vivi says.

"Yes, I know," Martha says. "We scoured your Instagram."

Vivi laughs. She can't believe it! This really *is* heaven! She would have loved a room like this in Money Pit (a velvet chaise! orange trees!), but it just didn't make sense in a Nantucket house, and Vivi had never saved enough to buy a pied-à-terre in New York or Paris.

There's a wall of books because every perfect room has a wall of books, at least in Vivi's opinion. Vivi strides over to check the titles. *Cloudstreet,* by Tim Winton; *Song of Solomon,* by Toni Morrison; *White Fur,* by Jardine Libaire; and—oh, baby—*Adultery and Other Choices,* by Andre Dubus, who might be the writer Vivi loves most.

"My favorites," Vivi says.

"Naturally."

Adjacent to the bookshelves is a green door. "Is this Benjamin Moore's Parsley Snips?" she asks. She's referring to the paint color.

"It is."

Gah! Vivi is in love with this room. "Where does the door lead to?"

"For me to know and you to find out," Martha says. "Don't be a snoop or I'll end your viewing window early." Martha opens the door and slips through before Vivi can peek at what's behind.

*Viewing window,* Vivi thinks. She moves to the edge of the room, and it *is* like standing at a large open window. Vivi can gaze into her old life from here. She can do *more* than gaze—she swoops right down into the action.

At Money Pit, Vivi finds her three children in the sitting room clinging to one another on the turquoise tweed sofa that they call "the

Girv," short for its product name, Girvin. Willa is in the middle, with Carson and Leo gripping hands across her midsection. Although Vivi might have imagined this moment in spite more than once ("You'll be sorry once I'm gone"), actually witnessing the raw urgency of her children's pain is more than she can bear.

*I'm right here, you guys!* But of course, nobody can hear her.

"We had a fight," Carson says, her voice staccato, hiccup-y. "I sent her an apology text, but I'm not sure she got to read it."

*Yes!* Vivi thinks. *Yes, sweetie, I did get it. Please don't worry about the fight. I had already forgiven you. I was going to make you avocado toast when I got home.*

"Where's her phone?" Leo asks.

"The police have it," Willa says. "They have her clothes, which they're sending to forensics, and I guess they might need her phone too, but I can ask Chief Kapenash."

"Would you call and ask if we can have it back?" Carson asks. "I need to know if she saw my text."

"Her phone is probably smashed," Leo says.

"It's not," Willa says. "The Chief made a point of telling me the phone was fine."

"I told her I loved her in the text," Carson says. She breaks down in fresh tears. "I want to go back and start over and be better. I want to make her laugh." She squeezes Willa. "I would give anything to hear her laugh right now. I would give anything to have her yell at me—I don't care, I just want her back. I mean, it's impossible that she's dead. It's impossible that we're *never going to see her again.*"

"Don't say that!" Leo is crying like he used to when he was a little boy. "Seriously, Carson, just please shut up."

*I'm here! I can see you! I can hear you! You aren't alone! I didn't leave you alone!* Vivi cranes her neck upward, searching for any sign of Martha. This is torture. She needs Martha's help. How does she let the kids know she's here?

"We were best friends," Willa says. "I told her everything and she listened. She didn't always agree but she listened."

Vivi notices Willa placing a hand on her belly and—aha!—Vivi can, in fact, detect a teensy-tiny heart beating inside of her.

Vivi glides over to the kitchen, where Willa's husband, Rip, is sitting at the table, staring at his hands. Vivi wonders what Rip is thinking. He's a pensive guy. Vivi might have remarked once or twice that he could use "more cowbell," but she has come to realize that Rip's strengths are underappreciated. Charles Evan Bonham III is a calm, steady presence, the perfect foil for Willa's manic desire to achieve. However, when Willa announced that she and Rip were getting married—something they'd been promising to do since the seventh grade—Vivi had thought, *It will never last. Willa will outgrow him.*

A month or so before Willa and Rip's wedding, Vivi took Willa out to Le Languedoc for a mother-daughter dinner. Because it was a weeknight in the spring, they were the only ones in the upstairs front room, which overlooked Broad Street and had a view of the charming lit windows of Nantucket Bookworks.

The aesthetics of that dinner had been sheer perfection. The dining room was lit only by candles; there was a bouquet of iris on the table; the restaurant smelled of butter, garlic, veal stock, freshly baked bread. They ordered an expensive bottle of champagne and then an even more extravagant bottle of white burgundy. Willa wasn't usually all that interested in food—she would eat or drink anything you put in front of her without complaint, but she never really seemed to *enjoy* it. However, that night, she swooned over the escargot en croûte and the pan-roasted lobster with parmesan polenta, and she allowed herself to get a little tipsy. This gave Vivi a chance to say her piece. Rip was the loveliest of humans, and the Bonhams were as admirable as they were established. Rip seemed content in the family's insurance business, and Willa would never want for anything materially.

But what about emotionally or intellectually? Vivi wondered. Rip had graduated from Amherst with a liberal arts degree; he was smart, but Vivi wouldn't call him *curious*. He'd been groomed to take over the family insurance business, and he would never be willing—or able—to live anywhere but on the island where he was born and raised. Rip had limits.

Vivi leaned across the table and wrapped her fingers around Willa's forearm. "You may wake up one day and decide you want a bigger world." Vivi thought about herself in high school riding shotgun in Brett Caspian's Skylark. What if that had been all she'd ever known? "You may want to move to Istanbul."

"I've been to Istanbul," Willa said. "During my summer abroad. I got robbed outside the Hagia Sophia, remember? I will never want to move to Istanbul."

"You may decide to pursue a master's in history or an MBA, and off you go to Harvard while Rip stays here on Nantucket. You may decide you like Boston—you ride the T, you get takeout Lebanese food, you spend an afternoon at the Isabella Stewart Gardner Museum. Then one day in class, a voice offers some brilliant insight, and you turn around to set eyes on some young man. Maybe he's not even your type. He's short and dark-skinned, not tall and pale like Rip; he has a mustache and a British accent instead of being clean-shaven and dropping his *r*'s like Rip, and yet you find yourself drawn to him..."

"I love how you're writing the novel of how I'll leave Rip," Willa said.

"You're so young, Willie. Twenty-three! Your prefrontal cortex isn't fully developed yet."

"Mother."

"It's the part of the brain responsible for sound decision-making," Vivi said. "It matures at twenty-five." This was a factoid Vivi had picked up while researching her novel *The Angle of Light*. "I just don't want you to shortchange yourself." She had split the last of the wine between their glasses. "Have you ever been with anyone else? Sexually?"

"Mother."

"Because if not..."

"Of course not, Mother. Well, I kissed Ryan Brickley in sixth grade."

"That doesn't count," Vivi said.

"Rip and I are meant to be together."

"I just worry that you got attached to Rip after Dad and I split, that he became your security blanket, and once you get a little older—"

"I'm not getting divorced," Willa said.

"Willie..."

"Please, Mom," Willa said. "Let's get dessert."

Vivi hovers so near Rip, she can see a raw, red hangnail on his thumb and hear his watch ticking. Vivi inches even closer. His head pivots in her direction, then he checks behind himself like he's looking for someone. Does he know she's here? Does he?

# Rip

Willa called Rip as he was walking out of the Field and Oar Club. She was crying so hard, he couldn't understand a word she was saying. He had instinctively pulled the phone away from his ear, and when he did this, his sister, Pamela, who had just walloped Rip in a brother-sister tennis match, groaned. She probably thought what he thought, that Willa had started bleeding.

But Willa wasn't calling about the baby. "Mama is dead, she's dead, she was hit by a car. She's dead, Rip, she's dead." This was followed by a guttural cry, and Rip felt like he'd been kicked in the stomach. *Vivi* was dead? Vivi was *dead?* She had been hit by a car on her run. Apparently, Leo had called Willa at home, waking her up, then he and Carson had gotten Willa and they all went to the hospital together. The ER doc told them that Vivi had been dead on arrival.

*Dead on arrival? Vivi?* There had to be a mistake. Things like this just didn't happen. Though, of course, they did happen—all the time, every day.

Rip had only one thought: he needed to be with his wife.

Pamela dropped Rip off at the hospital, and he was the one who had a substantive conversation with the doctor. There was internal bleeding, head trauma; by the time the paramedics arrived, she was gone. "It would have been nearly instant," the doc said. "There was no suffering."

The suffering, Rip thought, had only just begun.

He drove Willa, Carson, and Leo home. (They hadn't wanted to leave and it fell to Rip to point out that there was no reason to stay at the hospital, nothing left to wait for. Vivi was dead.) It was only a three-minute drive back to Money Pit, but it was three minutes Rip would never forget. Willa, Leo, and Carson all huddled in the back seat; Leo and Carson were bawling, clinging to Willa, and she had risen to the occasion, comforting them both, becoming the new mother figure as Rip watched her in the rearview.

When they got home, Willa led Leo and Carson into the front sitting room—and there, the three of them have stayed.

Dennis shows up wearing cargo shorts, a long-sleeved T-shirt from Cisco Brewers, a bandanna tied around his neck, and sunglasses. His steel-gray hair is standing on end; he's red-faced, sweating.

He looks at Rip and says, "What the hell happened? What *happened?*"

Rip blinks. Dennis and Vivi have been dating for a few years; he's the only guy Vivi has dated since she and JP split. Dennis is a few inches shorter than Rip and built like a fireplug—he's solid, stocky. When Vivi first started dating him, Rip didn't quite get it. Dennis is a tradesman who tells dirty jokes; he has a thick Southie accent and a freezer full of venison. He'd gotten drunk at Rip and Willa's wedding and given a long-winded toast, which everyone at the Field and Oar Club suffered through because they were too polite to tell him to sit down.

Willa once said, "Dennis clearly isn't Mr. Right, but he's Mr. Right Now. Mom likes him. She doesn't need someone complicated; she's complicated enough all by herself."

But in the past year, Rip has grown quite fond of Dennis. The insurance office's furnace went on the fritz in January, and Rip had called Dennis at six o'clock on a Tuesday evening. He'd shown up right away and stayed until almost midnight to get it up and running. Rip and Dennis were alone in the office for those hours and Dennis told great stories about hunting ducks over on Tuckernuck and about the Datsun 240Z he'd restored in high school before he was even old enough to drive.

Rip had gone home and woken Willa up just to tell her with wonderment, "Dennis is actually pretty cool."

"She got hit by a car at the end of Kingsley while she was running," Rip says to Dennis now. "I'm so sorry, man. I am just so...sorry." The words feel wrong in his mouth, like he's chewing on gristle.

Dennis's face crumples and he bends over, hands on knees, and starts sucking in air like he's just finished a dozen wind sprints on the practice field. Rip wants to vaporize. He can't even add something about how much Vivi cared for Dennis because Willa told Rip that her mother had broken up with Dennis a couple of weeks earlier.

At that second, Willa calls from the other room, "Rip?"

Rip puts a gentle hand on Dennis's shoulder and goes to his wife. "Dennis is here," he says.

"Who else have you told?"

"Just Pamela," he says. "I told her to call my parents." The elder Bonhams are on a Mediterranean cruise.

"I need to make a list," Willa says. "Mom's agent, her editor, her publicist. There's going to have to be some kind of formal announcement made by her publishing house. I need to find out if there's a will and who's allowed to access her bank accounts."

"Babe," Rip says. "There's time for that later. You're in shock right now."

Willa stares at him. Her pretty face is blank; her brown eyes are glazed over. "I am in shock."

There's a niggling thought in Rip's mind. "Have you told your father?"

Willa gasps. "Oh my God."

She has not told her father.

Willa's eyes widen and she turns around to look at Carson and Leo, who are sodden heaps on the sofa. "Did either of you text Dad?" Willa asks. "Or call him?"

Leo has his head between his knees like he's on a plane that's going down. "No," he says.

"No," Carson says. She's pressing tissues against her closed eyes. "And I'm not gonna."

"Would you do it, Rip, please?" Willa says. "We just can't."

Rip sighs. "Sure." He kisses Willa's forehead, then heads back to the kitchen. Dennis has disappeared, and Rip feels like he let the guy down—he should have been more comforting—and he decides he'll reach out to him later. He needs to call JP now before he hears the news from someone else, before JP's girlfriend, Amy, hears it from someone at the salon or JP's mother, Lucinda, finds out from someone as she's having lunch on the patio at the Field and Oar Club.

Rip steps outside the kitchen door and nearly trips over a pan filled with water on the flagstone path. Rip empties the water out of the pan and carries it to the kitchen; it has the scorched remains of something stuck to the bottom. He puts it in the sink to soak.

He's stalling.

When he steps outside again, his hands are shaking. He calls JP's cell phone but gets his voice mail. Leaving a message isn't an option. Rip tries to think. Should he call Amy? Amy is a stylist at RJ Miller. She has always been jealous of Vivi. She might offer lukewarm condolences, and that's not anything Rip wants to hear.

He tries JP's cell again—again, the call goes to voice mail—and then the ice cream parlor.

JP answers on the first ring. "Good morning, the Cone." In the background, Rip hears the Rolling Stones singing "Brown Sugar."

"JP?" Rip says. "It's Rip."

"Rip!" JP says. His voice is peppy. He's probably preparing the shop for a busy summer Saturday, checking inventory, making ten gallons of brownie-batter ice cream, the Cone's most popular flavor, writing out the specials on the board: Nantucket blackberry sorbet, peach cobbler, and lemon square, with ripples of curd and graham cracker bits. JP has no idea that in the next second, his life will be forever changed.

"I have some bad news," Rip says. "Tragic news."

The music stops. "Is it Willa?"

"It's Vivi, actually," Rip says. "She's...well, she was out running and she got hit by a car. On Kingsley. Right at the end of Kingsley."

"*What?*" JP says. "Is she okay? Did she break anything? Did she go to the *hospital?*"

"She's..." Rip clears his throat. "She's dead, JP. She died."

There's silence.

Rip feels the years fall away. He was only twelve years old when he asked Willa Quinboro to the Valentine's Day dance at the Nantucket Boys and Girls Club. Willa's parents had picked them up from the dance on their way home from dinner at Fifty-Six Union. Rip can still remember the smell of Vivi's perfume mixing with some other intriguing scent that Rip now knows was truffle oil from the fries in a to-go box. JP and Vivi were younger than Rip's parents by a good ten years and he remembers how loose and fun-loving and... *happy* they seemed. He'd spent days with them on the beach at Fortieth Pole, where they would grill salmon or chicken for lunch, and football Sundays at their house, when Vivi made hot artichoke dip and pepperoni bread and spicy mixed nuts. Vivi would sit on the arm of JP's chair, and JP would snake an arm around Vivi's waist as they yelled and cheered for the Patriots. They were a dynamic couple. Rip had been enthralled by them.

He'd been stunned two years later when Willa tearfully told him that her parents were getting a divorce. For a few weeks, it seemed like the earth had cracked open and the whole family would be sucked down into the crevasse. Carson had gone to see a counselor; Willa spent every waking second she could at Rip's, even though his parents' house was as cold as a museum; and Leo, at eight years old, had taken to riding his bike all over the island with Cruz DeSantis committing minor crimes, like stealing lollipops from the bowl at the dry cleaner's.

JP clears his throat. "Where are my children?" His voice is aggressive, like maybe Rip is holding them hostage.

"They're here at the house."

"Can I speak to them?"

"Um...they're pretty upset right now."

"Why are you the one who called me?" JP asks. "Why didn't one of them..."—his voice cracks—"call me?"

"They're a mess, JP," Rip says. He rolls his shoulders back and remembers that he's not twelve years old anymore. He's a grown man. At the insurance office, Rip handles claims. It's a job he's suited for because not much rattles him. Your pipes froze and burst with the thaw and so much water flooded the second floor of your house that it collapsed onto the first? Lightning struck your roof? You totaled your new Range Rover on the way home from the dealership? You drove your boat up onto the jetty and now there's a three-foot hole in the hull?

*No problem, let's file a claim,* Rip says all day every day. *We'll get this fixed.*

"They were too upset to call you. The three of them are in shock and so Willa asked me to let you know."

"Yes, well," JP says. "Thank you." He hangs up.

## Amy

It's a Saturday in June at the salon, and Amy arrives early because they have fifteen weddings. "You heard that right," she said to JP that morning. "Fifteen on the books, and we turned away at least fifteen more." It's an all-hands-on-deck day; the energy is high and it is happy. Champagne is popped with the first clients and the music is cranked up—Luke Combs—and Amy can't complain. She grew up in Alabama and was a Phi Mu at Auburn—LIOB! War Eagle!—so she loves not only country music but also the feel of a sorority house on the day of a big game.

She's on her fourth client at ten thirty, a mother of the bride, when the receptionist, Brandi, stands discreetly behind

Amy's shoulder and whispers, "JP is on the phone. He says it's urgent."

Amy turns a fraction of an inch toward Brandi. "On the phone here? He called the salon?"

"He says he's been trying your cell."

"Tell him I'm busy, please. I'll call when I take a break for lunch." Her lunch today will be a cheddar scone from Born and Bread stuffed into her mouth in about ten minutes. Amy has been fighting to get rid of fifteen extra pounds since she moved in with JP, and though she's tried bringing her own salad in a Tupperware for lunch, she keeps losing the battle of wills against the carbs and fat—the bagel boards, the bakery boxes, the cake because it's always someone's birthday—that are constantly under her nose here at the salon.

"He sounded... I really think you'd better..."

Amy shakes her head. She does *not* have time to talk to JP; right now, she feels what Santa Claus must feel on Christmas Eve. The client in Amy's chair, Mrs. Scaliti, is already upset because Amy started their interaction by calling her by her first name. Now she's giving Amy a baleful stare while her hair hangs in damp strands around her face. She needs to be at St. Paul's Episcopal by noon.

"I'll call him when I take a break for lunch," Amy repeats, and Brandi throws her hands up.

There isn't a break, not even a minute to think or sit down. Amy's lower back starts talking to her and she needs to pee. The flower girl is allergic to the lilies of the valley that Amy weaves into her French braid crown; the girl's neck splotches with hives. Amy tosses the flowers and sends the girl's mother to Dan's Pharmacy to buy Benadryl.

She's standing at the sinks washing the hair of a bridesmaid for the big Wauwinet hotel wedding—rumor has it, the whole do cost well over a million bucks—when her best friend at the salon, Lorna (a recent arrival from Ireland), says, "God bless you, Pigeon, I can't believe you're still here."

Amy laughs. "Where else would I be?"

"You haven't heard, then? Did JP not ring you?"

"He called, yes, but I haven't spoken to him." Amy makes an ill-advised quarter turn toward Lorna and accidentally sprays the bridesmaid in the face as she's rinsing; the girl sputters. She's very nice about it, but Amy is flustered. She doesn't have time for gossip! "Whatever it is can wait."

"Oh, Pigeon," Lorna says in the maternal voice she normally reserves for her Weimaraner, Cupid. "Promise me you'll ring him back as soon as you're finished here. Promise me."

"Yes, yes, I'll try, I promise I'll try," Amy says. She leads the bridesmaid—her name sifted in with the Chelseas and Madisons that Amy has seen already today—to her chair. She catches Brandi watching her. Jarred, working at the next chair, glances over at her. And Amy sees Molly the manicurist staring at her through the interior glass door of the nail sanctuary. Out of the blue, a woman two chairs down who is being blown out by Toni gasps and says, "Vivian Howe? The writer?"

Amy's good mood is about to be torpedoed right into the toilet. She doesn't want to hear about Vivi today. Plenty of times women come in here babbling about how it was reading *The Dune Daughters* that inspired them to visit Nantucket in the first place.

Just yesterday, a woman asked Amy if Vivi ever came into the salon to get her hair done. Amy had nearly answered, *No, she does it herself at home with clippers.* Instead she said, "She used to a long time ago but she switched to Darya's downtown." Amy didn't add that Vivi stopped patronizing RJ Miller the same week that Amy started working as a stylist there.

Amy knew JP was married when she'd met him ten years earlier. That was back when JP was running a wineshop called the Cork out of the cottage on Old South Wharf that now houses the Cone.

Amy had been unable to find a job when she graduated from Auburn and so she'd decided to spend a summer on Nantucket, a place she had become obsessed with after watching umpteen episodes of *Wings*. The second Amy stepped off the ferry, she saw JP's Help Wanted sign. She marched right into the shop and introduced herself to JP. He was tall with thick dark hair, arresting green eyes, and a dimple when he smiled. He'd asked Amy what she knew about wine and Amy winked at him and said, "You drink it, right?" JP said, "Your accent alone will sell cases. You're hired."

It was impossible not to work close together in the tight quarters of the wineshop. The cottage was only two hundred and fifty square feet, and much of this space was taken up with wine crates and casks and bottles artfully displayed in racks. There was a wrought-iron tower of champagne. JP sold cutting boards from Napa and French corkscrews and Caspari cocktail napkins. He bought an antique trestle table where they opened the bottles for that day's wine tasting. Sometimes (many times) nobody showed up, so Amy and JP would drink the wines themselves and describe them with sensuous words like *body* and *legs*. They would end up buzzed and giddy, and Amy would complain about her love life. It was easy to meet guys at the Chicken Box but they were all so immature, no more sophisticated than the frat boys she'd dated at Auburn.

"I'm looking for someone more seasoned," she said one day. "Someone like you."

She couldn't *believe* the words had popped out of her mouth. She was afraid JP would reprimand (or even fire) her, but he laughed it off. JP was married to the novelist Vivian Howe and they had three children. Amy reminded herself that these were more than just words—JP had taken a vow. He wore a ring and went home every night to Vivi, Willa, Carson, and Leo. Amy had been raised in a Southern Baptist family; she knew full well that it was a sin to covet her neighbor's husband. Even so, her romantic feelings for JP intensified by the day. He was so handsome and funny and knowledgeable about wine, and he was generous with his time and attention. He was eager to teach Amy what he knew about terroir, the vintners, the varietals; he watched her as she tasted, was interested to know what she thought, which wines she liked, which she didn't. Her opinion mattered to him.

As the summer wore on, they grew closer. Amy told JP when she had a quarrel with her mother over the phone or when she went on an awkward date. JP admitted to Amy that he was unhappy in his marriage. Vivi was either on deadline or traveling or signing ten thousand tip-in sheets or running or going to the farm to buy fresh mint for the iced tea she insisted on brewing herself or driving the kids to one of their seven thousand activities and playdates (and making him feel guilty because he rarely had time to pitch in) or inviting four other couples over for an evening of lobsters and rock anthems.

"Everyone else sees Superwoman," JP said. "I see someone who will do anything to avoid having sex with me."

One rainy day when there had been no customers, JP taught Amy to waltz, a skill left over from his finishing-school days, he told her. Amy had always been a good dancer. She took to it naturally and she could tell JP was impressed.

"Vivi has no rhythm," he said. "And no interest in touching me."

A couple of days before Amy was due to leave Nantucket—her job search had turned up nothing, so she was heading back to Alabama to enroll in cosmetology school at her mother's urging—JP insisted they pop a bottle of Cristal. This was a lavish gesture, but all summer Amy had watched JP spend money in careless ways (ordering this rare vintage, that crystal decanter, none of which ever sold), so what was one more bottle of bubbly? Amy had never tasted Cristal.

One bottle led to another and then to half of a third. Amy stood in the doorway that opened onto Nantucket Harbor. The sun was low in the sky; it looked like honey dripping off a spoon. There were fewer boats in slips, and the murmur across the way at Cru was subdued. Summer was ending. The view was heartbreakingly beautiful—seagulls standing on the wooden bollards, a glimpse of Brant Point Light in the distance.

"How can I go back to Alabama?" she said.

Suddenly, JP was beside her. When Amy turned, JP cupped her face and kissed her, softly, deeply, expertly. The kiss seemed to contain an entire summer of flirting, discovery, barely sublimated sexual energy. Amy thought of the kiss as a sweet goodbye to a relationship that could never be. She wanted to thank him; in many ways, JP had been *her* finishing school.

When they finally pulled apart, JP said, his voice husky, "I want you to stay here. With me."

It wasn't just lip service, and apparently it wasn't the Cristal talking either. JP was *serious.* He wanted Amy to stay on Nantucket; he wanted to *be* with her. The very next day, JP told Vivi that he had fallen for Amy Van Pelt, his employee.

It sometimes felt to Amy like JP was determined to change his life with a snap of his fingers. Vivi moved out; the wine store went belly-up; Amy commuted to cosmetology school on the Cape and rented a modest year-round apartment out by Nantucket Memorial Airport. When she graduated, she got a bottom-rung job at RJ Miller, sweeping up and washing hair. She also became the Hester Prynne of Nantucket; *everyone* knew she was the one who had broken up the Quinboro marriage. (*It wasn't like that!* Amy wanted to shout, but no one would have listened.) Because she was young and naive, Amy had hoped that, with time, she and Vivi could become friends, or if not friends, then friendly, or if not friendly, then civil. Amy had tried reading one of Vivi's books, *The Angle of Light*—JP kept first editions of all Vivi's books in chronological order on a shelf in the den—but she couldn't get into it. She wasn't much of a reader, and she made the mistake of telling Willa, then a freshman in college, that the book hadn't held her interest. Willa went home and told Vivi.

At some point, Amy began to suspect that JP hadn't meant to leave Vivi at all, that he had simply wanted her attention, because everywhere Amy looked, Vivi was present. Why did JP keep her books on such a prominent shelf? Why did he reach for the *Book Review* first when they spent Sunday mornings reading the *New York Times*? Why did he bring Vivi's name up in conversation whenever possible? Three years ago, when Amy moved in with JP (he'd made the offer only when Amy lost her year-round housing), Amy found two of Vivi's coats hanging in the closet. One was a pink wool belted driving coat, and the other was a flared white raincoat with three silver buckles that was lined with pale blue jacquard silk. Amy loved both coats so much that, if she'd had no pride, she might have worn them herself. She went through the pockets and found the stub of a movie ticket (*Eat, Pray, Love*) in one and a strawberry hard candy in another. Amy wondered if Vivi and JP had gone to see *Eat, Pray, Love* together or if Vivi had gone with her best friend, Savannah. Amy wondered where Vivi had picked up the hard candy as she unwrapped it and popped it in her mouth (she couldn't resist a strawberry hard candy, with its soft middle, or any candy, no matter how old and forlorn). Amy had asked JP about the coats and he said, "Yeah, sorry, she must have left them behind. Vivi has always been careless with her things." Amy gave the coats to Willa to take over to Vivi's house, but Willa brought them back, saying, "Mom doesn't want them."

"Well, what am *I* supposed to do with them?" Amy said. "They're her coats."

"She says you can have them." Willa had looked at Amy frankly then. "If they fit?"

Amy made a big show of stuffing both the coats into the kitchen trash as Willa looked on with cool eyes. No doubt Amy's adolescent behavior would be reported back to Vivi, and Amy thought, *Good! She doesn't care about her stupid (beautiful, stylish) coats and neither do I.* That evening when JP discovered the coats in the trash, covered with coffee grounds and eggshells, he'd cried out as though Amy had stuffed Vivi herself in the can.

In the divorce, Vivi was required to pay JP both child support and alimony. A lot of alimony. (She earned circles around him.) JP had left Vivi, and in the ensuing divorce, Vivi would be paying *him?* This seemed unfair, even to Amy.

Vivi's money has always been the elephant in the room. It only makes it worse that Vivi never complains about paying JP even though he has his own business and a wealthy mother, and she's never late with payments, or short. She never nickel-and-dimes him when she ends up paying for Leo's lacrosse equipment or Carson's car insurance. She just (graciously) pays for everything. Her generosity is a stranglehold. Amy hates that every time she takes a hot shower or goes to Ventuno for dinner with JP, Vivi is footing the bill.

If JP had any self-respect, he would stop accepting the alimony checks. But Amy knows he needs them; he still has a mortgage, and Leo is heading to college. And...he's accustomed to a certain lifestyle. He drives a vintage Land Rover that he fills with premium gas; he likes expensive coffee and organic fruit; he enjoys dinners out; he has dues to pay at the Field and Oar Club; he takes two vacations in the off-season—one ski trip and one tropical—and he wears nice clothes. (Amy recalls JP "taking a lunch" from the wineshop and returning an hour later with an eight-hundred-dollar cashmere-blend blazer that he'd bought at Ralph Lauren.)

Amy has been tempted to tell JP that he can spend Vivi's money but that she, Amy, will have no part of it.

But what would that mean? That Amy would move out? Find her own place? Or that Amy would stay but buy her own groceries, contribute her portion to the mortgage and utilities? She makes good money at the salon, but would it be enough? She figures she could pay for some of the life, but not all of it. As things stand now, she uses her salary and tips to pay for her car loan, her health insurance, her cell phone, her clothes, shoes, jewelry, and makeup, her barre and yoga classes, and some groceries, and she occasionally pays for dinners out. She has a small savings account that she will need (desperately) if she and JP ever break up.

But they won't break up—in fact, Amy knows there's a proposal in her future. Last December, Amy had been desperate to know if JP had bought her a ring for Christmas, so while he was doing errands one Saturday morning, she rifled through his dresser drawers and found *(Hallelujah!)* a velvet box containing a stunning sapphire-and-diamond engagement ring. Amy had put the box back exactly where she found it and tried to act natural. Inside, she was *soaring*. Finally! However, when Christmas Day arrived, the ring did not appear. (JP had gotten Amy a new makeup mirror for their bathroom, a cashmere hat, scarf, and gloves set, an OtterBox for her phone, and a very pretty necklace from Jessica Hicks.) At the next possible opportunity, Amy checked the drawer to make sure the ring was still there (it was), and she just figured JP was waiting for the right time.

Or…maybe JP was concerned because Amy's relationship with the kids had always been iffy, at best. (Willa was polite and formal with her, Carson ran hot and cold depending on what she needed from JP and Amy that day, and Leo was indifferent.) Amy usually took JP's lead when it came to his kids, which meant dinners once a month, showing up at their home games and staying for at least one quarter, and making plans for whichever holiday was JP's that year. It finally occurred to Amy that she should make an effort on her own. In the spring, she told both girls that she would give them free beauty services anytime. Willa had sniffed at the offer, but Carson jumped at the chance to come to the salon after hours. Carson was so pretty already that she was hard to improve upon, but Amy went all out, giving her a trim and a blow-dry, plus a tint and wax for her brows. Afterward, Carson asked Amy if she wanted to grab a drink at Petrichor, the wine bar.

"You could have knocked me over with a feather," Amy told Lorna later.

They each had two glasses of wine and shared the charcuterie platter. Carson talked about her bartending job at the Oyster-catcher, which would start in a few weeks. Amy asked Carson if she was dating anyone and Carson said, "No. Yes. Maybe. I can't talk about it." Which felt like a confidence. Amy had tactfully switched the topic to *Euphoria,* the show they were both binge-watching.

With that success under her belt, Amy moved on to Leo. She brought cupcakes to his final lacrosse game and offered to throw him a graduation party at the house. Leo made a squeamish face and then informed Amy that his mom was hosting a party.

"I'm sure you and Dad can come," Leo said.

"Of course we'll come!" Amy said.

Amy had never been invited to Vivi's new house (named Money Pit for the obvious reasons). She had mixed feelings about going, but JP double-checked with Vivi and confirmed it was fine, they were more than welcome. Amy promised herself she would act like a normal human being and not like a sociopath who stuffed the coats in the trash. Amy wore a new dress, black with white polka dots, and she bought Leo a graduation card and stuck one of her own hard-earned hundred-dollar bills inside. At the party, Amy tried to match Vivi's graciousness, even though Amy was uncomfortable and overdressed (Vivi wore white jeans and a University of Colorado T-shirt). She praised Vivi's hot bacon-and-blue-cheese dip (it was *delicious*); she offered to take a picture of JP, Vivi, and

Leo together; she chatted with the few people who didn't turn their backs or drift away when they saw Amy coming.

*I am finally fitting in!* she telegraphed to JP. *I've gotten the hang of it. Marry me!*

She might be imagining it, but it seems the more headway she makes with the kids, the more distant JP becomes. Amy feels him pulling away; she's been tempted to check his phone. JP has a lot of young women working for him at the Cone, some of whom wear cutoffs even though the Cone is kept at a brisk sixty-five degrees.

Another fear she has is that she and JP will get engaged but they will never get married because if they did, the money from Vivi would dry up. Vivi's money is like a noose placed lovingly around Amy's neck. There are times when Amy's jealousy of the woman gets so bad that she wishes Vivi would just disappear—move off-island or spontaneously combust. Then all of Amy's problems would be solved.

The good thing about Saturdays in June is that everyone is out of the salon by four o'clock. Amy finishes her last bride at quarter to four—the wedding is at six at the Sconset Chapel—and a hush comes over the place, which is nice, though Amy feels a little bit like Cinderella after the stepsisters leave for the ball. Her clients are off to pose for endless pictures, drink cocktails, eat hors d'oeuvres, listen to toasts, cut into beef Wellington, drink more cocktails, do the Electric Slide, and shamelessly hook up with the groom's third cousin or the bride's college roommate.

Amy takes a paper cup from the watercooler and fills it with the dregs of a bottle of champagne that is sitting in a bucket of melting ice near her chair. Amy hasn't had a thing to eat all day (which feels good) and the champagne goes straight to her head (which feels even better). Her top drawer is overflowing with manila tip envelopes.

Lorna comes over as soon as her last client leaves and says, "How are you holding up?"

"Great, but that was a hell of a day."

An incredulous expression washes over Lorna's face. "You didn't ring JP, did you?"

"No," Amy says. "I didn't have a second."

Lorna sighs. "Come outside, let's have a cig."

They step out onto the deck facing the back parking lot and light up. There's a table and chairs; Amy eats her lunch out here when the weather is nice and she has time. The first drag of her cigarette is a balm. She throws back what's left of the champagne and crumples the cup in her hand. "Should I sit down?"

"Yes." Lorna is so serious that Amy thinks for the first time that maybe she should be afraid.

"Is everything *okay?*" Amy says. She wonders if Willa miscarried again or if something happened to JP's mother, Lucinda. A stroke or a broken hip.

"Well." Lorna eyes Amy and blows smoke out of the side of her mouth. "No, not really. But jeezy, Pigeon, I'm not sure how you're going to take it."

"Take what?" Amy says. Her stomach squelches.

"Vivi was hit by a car this morning at the end of her road." Lorna pauses. "Pigeon, she's dead."

Amy opens her mouth. She knows Lorna isn't kidding and might not even be wrong, but sorry, hold on a second. *Vivi is dead? Vivi is dead. Vivi was hit by a car, and she's dead. Vivi is dead.*

Amy sits for a minute in complete stillness. She feels...she feels...her stomach...a horror...yes, she feels a thick, black, tar-like horror filling her insides. She wants to scream. Vivi is dead. JP called...*hours* ago. Said it was urgent. Because his ex-wife is dead.

The kids. The poor kids.

Lorna is watching her.

"I'm not going to sing out 'Ding-dong, the witch is dead,' if that's what you're thinking," Amy says. Her eyes fill with tears.

Lorna reaches out a hand. "I know you're not, honey. This must be...confusing for you?"

"A woman is dead. There's nothing confusing about that. It's tragic."

Lorna squeezes her hand.

"And, yes, confusing." Amy has to get her phone. She heads into the air-conditioned cool of the salon, but it's as if the salon has completely changed. Vivi is dead.

Her phone is clogged with texts from JP.

Call me ASAP
Urgent!!!
Amy, call me
Something terrible has happened
They won't put me through at the salon

There are also sixteen missed calls. Then more texts.

I'm at the house with the kids. Please come.
Don't come. I'll meet you at home.
Would you cancel our reservations at the Straight Wharf, please?
    I'll be home later. I can't leave the kids right now.
Text me when you get these messages but don't come to Vivi's.
    I'll meet you at home.

It's the last three texts that cut razor-thin lines into Amy's heart. JP doesn't want her at Vivi's. He's with his kids; the four of them are mourning together. Amy would be an interloper. She's self-aware enough to realize this.

Amy climbs into her car and closes her eyes. For ten years, Amy has told herself that what happened between JP and Vivi had nothing to do with her, but the stark truth is that Amy could have said no to JP, and by turning him down, she might have propelled him back to his family. She feels a monstrous guilt about her ungenerous thoughts and all the catty and awful comments she made to JP, to Lorna, and, on a few ill-advised occasions, to Vivi's own kids.

*I'm sorry, Vivi,* she thinks. *I was jealous. Insecure. You cast a long shadow. Your only flaw was that I couldn't compete. You were pretty and fun-loving and hardworking and magnetic, and I was jealous of you. I ate that jealousy (and a lot of doughnuts) for breakfast each day.*

*But you should know I admired you, though I was never confident enough to say it.*

Amy turns the key in the ignition. She'll call Straight Wharf in a minute. First, she's going to Hatch's for a bottle of wine, or maybe tequila, maybe the Casa Dragones that was Vivi's favorite. She will go home alone and drink with her demons.

# Leo

Leo can't eat; he may never eat again. When Carson says she has a pill, an Ativan, he asks her for two and she brings them with a glass of his mother's fresh-brewed iced tea with mint. A little while later, the world slows down and grows softer at the edges.

Leo's father shows up; he's normally an even-keeled, glass-half-full kind of guy but now he looks the way that Leo feels—like his heart has been firebombed, his spirit razed. JP starts out with a statement that he must have composed in his head on the ride over.

"We're going to figure this out, you aren't alone, I'm here for all of you," JP says.

"I'm not your mother, of course," he adds, and then he starts to cry so hard that Willa leads him over to the sofa.

He loved her, Leo thinks. He really loved her despite hating her also, which Leo understands a little better after last night.

Last night. Marissa. Cruz. Leo was so drunk that there are blank spots, but there are also indelible images, things he wishes were from a dream but that he knows really happened. Leo isn't sure how he got home, but he does remember pulling his mother's bottle of tequila off the shelf and doing a couple of shots once he was safely in his own kitchen. He wanted what happened at Fortieth Pole to go away. He wanted the tequila to erase it.

For the rest of his life, he will be haunted by the pounding on his door this morning and Cruz shouting, "Wake up, man! Wake up!" Leo had thought Cruz wanted to talk about the night before. It took him whole seconds to process what Cruz was saying: "Your mom went to the hospital. She's hurt, man. Hurt bad."

Leo called Willa right away, thinking she would know what to do; she was their mother's second in command. Leo's call woke her up; she didn't know anything about an accident. Cruz was insistent, damn near bawling. He saw Vivi lying on Kingsley, he'd called the paramedics, Vivi was taken away in an ambulance, and they all had to get to the hospital *now. Right now!* Leo woke up Carson, and they'd picked up Willa on the way.

Cruz drove his own car, and Leo was glad about that.

At the hospital, an unfamiliar doctor told them that Vivi hadn't made it. *She didn't make it* was too gentle a phrase because it sounded like Vivi hadn't made it this time but could maybe try again.

"She didn't make it?" Willa said.

"She was dead on arrival," the doctor said. Who was this doctor? Someone from off-island, a traveler. This doctor had no idea who

Vivi was, so how could he pronounce her dead? Lots of times people from off-island didn't understand the way things were done on Nantucket. Leo wanted to hear from someone he knew. Like Dr. Fields.

"Where's Dr. Fields?" Leo asked.

"Dr. Fields retired last year, I was told," the doctor said. "Would you like me to get the social worker?"

Rip showed up and drove Leo and his sisters home. Cruz went to the station to talk to the police because he had been the one to find Vivi on the ground.

Leo closes his eyes and when he opens them again, his father is gone and his mother's best friend, Savannah Hamilton, is walking into the front room. Savannah takes in Leo and his sisters—they haven't moved in what feels like hours; Leo has no idea what time it is—then she kneels in front of them, opening her arms. They fall into her. Savannah has a history so broad and so deep with their mother that hugging her and inhaling her familiar perfume is like getting Vivi back for a second. Savannah is single and sophisticated; she has no children and is the founder of Rise, an international children's charity. She owns a town house on Marlborough Street in Boston, a place so big that the three Quinboro children have their own bedrooms there. She is the godmother of all three of them.

Whenever the kids asked her why they all had the same godmother, she'd tell them, "Because I'm your mother's only friend."

And then, on cue, their mother would say, "When you have a friend like Savannah Hamilton, you don't need anyone else."

Everyone knew that Vivi put a version of Savannah in each of her books, the only differences being that the friend was named something like Samantha or Hannah and ran a PR firm or an advertising agency instead of a nonprofit. The best friend in Vivi's books was always tall and blond, like Savannah, and stylish, wearing only neutral colors. She was fiercely loyal and able to drop everything at any moment to drink coffee or tequila and talk through the protagonist's dramas.

The real Savannah was like that, especially the "fiercely loyal" part, though there were three people Savannah championed above Vivi—and those people were Willa, Carson, and Leo. Savannah had made it clear all through their growing up that she would always take their side, even against their mother. "I want to be the adult in your life that I never had," she said.

When their crying subsides now, Savannah wipes at her eyes then pulls a packet of tissues out of her clutch. "Let's blow our noses and try to focus for one minute."

Leo likes being given instructions.

Savannah says, "I will take care of everything. That way we don't have to get into the messy business of your father or Dennis doing it. Where is your mother's phone?"

"The police have it," Willa says.

"Why is that?" Savannah says.

"They have to check it out in case she took a picture or recording or something as she was hit," Willa says. "It's a long shot but they said they've solved hit-and-runs that way. They'll return the phone when they're finished with it."

"Bring it straight to me, please," Savannah says.

"I need to check it," Carson says. "We had a fight this morning and I sent her an apology text and I want to make sure she read it."

"Oh, Angel Bear," Savannah says. She calls all three of them Angel Bear, which started embarrassing Leo in the fifth grade, so she calls him just Bear. "Your mom knows you're sorry. Your mom was one of the most forgiving women I have ever met." Savannah lowers her voice. "Did you happen to notice how lovely and gracious she was with Amy at Leo's graduation party? And throwing it back even further, you do know I had to kick your mother out of my parents' house with nowhere to go her first summer here and she still stayed my best friend for"—Savannah's voice breaks—"thirty years."

"I want to make sure, though," Carson says.

"We will make sure, baby, I promise," Savannah says. "I'm going to contact Vivi's publisher. Her book comes out July thirteenth— that will likely go on ahead but we have to make a formal announcement by Monday, I think. And I will arrange for the funeral at St. Mary's followed by a reception at the Field and Oar." She pauses. "On my family's membership."

"Oh, man," Carson whispers, and she actually kind of smiles. "Mom would *love* that."

She *would* love it, Leo thinks. When his parents split, the Field and Oar Club membership went to Leo's dad, and the board of governors decided not to let Vivi rejoin on her own. When Willa and Rip got married at the club, Vivi had pretended like everything was just fine but right before the dancing started, Leo's girlfriend, Marissa, reported that she'd seen Vivi crying in the ladies' room.

"I wish she knew it," Willa says. "I wish we could tell her."

"She knows," Savannah says. "I'm not sure about you guys, but I feel her here."

Leo takes in the room—the fireplace that Vivi had repointed, the new hearth, the bookshelves built on the diagonal that Vivi insisted on because she'd seen them on Kelly Wearstler's Instagram feed, the giant clock made from salvaged barn boards, the turquoise tweed midcentury sofa that they all called the Girv. This room reflected Vivi's eclectic taste—as did every room on the first floor of Money Pit. She hadn't renovated the upstairs yet; she was waiting for "an unexpected windfall." She'd died without ever getting the walk-in closet of her dreams.

Leo loves Savannah and he's glad she's here but he can't stay awake another second.

"I have to go upstairs," he says. "I have to sleep. My head is pounding."

"You drank Mom's tequila," Carson says.

"You go to bed, Bear," Savannah says to Leo as she gives him a squeeze. "Frankly, I could use a shot of Vivi's tequila. I wonder where she hid it."

Leo climbs the stairs feeling eighty years old instead of eighteen. His mother is dead. That feels like a big nut he's expected to swallow even though it's physically impossible.

His bedroom is dark with just an outline of fire pink around his window shade. The sun is going down. His mother woke up today. Today was the last day she was ever alive.

He reaches for his phone, and wow—there are a lot of messages. He suspects most of them are from Marissa.

Leo broke up with Marissa Lopresti, his girlfriend of nearly two years, last night during a bonfire at Fortieth Pole. Most of the just-graduated senior class was there and although it wasn't a graduation party per se—those had ended a couple of weeks earlier—it still had a nostalgic feel to it, like, *We only have so long before we go our separate ways and things will never be the same so we'd better enjoy this now.*

Leo was having a beer a few yards away from the lip of the firepit and talking to Cruz. Because Dartmouth was on the quarter system, Cruz would have a week free in November when he could come out to Boulder and they could ski Loveland Pass.

Marissa had overheard the conversation. "I can't believe you're making plans with Cruz and not me," she said. Then she smirked at Cruz. "Black people don't even ski."

Cruz had laughed the comment off. "This one does."

Leo finished his beer and crumpled the can. He was sick of Marissa's jealousy and her insecurity and the casually racist remarks she tossed at Cruz.

He said to Marissa, "Apologize to the man, please."

"I was joking," Marissa said, and she hugged Cruz. "He knows

I'm joking. I obviously realize that Cruz skis. He went with you to Stowe last year."

"Then why say it?" Leo asked.

"It's cool, bruh," Cruz said. He held up his palms. "I'm impossible to offend, Marissa. I thought you'd learned that."

But Leo couldn't shake it off this time. "Marissa, come with me for a second." Leo led Marissa down the beach away from the raging fire and the bass line of Lil Uzi Vert, and she reached for his hand, maybe thinking he wanted to fool around in the dunes. He stuffed his hands in his pants pockets, and once they were at the waterline, well out of earshot of everyone, he said—simply, so there could be no misunderstanding—"I want to break up."

She laughed. "What? Because of *that?* He knew I was kidding, Leo."

"I'm tired of your jabs and your cute little comments. It's like you can't help yourself, you have to find a way to throw shade at Cruz."

"He hogs your attention, you have to admit—"

"He's my best friend. I've known him way longer than I've known you." Leo shook his head. "But that's not the point. The point is I think we'll both be happier if we spend the summer apart and then go our own ways without any emotional entanglements."

"You sound like your mother," Marissa said. "She hates me, you know. She never wanted us to get this serious."

"She thinks we're too young."

"What about Willa and Rip? They're *married.*" Marissa wrapped her arms around Leo. "And we're getting married. You even said so."

Leo knew he was guilty of indulging Marissa's fantasy of the two of them getting married after they graduated from college. For most of their relationship, Leo had been content to go along with whatever Marissa wanted just to keep the peace. But those days were over.

"Sorry, Marissa. I don't want to be with you anymore."

"You're drunk."

"I've had one beer. I know what I'm saying. I know what I'm doing." He sighed. "I just want to be free."

There had been more discussion, Marissa trying to persuade him to take it back, Marissa telling him he'd be sorry, Marissa apologizing for the times she'd been cruel—she couldn't help it, she said; she had father issues—Marissa getting angry and calling Leo names, Marissa crying, and, finally, Marissa storming off, which came as a relief. Leo pulled another beer out of the ice-filled trash can and found Cruz, who was sitting by the fire talking to his girlfriend, Jasmine Kelly, who was going to Vanderbilt in the fall.

"That's done," Leo said. "I broke up with her."

Jasmine made a noise of disbelief with her lips and Leo said, "I'm serious. It's over. No turning back."

"Whoa," Cruz said. "Are we staying or going?"

"Staying," Leo said. "But I need something stronger than this beer."

There are at least a dozen missed calls from Marissa in the midnight hour while Leo was still at the party. The last missed call was at 1:27, and then they dropped off; she must have fallen asleep.

There's one text from her, sent at noon today. It says: Alexis told me what happened to your mom. I'm so sorry. Alexis says Cruz is a suspect.

*Cruz is* not *a suspect,* Leo thinks. Cruz was the one who found Vivi.

There's a string of texts from Cruz:

The police impounded my car. Forensics has to check it. My dad came and got me. I'm home.

I'm not sure when you'll get this, but you need to clean your phone.

There's gonna be a text from Peter Bridgeman, a photo. Delete it.

I'm home. Call me.

She was my mom too.

Delete that photo, man. Please. We can talk about it later. Or not.

Leo scrolls back to a time he now thinks of not as "morning" or "last night" but "when Mom was alive."

Sure enough, a text from Maybe: Peter. Attachment: 1 image.

Leo clicks on it and immediately leans over to dry-heave.

*No!* he thinks. He breaks out in a sweat. Peter Bridgeman took this? Leo races for the bathroom and dry-heaves into the toilet, then realizes he has left the photo open on his bed where anyone could see it.

He runs back out, snaps up his phone, deletes the photo, then deletes it from his deleted file.

Should he call Peter? He has never liked the kid and they had that fight last fall when Peter got in Leo's face. Leo had wanted to whip him so badly but there were people around to break it up and Leo supposed he was grateful for that. Peter is sort of family; Willa's husband, Rip, is Peter's uncle.

Who else did Peter send this picture to other than Cruz? Leo could call and threaten Peter—but by now, Peter would have heard about Vivi, and even lowlife Peter Bridgeman would feel bad for Leo, so hopefully he'll delete the picture and that will be the end of that.

But Leo fears it's just the beginning.

# Nantucket

When the news breaks that the writer Vivian Howe has been killed in a hit-and-run off the Madaket Road, everyone has something to say.

She was a local—she had lived on Nantucket for over twenty-five years—but she wasn't a native. She was from...Pennsylvania? Ohio? That made her a wash-ashore.

A few years earlier, the editor of the *Nantucket Standard,* Jordan Randolph, had pointed out an error in one of Vivian Howe's novels. She had referred to a ferry unloading at Steamship Wharf rather than Steamboat Wharf, and he'd verbally flogged her in his weekly editorial, saying that if she couldn't get the basics of Nantucket correct then she had no place writing about this island. This was met with backlash. The ferries were run by the Steamship Authority so nearly all of us—wash-ashore and native—called it Steamship Wharf. Honor Prentice, who was a fifth-generation Nantucketer, wrote a letter to the editor saying that even *he* called it Steamship Wharf.

Advantage, Vivi.

Most of the small-business owners in town loved Vivi because her books drove tourism—in particular, they brought in day-trippers with money to spend. When Vivi set a scene in her books at a specific restaurant, people wanted to eat there. When a character bought a dress at a certain boutique, her readers wanted to shop there.

Vivi was also blamed for the downside of tourism. As Lucinda

Quinboro sat in a line of cars at the intersection by the high school, she said to her best friend and bridge partner, Penny Rosen, "This is all Vivi's fault, you know."

And Penny said, "You'll blame anything on Vivi."

It had been a big deal ten years earlier when Vivi and her husband, JP Quinboro, divorced. Some of us knew it was because JP fell for Amy Van Pelt, his young employee at the wineshop (which we never set foot in because the prices were so inflated). JP caused conversations to awkwardly stop wherever he went—the Nickel for sandwiches, Marine Home Center for paint, the Chamber of Commerce for Business After Hours—because no one knew what to say to him except *Wake up, man.* Vivi moved out, and when her new novel *Along the South Shore* proved to be a "breakout book," she went on tour for so long that some of us thought she had left the island for good.

But eventually Vivi returned, and after a while, she seemed to recover. She bought a house on Kingsley that looked great on paper, though once Vivi moved in, leaks sprung and she discovered the fancy wine fridge was on the fritz and there was a pervasive smell of rot at the base of the stairs and she could hear mice (or rats) in the ceiling and she realized she had bought a money pit and decided that would become the official name of the house. She kept the tradespeople among us busy for years—her contractor Marky Mark, her plumber, her cute electrician Surfer Boy, and the person she revered above everyone else: her landscaper, Anastasia.

Vivi seemed to be flourishing and we cheered her on.

The news of her death was a shock.

The Springers had seen Cruz DeSantis kneeling by the body at the scene. They pulled over to ask what happened, but Cruz was too upset to say anything other than that the ambulance was on its way. Had Cruz DeSantis been the one to hit her?

We hoped not.

Cruz DeSantis was a shining star of the just-graduated senior class. He was going to Dartmouth on a full ride, which is a testament to his father, Joe, who owns the Nickel sandwich shop on Oak Street. The Nickel is tiny, but its influence in our community is outsize. Anyone who has ever had Joe's deviled-egg salad with crispy bacon and lamb's lettuce on toasted olive sourdough or his grilled salmon with fresh spinach and raspberry-dill aioli on a soft brioche roll will tell you—they may be "just sandwiches," but there's a reason why the Nickel is number one on Nantucket's Tripadvisor in the category "Restaurants, Downtown."

Joe DeSantis served in Iraq with the storied Eighty-Second Airborne. He's not only an American hero, he's a Nantucket hero. He brings the day's leftover sandwiches (when there are any) to the fire station or to Nantucket Cottage Hospital or to the AA meetings at St. Paul's Episcopal. He donates gift certificates to every island nonprofit. You (almost) hated to ask the man for anything because he never said no. Joe is also an extremely good listener. He called the sandwich shop the Nickel because of the old *Peanuts* cartoon of Lucy offering advice for five cents. (A framed picture of this cartoon hangs on the wall of the shop.)

Cruz is as generous, good-hearted, and hardworking as Joe. Cruz bought the Jeep he drives with money he earned at his two summer jobs—he stocks shelves at the Stop and Shop and tutors kids in math and science.

We can't stand the thought of Cruz's future in jeopardy because of this accident. All we know for sure is that he was at the scene.

Alexis Lopresti was working the desk at the Nantucket Police Department when the call came in that Vivi had been killed. She has been trained not to divulge any police business under penalty of losing her job, but those of us who know Alexis realize that she does not believe the rules apply to her.

She texted her sister, Marissa, immediately. Vivi Howe was killed in a hit-and-run. They're questioning Cruz. Falco saw him run a stop sign a couple minutes before it happened.

Marissa Lopresti had driven out Eel Point Road to a sheltered, shallow saltwater pond called the Bathtub where her mother used to bring her and Alexis when they were little. Almost nobody hung out at the Bathtub—*buggy* and *stagnant* were words that came to mind—and sure enough, Marissa found it deserted. Once there, she searched through the Jeep, found her phone—it had fallen under the passenger-side seat—and studied the picture that had been sent to her by Peter Bridgeman.

At that moment, the text from Alexis came in. Vivi was *dead.* The police were questioning *Cruz.* An officer had seen Cruz run a stop sign and go speeding down Surfside Road.

*Oh my God,* Marissa thought.

Marissa drove her Jeep straight into the Bathtub, then sacrificed her phone to the icky, squelchy bottom, waded out, and walked, soaking wet, over the dunes to Eel Point to find help.

# The Chief

The traffic homicide investigator arrives from the Cape. Her name is Lisa Hitt; she's fifty or so and what some people might call a dynamo. She has long brunette hair, lots of energy, and always a big smile, even in the gravest of circumstances.

As the Chief is driving her to the scene, he tells her what he knows. When he says the name of the deceased—Vivian Howe—Lisa cries out.

"No!" She slaps the dashboard in front of her. "No, no, no! She's my favorite author. This is going to sound so stupid, but I follow her on Instagram. I've seen pictures of her kids. I've watched videos of her home improvements. In fact, when I heard I was needed over here, I booked a room at the Nantucket Hotel because that's the hotel Vivi mentions in her books—she calls it the Castle—and I made a reservation at Nautilus because that's Vivi's favorite restaurant." Lisa pauses. "I can't believe Vivian Howe is dead. I think I'm going to cry."

*There's no crying in forensics,* the Chief thinks. "We're here," he says. He pulls over just shy of the turnoff to Kingsley. Smith has replaced Falco and is directing traffic around the cordoned-off area. The Chief sees that bouquets are already piling up on the corner. He hasn't yet told Andrea that Vivian Howe is dead, but she might know by now. It's a small island.

The Nantucket forensics van pulls in right behind them, and Lisa Hitt gets to work (they call her Lisa Hitt-and-Run, the Chief remembers now) taking photographs, measuring what tracks she can find in the road, collecting samples of Vivian Howe's blood from the sand and dirt.

"It looks like the person backed up here," Lisa says, pointing to a section of tracks. "But there aren't any skid marks, and there's more than one set of tires here. It's impossible to know if these are from the vehicle that hit the victim, the vehicle of the person who found her, or someone else entirely." She stands up. "You have one vehicle impounded?"

The Chief nods. Cruz's Jeep.

"And we'll get her clothes from the ME? The body is being sent to the mainland for an autopsy?"

"Yes." The Chief has a bad feeling in the pit of his stomach. He hates what Falco said about Cruz running a stop sign and then taking off like a bat out of hell down Surfside. Falco should have pulled him over! That's why police stop speeding cars, so something like this doesn't happen. Why hadn't Falco just done his job?

"Vivi was—what? Five three? And weighed a hundred pounds

soaking wet? If she got hit head-on by a car going twenty-five or so, there might not even be a dent in the fender."

"But there might be," the Chief says.

"But there might be," Lisa agrees. "You recall the words of Edmond Locard, right, Chief?"

The Chief hasn't the foggiest.

" 'Every contact leaves a trace,' " Lisa says.

Ed feels sick. He has arrested friends before, even assisted in FBI stings of friends. But he has never experienced the conflicting emotions that he feels now.

"Let me look at the car you have," Lisa says. "You know the driver?"

"I do. Ms. Howe knew him well. He's friends with her son."

Lisa gasps. "I hope you aren't talking about Cruz? Vivi posted pictures of Cruz all the time. She called him her fourth child."

The Chief nods.

Lisa sighs. "This is all very life-imitating-art here, Chief. I feel like I'm living in one of Vivian Howe's novels." She smiles wistfully. "They usually have happy endings."

"Not today," the Chief says. Falco seeing Cruz run the stop sign isn't the only thing bothering the Chief. The other is Cruz claiming he was driving to the Howe residence from his house, which is nowhere near Hooper Farm. So one of them is either mistaken or lying. The Chief doesn't like this one bit.

And, of course, no matter who did it, a woman is still dead. And three children are left without a mother.

# Vivi

The green door opens and Martha enters Vivi's boho-chic paradise with a different Hermès scarf wound through her hair and knotted at her neck in a way you couldn't possibly get right unless you worked for Hermès or were the editor of French *Vogue*.

"I like what you did with the scarf" is what Vivi says instead of *What are you doing here* or *Why are you always sneaking up on me?*

"I come when you need me," Martha says, because apparently Martha can read her mind.

"Do I need you now?"

"Yes. Today is your funeral, Vivian."

"I know." Vivi has been watching the preparations below. The police have closed Federal Street between India and Cambridge. They do that only when they're expecting a very large crowd.

Vivi and Martha stand at the big window and peer down just as Rip's Yukon is ushered through the crowd by the police. Vivi watches her children clamber out and onto the sidewalk in front of the church.

Vivi stifles a sob. She isn't sure why she still has emotions and such strong, soul-searing pain. Isn't that something you let go of when you die?

"Only once you join the choir," Martha says. "While you're watching from here, you remain hostage to your feelings."

"Ugh," Vivi says. "I can't bear it."

"We don't have to watch," Martha says. "Lots of people choose to pass on this part."

"They do?" Vivi says. That seems absurd; she isn't going to miss her own funeral. No way. It's bad enough her body isn't there. Her body has been sent to the Cape in the cargo hold of the Steamship (no dignity) for an autopsy, but the kids and Savannah decided to hold the memorial service today, Wednesday, which Vivi agrees is wise. To drag out holding a service would mean to drag out everyone's grief and mourning. Vivi's publisher, Midst and Hupa (which Vivi long ago nicknamed "Mr. Hooper," an homage to the *Sesame Street* grocer of her childhood), has arranged for an online memorial service tomorrow.

*Boom, boom,* Vivi thinks. She'll be old news by the end of the week.

"Stop feeling sorry for yourself," Martha says. "Let's stay in the moment, shall we, and appreciate the wonderful turnout."

Rip and Leo are wearing navy blazers and khaki pants. Leo's pants have a ketchup stain on the thigh. Vivi knows those pants were last worn during graduation; right after the ceremony, Leo and Cruz and a bunch of their other buddies went to Lola Burger. The pants have been sitting on the floor of Leo's bedroom since then. Vivi sighs. She did her kids' laundry (reluctantly), but only if the clothes made it into the hamper in the hallway. She didn't go into Leo's or Carson's room looking for them (when Willa lived at home, she always did her own laundry). This seemed like a reasonable rule while Vivi was alive, but now she regrets not doing a better job. Already, Leo looks like a kid without a mother.

Willa is wearing some black linen Eileen Fisher frock that couldn't be less flattering. It's always been Willa's style to hide her body rather than flaunt it. Carson is the flaunter. She has raided Vivi's closet and chosen the most inappropriate black dress imaginable: a see-through lace Collette Dinnigan, vintage 2007, that Vivi splurged on after she sold the Hungarian rights to *Five-Star Island.* The dress is supposed to be worn with a strapless black slip but Carson is wearing it with a strapless nude slip so it appears, at first glance, that Carson is naked underneath. She's also wearing Vivi's black studded Christian Louboutin stilettos. Carson looks like she's heading to an S and M club in East Berlin. She's gorgeous, breathtaking, but wow—inappropriate. Why didn't Savannah steer her toward something a little more subdued?

At that moment, Savannah steps out of the church. She's in a navy sheath that has a block of happy yellow at the hem; when Vivi blinks, tears fall. Savannah only wears clothes that are black, white, beige, or denim blue (with gold and silver thrown in for evening), and Vivi recalls telling Savannah many times in late-night drunken conversations that when she died (in the vague and distant future), she wanted Savannah to wear *color* to her funeral.

Savannah remembered. And she'd done it. Because Savannah Hamilton is a best friend for the ages.

The expression on Savannah's face when she sees Carson's outfit tells Vivi that Savannah *did* suggest something more modest and Carson ignored her. Surprise, surprise.

Savannah beckons and the kids trudge up the steps. Willa and Carson are...holding *hands?* Has Vivi's death brought them together? Was that what it took for them to realize they're sisters? How many times had Vivi pulled her girls away from each other, their faces flushed, Willa with angry pink scratch marks down her cheeks, Carson's green eyes flashing with fury and guilt? After one of their slapping-and-hair-pulling fights, she'd said to them, "I would have given anything in this world to have been blessed with a sister."

Martha pipes up. "Sisters can be a mixed bag." She gives a weary laugh. "Having a sister doesn't always mean an automatic best friend."

"Did something happen between you and Maribeth?" Vivi asks.

"Story for another day," Martha says.

Savannah shepherds the kids inside and the doors close behind them, leaving everyone else to bake out on the street.

Dennis arrives; he's wearing his gray suit even though Vivi told him at Willa's wedding that the pants were a bit tight in the seat and the gray a little too corporate for Nantucket. Despite the grown-up attire, Dennis looks as lost and sad as a little boy. The only person Vivi confided to about her split from Dennis (*I need space, the book is coming out, away on tour, think it would be best if you stopped spending the night, you might want to start dating someone else and if you do, I totally understand*) was Savannah. Savannah felt Vivi needed to pull out the hatchet and make a swift, clean break. "It will feel cruel in the moment," Savannah said. "But it's kinder in the long run."

*I'm sorry, Dennis,* Vivi thinks. If she had known she was going to die, she might have spared him the indignity of the breakup. She wishes she could set Dennis up with one of the single women from her barre class.

"You can make that happen," Martha says. "But you'll have to use one of your nudges."

*No, no,* Vivi thinks. She isn't going to squander one of her nudges on Dennis's future romantic happiness. He'll have to find someone on his own.

Vivi sees Marissa Lopresti show up. Her dress gives the Collette Dinnigan a run for its money—it's a backless black minidress with a plunging neckline and cutouts at the sides. It's the same dress Marissa wore to Money Pit for Christmas dinner last year. Vivi had raised her eyebrows then and offered Marissa a sweater, and Marissa had given Vivi an incredulous look, as if to say that a sweater would completely negate the point of the dress.

Marissa is attended by her sister, Alexis, five years older, and her mother, Candace, who, thanks to a lot of Botox, looks only five years older than Alexis. Candace Lopresti is a consultant for the luxury-hotel industry. She travels all the time for work—to the Oberoi in Mumbai, to the Mandarin Oriental in Canouan. While the girls were in middle school and high school, respectively, she left them at home with *her* mother, who was quite elderly (and senile). This arrangement had the appearance of propriety, of checking the box of "girls, chaperoned," but Vivi happens to know that Alexis, at least, had run wild. It is oh so ironic that Alexis now works at the police station, because Alexis Lopresti was a very bad teenager.

"You shouldn't judge," Martha says.

*True,* Vivi thinks. Carson wasn't much better.

Once Leo and Marissa started dating, Marissa handled her mother's absences by basically living at Money Pit, often staying an entire weekend. "My mom's away," she would say on Friday afternoon when she showed up with her Louis Vuitton Keepall, an exorbitantly expensive piece of luggage that her mother had given her in place of love, manners, and a sense of responsibility. (Wow, Vivi really *is* judgy today!)

Alexis and Marissa let their mother lead them into the church. Vivi wonders why Marissa didn't come with Leo.

And where is Cruz?

Vivi sees JP ascending the stairs. Vivi wonders if he'll start slapping backs and chatting people up. But no—he slips into the church without so much as a wave to anyone.

Where is Amy? Vivi wonders. Did JP leave her to the tedious business of parking the car, or did she (wisely) decide not to come?

Martha clears her throat.

"She's not coming?" Vivi says.

Martha ever so slightly shakes her head and Vivi feels relief. Maybe she is an evil and vengeful person, but she is happy that the woman who stole her husband isn't going to sit in church, up front with her children, and pretend to mourn.

The doors to the church open and people file inside.

There are a few late arrivals.

Vivi notices Cruz and Joe DeSantis marching down India Street. Joe has a firm hand on Cruz's back and is pushing him along.

*Cruz!* Vivi thinks. She'd expected him to be inside already, sitting with her kids.

Cruz says, "I'll wait out here."

Joe says, "After all that woman did for you, after all the meals she fed you, all the books she lent you, that beautiful letter of recommendation she wrote, the genuine love she showed you day in and day out since you've been in short pants? You're coming inside, son."

"No," Cruz says. He squares his shoulders and locks his arms across his chest.

Vivi can hardly believe her eyes. Cruz never defies his father, and for good reason. Joe DeSantis is as tall and unyielding as a brick wall and he has a deep, commanding voice. He's not scary, exactly, or intimidating, but the man has a distinguished presence. Cruz usually respects—and obeys—him.

"I never thought the day would come that I would say this, but I'm disappointed in you." Joe opens the church door, dips his fingers in the holy water, and genuflects, then the door closes.

Cruz takes a shuddering breath. Something is wrong, Vivi thinks. Something is *really* wrong. He looks skyward, squinting behind his glasses.

*Does he see me?* Vivi wonders.

"No," Martha says. "We've been over this."

*Does he sense me?* she wonders.

Cruz follows his father into the church.

Vivi spies a man hurrying down Main Street; he turns left at the Hub, heading for the church.

It's...Zach Bridgeman.

Well, okay, there have been latecomers to every church service in the history of the world, and today, for Vivi's memorial, the latecomer is Zach. Pamela must already be inside, seated with the elder Bonhams. Zach takes the church steps two at a time on the diagonal. When he opens the door, Vivi hears organ music and sees everyone rise. Time to go inside.

But instead of going up to the front, Zach slides into the far corner of the vestibule.

"Huh," Vivi says. Maybe he has to get back to the control tower, maybe he wants to sneak a cigarette, maybe he doesn't want to call attention to his tardiness by walking to the front of the church while everyone is watching.

"This will make sense to you later," Martha says.

Martha is starting to annoy Vivi. She knows everything. She's the omniscient narrator that Vivi never asked for. (Vivi prefers close third-person.)

"Sorry, not sorry," Martha says.

"Is there something going on with Zach?" Vivi says.

Martha nods.

*Well, okay, then,* Vivi thinks. She's a novelist. She's intrigued.

The processional hymn is "Love Divine, All Loves Excelling," one of Vivi's favorites. So someone (Willa) listened to Vivi on the rare occasions when they made it to church and Vivi mentioned that she'd like this hymn sung at her funeral.

After the hymn, everyone sits.

The kids are in the first pew, sandwiched between JP and Savannah. The three of them are a soggy, weeping mess.

As a mother, Vivi wasn't perfect, not even close. Willa, for example, wanted Vivi to be more like Rip's mother, Tink Bonham— cool, elegant, reserved. Vivi was, admittedly, none of these things. She occasionally ate noisily and snorted when she laughed and she swore like a sailor and she honked and flipped people off when she drove (but only off-island) and she ugly-cried at sad movies and video clips of servicemen and -women returning from overseas and surprising their kids at school. All of this embarrassed Willa and, Vivi thought, inspired just the tiniest bit of disdain.

Carson, meanwhile, wore her disdain for Vivi like a neon feather boa. Vivi often felt like she could do nothing right in Carson's eyes. Any détente, any period of friendship and affection, was always temporary and followed by a blowup (such as the fight they had the morning Vivi died). And yet, Carson is sobbing like she's holding her own broken heart in her hands.

Leo is usually the stoic. When he dislocated his shoulder in a middle-school lacrosse game, he didn't make a sound. He never cried getting shots as a baby. He had a high tolerance for pain and discomfort; his sisters used to fling him around, draw on him, dress him up. Willa once dropped him on his head in their gravel drive-way. Vivi thought Leo might meet the fact of her death with quiet strength, and while there are occasional flickers of that—he takes a breath, mops his face, focuses—he always dissolves again.

*My babies,* she thinks. *They need me. I never had to be their best friend, I never had to be cool or funny, I didn't have to make all those snacks or bring them treats from the grocery store or lavish them with gifts the Christmas that JP and I split; I didn't have to drive them to the beach, picking up half a dozen friends on the way, when they could just as easily have ridden their bikes.*

*All I had to do was hug them, kiss them, rock them to sleep, read to them, tell them I was proud of them and that I was happy, so happy, that they were mine.*

*I'm here,* she thinks. *I'm here.*

Vivi wants to let the kids know she's watching. Should she use one of the nudges? What would she do? Have a car drive past blaring "Spirit in the Night," by the Boss? Create a spontaneous, out-of-nowhere lightning storm?

"I want to use one of my nudges," Vivi says. "Let the kids know I'm here."

"I'd wait," Martha says. "Until they need you."

"Are you not watching? They need me now."

"They're fine," Martha says. "This is normal."

Vivi supposes it is normal—their mother died suddenly, without warning, and they had no time to prepare or say goodbye.

The thing is, Vivi knows exactly how they feel.

Just like that, she's sucked out of this church and plopped into the front row at St. John Bosco Catholic Church in Parma, Ohio. It's February 18, 1987. Vivi is seventeen years old, a senior in high school. Her applications to college have all been mailed in, and her father has just killed himself by running the family car, a 1982 Ford Country Squire station wagon, in the garage.

Her father's death is not only a tragedy (a person dying in the prime of his life); it's also a scandal. There are whispers in the church, in the neighborhood, and in the community as a whole. *Why did he do it? Was there a note?*

There was no note, no explanation.

Vivi's father, Frank Howe, works for the phone company, Ohio Bell. He's a "manager," so he wears a shirt and tie to the office but no jacket. Vivi knows nothing about his work life; what it is he manages, she has no idea and doesn't ask. Once a year, Vivi and her mother, Nancy, go to the "company picnic," which is held at Frank's boss's house in a subdivision that's nicer than the Howes'. Mr. Ricard, the boss, has an in-ground pool and a tiki bar, and Vivi appreciates these things even though she dreads the company picnic because she's expected to hang out with the other employee kids, none of whom she knows. She always brings a book and spends the afternoon on a chaise, reading. On the way home, her mother always calls her "antisocial," and Vivi shrugs and says under her breath, "Sit on it." One year when Vivi attends this picnic, her reading is interrupted by the sound of a barbershop quartet singing "Coney Island Baby." This is startling enough, but Vivi sits bolt upright when she realizes that the man singing the baritone part is her father.

Vivi didn't know her father could sing! How and when did he learn the harmonies, the lyrics? This is the first time Vivi thinks of her father as a *person,* someone who has talents and interests of his own.

Vivi's mother is deeply, almost painfully religious; her idea of interior decorating is to hang up as many crucifixes as possible. She's the head secretary at the church rectory; she's on a first-name basis with the priests and knows the business of all of the parishioners. Everyone calls her a saint—she organizes the canned-food drives, the clothing drives, the relief for the famine in Ethiopia. She ministers to the sick and the elderly when the priests are busy; she volunteers at the battered women's shelter. She runs the soup kitchen and leads the women's Bible study.

Only Vivi and her father know that Nancy isn't a saint. At home, she's dictatorial and impatient. It's her way or the highway. Nancy Howe is in a constant battle with her weight, and Vivi and Frank are casualties, even though they're both thin as rails. If Nancy is on a diet (which she always is), Vivi and Frank are on a diet. They eat bizarre and awful dishes like lasagna made with cottage cheese, dry-broiled fish fillets, sugar-free cake. They say grace before dinner, holding hands; Vivi's mother goes on and on for full minutes while dinner grows cold.

Nancy smokes like a chimney, though always outside in the garage. Everyone is allowed one vice, she says. This is the only thing that lets Vivi know her mother is human.

On Saturday mornings, Vivi and her father go to the Perkins in Middleburg Heights for breakfast while her mother works at the soup kitchen or picks up floral arrangements for the weekend services. Both Vivi and her father look forward to these breakfasts all week. They always sit in the same hunter-green vinyl booth and have the same waitress, Cindy, who has a high ponytail and wears bright pink lipstick. "It wouldn't be Saturday without my two favorite customers," Cindy always says. "Coffee?"

Yes, Vivi is allowed to drink coffee at these breakfasts. Cindy brings Vivi her own silver pitcher of cream and the sugar dispenser. Then Vivi and Frank pore over the huge laminated menu and order whatever they want: scrambled eggs and bacon and sausage or hash browns and lightly buttered rye toast that comes with little packets of jelly or pancakes that have a fluffy dollop of butter on top or waffles with strawberries and whipped cream or French toast sprinkled with powdered sugar or omelets oozing with cheese and soft brown onions and tomato and green pepper. Frank brings the *Plain Dealer* and he gives Vivi a section to read, which makes her feel grown up and also keeps her from eating too fast. They savor not only the food but the freedom from Vivi's mother's rules and regulations, her diets and diatribes. The real grace that Vivi experiences growing up are these stolen hours in a chain restaurant sitting across from her father as they scrape the syrup off their plates with the backs of their forks and Frank winks at his daughter and slides two quarters across the table so Vivi can go buy her horoscope from the vending machine in the breezeway while he pays their bill and leaves Cindy a tip.

At seventeen years old, Vivi can't understand why her father would kill himself, so she assumes that, like the barbershop quartet, he had been keeping some things secret. Had he been fired? (No.) Had he been in financial trouble? (No, although because he committed suicide, the life-insurance policy is null and void, and Vivi and her mother have lost their main breadwinner.) Did he have a lover? (This doesn't seem likely, though Vivi wonders about their waitress Cindy, because she's the only other woman Vivi saw her father interact with on a regular basis.)

What can Vivi do but blame the only person left, her mother? Nancy Howe is responsible for Frank's suicide because she made their lives so cheerless and dull.

There are bitter fights in the days that follow Frank Howe's death. One starts when Vivi overhears her mother telling someone on the phone that by killing himself, Frank had "chosen to spend eternity in hell."

"How dare you!" Vivi screams once her mother hangs up. "My father is not in hell!"

Nancy Howe's expression remains unchanged as she lights a cigarette; now that Frank is dead, she has started smoking in the house. "He committed a cardinal sin." She exhales. "I don't make the rules, Vivian Rose. God does."

Vivi has a boyfriend named Brett Caspian. They started dating back in September, right as senior year began. They're a bit of an odd couple because Vivi is a "goody-two-shoes"; she takes honors classes and she's the editor of the school literary magazine. Brett Caspian is a "druggie." He has long, feathered hair; he wears flannel shirts and jeans and clunky Timberland boots; he smokes and is the lead singer and guitarist for a band called Escape from Ohio. Escape from Ohio plays at all the high-school beer parties, and although Vivi rarely goes to the beer parties—she's usually home studying— she has been to one or two and thinks the band is pretty good.

The second week of school, Vivi is chosen to attend a fiction-writing workshop given by a Famous Author over at Normandy High. The three-day workshop is transformative. Vivi is something of a shining star, singled out by the Famous Author for her short story about an overweight housewife who thinks her husband is having an affair only to discover that he's been singing in a barbershop quartet.

The only problem with the three-day workshop is that Vivi has missed three days of her regular classes—AP European history, AP physics, and AP calculus.

She stays after school to make up a quiz in calculus; it's the first quiz of the year, on derivatives. Vivi's calculus teacher, Mr. Emery, also happens to have detention duty—and the only kid in detention that day is Brett Caspian.

Brett is sitting two rows ahead and one seat to Vivi's left, lounging like he's at the beach, his feet up on the chair in front of him. He has his binder on the desk and a pen with a chewed cap in his hand but he makes no move to do any homework. Instead, he taps the pen in a complicated drum rhythm, staring at the ceiling first and then at Mr. Emery, who is completely immersed in grading papers. Vivi does her best to ignore Brett Caspian, though the tapping is distracting. She looks up and starts to ask him to please stop, but as soon as she takes a breath, he turns and winks at her.

Is it fair to say this wink changes Vivi's life?

Her whole body flushes and she can no longer concentrate on derivatives. It must have been a sarcastic wink because, in high school in 1986, Vivian Howe isn't someone who gets winked at. She's wearing a khaki A-line skirt and a petal-pink polo and a pair of off-brand boat shoes that she begged her mother for at Higbee's. She's a devotee of *The Official Preppy Handbook* and tries to create the looks on a budget. The looks are not sexy or inviting.

Mrs. Shepherd from the office buzzes through on the intercom. "Dave, you have a phone call."

Mr. Emery's head pops up. He looks disoriented, like he's been asleep or underwater. He blinks at Vivi and Brett as though he has no idea who they are or what they're doing in his classroom.

He stands up. "Be right back. Vivi, when you're finished, leave the quiz on my desk, please."

Brett says, "Aren't you afraid I'm going to tell her all the answers?"

Mr. Emery surprises them both by laughing, then leaves the room.

Now they're alone. Vivi tries to concentrate on the numbers and letters. The derivative of $x^2$ is $2x$. The derivative of $2x$ is 2. She finishes the quiz, no problem. Ten minutes has passed and Mr. Emery still isn't back. Vivi finds herself reluctant to leave. She double-checks then triple-checks her answers. Finally, she can dawdle no longer. She drops her quiz on Mr. Emery's desk.

She knows that Brett Caspian is watching her. He's cute, she decides. She never realized this before because he's a druggie and therefore not her type, not even her species.

When she collects her books, he says, "Well, I'm not hanging out here any longer."

Vivi says, "You're going to leave detention? Aren't you afraid they'll double-down if you do that?"

"Nah," Brett says. "Dave will let me slide."

"Dave?"

"He's friends with my parents," Brett says. "They bowl together at Maple Lanes."

Vivi is astonished to hear this. She doesn't think of someone like Brett Caspian as even having parents, never mind parents who bowl with a teacher.

"Anyway, if you don't want to wait for the sports bus, I can drive you home," Brett says.

Vivi practically has to pick herself up off the floor. "Okay?" she says.

They're like Judd Nelson and Molly Ringwald from *The Breakfast Club*. Or close enough. They become a couple. By October, Vivi has traded in her A-line skirts for Jordache jeans and her boat shoes for Chuck Taylors. Brett picks her up on Friday nights and they go together to Byers Field to watch the football games, though neither of them is the rah-rah type, and then they head to Antonio's for pizza. On Saturdays, they do a few laps around the Parmatown Mall, one of Brett's hands possessively in the back pocket of Vivi's new jeans and his other hand holding a cigarette. Sometimes they go to a movie at the mall; sometimes Vivi goes to the high-school parties where Brett's band is playing. Afterward, they drive around Parma and Seven Hills in Brett's Buick Skylark playing 100.7 WMMS (the greatest rock station in America, right there in Cleveland) so loud that the soles of Vivi's shoes vibrate against the dashboard as the crisp Ohio air rushes in through the open windows. They park on State Road Hill or the Canal Road over in Independence and make out. They go to second base; they go to third base. They say, *I love you, I love you too, I love you more, I am so in love with you.* The feeling is so fresh out of the box, so wondrous, that they believe they are the first people ever to experience *this* kind of love. They believe they invented it.

Vivi goes with Brett to band practice, which is held in his buddy Wayne Curtis's garage. Wayne Curtis plays bass, and Roy, who has already graduated, plays the drums. Vivi knows Roy; he has a smart sister in the grade below Vivi.

Wayne and Roy don't act one way or another when Vivi comes to practice. They mostly ignore her, though once, Roy asks where she's applying to college, and when she tells him—Duke, UNC, UVA—he whistles.

"Anywhere is fine as long as it's not here," Vivi says.

"I hear ya," Roy says. The band's name, after all, is Escape from Ohio.

The secret truth is that after Vivi falls in love with Brett, she falls in love with Ohio. With only her guidance counselor's knowledge, she applies to Denison, Kenyon, Oberlin. She and Brett talk about getting married when they're in their twenties and moving downtown into a condo with a view of the lake; then, when they have children, they'll buy a house in Shaker Heights. Their kids will have the same sensible Midwestern upbringing that they've had.

At the beginning of November, they go all the way. They're in the back seat of the Skylark, parked in the woods by the Canal trail entrance, and the key is turned in the ignition just enough to keep the heater blowing its dry hot air. There's some positioning required, and for a second, it's like a game of Twister; Vivi feels the ridged vinyl against her bare back, her clothes now mixed with Brett's in the shallow wells of the car floor. Vivi pulses like a white-hot star. The pleasure and ache of Brett inside of her brings her to tears, and she ends up crying. They are both crying a little, because it's Brett's first time as well. And wow. Just . . . wow.

After Vivi's father dies in February, Brett writes her a song. It's called "Golden Girl," and at first, Vivi is confused by the title because she has very long, very dark hair. But once she hears the lyrics, she realizes the *golden* is metaphorical. Vivi is Brett's golden girl; she's his sunshine, his light, his treasure, his prize. She's the fire in his eyes.

Vivi would have loved the song even if it stunk—but she can tell it's good. Very good. Maybe even good enough to be played on WMMS.

With Vivi's father gone, Brett Caspian becomes everything to her. He's her sword and shield, her security blanket, her therapist, her best friend. His love is her oxygen. She will do whatever she must in order to keep him.

Back on Nantucket, at Our Lady of the Isle, the priest gives the Gospel reading and then the homily, which feels sort of generic to Vivi, but it's her own fault for going to church only on Christmas Eve and Easter. Father Reed once mentioned to Vivi that his elderly aunt enjoyed her novels, and Vivi dropped off a signed, large-print edition of *The Photographer* at the rectory the very next day—but Father Reed doesn't mention that in the homily; it's more about death in general and how it's really a birth into the Kingdom of God.

The homily is boring enough that the crying stops, but once Father is finished, Savannah ascends to the pulpit and you can hear a pin drop. Vivi takes the moment when Savannah is reviewing her notes to scan the church. Her gaze alights briefly on the front row. The kids are watching Savannah with rapt attention; JP is bent over with his head in his hands. Dennis is on the other side of the church sitting next to Candace Lopresti, Alexis, and Marissa, which is as good a place for him as any.

Joe DeSantis is on the aisle about three-quarters of the way back. He has been absorbed by the parents of the kids in Leo and Cruz's class. Willa's boss is here, and a group of people Vivi recognizes from the Oystercatcher. There are teachers, coaches, a bunch of real estate agents and business owners from downtown, all the guys who have worked on Money Pit, including Marky Mark, Vivi's contractor, and Surfer Boy, the electrician, both of whom put on ties for this.

There's Jodi, Vivi's agent, sitting with Wendy, Tim, and Cristina from Mitchell's Book Corner. There are the women from Vivi's barre class (exhibiting excellent posture). She will never have to suffer through thigh work again—is that a good thing? Her dentist and dental hygienist are here. Vivi will never have another cavity or another torturous root canal. No more ob-gyn exams. She has escaped the indignities of menopause. What does a hot flash feel like? Vivi will never know.

Sitting in the second row behind the kids is...Lucinda Quinboro, Vivi's ex-mother-in-law. *Well, that's rich,* Vivi thinks. She *is* the children's grandmother but...well, Lucinda was never a fan of Vivi's. She looks happier now than she did on Vivi and JP's wedding day.

"That's not true," Martha says. "And you know it."

"She never thought I was good enough for him," Vivi says. "Her little Jackie Paper."

"She prefers you to Amy," Martha says. "She thinks Amy is a gold digger." Martha pauses. "Sorry, that was very indiscreet."

"What else can you tell me?" Vivi says.

"Nothing."

"Oh, come on."

"You know as well as I do that it won't do you any good to find out what everyone thinks of you."

Savannah clears her throat.

Yes, yes, let's get to the eulogy—but first, Vivi seeks out Cruz. He's skulking in the doorway, his head hanging.

*Cruz! Go sit where you belong, up front, with my kids!* Vivi thinks. What is going on?

Zach Bridgeman is still in the back corner of the vestibule, hands stuffed in his pockets, looking supremely uncomfortable. As Savannah draws a breath to speak, he slides past Cruz and out of the church.

"I'm sure many of you are wondering how I'm going to get through this," Savannah says. "The answer is…I took a pill. I may fall asleep up here, but I won't cry."

There's a ripple of laughter that soothes like light rain.

"I need to ask your indulgence. I'm not the writer. Vivi was the writer. So if the universe were working the way it's supposed to, she would be up here eulogizing me, making me sound like a much more wonderful person than I actually am. Because, see? I've been at this five seconds and I've already made it all about me."

More laughs.

"Vivi and I were best friends. That phrase is hackneyed, overused; it has been acronym-ed into BFFs. As girls, we learn from our earliest social interactions that we are supposed to have a best friend. Someone to chant while we jump rope, someone to confide in about our secret crush. I'm not going to snow you. I didn't have a best friend growing up. Well, I did, but it was my dachshund, Herman Munster."

People laugh, though Vivi knows this is a sore spot with Savannah.

"That changed my first week at Duke University, in the Craven Quad dorm, when I met a girl from down the hall, Vivian Howe. We were in the bathroom; Vivi asked to borrow shampoo. She had arrived at college woefully under-provisioned, whereas I had an entire CVS stuffed beneath my extra-long twin bed. Vivi was from a town called Parma, Ohio. She was a tiny thing with long straight coal-black hair and cute freckles across her nose, and she had a thin silver hoop pierced through the top of her ear that I was jealous of. The second Vivi accepted the bottle of Breck from me, I felt a recognition: here was the best friend I'd been looking for.

"In the summers during college, Vivi stayed in Durham and wait-ressed at the Flying Burrito in order to save money for the following school year. I didn't get her to Nantucket until we'd both graduated. My parents had a rule at our Nantucket house: houseguests stayed one week, not a minute longer. I had other ideas about Vivi; I thought she might be allowed to live in my room for the entire summer. She wasn't a houseguest and she wasn't just a friend, she was a sister." Savannah stops, takes a breath. "My parents saw things differently, and after a week, they insisted that Vivi had to go. I thought Vivi would head back to Durham to sling chips and salsa, but in the seven days of her visit, she had fallen in love with Nantucket Island. She said she had…*found her home.*" Deep breath. "So…what happened? She rented a room in a house on Fairgrounds Road and found a job at Fair Isle Dry Cleaning. Anyone who has ever been to Fair Isle Dry Cleaning," Savannah says, casting her eyes around the church, "which seems to be only half of you"—laughter—"knows how hot it can get in there. So that first summer, Vivi chopped off all her hair and got a pixie cut. She started studying the locals and summer people so she could put you all in her future novels." Laughter. Uncomfortable? "Oh, you think I'm kidding? Clearly no one here has read *The Season of Scandal.*" Laughter. *She's got them in the palm of her hand,* Vivi thinks. *Go, Savannah!*

"Vivian Howe has been called a wash-ashore. But she was more of a Nantucketer than people who have lived here their entire lives because of how *deeply,* how *profoundly,* and how *unconditionally* she loved this island and our way of life." Savannah is stabbing the podium with her finger. "She wrote thirteen novels, and each one is a love letter to Nantucket. It is a small but real comfort to know that although Vivi is gone, her words remain."

Vivi smiles at Martha, who rolls her eyes. "Modesty, Vivian," she whispers.

"However, the most important works that Vivi has left behind are...her three beautiful children—her daughter Willa, her daughter Carson, and her son, Leo." Savannah turns her focus to the front pew. "Kids, your mom was a busy lady. She was writing or she was running or she was making chicken salad or she was swimming at Ram Pasture. The woman didn't have five minutes in her day that wasn't accounted for. Sometimes even while we were talking, I knew she was working out a plot point in her head or wondering how she would ever persuade her publisher to send her to Winnipeg on tour because her Canadian readers deserved a visit. However, I'm here to tell you that, at the end of the day, the only thing that mattered to your mom was the three of you. She was so, so proud of you and she loved you so, so much."

*Yes,* Vivi thinks.

People are openly crying.

"My job, as your mom's best friend, is not to make this loss easier. Nobody can do that. My job is to talk to you every day about your mom, to share my memories, and not only the good memories. Nobody wants to hear about a sainted, squeaky-clean Vivi. Has anyone here seen Vivian Howe get angry? Has anyone here seen Vivian Howe get angry after drinking tequila? Not pretty. But real."

Martha chuckles again.

"Glad you find that funny," Vivi says.

"I promise you, Willa, Carson, and Leo, that for as long as I live, I will talk to you about your mom. I will text you or call you when I have a vivid memory; I will advise you the way I think Vivi would have advised you; I will always, always remind you that wherever she is, she loves you. The love never goes away. Your mom is watching you right now. There is no way she would ever leave you."

Vivi gasps. "Does she know?"

"Of course not," Martha says.

There are soft sobs, sniffling.

Savannah looks up into the soaring rafters of the church. "Vivi,

I'm talking to you now. I have given a lot of thought over the past few days to what we, as humans, can be to one another. Can we cross boundaries to fully understand—or even *become*—another person? I decided the answer is no, we can't. I'm here, alive, and you are somewhere else. But of all the people I have known in this life, I felt the closest to you. You *were* and *are* and *always will be* my best. Friend. Forever. Thank you."

"Wow," Vivi says.

"That's the best one I've heard so far this year," Martha says.

*Only this year?* Vivi thinks. Inside, she's cheering like Savannah just caught Cam Newton's touchdown pass in the end zone to win the Super Bowl in overtime!

The priest takes the pulpit, lifts his hands, and says, "Let us pray."

# Nantucket

The service, we agreed, was lovely. Savannah Hamilton had done such a good job that we all looked around and wondered who in our own lives might represent us half as well.

And, boy, did Savannah know how to throw a party—because that's what Vivian Howe's "memorial reception" at the Field and Oar Club ended up being: a party. The expansive green lawn that led from the brick patio to the lip of the harbor had a bar running along one side and a buffet along the other. We ordered Mount Gay and tonics or glasses of crisp Riesling and accepted tiny lobster-and-corn cakes dotted with avocado crème fraîche from passing trays. We were lured to the smoking grill by the irresistible scent of the lamb lollipops and riblets slathered with tangy sauce. In the center of the buffet was a tiered silver tower laden with seafood—jumbo shrimp, plump oysters on the half shell, cherrystone clams, Alaskan king crab legs. There was a wooden board, as big as a wagon wheel, featuring an artful spiral of finger sandwiches; it was so beautiful, we felt bad disrupting it, but the horseradish roast beef on tiny rounds of rye was too delicious to resist.

Sean Lee played the guitar and sang acoustic covers of Springsteen, Clapton, Billy Joel, and Crosby, Stills, and Nash, Vivi's favorite kind of singalong music. Although she didn't play an instrument and could *not* carry a tune, she was a fiend for rock and roll. In her most underappreciated book, *Summer Days Again,* the chapter titles were all songs from the 1950s and '60s.

The air was sparkling; the water shimmered; the flag snapped in the breeze. There was no view on Nantucket more glorious than the one from the lawn of the Field and Oar Club. The club was exclusive and old-money; there was a twenty-year waiting list to get in and a ruthless membership committee to persuade. The Quinboros had been members since the 1940s and Vivi became a member automatically when she married JP. She'd bristled at some of the rules—she once wore a red polo to play tennis, which was a no-no, and there was the time she accidentally spat her cocktail all over the commodore's navy double-breasted blazer because he'd said something she found absurd. When Vivi and JP got divorced, the membership committee voted five to four against readmitting Vivi on her own. Some felt this was a harsh decision, especially since everyone knew why the marriage had ended, but Lucinda Quinboro wrote the committee a letter stating that she did not want to encounter her former daughter-in-law at the club under any circumstances.

*Even when they were married, it was clear she didn't belong here,* Lucinda wrote.

Some people on the committee thought that Vivi brought a freshness and a frankness to a place that could be straitlaced and fusty, but the man with the deciding vote, Gordy Hastings, had read Vivian Howe's novel *The Angle of Light,* and he was not amused by the way she'd depicted their club in that book, thinly disguised as "the Lawn and Anchor Club." The members of the Lawn and Anchor Club were self-absorbed and obnoxious, and although Gordy's wife, Amelia, told him to relax, it was *fiction,* Gordy saw through the pretense. If Vivian Howe thought so poorly of the club, he felt no need to invite her to join on her own.

And he didn't.

Vivi's ex-husband, JP Quinboro, had been shocked by the committee's decision, but his girlfriend, Amy Van Pelt, who quickly replaced Vivi on JP's arm, felt as Lucinda Quinboro did. She was thrilled not to have to worry about bumping into Vivi in the powder room.

Savannah Hamilton, whose family had been members of the Field and Oar since its inception in 1905, told Vivi she could sign under H-1 whenever she damn well pleased.

Lucinda Quinboro and her best friend and bridge partner, Penny Rosen, attend the memorial service reception, and when Lucinda orders two Hendrick's martinis, dry, from Marshall the bartender, he says, "Right away, Mrs. Quinboro. I'll put that on your chit, Q-ten?"

"*My* chit?" Lucinda says. "Aren't the drinks free today?"

"Ms. Hamilton is picking up the tab for non–club members only," Marshall says.

Lucinda looks around. Everyone here is a non–club member except for herself, Penny, JP, and the Bonhams. "That seems calculating," she says.

"Oh, come off it, Lucy," Penny says. Penny and Lucinda have been friends for five decades and Penny is the only person left alive who calls her "Lucy." "You never liked Vivian, you had her blackballed from this club, and now you're complaining because you have to pay for a drink at her memorial reception? Shame on you."

"Yes, Marshall, Q-ten," Lucinda says. She scowls at Penny. "I suppose you'll be the person who speaks at my funeral and tells everyone how wretched I was."

Penny suppresses a smile. The thought delights her.

"I look forward to *you* buying the next round," Lucinda says.

Although it's easy to get swept up by the food, the music, and the beauty of the day, many of us are keeping our eyes on Vivi's children. Willa Quinboro Bonham is sitting at a table in the shade of an umbrella between her husband, Rip, and her mother-in-law, Tink. The Bonhams, like the Quinboros, are longtime members of the Field and Oar Club—Tink plays tennis, Chas Bonham sails— but unlike the Quinboros, they stay out of the sticky politics of the place.

Tink is worried about only one thing: the health and safety of her daughter-in-law, who is once again pregnant. Tink, as many of us know, is keen for a Bonham heir—preferably a boy.

"Is there anything else I can get you, dear?" Tink asks Willa. Willa has a glass of ginger ale in front of her. "What about a cucumber sandwich?"

"I can't eat."

Rip holds his wife's hand. "Do you want to leave?" he asks. "We can go home and you can lie down in the air-conditioning."

"I need to make sure Carson and Leo are okay," Willa says.

Marshall the bartender notes that Carson Quinboro is on her fifth Tom Collins. He knows that Carson is slinging drinks at the Oystercatcher and he tries to strike up a conversation with her about the business, but she shuts him down, and he can't really blame her. Her mother just died. She thrusts the glass in his face and says, "Stronger, please, bruh." Marshall believes a Tom Collins should be light to medium strength; it's supposed to be refreshing enough that you can drink several of them over the course of an afternoon and not get drunk. But the customer is always right. He hands her a cocktail that's practically all gin.

Carson avoids her father, avoids her grandmother and Penny, avoids Leo, avoids Dennis. She uses Savannah as a touchstone, checking in, then spiraling out. After cocktail number four, she heads to the water and pulls out her cell phone and her vape pen. She starts sending off a string of texts and takes a few quick puffs off her Juul, but before she can even exhale, the assistant GM is striding across the lawn toward her.

She tucks both her phone and her Juul into her mother's clutch and leans over to unbuckle her mother's Louboutins. She has done a fine job of aerating the club's lawn with the stilettos. She smirks at the assistant GM, and when he opens his mouth to remind her that bare feet, cell phones, and vaping are not allowed on club premises, she discreetly flips him off. Although this is unbecoming behavior, it's the assistant GM who feels he's made a faux pas. The young woman has, after all, just lost her mother.

Leo Quinboro is still in his blazer despite the sweltering heat and despite the fact that the ranking member—former commodore Chas Bonham—has taken his jacket off. Like his sister Willa, Leo has always followed the rules.

Leo's school friends Christopher and Mitch pull him aside to ask if it's true that Cruz was the one who hit Vivi.

"That's what Marissa said." This from Mitch.

"Yeah," Christopher says. "Alexis told her that one of the officers saw Cruz blow through a stop sign and take off speeding a few minutes before your mom was hit."

"Marissa should keep her mouth shut," Leo says, and Christopher figures the rumors he's heard about Leo and Marissa breaking up are true, even though they were voted Cutest Couple in the senior-class superlatives. Marissa was at the service, but she sat with her mom and Alexis, and she's not here at the reception.

Even stranger, Christopher thinks, is that Cruz isn't here, though Mitch said he saw Cruz at the church, standing in the back. Joe DeSantis isn't here either. Christopher wonders if they aren't comfortable at the club—it's not exactly a diverse place; every single person here is white—or if there's more to it. *Was* Cruz DeSantis the one to hit Vivian Howe? The rumor about him running the stop sign and speeding is pretty damning, and Christopher can't think of any other reason why Cruz would not show up for Leo. His absence is . . . conspicuous.

As with any party where alcohol and heavy emotions mix, things eventually come to a head. None of us has really been paying attention to Dennis Letty, Vivi's former boyfriend, but he has been circling JP Quinboro like a shark. Unlike Leo, Dennis shed his jacket long ago (before Chas Bonham removed his, a few of us noticed) and loosened his tie, and he's sweated through his white dress shirt. We can't say we're surprised. When he's drinking bourbon like he is today, Dennis can be a bit of a wild card. Does anyone remember Willa and Rip's wedding?

Dennis steps right up to JP; he's a few inches shorter but he has at least forty pounds on JP. "I hope you know, you broke Vivi's heart. You had a good thing and you wrecked it."

JP nods thoughtfully. "What happened between Vivi and me is none of your business, Dennis. You should probably think about heading home. I can call you a cab if you like."

"If I *like?*" Dennis says. He might not have grown up on Hulbert Avenue, he might not know a sloop from a cutter, but he knows when he's being talked down to and he also knows that over the past three years, Vivi forked over half a million dollars of her hard-earned money to this clown. JP can act like Richie Rich—all well-bred and knowing which fork to use and his loafers-without-socks and his Wayfarers perched in his Kennedy-thick hair—but the fact is, JP Quinboro is unfamiliar with an honest day's work.

Dennis had tried to persuade Vivi to drag JP back to court just on principle—it wasn't right that the guy cheated on her and *she* was paying *him*—but Vivi said she was too busy with deadlines and that a prolonged court battle would be too distracting.

"I know you're standing up for me," Vivi said. "And I love you for it, but that crusade ended long ago. It's over, Denny. Let it be."

The thing is, JP wasn't even grateful. He acted like the money was his due.

Dennis pulls his arm back and, without warning, punches JP in the jaw just as he's bringing his Mount Gay and tonic to his mouth, so the glass goes flying and smashes against the brick walk. JP is taken by surprise, and Dennis has such a long history of bar fighting that he crosses with his left and hits JP in the nose. There's blood everywhere.

Rip Bonham sees what's happening and steps in. "Whoa, Dennis, come on, buddy, that's enough."

Dennis lets Rip pull him aside while Willa hurries over to her father with a wad of paper napkins. JP presses the napkins to his nose and there's a red bloom through to the other side.

Willa says, "Do you need an ambulance?"

JP shakes his head and Rip escorts Dennis out to the parking lot. Those of us remaining gather our things and fold a few of the club's famous chocolate chunk cookies into napkins to enjoy later.

It's fitting, we suppose, maybe even flattering that Vivi has men fighting over her to the very end.

Our hostess, Savannah, leads JP into the dark, cool, and empty ballroom, where they sit on two banquet chairs off to the side. Savannah has known JP since they were children on the tennis courts here— ankle-biters, they were called, the kids who volleyed and learned to serve and then ate pizza in a circle on the sun-warmed clay. JP was just one of the crowd, indistinguishable from the other sons of privilege Savannah had grown up with, until he started dating her best friend. And then married her, had children with her, cheated on her, and caused her all kinds of heartache. Savannah is annoyed to be in the position of having to comfort him, and yet she knows this is what's called for.

"I'm sorry that happened," she says. "I should have been watching Dennis more closely. He was a ticking time bomb."

"I never understood what she saw in him."

"He's salt of the earth—she liked that. Plus, he worshipped her, and after what she'd been through…"

"She wanted the opposite of me," JP says. "Well, that she got." He looks at Savannah; she sees a pair of bloodshot green eyes above the bloody napkin. "You know, my relationship with Vivi wasn't exactly black and white. It was probably the most complicated relationship in the history of the world."

This makes Savannah laugh. "You sound like such a pompous ass."

"I know," JP says, then he starts to cry. "I loved her so much. From the instant I set eyes on her, when I picked up those clothes at the dry cleaner's…"

"You were picking up your mother's dresses," Savannah says. "That alone should have warned her to stay away from you."

"I made such a mess of things," JP says. "Dennis wasn't *wrong*— I did break Vivi's heart. I know I did."

Savannah relieves JP of his bloody napkin. His nose looks like a rotten strawberry, and a bruise is forming at his jawline. That's going to hurt in the morning. "I'd love to parse it all out with you, JP, but I'm not in the right frame of mind right now. We need to focus on what's important—"

"Finding out who hit her," JP says. "Seeing justice done."

Savannah takes a breath for patience. "The police are handling that. You and I have the kids to worry about."

"The kids love me," JP says. "But they don't like me. They liked Vivi. They talked to Vivi." He offers Savannah the slow, handsome half smile that, Savannah knows, was one of the things that hooked Vivi in the first place. "And they like you. They talk to you."

"They do," Savannah says, standing up. "Do you need me to give you a ride home or are you going to call Amy?"

"Amy?" he says as though he has no idea who that is.

"I'm parked out front," Savannah says. "Let's go."


# Amy


Amy asks for the day of Vivi's memorial service off and so does Lorna, claiming that she needs to support her friend, and thankfully, Wednesdays are slow at the salon. Brandi, the receptionist, reluctantly takes them off the schedule, thinking they will be attending Vivi's service.

Instead, the two of them head to Cru, located on the end of Straight Wharf, which is the best place for day-drinking on Nantucket.

They settle in at the back bar and order a bottle of champagne, the Pol Roger, "in honor of Vivi." They also order a dozen oysters and, what the hell, while they're at it, the caviar service—osetra, with all the trimmings. When the glass doors swing open, diners have an unimpeded view across the water. There's a narrow strip of boardwalk around the back bar, and Amy knows that plenty of people have fallen in; she used to hear the ruckus when she worked across the way at the Cork with JP. The ocean is spangled with sunlight; boats are tilting from side to side in the nearby slips; the ferry's horn sounds, and seagulls cry out like jealous girls. Tommy the bartender pops the cork on their bottle of champagne.

"Celebrating, ladies?" he asks.

Amy hasn't thought about the optics of this until now. She's taking a day off work so she can mourn her boyfriend's ex-wife, but her version of "mourning" is drinking champagne she can't afford and eating caviar she *really* can't afford. What if someone sees her?

"That's right," Lorna says, raising her flute of platinum bubbles. "Celebrating a life."

Amy had offered to skip the service and reception before JP even asked. "I think everyone, the kids especially, would be more comfortable if I stayed away."

Amy sensed JP's relief immediately. "You're probably right," he said.

Will the kids miss her? Carson, maybe. But if Amy attended the service, everyone would be watching her because she would be in the uniquely awful position of mourning a woman she had not always spoken of in the most generous of terms. Amy couldn't bear the scrutiny.

She raises her flute and clinks it against Lorna's without words. All she wants to do today is drink and forget.

At some point in the future, JP will be able to think about something other than Vivi's death. The summer will march on, the kids will adjust, Leo will leave for college. Amy will reach out to Carson—this might be a chance for them to grow closer. And JP will be free to propose. Amy just has to wait a little longer.

The champagne is gone before they know it and Lorna orders a bottle of rosé. Tommy asks if they're thinking about more food. The oysters slipped down Amy's throat in six briny swallows and the caviar provided three bites apiece. Amy orders two buttery lobster rolls with fries.

She turns to Lorna. "Don't worry, this is all my treat." She does some mental calculations and realizes that even if they stop eating and drinking now, their bill will be four hundred dollars. This lunch is extravagant, but she has reached the point of no return. "We could be dead tomorrow."

As the afternoon wears on, the bar becomes more crowded. The demographic is handsome men, suntanned after a day of sailing or fishing, in groups of three or four. One cute guy in a Torrey Pines visor starts chatting with Lorna. He likes her accent, he says. His grandfather was an Irishman, from Wexford.

"Ha!" Lorna says. "That's where I grew up!"

Amy tries to contribute to their conversation, piping up in her own accent—Alabama!—but her Southern drawl has dried up in the past ten years and now when she says "Y'all," it sounds forced. She turns to the remaining warm rosé in her glass and wills one of the other gentlemen to come over and rescue her, but nobody does. She arrived on Nantucket a svelte twenty-three-year-old; now, she's ten years older and fifteen (no, twenty) pounds heavier, and she looks…worn out. She *is* worn out. Dealing with JP and his kids and his mother and his struggle to find himself has been exhausting, and wondering when she will stop being the girlfriend (mistress) and start being the wife has left her disenchanted. Her light has dimmed. No wonder all the men at this bar are steering clear of her. She might as well have a sticker across her forehead that says USED UP.

She throws back some more wine just as a man in a white undershirt and a pair of tight gray suit pants takes the stool to her left. He signals the bartender, orders a Cisco Whale's Tale, and only then seems to notice Amy.

"Oops, this seat taken?"

Amy shakes her head. She's happy that there's someone in this bar who doesn't think she's a leper, even if he's not one of the gorgeous sailing men. Amy didn't get a good look at the guy and she's afraid to turn her head lest she seem too obvious, though she does notice blood on his knuckles.

She's had so much to drink that she thinks nothing of grabbing the guy's wrist. "Did you hurt yourself? Or…were you in a fight?"

"Fight," the guy says. His beer arrives and he stands up and throws back the whole thing in one long gulp. This gives Amy a chance to look at him; when he finishes, he takes a long look at her.

"Oh," he says. "Hey, Amy."

"Dennis!" she says. Her voice sounds enthusiastic, which is strange because she doesn't know Dennis very well. He was Vivi's boyfriend, although Amy heard from JP that apparently Vivi and Dennis had broken up or were breaking up in stages.

Amy owes Dennis a debt of gratitude. Last June, at Willa and Rip's wedding, JP and Vivi had danced together to the first song along with Willa and Rip and Mr. and Mrs. Bonham. It was at the top of Amy's Worst Moments of the Relationship. Vivi fit right into JP's arms and they danced so fluidly (hadn't JP told Amy the very first summer that Vivi *couldn't* dance?) and they were laughing and so visibly joyful that Amy thought, *What am I even doing here?* She might have left the Field and Oar Club altogether had Dennis not come over to her with a fresh drink, had he not rested his hand lightly on her back and clinked a cheers and whispered a joke in her ear that she hadn't been able to hear over the music but laughed at anyway.

"I'll have another," Dennis says to the bartender now.

"So, wait, you were at the memorial service, right? And the reception?"

Dennis nods.

If he's here at Cru then the reception must be over. Amy wonders if JP has called. She wonders if he missed her, if she did the right thing by staying away. She wants to know if anyone asked where she was. She is hopelessly self-centered, she realizes. Today has nothing to do with her. Today is about Vivi and the people she loved and the people who loved her. Which leaves Amy out.

Poor Dennis. Amy tries to imagine how he must feel. Vivi broke up with him and then died. It's two completely different kinds of pain, one layered on top of the other.

"How are you doing?" Amy asks.

Dennis shrugs.

"How are the kids?"

"I didn't talk to the kids. They were up front with Savannah and your boyfriend."

"Oh, Savannah," Amy says. "She must be really upset."

"She is. She gave one hell of a speech at the church."

Amy wishes she'd been there to hear it; she has always been slightly obsessed with Savannah. Savannah Hamilton has that elusive thing known as class; it's visible from every angle. It's her hair, her clothes, her manner of speaking, her graciousness, her taste, her effortlessness in the world. Why has she never married? Amy asked JP this once and he said, "Her standards are too high." She dated Michael DelRay, a bigwig at JPMorgan, for a while, Amy knew, but broke up with him because he was too mercenary. Savannah is a do-gooder. She took her family money and started a nonprofit that feeds and educates children in places like Niger and Bangladesh. Even if Amy wanted to hate her, she couldn't.

"So did you get into a fight at the *funeral?*" Amy asks.

"The reception."

"You got into a fistfight at the Field and Oar Club?" Amy is titillated by the mere thought. The club intimidates her. JP always talked about how Vivi used to flout the club rules, so every time Amy sets foot in the place she feels the stifling need to *behave.* Amy doesn't belong there any more than Vivi did. Amy hails from Potter, Alabama. People know Montgomery and Mobile, but no one has ever heard of Potter. It's as country as catfish.

"I did."

"Did they throw you out?"

"They did."

"Who'd you fight with?"

Dennis brings his second beer to his mouth and drains half in one swallow. "Who do you think?"

Amy stares at the puddle of pink wine left in her lipstick-smudged glass. "JP?"

"Yep."

Amy takes stock of her surroundings. Lorna's in deep conversation with the sailor; Amy can easily leave her here if she wants to go home and tend to JP. If there's blood on Dennis's knuckles, what must JP's face look like? "Is he badly hurt?"

"He might have a shiner," Dennis says. "I hit him twice. He didn't really fight back."

*No, he wouldn't,* Amy thinks. JP doesn't like confrontation. If he has a problem, he throws money at it.

She should probably go home and tend to his wounds.

But...she doesn't want to.

"I had a lot of pent-up anger toward the guy," Dennis says. "Though I feel bad about hitting him now." He eyes Amy's glass. "What if I bought you an apology drink for ruining your boyfriend's face?"

"I wouldn't say no," Amy says.

# The Chief

The national average of hit-and-run homicides that end in convictions is under 50 percent, but that doesn't make the Chief feel any better. Nor does the fact that his wife, Andrea, spent an hour on Thursday watching the virtual memorial service for Vivian Howe, then spent another hour (or more) on the Vivian Howe Memorial Facebook page reading through the comments from her readers.

"They want the Nantucket Police to figure out who did it," Andrea says. "They want justice. I felt shady—there I was on the page, posing as a normal, everyday reader, which I am, except that I'm also married to the Nantucket chief of police."

"I'm doing the best I can," Ed says.

But the truth is, he's getting nowhere with this investigation.

The tire tracks were no help. The pattern had been compromised by Cruz's footprints, the arrival of the ambulance, and the footprints of the paramedics.

Lisa Hitt found Vivian Howe's blood on Cruz DeSantis's car. On the door handle. Likely, Cruz had Vivi's blood on his hands when he climbed into his Jeep after the ambulance took her to the hospital. The luminol turned up nothing on the bumper or grille, which was a relief, though frankly, the Chief would have felt better if the car were completely clean. He doesn't want the statement "Vivian Howe's blood was on Cruz DeSantis's Jeep" to get out into the community without context. Already, Falco's report of seeing the kid run a stop sign and speed down Surfside is everywhere. Finn told the Chief he'd heard people talking about it on the beach at Cisco.

"They're all saying Cruz hit her," Finn said.

"There's no evidence of that," the Chief said. "People talk. We might as well call this Rumor Island."

The only member of Vivian Howe's family who has called Ed is Rip Bonham, her son-in-law. The Chief knows Rip and his father, Chas, and his sister, Pamela Bonham Bridgeman, because the department works with the Bonhams' insurance company on regular traffic accidents. Rip's phone call was gentle, just asking if the police had any leads.

The next steps would be examining Vivi's clothes for flecks of paint from the Jeep and looking for fibers from those clothes on Cruz's bumper. Every contact leaves a trace.

Here is where the investigation hit a major snafu. Vivi's clothes are missing. The ME says he followed protocol—he cut the clothes off the deceased, bagged them, and had them delivered to the police station, where they would be processed and sent to Lisa Hitt on the Cape. But the clothes never made it to the station, according to Alexis Lopresti, who was working the processing desk. The Chief went back to the ME—the guy was new, replacing longtime ME Dr. Fields—to ask who exactly he'd sent to deliver the clothes, and the ME admitted he wasn't sure. He'd handed them off and assumed they would be dealt with.

"Well, where are they, then?" the Chief said. He was about to blow his stack, but the last thing he needed was an ME with a grudge against him. "Never mind—they must be at the station."

Ed drove to work and stormed up to Alexis Lopresti at the processing desk.

"You did not see or receive the bag containing Vivian Howe's clothes from the hospital, is that correct?"

"Nope," Alexis said. "Did you check the evidence room?"

"Yes," he said. "Twice. Who was on the schedule last Saturday?"

Alexis looked put out by this question. "I don't know."

The Chief was tempted to fire her on the spot. She must have noticed his expression because she clickety-clacked on her computer and said, "Dixon and...Pitcher."

Pitcher was green; he'd been on the force for only nine months. It was entirely possible Pitcher had left the clothes in the back of his squad car.

When the Chief called Pitcher, there was loud music and laughing in the background; it sounded like he was out on the town. He was very young; the Chief remembered that he'd seen Pitcher hanging around Alexis Lopresti's desk with unusual frequency, probably trying to get a date.

Pitcher said that he hadn't been the one to pick up the clothes. "I definitely would have remembered that. Clothes and running shoes too, right?"

"Right," the Chief said. "So you did see them?"

"No," Pitcher said. "But I know she got hit while running. So there would have been running shoes. What I'm saying is, shoes would have been hard to miss."

In a last-ditch effort, the Chief called Lisa Hitt to see if, maybe by the grace of God, the clothes had landed in her hands.

"No," she said. "Why, are they missing?"

The Chief can't release Cruz's car until they find the clothes, and he knows he owes Joe DeSantis an explanation, one that should be offered in person.

He swings by the Nickel at two thirty, after the lunch crowd has dispersed. He's relieved to find only Joe in the place, slicing up a prime rib in the back.

When Joe sees the Chief, a concerned look crosses his face, but he smiles. "The tuna niçoise baguette is sold out, Ed, sorry. You know you gotta get here earlier than this."

Ed's stomach rumbles. He could do with a prime rib sliced thin, lacy Swiss, and arugula with some of Joe's wickedly spicy horseradish sauce on a warm pretzel roll—but that's not why he's here.

There are days he hates his job, and he has just lived through a handful of them.

"Do you have a minute, Joe?"

Joe strides across the shop, flips the sign to say CLOSED, and pulls two Cokes out of the cooler. There's nowhere to sit, so they lean on the counter.

"If you're not here for lunch, there must be trouble."

The Chief sighs. "Has Cruz talked to you at all about what happened when he found Vivian Howe?"

Joe shakes his head, cracks open his Coke. "He hasn't said a word about it except that he told you everything." Joe takes a drink. "I guess I don't understand why you still have his car."

"There are a few things that look bad," the Chief says. "One of the officers saw him run the stop sign at Hooper Farm and Surfside and then haul ass down Surfside only a few minutes before he called 911."

Joe is silent.

"When I asked Cruz where he was coming from, he said home, which doesn't match up."

"Your officer is sure it was him? There are a lot of white Jeeps on this island, Ed."

"The officer said it was him, though he could have been mistaken." The Chief cracks open his own can of Coke and tries to enjoy the first cold, spicy sip. "The tire tracks were no help. Luminol turned up Ms. Howe's blood on the door handle but not on the bumper or grille—and because of the gash on Ms. Howe's leg, there would almost definitely be blood on the bumper."

"Cruz didn't hit her," Joe says. "That child..." Joe spins the can in his hands. "He doesn't lie, Ed. If he'd hit Vivi, he would have told us."

"Why was he going over to the Howes' place so early on a Saturday morning?" the Chief says. "Seven fifteen? I asked him but he didn't answer."

Joe says, "I take it he and Leo had a fight. Something must have gone down the night before—that happens around graduation, emotions are high, people say things they don't mean. Cruz hasn't seen Leo since the hospital. I could barely get him to go to the memorial service."

"Cruz was very emotional at the station, and I wondered if something else was going on," the Chief says.

"Vivian Howe was, for all intents and purposes, Cruz's mother. He loved her." Joe clears his throat. "Vivi was very good about making him feel like a part of things, about taking care of him the way only a mom can. Vivi's death is a big loss to my boy, and to me as well. But Ed, he didn't hit her."

"Okay."

"You're not convinced?" Joe straightens to his full height, and suddenly the room grows smaller. "You think he's hiding something? *Lying* to you?"

"He has a lot to lose."

"Damn straight he has a lot to lose," Joe says. "The kid has achieved beyond anyone's wildest dreams. I don't understand why Cruz is being treated like a suspect rather than a heartbroken kid who happened to be the first one to find the woman. Or is he a suspect because he's Black, and when someone Black is close to the scene of a crime, he must have committed it?"

The Chief recoils. "This isn't about race," he says. He sits with his discomfort and checks himself. Did Falco actually see *Cruz* or was there some other Black kid driving a white Jeep? Did Falco notice Cruz primarily because he was Black? Was it easier for the Nantucket community to say that Cruz DeSantis did a bad thing because he was Black? The Chief will *not* lead a department where Black citizens are treated differently than white. He has learned, however, that racism is systemic. It's often so deeply buried that you can't even see it, but it's there.

"I like you, Ed. I count you as a friend. I would never take advantage of that friendship. But my son didn't hit Vivi. He's the kind of kid who would have confessed right away and presented his wrists for the cuffs. He loved Vivi Howe so much that he would never forgive himself. Now, I know there's something unresolved between him and Leo Quinboro. I can see that on his face without even asking. But what I don't see is guilt over killing a woman. He has been very patient while you check his car. He's been riding his old bike to work without complaint—because he trusts the system. But I'm not going to stand by and let you make him a scapegoat because you need a conviction in this case. Cruz didn't hit her, Ed."

These words land, and in that instant, the Chief knows in his heart that Cruz DeSantis didn't hit the woman. Someone else hit her and *ran,* probably only a few seconds before Cruz found her.

"I'll release the car this afternoon," the Chief says.

"Thank you, Ed," Joe says, and the men shake hands.

## Vivi

Vivi is relaxing on the velvet chaise when Martha enters through the green door, holding her clipboard. "There are some lovely posts on your memorial Facebook page," she says. "Would you like to take a look?"

"Are they *all* lovely?" Vivi asks. If there's one thing she's learned about Facebook, it's that people think it's just fine to post things that they would never *dream* of saying to someone's face. In recent years, Vivi had become something of an online manners stickler: If you don't have something nice to say, keep scrolling!

"Well," Martha says.

Vivi's interest is piqued. She takes the clipboard.

### VIVIAN HOWE MEMORIAL FACEBOOK PAGE

Please share your thoughts and memories of Vivian Howe below. We encourage you all to stay positive! Vivian's family and close friends will look at this page as a way to seek solace from her readers. Thank you.

This past winter, I was diagnosed with stage two triple-positive intraductal carcinoma and underwent eighteen rounds of chemotherapy at MD Anderson in Houston. I brought a Vivian Howe novel to each of my three-hour appointments. My chemo nurses always asked how I was enjoying the book and this gave us something to chat about other than my cancer. I will always be grateful to Vivian Howe for being "with" me in my darkest hours.—Crista J., Katy, TX

VIVIAN HOWE IS A QUEEN! REST IN PEACE, VIVI!—Megan R., Wiscasset, ME

I don't even want to read *Golden Girl* because when I do, I won't have any more Vivi to read and that's when the loss of her will sink in. Is anyone else feeling that way?—Lloret A., Bowmore, Scotland

Reply: Me too!—Taffy H., Kalamazoo, MI

Reply: Me too! 🙌 —Beth H., Sharon, MA

## "So far so good," Vivi says.

Hello! While I'm sad about the loss of one of my favorite authors, I would also like to offer a suggestion. Please will someone go back into Ms. Howe's novels and fix the copyediting mistakes? On page 201, line 21 of *The Photographer* it says "Truman" where it should say "Davis." Also, I've long been shocked that the copyeditor let the interrobangs stay throughout Ms. Howe's work. For those of you who don't know, an interrobang is an unorthodox combination of question mark and exclamation point. How did this happen?!!!??? (You can see from my example how unseemly this looks.) Thank you, and my sympathies to the family.—Pauline F., Homestead, FL

Reply: "Interrobang" sounds like what happens when one of my kids knocks on the door while I'm having sex with my husband. (Sorry, couldn't resist. I like to think this is a Vivi-type joke.)— Kerry H., Grand Island, NE

"She's right," Vivi says. "That is the kind of joke I would make." Martha says nothing.

Hello, I'm new to Facebook as of right this minute. I was wondering if anyone knows how to get ahold of someone in Vivi's family? I'm not some weirdo stalker, I promise. I went to Parma High School with Vivi from 1983 to 1987. She was my girlfriend for eleven months. I haven't seen her since August of '87 but I heard from the sister of my former bandmate that she passed away suddenly and I'd like to express my condolences and share my memories with the family. I also just found out that she's a writer, and kind of famous. (I don't read much.) I went on Amazon and read the description of her book that's coming out next month and I would like to talk to her family about that as well. So if anyone here can help, I'd appreciate it. I don't have a Facebook page (this is my coworker's page I'm writing from now) but my name is Brett Caspian and I'm the GM of the Holiday Inn by the University of Tennessee in Knoxville. You can call the front desk and ask for me. I'm sorry about Vivi. She was a special girl.

*Oh no!* Vivi thinks. *Nooooooo!* Brett Caspian found out about the book.

Vivi's hunch had been correct: Brett didn't know she was a writer. He knows now only because someone told him she died. His bandmate's sister—Roy's sister Renata, if Vivi had to guess. *Aaaaaaaah!* She realizes how *naive* she was to think that Brett would never hear about this book. The whole world is connected; everybody knows everything, thanks to the internet. Brett isn't on Facebook but that doesn't mean he lives in a cabin in the woods or in the middle of the Brazilian rain forest. He's the GM at a Holiday Inn in Knoxville, Tennessee. (This seems so random. If Vivi had to guess what Brett was doing with his life, she would have said he was working on a production crew doing lights and sound for the bands they'd loved—Foreigner, Blue Öyster Cult—on their summer-outdoor-venue-reunion tours.)

Brett doesn't sound angry in the message. He doesn't sound like he hates her.

But he will—if he reads *Golden Girl*.

Vivi remembers how Brett used to wait on a bench and smoke every time she went into B. Dalton at the Parmatown Mall. He wouldn't even set foot in the bookstore.

There's no way he'll read *Golden Girl*.

Vivi hands the clipboard back to Martha with a smile. "Better than I expected!" she says.

# Willa

Willa and Rip are moving for the summer. They're leaving their house on Quaker Road—purchased just after their wedding with help from the elder Bonhams—for a cottage situated on the beach at the entrance to Smith's Point. Their house on Quaker Road is forty-five hundred square feet and has five bedrooms. The cottage is tiny; it's a dollhouse. It used to be the "summer residence" for Rip's grandparents, and Willa and Rip would ride their bikes there when they were in middle school and high school. Rip's grandmother would serve them lemonade garnished with fresh mint, but they had to drink it at the picnic table on the deck because the house was too small for them all to hang out inside. The cottage is called Wee Bit. It has a teensy-tiny sitting room, one wall of which is a galley kitchen, a bedroom that is big enough to hold one bed and one nightstand, and a powder room with a sink and toilet. There's a deck with a picnic table and a gas grill that Rip's grandfather splurged on sometime in the mid-1990s, and three stairs down, there's a flagstone patio in front of an outdoor shower. Beyond the deck and the shower are dunes with a path that cuts over and onto the beach.

After Rip's grandparents went into assisted living, Wee Bit sat unused. Nobody in the Bonham family wanted to stay there. They were a tall family; Chas and Rip couldn't even stand to their full height unless they were right in the center of the room where the ceiling peaked. Both of Rip's grandparents passed away over that winter and Rip officially inherited the cottage. It was infested with mice and everything was mildewed. The floor in the sitting room was rotted; the bathroom was unspeakable. Willa thought that they could—*maybe*—use the cottage as a staging area if they ever wanted to throw a beach party, but Rip was set on living there.

Without telling Willa, Rip had hired Vivi's contractor, Marky Mark, to replace the floors, repaint, tile the powder room, and update the appliances in the kitchen (three-quarter fridge, miniature stovetop and oven, microwave) and he'd bought a new bed, a queen instead of a king so there was marginally more room to move around. He also bought an AC unit. Marky Mark rebuilt the enclosure around the outdoor shower. Rip picked out a new love seat, seagrass rugs, a round wooden coffee table. When he took Willa to look at it, saying only that he'd "spruced it up," she had been blown away. It was so much better. It was adorable, like something from the HGTV show *Tiny Paradise.*

It was still way too small to live in.

After Willa's second miscarriage, she started to change her mind about that, and after her third, she was counting the days until they could move out of the house on Quaker and into Wee Bit. The house on Quaker was enormous, the rooms yawning and empty, waiting to be filled with children. The house was tapping its foot like an impatient friend—*What's taking you so long? What's wrong with you?*

They move out to Wee Bit exactly one week after Vivi's memorial service. Willa is even happier to escape the house now because all she sees is the ghost of her mother dropping by with banana bread or a bunch of chives from her herb garden or a book that she wants Willa to read so they can discuss it. Her mother never called or even texted before she popped by, which was fine most of the time. Once, back in February, Vivi let herself into the house while Willa and Rip were in the bedroom having sex. They'd heard her calling out, they'd heard her climbing the stairs, and Rip had nearly lost his erection but Willa begged him to finish because she was ovulating and he had paddle tennis that night and by the time he got home, she would be asleep.

Rip said, "She's going to come into the bedroom, Will, and the door isn't locked."

Willa had shouted, "Go away, Mom, please! We're busy!"

"Getting busy?" Vivi said. "Sorry, guys! Have fun!"

They could hear her retreat and Rip came, then fell on top of Willa, saying, "That was the ultimate test of my manhood." And a couple of weeks later, Willa discovered she was pregnant. They called it the Bad Timing Baby until Willa started bleeding at eight weeks.

Vivi stopped by so often because, Willa realized tearfully, the two of them had become friends. They'd emerged out of the dark, confusing tunnel-maze of mother-daughter relationships to discover that they liked each other and had fun hanging out. Vivi hadn't enjoyed a friendship with her own mother at all; they remained in the maze until Nancy Howe died, during Vivi's first winter on Nantucket.

Vivi admitted to Willa recently that she had been worried when she gave birth to a girl because her own relationship with her mother had been so unpleasant.

"Then I realized I didn't have to do things the way my mother did them. I could become the mother I wish I'd had." Vivi laughed. "Your father and I quickly figured out that you were going to raise us rather than the other way around."

Yes, much has been made of "the way Willa is"—a super-achiever, responsible, reliable, mature, a leader. She's the youngest assistant director the Nantucket Historical Association has ever had and she will take over there in five years when the present director retires. She'll be executive director before she turns thirty.

Or she might leave the NHA once she gets pregnant and work on her pet project, a biography of Anna Gardner, a Nantucket abolitionist who'd organized three antislavery conventions in the early 1840s (Frederick Douglass spoke at all three).

In their conversations at the kitchen island—Willa drinking herbal tea and Vivi drinking tequila over ice (Willa kept a bottle of Casa Dragones on hand just for her mother), they would talk about what path Willa's life might take. Vivi was of the opinion that Willa could have it all—she could work at the NHA for thirty-five years and leave her stamp on the historical legacy of the island *and* she could write the biographies of Anna Gardner, Eunice Ross, and any other remarkable (and overlooked) Nantucket woman that she wanted to. She could ask for a sabbatical or she could set up flex time.

"What about kids?" Willa said. She wanted five, four at the very least, but every time she said this, Vivi groaned and said she'd feel differently about having five after the first one was born.

"You'll get a nanny," Vivi said. "And unlike me, you'll use your time to write. I used the times when I had babysitters to clean or take a nap. Kids are hard, Willie, I won't lie." Willa can see her mother clearly: her stylish dark pixie cut, her brown eyes, the freckles across her nose, her dangly earrings. She wore clothes that were meant for a person twenty years younger but that looked good on Vivi—tight white T-shirts, skinny jeans, suede high-heeled boots. Willa was hesitant to use the word *beautiful* to describe her mother because it didn't quite fit. She was cute, spunky, *alive*. And she had near-perfect instincts about people. If her mother believed Willa could do it all, then it was so.

Where does Willa see herself five years from now, at age twenty-nine?

She is the executive director of the NHA and she has just published her biography of Anna Gardner to great critical acclaim (even her fantasy does not include the book becoming a commercial success). She has three children: Charles Evan Bonham III (Charlie), age five, Lucinda Vivian (Lucy), age four and a half, and Edward William (Teddy), age three. Charlie is in kindergarten and the other two go to Montessori preschool, leaving Willa free to split her days between work on NHA business and her second book, which is about Eunice Ross, the young Black woman who petitioned for entry into Nantucket High School in 1847, nearly a century before *Brown v. Board of Education.* She picks the kids up from school and fixes them a snack of freshly baked banana bread, then they have quiet time doing puzzles and reading while Willa makes dinner. Tonight, it's grilled steak tips, parmesan fondant potatoes, pan-roasted asparagus, a crisp green salad, and popovers, and for dessert, a strawberry-rhubarb galette. Rip comes home from work and changes into the soft gray Amherst T-shirt that Willa loves. He kisses Willa long and deep, the way he used to when they were in junior high, then he puts his finger to her lips and says, "We'll finish that later." After dinner, Rip gives the kids a bath, puts them in their pajamas, and supervises teeth-brushing while Willa cleans the kitchen, makes lunches for the following day, and gets the dishwasher humming. Then she goes in to read to the kids—three books per night, chosen by theme. Tonight's theme is pigs: *If You Give a Pig a Pancake, Olivia Saves the Circus,* and *Toot and Puddle.*

After the children are tucked in and on their way to dreamland, Willa and Rip reunite in front of the TV, Willa in a silk nightie because she's lost all the baby weight and then some (she gets up before dawn to ride her Peloton on Tuesdays and Thursdays; that's all it takes!). Rip cracks open a beer and pours Willa a glass of the Cloudy Bay sauvignon blanc. They start watching the first episode of the hot new show on Peacock, but before they can figure out who the main characters are, they're all over each other on the sofa, and the silent furtiveness of it (they can't wake the children!) makes it just as hot as the sex used to be in high school when they were under a blanket on the sofa in Rip's basement rec room.

After that, sweaty and spent, they split a piece of the strawberry-rhubarb galette dolloped with freshly whipped cream and then decide that sleep is more important than finishing the show. They head to the bedroom; Willa picks up the novel on her nightstand, and Rip is snoring before she turns the page.

When Willa reaches up to turn off the light, she feels a tiny burst of light and energy inside of her, and she knows she's pregnant again.

This is the life Willa wants.

It feels a long way off from the life Willa presently has, the one where she's heartbroken and lost. Her mother is gone. Five years from now, even if Willa has attained the kind of perfection she dreams of, Vivi will still be gone. She's gone forever. Willa *will never see her again.* It seems impossible. Someone snuffed out her life and then, in an act so unconscionable Willa can't even imagine it, drove away.

Someone *on this island* got away with murder.

Willa wants justice. There was a rumor going around that Cruz DeSantis had been the one to hit Vivi and was just pretending that he'd found her—but Willa refuses to entertain this possibility.

"People are just gossiping," Willa says. "They don't know Cruz like we do."

Rip isn't so sure. "I heard there are some funny things about his story. Even your brother thinks it might be him."

"No, he doesn't," Willa says.

"I think he does," Rip says. "I guess Cruz and Leo had a fight the night before, so maybe Cruz came over so early because he was upset, and he turned onto Kingsley going too fast without paying attention, and...*boom.*"

"Don't say *boom.*" Willa closes her eyes. She can't let herself imagine the moment of impact but she can't block it out either. "It wasn't Cruz. It was someone else. Just keep checking with the police, please. I want them to get this guy behind bars."

Willa is eight weeks pregnant, and although she has by now trained herself not to get her hopes up, she *cannot* lose this pregnancy.

This is the last pregnancy Vivi knew about; this baby and Willa's mother were alive at the same time. This pregnancy must continue; it must thrive.

Willa doesn't feel sick, or tired, or dizzy. Her breasts might be a bit tender, but that could be because she's constantly pressing and pinching them to see if they feel tender.

*I cannot lose this baby. I cannot lose this baby.* Willa knows she's obsessing and that obsessing is bad for her. She obsesses about obsessing.

Moving into Wee Bit is a good distraction. Willa does her favorite thing: she makes a list. She writes down all the essentials they need to bring and checks them off as she packs them up. Five linen dresses for work; T-shirts; her short overalls; five bathing suits; her straw hat; her Lululemon shorts; and tanks for exercising, which she is going to do more often. And a cotton open-weave sweater because it gets chilly at night by the ocean.

Wee Bit has a sandy front yard separated from the entrance to Smith's Point by a split-rail fence. Up over the rise is the prettiest stretch of beach on Nantucket—a wide swath of golden sand as far as the eye can see, blue-green water, gentle waves.

On her first afternoon at Wee Bit, Willa goes for a barefoot walk at the waterline. She's the only person on the beach; it feels like she has the entire island to herself. Because she works at the Nantucket Historical Association, she can't help but think of all the lives and stories that have played out on this island. She's a native; this land, in some sense, belongs to her.

She picks up her pace until her heart rate increases. Blood flow is good for the baby; so is fresh air, sunshine. Can these things combat her indescribable grief?

*Mom,* she thinks. *Where are you? Where did you go?*

The waves encroach and recede over and over again, just as they did hundreds of years ago when the Wampanoag tribe swam in these waters, in the 1860s during the height of the whaling industry, in the 1920s when artists and actors from New York came to Nantucket to escape the heat of the city. The waves will keep rolling in and out for all eternity, long after Willa is gone, after her children and grandchildren and great-grandchildren are gone.

Willa feels dizzy.

When she heads back to Wee Bit, it's six thirty, and despite her fantasy of a life where everything is made from scratch, she can't manage anything more complicated than peanut butter crackers. Millie's, a Mexican restaurant, is a short bike ride away and Willa is craving their guacamole. This is a good sign, she thinks. She has lost four pounds since her mother died.

As she comes up over the rise, she blinks. There's a red Range Rover parked alongside the split-rail fence. Pamela's car.

What is *she* doing here? Willa wonders.

Pamela and Zach made a bet about how long Willa and Rip would last out in Smith's Point. "Zach gives it a week," Pamela said. "I give it two days."

Is she here to check?

The only downside to marrying Rip Bonham is having Pamela Bonham Bridgeman—she likes to refer to herself by all three names—as a sister-in-law. Willa despises her. Willa has always despised her. Pamela is sixteen years older than Rip. Mrs. Bonham, Tink, suffered three miscarriages, which is the number Willa rests at presently. But Tink was "bound and determined" to give birth to "an heir." Wasn't Pamela an heir? Yes, technically, but male primogeniture reigned supreme in the Bonham household. As Willa had learned from studying so many of Nantucket's family trees, if Tink hadn't given birth to Rip, the Bonham name would have splintered off into a distaff Bridgeman line.

But Tink had, at last, been successful, and on March 11, 1997, she gave birth to a ten-pound baby boy. Pamela, at the time a sophomore in boarding school, had both doted on and greatly resented Rip, and she has vacillated between love and bitterness ever since. She probably sensed that her own presence in the family wasn't enough and this left a permanent chip on her shoulder.

She's prickly, tough, difficult to please.

Pamela has never been a fan of Willa's and huffs in disbelief with each passing year that Willa and Rip stay together. While Rip was at Amherst College, Pamela encouraged him to date girls from Smith and Holyoke. When Rip proposed to Willa, Pamela launched a campaign to make him reconsider. She said she didn't want Rip to "limit" himself. Pamela didn't think Willa was good enough. Willa was the product of a broken home; she had needed three years of orthodonture; she didn't ski; she wasn't competitive in games like the Bonhams were; her political views were too far left; she was bookish, bordering on antisocial—the list of objections went on and on.

There had been moments when Willa was certain Rip would submit to his sister and ask for his ring back. He held his sister in the highest regard. Both of them now worked together at the family insurance company under Chas—Pamela was vice president of homeowners' insurance while Rip handled claims. Pamela was smart, savvy, decisive, and strategic about how to grow the business beyond what her great-great-grandfather could ever have dreamed of. Willa had to hear about her genius incessantly.

But Rip had stuck to his guns, as the saying went. Pamela wore black to the wedding, and Willa accepted Pamela as the burden she must bear for the treasure that was her new husband.

Lots of people had trouble with their in-laws. Willa was hardly alone in this.

Willa reminds herself that Pamela's life is hardly perfect. There's a good chance that Pamela's ill will toward Willa is stoked by jealousy. Pamela's husband, Zach, the head of air traffic control at Nantucket Memorial, is way more handsome than Pamela is pretty. Their looks are so uneven that it brings up questions, the first one being: How did they get together? (Willa knows the answer—Zach waited tables at the Field and Oar Club in the summer of 1999 and Pamela was so smitten by him that she walked right into the help's quarters one night and asked him out.) Zach is also cool and funny. He reads for pleasure (including all of Vivi's books) and he's a licensed pilot in addition to being the head of ATC. Willa likes Zach tremendously; having him around balances out the unpleasantness of Pamela.

Their son, Peter, looks like Zach—he's a handsome kid—but he has inherited Pamela's temperament. He's a jerk—sorry, but he is. He has always been a jerk. Back when Willa and Rip used to babysit Peter, they were constantly doing damage control. Peter was a biter and a toy-stealer and a sand-thrower, and no amount of reprimands or time-outs ever changed his behavior. In school, he was diagnosed with ADHD, put on Adderall, taken off Adderall, sent to Proctor Academy his sophomore year, kicked out of Proctor for smoking (and selling) weed, then sent back to Nantucket High School. He had to repeat a grade, which put him in the same class as Leo. Leo loathed Peter. "I know he's sort of family," Leo said. "But he's a prick."

Willa can't imagine why Pamela is out here in Smith's Point. She never stopped by the house at Quaker Road, and that was infinitely closer.

"Hi?" Willa says. Pamela is still in the Rover but her window is down; she's typing something on her phone. "Everything okay?"

Pamela looks up. "Fine."

"Okay?" Willa says. Is this a *social* visit, then? It's a stunning evening, filled with the mellow golden light of early summer. "Do you want a tour? It looks a lot better..."

"Not right now," Pamela says. She offers Willa a rare smile. "How are you feeling?"

Willa isn't sure what Pamela is asking. Is she talking about Willa's earth-shattering loss? Or about her pregnancy? Rip told his sister that Willa was pregnant again, which was (sort of) fine, except

Pamela then went and shared the news with the elder Bonhams and so now Tink and Chas are treating Willa like she's made of bone china. Their desire to pass along the family name has grown only more fervent with time.

Willa hasn't told her brother and sister, her father, or even Savannah that she's pregnant. She's going to wait until after she gets her ultrasound, which is in another six weeks.

"I'm okay, I guess," Willa says. (Not eating, not sleeping.) "I was glad to move out here."

Pamela sniffs. "It's quiet, anyway. Peaceful."

Willa nods, wondering what Pamela wants. Maybe she's just checking in. Maybe she feels bad for Willa and intends to offer herself as a mother substitute. The idea is nearly laughable.

"You're sure you don't want to come in?" Willa says. "I wish I had something other than tap water to offer you. I think Rip and I are just going to get takeout from Millie's. I can't handle the grocery store yet. Too many people. Their eyes give them away—I know they feel sorry for me. Some of them come up and offer their sympathies. Others wave and say hello like everything is normal."

Pamela looks at Willa and an amazing thing happens: Pamela's eyes fill with tears. Pamela Bonham Bridgeman is displaying human emotion. Willa tries to abandon her cynicism. Had Pamela *liked* Vivi? Admired her, maybe? Willa remembers no special connection. Pamela habitually referred to Vivi's books as "fluff" and always seemed a little pissed off that her husband was such a fan.

"If I share something with you, do you promise not to tell anyone?" Pamela asks. "Even Rip?"

*What is this?* Willa thinks. *A confidence? A ... secret?* Willa's mind starts racing. What is *happening* here? Is Willa's dream for the past twelve years—half her life—of having a normal relationship with her sister-in-law finally coming true?

"Of course," Willa says. She isn't sure she'll be able to keep whatever this is from Rip, but she'll try.

"I think Zach is having an affair," Pamela says.

Willa feels a surge of what she can only describe as lurid excitement. Though she's aghast too, of course.

"In fact, I'm sure he is," Pamela says.

# Vivi

"This is getting good," Vivi says. She has pulled one of the peach silk soufflé chairs right up to the edge of the room. "We need popcorn." She tilts her head. "Why isn't there food up here? Why isn't there *wine?*"

"Heavenly banquet," Martha says. "Once you join the choir."

"Only then?"

"Reward for all that singing."

"Will there be truffle fries?" Vivi asks. "Tequila?"

"Vivian, please," Martha says. "Let's focus on the matter at hand."

The matter at hand: Pamela thinks Zach is having an affair. Vivi knows she should be more sympathetic toward Pamela. After all, Vivi has been in the exact same spot, except Vivi didn't have to figure it out. JP had marched into the house one late-summer evening and told Vivi he'd "fallen" for Amy, sounding almost proud of himself.

But Pamela is an unsympathetic character in this story. If Vivi were still alive and Willa had confided Pamela's suspicions about Zach to Vivi, Vivi might have said, *Good for him.*

Vivi is an absolutely wretched person. How did she end up ascending instead of descending?

Martha chuckles. She's an unapologetic mind reader.

"Is there more?" Vivi asks.

Martha pulls the second soufflé chair up next to Vivi's. "Oh, there's more."

# Carson

The owner of the Oystercatcher gives her two weeks off after her mother dies, but then she has to make a decision: return to work or quit. It's the Fourth of July weekend, the Oystercatcher is pumping, and they need their bartender. The owner, George, has been subbing in but if Carson doesn't return for her weekend shifts, he'll have no choice but to replace her.

She shows up on Saturday at three o'clock, right before buck-a-shuck. George puts his hands on her shoulders. "You can do this." He sounds like he's sending her out into the ring with Floyd Mayweather.

"I can *totally* do this." Before Carson left her mother's house, she made herself a double espresso and did a shot of her mother's tequila, which Savannah had found in the laundry room. ("I figured your mom would hide it someplace you would never look," Savannah said.)

Carson steps behind the bar and jumps right in: a dozen Island Creeks, a dozen cherrystones, four Whale's Tale Pale Ale drafts, "Vodka soda, close it" for the Chad in the pink polo shirt, a dozen East Beach Blondes, two chardonnays, a planter's punch. Carson fields the orders like they're pop flies. She won't think about her mother. She won't check her phone. When she gets a second to breathe, she makes herself an espresso and takes an Ativan. She can do this.

The crowd thickens with every passing minute. It's like eating a plate of spaghetti—you think you're making headway but you can't clean your plate. (Maybe that's the Ativan talking?) No, there are people pouring in, drawn to the bar like iron shavings to a magnet. Sean Lee, the guitar player, starts singing and Carson curses herself because she meant to request "Stone in Love," by Journey. Sean had sent her a text saying If there's anything I can do, let me know, and Carson texted back and asked him to learn this song because, it turns out, this is the song that Vivi was listening to when she got hit.

*Burning love comes once in a lifetime.*

Carson could tell from looking at Vivi's phone that she had gotten Carson's last text. Sorry about the pan, Mama, and the tequila wasn't me. I love you. The timing of the text was so close to what the police said was the point of impact that Carson wondered if Vivi had been reading her text instead of watching the road, and that Carson's apology was the reason her mother was killed. *You'll be the death of me, Carson Marie.* Savannah assured Carson that the place where the police found the phone indicated that the phone had not been held in front of Vivi's face but rather at her side. Was Savannah making that up? It was possible but Carson clung to the maybe-a-lie like a lifebuoy. She couldn't take another breath otherwise.

By seven o'clock, as the sun is starting to slant toward its descent, the Oystercatcher is at maximum capacity and all the customers are deliriously happy—eating, drinking, taking selfies, singing along with Sean, talking and laughing as though nothing bad could ever happen, as though they were all going to live forever.

Carson gets lots of tips but she can't bring herself to ring the damn bell; it feels like a button that's out of her reach, a bar she can't clear. She asks the kiss-ass barback, Jamey (boy), to cover while she goes to the bathroom. She needs something. The Ativan took the edge off, but the downside is she's in a fog. She has some coke but she isn't sure how it will mix with her grief. Still, she's back at work; she needs to be up, up, up. She's only halfway through her shift.

She taps some out on her thumb, snorts. Ah, okay. Her eyes water; it's bitter, sharp. She sits on the toilet waiting for the rush but it's slow to come, so she bumps. She feels her heart kick-start. Great, she's back in the game.

She reaches into her purse for her phone, which might as well be radioactively glowing. *Don't touch it!* she thinks.

She touches it. Has he texted? Yes, he has.

She hasn't heard from him since the day her mother died. That night, she sent him two texts. The first said, I can't do this anymore. The second said, Please don't come to the service. Say you're sick or you have to work, idc, but please DO NOT show your face at the church or the reception.

Immediately after she sent the texts, she wanted to snatch them back because she was hurting and she needed him.

But the affair *had to end,* because how was Carson to know that Vivi's death wasn't the universe's way of punishing her?

When Carson talked to Savannah about this—"Do you think Mom died because of something I did?"—Savannah took Carson's cheeks between her palms and squished them together so that Carson had fish lips, something she used to do when Carson was little. "It was an accident, baby. A senseless accident. It didn't have anything to do with you or me or even Vivi herself."

This sounded rational and even like something Vivi might say in her sweet-tart way ("Not everything is about you, darling"), but she couldn't be sure, and Savannah didn't know the depths of Carson's treachery.

Carson washes her hands and checks her reflection in the mirror. Her green eyes flash wickedly; that's from the blow. Her cheeks have color. She looks better, she feels better, she can do this. She goes back to work.

\*     \*     \*

"Mount Gay and tonic, strong, please, bruh." This is from a young guy in the corner seat.

Carson rolls her eyes. "All my drinks are strong."

"That was a joke," the guy says. "Because of...last week? At your—" He stops suddenly. "Never mind. Mount Gay and tonic, regular strength is fine."

Carson narrows her eyes at him. He's cute if you like golfers and preppies. His golden-blond hair is a little long in the back and curls up under his baseball cap—DUCKS, the cap says on the front—and he has a strong chin, which Carson likes. What does he mean, "last week"?

She makes him a drink using a little more rum than she might normally, and when she sets the glass down, it dawns on her that she has gone only one place. "The Field and Oar?"

"Yes," he says. "I'm Marshall. I bartend there? I'm really sorry about your mom."

Carson isn't sure how to react. She didn't anticipate being faced with anyone here who knew about her mom. Her customers are primarily tourists—day-trippers, hotel guests, Airbnb dwellers, renters, summer residents. The locals stopped coming once the two-hour wait for a table started a few weeks ago.

Carson decides to smile through her agonizing pain. Her mother is dead. How can she be standing here? "Thank you," she says. "I appreciate it."

Marshall takes a sip of his Mount Gay, then asks for a menu.

"Are you waiting for someone?" Carson asks. He looks up at her with an expression that is both alarmed and embarrassed and she feels like a jerk for asking.

She reaches into her bag under the bar and pulls out her phone. Nothing for nearly a week and now there are two texts from him. She clicks on her camera and turns around to snap a selfie with Marshall. He grins and the picture is cute so she posts it to her Instagram with the caption

Taking care of Marshall from the #fieldandoarclub on his night off! 😊

A dozen Island Creeks, four Bud Lights, two dirty martinis, and then three tables' orders come into the service bar and Carson regrets taking the thirty seconds to post because now she's in the weeds.

When she finally pops her head above water, Marshall says he wants to order dinner—the fish sando, extra tartar, and fries and coleslaw, and the chowder to start. Carson gives him a second Mount Gay and tonic on the house. She's hitting the top of her high now; nothing can stop her. She's moving like lightning, shaking up martinis and cosmos, joking with the couple on the far left side of the bar, pounding some high fives, delivering platters of oysters and clams, extra lemon, extra horseradish, extra crackers.

"You're on fire," Marshall says. "Is it always like this?"

"Always," Carson says, though she's showing off. She knows what Marshall's bartending job at the club looks like—it's making cocktails for Carson's grandmother and Penny Rosen when they arrive at four thirty for dinner and pulling draft beers for New York investment bankers after they come off the tennis court.

Marshall's food is up and Carson takes extra care in setting down the plate. "Fish sando, extra tartar, fries, and slaw. What else can I get you?"

"I never saw the chowder," he says.

"Oh, wait..." Carson checks the slip. She forgot to put in the chowder. How is this possible? "I forgot to put it in. I am *so* sorry." She feels like a fraud; she isn't such a superstar after all. She's a crummy server.

"Don't worry about it," he says. "This looks great."

Carson hesitates. "Let me put it in, please. I feel awful."

"What if you let me buy you a drink when you get off tonight?" he says. "You finish around eleven? We can hit the back bar at Ventuno."

Carson nearly laughs. He's asking her *out?* Marshall from the

Field and Oar? Oh, how cute. He's probably a year or two older than she is but she knows she would eat him alive. DUCKS means the University of Oregon—this comes to Carson out of nowhere. He's fresh and piney like the Pacific Northwest.

"Let me see how I'm feeling, okay?"

"Whatever works." Marshall stares down at his plate and Carson can tell he's stung. He put himself out there and she turned him down and he doesn't have any other friends, or if he does, they're all working at the Field and Oar.

"I'll let you know before you finish eating," Carson says. She flags the other barback, Jaime, who is a girl and not a kiss-ass, to cover her, grabs her bag, and goes to the bathroom.

She takes one bump, then another. Tomorrow, she'll have to call her guy. She needs to get back out there and finish the dinner rush strong, but she sees her phone and it's like falling into a hole. She checks her texts.

Can I see you tonight? End of Kingsley?

We should probably talk.

Carson's head pitches forward; she loves her phone so much in that moment that she'd like to take a bite of it. These texts are like cool water on a bad sunburn, like a soft pillow when she can't keep her eyes open. A balm, a relief. He wants to see her.

She sends back a text: No.

She counts to ten, which is all it takes for three dots to appear. And then—

I can't go another day without seeing you. Meet me, please.

She hesitates. Giddiness bubbles up inside her; she's a shaken can of seltzer about to spew. But no. It has to end. While it's still a secret. They have done enough damage. Her mother is dead.

Okay, she texts back. See you at midnight.

Carson heads back out to the bar. Marshall finished his dinner and Jaime has gotten him a fresh drink.

"I can't meet you tonight," Carson says. "But maybe another time. And, hey, your dinner is on me." She takes his tab and slips it into her apron pocket.

"There's no need—"

"Oh, but there is." She winks at him. "We have to take care of each other." She heads to the other side of the bar to take orders. When she comes back, Marshall is gone. A fifty-dollar bill and a napkin with his phone number are in his place.

Carson shakes her head. Bold move; she likes it. She throws the napkin away, tosses the fifty in the bucket, and rings the bell.

Midnight finds her in cutoffs and Chuck Taylors walking down Kingsley toward the dead end. There's a space in the bushes big enough (almost) to hide one car and that's where Zach Bridgeman is waiting for her in his Audi Q7. She climbs into the back seat with him, and when she sees him, smells him—he smoked a cigarette on the way over, another secret he keeps from his wife—she starts to cry. He gently takes her face in his hands and licks her tears and then they're kissing like it's the only thing keeping them alive. Carson wants to straddle his lap; she wants to wriggle out of her shorts or even rip them in half to get them off; she wants to slide down on top of him and bounce up and down, his hands grasping her ass, until they both climax in a burst of heat and light.

But instead, she pulls away. "She's dead."

"I know, baby. I'm so sorry."

"And I have nobody to hold me."

"I'll hold you."

"This is our fault."

He flinches at this as she knew he would. Zach refuses to acknowledge the dark side of what they're doing. All he ever talks about is how happy Carson makes him, how his life has new meaning, how each day is filled with possibility instead of despair. He's the one who's married; he's the one who has to lie, sneak out, delete everything on his phone. But he would never accept that their union was evil enough to bring about this kind of retribution.

"Don't be ridiculous, Carson. Our relationship has nothing to do with your mother."

"I believe otherwise. You can tell me I'm wrong but you can't *prove* I'm wrong."

"I came to the service," Zach says. "I was in the back. I could only see the side of your face, but I was there. I cut out of work. I left Yeats in charge, which was irresponsible, but I needed to see you, if only from afar."

He does this all the time, speaks like he's writing a sonnet. *If only from afar.*

"I specifically asked you not to come. I don't know why you think I would be happy to hear you came anyway."

Zach sighs, rests his head against the seat. His skin is pale and beautiful in the dark. He has long, thick eyelashes and a few gray hairs around his ears. She is twenty-one years old and her lover has gray hair. But his age is third or fourth down the list of what makes him inappropriate.

"Let's say what we're doing has nothing to do with my mother's death. There's still no good ending to this, only destructive, scandalous endings. We need to walk away tonight and never speak of it again."

"What about the ending where I leave Pamela and we run away together? Hawaii, Alaska, Paris. I can find work anywhere. So can you. Peter is going off to college in eight weeks. Can't we hang on for eight weeks?"

"We would still destroy two families—yours and what's left of mine. It has to end, Zach." She forces the words out. She doesn't want it to end. She wants Alaska, Hawaii, Paris, however improbable that sounds. "I had a very handsome man ask me out at work. He lives here, he's single, he's closer to my age."

Zach closes his eyes. "Yes, I saw your Instagram."

Well, that was why she'd posted it, wasn't it? Carson doesn't care a whit about her social media except as a way of agitating Zach.

Carson kisses Zach's cheek and opens her door. "I'll see you at the next family gathering." She closes the door gently but firmly and starts walking down the dirt road to her house. She hears one door open and close, then another; he's moving to the front seat. The engine starts up. She wills him to drive right past her, but if he does, she knows tonight will end with her leaving him desperate voice mails, and in the final one, she'll threaten to tell Pamela everything if he doesn't meet her again tomorrow.

The car slows down; she hears the electric hum of his window. "You know I can't live without you and I can't stand the thought of anyone else touching you."

She keeps walking. She wants to be with him but it's wrong—so wrong that her mother is now dead.

"Carson!" he whispers. It's risky for them to be out here on the road together. Carson has no idea what Leo is up to—it's like they're sad motel guests whose paths cross occasionally—but he could come driving down the road any second, and what would he make of this? Carson at a quarter past midnight communing with their sister's brother-in-law. "Carson, please stop."

She keeps walking.

"Please, Carson. I love you."

*I love you too,* she thinks. She has never been in love before and has never said the words to a man; she's a late bloomer in this, but she knows that this is what love feels like. It feels like jumping out of a plane with a parachute that has been packed by someone who's assured you that, yes, it will open, and you will float safely to the ground.

She walks over to where Zach's Audi is idling and kisses him, right out in the open.

"See you tomorrow?" he asks.

She nods, and he drives away.

# Vivi

Vivi leaps out of her chair. "No," she says. "Absolutely not. I refuse to believe it."

"Believe it," Martha says.

"Carson and Zach Bridgeman?"

"Yes."

Vivi is...stunned. She's...aghast. Carson and Zach? This had been going on while Vivi was *alive?* While Carson was living under Vivi's *roof?* Vivi thinks about her final morning on Earth, of Carson coming home at five thirty a.m. Had she been out with Zach? Vivi thinks back to the night at the Oystercatcher when Zach and Pamela sat down at the bar. Carson had been flustered, there was no denying it; she'd stammered, knocked over the menus, spilled bourbon over the rim of the glass. Had they planned that cute little meeting or had Zach ambushed her? Was he cruel enough to bring his *wife* to the bar where Carson was *working* without warning her?

Vivi has depicted some scandalous affairs in her novels, but never anything quite *this* sordid.

"Eh," Martha says. "Some of them were pretty sordid. Let's not forget Clay and Meghan in *Main Street Gossip.*"

"But he's"—Vivi calculates. She thinks Zach is a year older than Pamela, so he's about forty-two. And Carson is twenty-one— "twice her age."

"It happens."

"I'm the novelist," Vivi says. "I know it happens. But no, sorry, this I can't abide." How long has this been going on? Who else knows? Does Willa know? (Definitely not.) Vivi thinks back. Did Carson and Zach have a close relationship in the past? Not that she'd noticed. Was this thing going on when Willa got married? At the wedding, Vivi had been too consumed with herself, JP, Amy, Dennis, and Lucinda to worry about Carson. "I'm glad you advised me to save my nudges. Because I'm putting an end to this."

"You can't," Martha says. "They've fallen in love. Breaking that up requires more than just a nudge."

"So now you're telling me my nudges won't work?"

"They'll work," Martha says. "What I'm telling you is a nudge is a nudge. It's exactly what a parent tries to do in real life. But you don't have the power to stop love or change it."

"You've *got* to be kidding me!"

"I'm sorry, Vivian." And with that, Martha disappears through the green door.

Vivi is allowed to use the hours when her world is asleep to travel back in her memories. Every single moment of her life—days, weeks, months, even entire years that she has long forgotten—can be revisited in crystal-clear detail, as though she's living it again. She isn't bound by chronology. She's like a contestant on a game show—she spins the wheel and sees where it lands.

*My first summer on Nantucket.* Sure, why not.

It's 1991; she has just graduated from Duke, she has no job and no prospects, but she did win the creative-writing award at graduation, which came with a five-thousand-dollar prize. Five thousand dollars is a fortune. It's enough that she can ignore her mother's pleas to come home to Parma ("You can get a job at the mall, take a typing class...") and go with Savannah to Nantucket for the summer.

"It'll be so great," Savannah said when they were back in Durham packing up their dorm room. "I have a part-time job in a needlepoint store on Main Street and when I'm not working, we can hang out on Madequecham Beach. We can go to the Chicken Box and the Muse at night."

"I'll have to get a job too," Vivi said.

"You'll be writing," Savannah said. "You're bringing your word processor, right?"

"Right," Vivi said, but her voice faltered because she wasn't sure she considered "writing" a job—a job was supposed to produce income. Maybe she could write in the mornings, then wait tables or work retail. She wanted to use the five thousand dollars as a nest egg, not as pocket money to blow through during her fun Nantucket summer.

Her fun Nantucket summer! On the ferry, Vivi and Savannah sit on the top deck with the sun in their faces and the wind blowing their hair back like they're a couple of J. Crew models. The island comes into view—sailboats in the harbor, the town skyline, such as it is, consisting of two church steeples. When the girls disembark, Savannah waves at her mother, Mary Catherine, who is driving an ancient Jeep Wagoneer with wood-panel sides. Mrs. Hamilton helps them load their luggage into the back while Savannah's yellow Lab, Bromley, chases his tail in excitement.

"I swear, Vivian, you brought so much luggage, I'd think you were planning on spending the summer!" Mary Catherine says.

Vivi's mouth opens. Savannah squeezes Vivi's wrist in a way that Vivi knows means *Don't respond* and says, "You sit up front, Vivi, so you can see. I'll sit in the back with Bromley."

On the way to the house, Vivi cranes her neck trying to take it all in: the bike shops, the pizza place, the Nantucket Whaling Museum, a young woman in a yellow sundress crossing the street with an armload of flowers. When Mary Catherine said Vivi brought enough luggage to make her think she was spending the summer, what did *that* mean? *Isn't* she spending the summer? Vivi tries not to panic, although she has nowhere to go except back to Ohio, where she'll end up working at one of the Parmatown Mall kiosks that sell markers with disappearing ink or paper planes that fly in loop-the-loops or, even worse, she'll be stuffing her legs into nylons and showing up at some blocky office building to become a Kelly girl.

But she has her heart set on a summer at the beach.

The Hamilton summer home, Entre Nous, is on Union Street in a row of what Mary Catherine calls "antiques." (Vivi thought antiques were pieces of furniture or cars, not houses.) The home was built in 1822 by Oliver Hamilton. It has white clapboard siding, black shutters, a black front door with a silver scallop-shell knocker, and huge blooming hydrangea bushes flanking the "friendship stairs"—seven steps on either side of the door that ascend to meet at a landing.

When Vivi enters, she holds her breath. She knows, somehow, that this is a moment she'll remember until the day she dies (and beyond, as it turns out!). Vivi had thought the house would be beachy, like an upscale version of the place they rented in Wrightsville during spring break, but this house has Persian rugs, chandeliers, a grandfather clock, and a huge vase of Asiatic lilies on a marble-topped table in the foyer. The dog bounds inside and sniffs at Vivi's crotch for what seems like an indecent amount of time while Vivi tries to pry his muzzle away. Nobody else seems to notice, but Vivi feels exposed, as if even the dog has rooted her out as a stranger. The house is the grandest Vivi has ever been inside. The staircase has a runner held across each step with a brass rail and Savannah points at the scrimshaw button embedded in the cap of the newel post at the bottom of the balustrade; it was placed there when "good old Ollie" paid off the mortgage in 1826.

Vivi peers into the formal living room to the right of the stairs and the dining room to the left, each room with a brick fireplace. Savannah leads her down the hall to a library, which is everything you'd want an at-home library to be. Built-in shelves hold rows and rows of books—the requisite leather-bound kind but also the rainbow spines of popular hardbacks and an entire swath of battered paperbacks. There's a deep leather armchair where apparently someone has been sitting recently—a copy of *Moby Dick* lies splayed open on the seat. Vivi can't help herself; she picks the book up. In the margins are notes in faded pencil.

"I was just revisiting Melville," Mary Catherine says. "That's the copy I studied from at Smith, if you can believe it."

Vivi sets the book down with some reverence now. The library isn't just for show; it's the place where Mary Catherine can revisit Melville and reflect on the thoughts she had as a younger person. Vivi understands that she's in a home where things aren't put out for show; the furnishings have meaning, *provenance*. It's mortifying to compare this home—Savannah's *second* home—to the place Vivi grew up, with its wall-to-wall carpeting, crucifixes everywhere, the long, fancy mirror at the end of the hall bought on sale from the furniture department at Higbee's.

Vivi wishes she hadn't sold all her books back to the student bookstore at the end of the year. She, too, wrote in the margins (this was a detriment to their resale value) and now she will never be able to revisit her musings; she will never be able to hand off her copy of *Franny and Zooey* to one of her children and say, *I read this at nineteen, let me know what you think.*

From now on, she decides, she's saving her books.

Beyond the library is a huge, wide, bright kitchen, which is many different rooms in one. In front of a row of windows is a harvest table set with ten Windsor chairs. Against the opposite wall is an enormous cast-iron range with an imposing hood; the backsplash tile is painted with pictures of fruits and vegetables labeled in French: *haricot vert, artichaut, pêche*. There's a plaid Orvis dog bed in the corner and beyond that a mudroom where Bromley's leashes hang alongside yellow rain slickers. A straw market basket rests on a simple wooden bench that is probably where good old Ollie Hamilton used to sit to put on his boots.

The kitchen has a square island topped in dark marble. There's a prep sink at one end and three barstools at the other. Someone has set out a cutting board with a block of pale cheese, a stick of salami, and a dish of purplish olives.

"Alcohol?" Savannah asks. She pulls a bottle of wine from a fridge that seems to hold only wine, and Vivi can tell it's not the cheap stuff that she and Savannah used to buy at Kroger and drink in the dorms before they went out.

Savannah takes two wine goblets down from a rack over their heads that Vivi hadn't even noticed and says, "Let me show you upstairs."

The hallway of the second floor is long, with a barrel-vaulted roof. Doors that lead to bedrooms—or bathrooms? or closets?—are all closed. At the end of the hall is a rounded niche holding the most impressive model ship Vivi has ever seen. This house is like a museum; there isn't one cheap or inauthentic thing in it.

They ascend another set of stairs to the third floor, Savannah's floor, the renovated attic. The massive, airy, slope-ceilinged space is entirely white—walls, trim, curtains, king canopy bed. The rag rug is done in vivid rainbow stripes, and hanging on the walls is Savannah's childhood artwork—finger-paintings, crayon drawings.

It's a "self-portrait"—Savannah with green hair and red pants drawn like two long boxes—that finally moves Vivi to tears. She brought home school projects—turkeys created by tracing her hand, Easter bunnies with cotton-ball tails, even a tessellation Vivi slaved over for her geometry class in ninth grade—and she's certain they all went into the trash. Vivi's family never documented or celebrated itself because neither of her parents believed their family was worth it. They were just trying to survive, and they didn't even succeed at that.

"What's wrong?" Savannah asks.

Vivi can't explain what she's feeling without sounding petty. *My*

*mother didn't keep my artwork. I have no personal history to display.*
Savannah will no doubt say she's envious because Vivi's parents
aren't "all over" her. Vivi has what Savannah wants: freedom.

"Your mother doesn't know I'm staying all summer," Vivi says.
"Does she?"

"I don't care about my mother," Savannah says, waving a hand.
"Her opinion matters not. And you don't have to worry about
sharing my bed because..." She strides over to a door that Vivi
thinks is a closet and opens it to reveal another bedroom, this one
just big enough to hold a double bed, a dresser, and a desk set
by a tiny window. Vivi gazes out—she can see the harbor in the
distance. The tiny room is perfect. It's compact and sensible. She
can write here while looking at the water for inspiration.

Tears drip down Vivi's face. "How long does she think I'm
staying?"

"Oh, it's this stupid family rule. Houseguests get one week."

"Why didn't you *tell* me this?" Vivi says. "You said I could stay
for the summer."

"You *can* stay for the summer," Savannah says. "I just have to
speak to my father in person."

Mr. Hamilton lives and works in Boston during the week; he
arrives on Friday afternoons and leaves on Monday mornings.

"What if that doesn't work?"

"It always works," Savannah says.

"But what if it *doesn't?*" Vivi says. "Just give me the plan for the
worst-case scenario."

"Worst-case scenario?" Savannah says. "Listen, my parents never,
ever come up here. And they go to bed early. We could just say
that you've found a place to rent and that every once in a while you
sleep over. I'll take care of cleaning your room, doing the sheets,
and whatnot while my mother is at the club—"

"You're suggesting I *hide* here all summer?" Vivi asks.
"Like...like *Anne Frank?*"

This makes them both laugh—but is it really funny, and is Vivi really so far off base?

After spending a few days on Nantucket—lounging on Nobadeer Beach, driving around town in Savannah's bare-bones Jeep (no top, no doors, no back seat), riding a couple of the old Schwinns in the garage out to Sconset to see the first bloom of the climbing roses, dancing all night at the Chicken Box—Vivi is ready to consider the hidden refugee plan.

When Mr. Hamilton shows up on Friday afternoon, still in his pin-striped business suit—he's the managing partner in a big law firm on State Street—the household becomes far more festive. Mr. Hamilton makes his famous frozen margaritas and they drink them while sitting at a table by the pool.

"How are you liking Nantucket?" Mr. Hamilton asks Vivi.

"I love it," she says. "I never want to leave."

"Ah, but leave you must," Mrs. Hamilton says. "Monday, yes? Have you booked your ferry?"

"Can't Vivi stay a few more days?" Savannah asks. "Please?"

"A few more days won't hurt," Mr. Hamilton says, filling enormous tulip-shaped glasses from the blender.

"You've both clearly forgotten that Patrick and Deborah are coming with the children," Mary Catherine says. She offers Vivi a close-lipped smile. "My brother, his second wife, their blended family of six children. I'm afraid there won't be an inch of extra space."

Vivi mumbles, "Excuse me," and slips away from the table. The margarita is churning in her stomach. Patrick and Deborah and their six kids are family and Vivi is not. She has to go. Bromley follows Vivi into the house—he has become her devotee this week, always at her heels, and she has to shoo him away so she can close the powder-room door.

Of all the rooms in this remarkable house, the downstairs powder room is the one Vivi loves the most. The walls are plastered from floor to ceiling with framed snapshots of the Hamilton family on Nantucket. There must be over two hundred pictures, and Vivi has spent a long time studying them. Most are from when Savannah was growing up. There are photos taken on the beach, on sailboats, at picnics, on the tennis court, in the pool, at the Fourth of July festivities on Main Street; there's a picture of Savannah's old dachshund, Herman Munster, lying across the sofa in the library. There are pictures of a younger Mr. and Mrs. Hamilton hugging, kissing, hoisting cocktails. Vivi has scrutinized each photograph like a detective looking for clues.

Now, she scans the wall for people who might be Patrick and Deborah or Patrick and his first wife.

There's a knock on the door: Savannah. "Are you okay? Please don't hate me. This is all my fault."

It *is* all Savannah's fault. Who invites someone to spend the summer at her parents' house without *checking with them first?* Savannah knew the family rule about houseguests and yet made no mention of it. She led Vivi to believe that this Nantucket life could, for one summer, be hers. This wouldn't be so bad if Vivi hadn't fallen so completely, irrevocably in love with the island and all its wonders.

"I'll be right out," Vivi says in a carefree, singsong voice.

She studies the Hamilton family picture that is right above the light switch. It's of Mr. and Mrs. Hamilton and Savannah when Savannah is seventeen or eighteen, so maybe the summer before Duke, which was the summer that Vivi spent every waking moment with Brett Caspian. The Hamiltons are at a bonfire on the beach; they're all end-of-summer tan, and Savannah appears to be shoving the last bite of a hot dog into her mouth.

Vivi's and Savannah's lives could not have been more different that summer, but since then their lives have converged, and now, four years later, they are best friends. Change happens in an instant—one girl offers another her bottle of Breck shampoo, and a friendship is formed.

Vivi has money in the bank. She can use some of it to rent a room and buy a secondhand bike. She can get a job. She can stay here on her own.

She will stay, she decides. Somehow, some way, she will make this island hers. She will become a Nantucketer. Twenty or thirty years from now, she will be able to tell the story of how she refused to overstay her welcome at the Hamiltons' and so she forged her own way.

*Between us,* she imagined saying to friends, *it was the best thing that ever happened to me. It was the defining moment of my life.* This week has been about more than Vivi from Ohio being exposed to wealth and privilege. It has been about Vivi finding a home.

And someday, she tells herself, she will have a powder room just like this one—with pictures of her and her husband and their children, all of them smiling in gratitude at their own good fortune.

*Well!* Vivi-in-the-sky thinks. She had forgotten the intensity of her emotion when she'd learned she would have to leave the Hamiltons back in June of 1991. Savannah has never forgiven herself; she has apologized at least a hundred times over the years.

Vivi succeeded. She stayed on Nantucket and created a life and family. How that happened is a memory for a different night.

Vivi wishes she had taken the time to decorate the powder room in Money Pit with family photographs like the Hamiltons'. But who was she kidding? That house had a hundred projects more pressing—like Leo's shower leaking onto the dining-room table and a family of mice living behind the washer and dryer. Maybe one of the kids would do the project now that Vivi was gone. Maybe Savannah would recall the umpteen times Vivi said she wanted to re-create the powder room of Entre Nous and she would prompt the kids to do it.

Not doing the powder room is a regret, albeit a small one. There are other, far bigger regrets. But Vivi will think about those later.

# Leo

After two full weeks of radio silence, Marissa shows up at the house on a Monday, Leo's only day off from the Boat Basin. He opens the door to find her holding a Bakewell tart with feathered pink and white icing. The fluted crust is golden brown but there's one imperfection where it looks like the crust crumbled and has been pinched together.

"Did you"—Leo swallows. He's happy to have the tart to look at instead of Marissa's face—"make Mary Berry's Bakewell tart? Did you make that *yourself?*"

"Not exactly," Marissa says. "I took a picture of it to the Bake Shop and asked them to make it because I know you've always wanted to try it."

"Oh," Leo says. "So you paid someone to do it for you."

"It's an apology, Leo. I'm sorry about what I said to Cruz on the beach and I'm obviously sorry about your mom. Just let me in, please?"

Leo takes a deep breath and holds open the door.

They pick up right where they left off, hanging out all the time. They used to watch *The Great British Baking Show* ironically—they would imitate the accents and use words like *arduous* and *intuitive*—but now Leo watches it as an escape. The biggest disaster under the tent is dough not rising, or pastry cream curdling, or fruit that is too soft or watery leading to a soggy crust. Leo doesn't have to think about his mother, dead, or about his former best friend, who is quite possibly the reason his mother is dead. The one time that Marissa and Leo tiptoe close to the topic of Cruz, Marissa whispers, "I hate even thinking this…but it must have been him. Alexis said Officer Falco saw him run a stop sign and then speeding less than five minutes before your mom got hit. He was driving recklessly before he turned onto Kingsley, boo. I'm sure he was so upset that he might just have erased what actually happened from his mind. He might be in complete denial, like a case of temporary insanity."

Leo has blocked Cruz on his phone and on Instagram and Snapchat. He expects Cruz to show up at the house like Marissa did, but so far he hasn't.

Leo has also blocked Peter Bridgeman from his phone. He wants to pretend that the night before his mother's death—the bonfire at Fortieth Pole, his breakup with Marissa, and the photograph that Peter sent him—never happened.

Marissa tells Leo that Alexis has a new boyfriend. He's an officer in the department, and things are moving so fast that Alexis has created a Pinterest board for her wedding.

"And I decided to make one too," Marissa says. "You know, for the future."

"Make what?" Leo says, because he's only half listening.

"A Pinterest board for our wedding," Marissa says. "Here, look." They're lying on the Girv. Leo is spooning Marissa and Marissa is spooning her laptop. "I chose bridesmaid dresses and flowers, though I'm thinking of switching the palette from pink to peach."

"Good idea," Leo says with false enthusiasm. He knows he won't be marrying Marissa, but he needs her right now, is the thing. He needs her badly.

Without Vivi, Leo is not only lost but confused. Who's in charge of his day-to-day life now? Everyone, it seems, and no one.

Leo's father, JP, suggests that Leo spend the summer at his house and maybe trade his job at the Boat Basin for one scooping ice cream at the Cone.

No and no, Leo says. Then, because he's angry and has no place to vent, he says, "I hate Amy." He's instantly ashamed. He doesn't like Amy, but *hate* is a strong word and he would never say it to her face.

JP clears his throat. "What if Amy weren't around?"

"Where is she going?"

His father doesn't answer, and Leo doesn't care. He won't live with his father because he can't bear to leave his mother's house. A part of her is still here. There's Tupperware in the refrigerator that still holds her grilled zucchini dip; half a bottle of her Drybar shampoo is on the shelf in the outdoor shower. It's like she's away on a book tour and might be back at any moment.

Carson has been sleeping in Vivi's room. She just moved in like it was her right, and when she's not at work, she wears Vivi's clothes. This is either a healthy way to grieve or a sign of mental illness.

Both Leo and Willa understand that Carson is a renegade. She acts out, demands attention, gets in nonstop trouble, makes questionable decisions, drinks, vapes, smokes weed, and was an expert at pushing every single one of their mother's buttons. However…Carson is also cool, funny, and very, very pretty; people comment on it all the time. Leo's friends always tell him how hot Carson is. Cruz had a wicked crush on her for years.

Leo can't think about Cruz.

Carson isn't in charge of anything following Vivi's death except going back to work and keeping herself alive. Once the zucchini dip is gone and people have stopped dropping off lasagna and clam chowder, Leo wonders what they're supposed to eat. What will they do for money? Who's going to pay the mortgage?

That's where Savannah comes in. She's handling all the business stuff, figuring out Vivi's finances, and dealing with the publication of the new book. She's the administrator of the Vivian Howe Memorial Facebook page.

"Do you want to read the comments people have been posting?" she asks one morning when Carson and Leo happen to be in the kitchen foraging at the same time.

"No," Leo says.

"No," Carson says. "That sounds like Willa's kind of thing."

"Have either of you heard of a boyfriend your mom had in high school named Brett Caspian?"

"Negative," Leo says.

"Mom didn't have boyfriends in high school," Carson says. "She was a total nerd."

"That's the story she always told me too," Savannah says. "But this guy is insisting he dated her for most of their senior year and into the summer before she left for Duke. He says he has pictures."

"Ask him to send the pictures," Carson says. "Because I've never heard of any guy named Brett Kardashian."

"Caspian," Savannah says. "He wants to talk to someone about the new book."

"Crackpot," Carson says. "Dead-celebrity chaser. But ask for the pics."

"I think I will," Savannah says. "Your dad has never heard of him either. He said *he* was your mother's first boyfriend, wink-wink, nudge-nudge."

"Can we not talk about this anymore?" Leo says.

Savannah leaves envelopes filled with cash for them to divvy up.

Marissa takes some of the money and does a grocery-shop for the house. Leo is relieved. If he goes to the Stop and Shop, he might see Cruz working. He wants to ask Marissa if she saw Cruz when she went, but he doesn't.

He can't even say Cruz's name out loud.

Leo eats a lot of toast with peanut butter. He gets takeout, but he has to avoid the Nickel, even though all he's craving is a corned beef Reuben on marble rye with Joe's homemade Thousand Island dressing. Leo knows that *he's* avoiding the DeSantises but he's surprised, even hurt, that neither Cruz nor Joe has swung by the house to check on him and that Joe hasn't dropped off a platter of sandwiches even though he does this every time someone on this island so much as breaks a toe. Aren't they worried about him? Don't they care?

Willa and Rip have moved out to Smith's Point, but Willa stops by every once in a while to check in. Rip is handling the police investigation because he's used to logistics and following up in his job for the insurance company. He handled the claim for the Jeep Marissa totaled the night before Vivi died. She was so upset about Leo breaking up with her that she drove the Jeep right into the Bathtub out at Eel Point.

"How did you get home, then?" Leo had asked.

"I walked."

This seemed very unlikely and Leo said so, then Marissa admitted that she'd hitched a ride with some rando coming down the Madaket Road. She couldn't call anyone because her phone had been in the car. This explained why her calls stopped that night, and it also meant that Marissa hadn't seen the photo from Peter Bridgeman.

Rip had Marissa's Jeep towed and taken off-island. Marissa's mother, Candace, not only replaced Marissa's phone but bought Marissa a brand-new Jeep, an outlay of fifty grand, at least.

"Wasn't your mom angry about the Jeep?" Leo asks. "You ruined it yourself."

"So?"

"So it seems like another parent might have made you deal with the consequences of your actions."

Marissa shrugs. "I was upset about our breakup. She understands."

Leo and Marissa have been together long enough for Leo to realize that Candace Lopresti is the kind of mother who wants more than anything to be friends with her daughters. She never created any rules, mostly because she wasn't home to enforce them; she was always traveling for work. She gives Marissa and her older sister, Alexis, whatever they want whenever they want it. A brand-new phone and a brand-new Jeep to replace the ones that Marissa willfully trashed is Candace's way of saying *I'm here for you, honey.*

Nothing is normal, nothing will ever be normal again, but Leo tries to immerse himself in work at the Boat Basin—the clients, his golf cart, his walkie-talkie. He smiles and chats like everything is just dandy; for all the boat owners know, Leo is a cheerful, friendly Nantucket kid who is heading to the University of Colorado in the fall and doesn't have a care in the world. Every time he pockets a tip, he thinks to himself, *I deserve an Oscar.*

Then, one morning when he's at work, Marissa calls to say that Alexis had news. Vivi's running shoes, which had mysteriously gone missing, were just found in the trash can of the Stop and Shop break room. The custodian who takes out the trash noticed them because—and no one was happy to hear this—he sometimes went through the trash looking for things of value that people threw away. He found Vivi's sneakers, which he thought might be worth saving until he saw they were stained with blood. Then he called the police.

"I hate to say this but it's not looking good for Cruz," Marissa says.

"Why would you automatically think of Cruz?" Leo says. "Other people work at that store, you know."

"Leo," Marissa says. "Come on."

# Vivi

She needs Martha! She needs Martha! Where's Martha?

Vivi approaches the green door. She puts her ear to the panel and hears faint singing. It sounds like...like "Fool in the Rain," by Led Zeppelin. Is Vivi imagining this? It's *such* a great song, a song totally worthy of the afterlife, but shouldn't the choir be singing hymns or madrigals?

Ever so slowly, Vivi takes hold of the knob and turns...

"Vivian!"

Suddenly, Martha swings open the door from the other side, pushing Vivi back toward the bookshelves. A new scarf, lavender in hue, is tied around Martha's ponytail, a 1950s-sock-hop look.

"What did I tell you about the door, Vivian?"

"I'm not supposed to open it."

"I should dock you a week of viewing time," Martha says.

"No, please don't! I'm sorry! You said you would come when I needed you and I need you now. I want you to assure me that Cruz wasn't the one who hit me. I would forgive him—I would forgive that child *anything*. But I'm afraid the world won't forgive him. I'm afraid the court system, the judge, the Nantucket Police, and my own kids won't forgive him. Please, Martha, tell me Cruz wasn't the one who hit me."

"You seem a little slow in learning the rules," Martha says. "I can't tell you who hit you or didn't hit you."

"Is that because you don't know or because you don't want to tell me?"

"Oh, Vivian, the same rules apply to us here as down there."

*That's not really true,* Vivian thinks.

Martha shakes her head and the scarf moves like a curtain in the breeze. "Some things you have to figure out on your own."

# The Chief

Dixon, again with the bad news. A janitor at the Stop and Shop found bloodstained sneakers in the trash in the break room and he called the police to report it. Dixon went himself to retrieve the sneakers, and they exactly matched the description of Vivi's missing sneakers.

"For crying out loud!" the Chief says, because his mind travels right to Cruz DeSantis.

"This is good," Dixon says. "They were lost, now they're found. And you know, Chief, the DeSantis kid works at the Stop and Shop."

"Did the janitor find the clothes as well?"

"No, just the shoes."

Just the shoes. That makes no sense. And what's valuable, from a forensics standpoint, is the clothes—the shorts and the tank—in case there are flecks of paint. Every contact leaves a trace.

"Do you want me to bring the DeSantis kid in?" Dixon asks.

"Not yet," the Chief says. "I need to think."

The Chief asks Dixon to air-freight the shoes to Lisa Hitt on the Cape. He should probably request a homicide detective from the state police—the Greek would be his best option—but he doesn't want to call one in just yet. The Greek is a busy man and they have no forensic evidence tying this death to any suspects.

Cruz DeSantis is a smart kid—he's too smart to tamper with evidence, too smart to throw bloody sneakers into the trash at his place of employment. Right? The Chief will go talk to him.

It's eleven o'clock in the morning. A phone call to the Stop and Shop confirms that Cruz is working. The Chief arranges for him to take a break so that Cruz can help with an ongoing investigation.

The Chief is waiting out back by the employee entrance when Cruz comes out. He looks...tired, sick, traumatized.

"Cruz."

"I heard the news already," Cruz says. "I work here, Chief Kapenash."

"Right," the Chief says. "Let's take a drive."

They have only thirty minutes, so they can't go far. The Chief goes around the small rotary, then the big rotary. Traffic is bad; everyone is driving while talking on a cell phone or texting. It's amazing there aren't motor-vehicle homicides every day.

"I know Donald found running shoes in the trash of the break room," Cruz says. "I didn't put them there. Why would I have Vivi's sneakers?"

"They went missing from the hospital," the Chief says. "Somewhere between the hospital and the station, we lost track of them. The clothes still haven't been recovered."

"Check my car, check my house—I don't have the clothes. I never touched or saw or knew about any of this. Why would I?"

"Calm down, son," the Chief says.

"I've been pulled out of work to ride around with the chief of police," Cruz says. "Would you be calm in this situation?"

"No."

"I didn't hit Vivi," Cruz says, and again, there's something in the tone and timbre of his voice that makes the Chief want to believe him. "I *found* her. Finding her wasn't a crime."

The Chief takes a left off Polpis Road toward Monomoy. It's been three years since the last homicide on Nantucket. The maid of honor in a lavish wedding at a waterfront estate called Summerland was found floating in the harbor. They chalked that up to an accident, but it still irks the Chief and he knows it bothers the Greek as well. If Ed called the Greek now, he would jump at the chance to investigate this hit-and-run—maybe. Or maybe he'd think it was a lost cause, or maybe he'd think the answer was sitting right there in the front seat.

"You lied to me, Cruz."

The kid says nothing.

"You told me you were driving to the Howes' from your house. But you weren't."

"No."

This admission is a start. "Where were you coming from?"

"Hooper Farm."

"What were you doing on Hooper Farm?"

"Does it matter?"

"I wouldn't be asking if it didn't."

"I went to see someone."

"A girl?"

"This kid, Peter Bridgeman."

*Bridgeman?* Ed thinks. "He's Zach and Pamela's kid?"

"Yeah, he's my year. Just graduated. I needed to talk to him."

"At seven in the morning? What was so urgent?"

"Something."

"Son."

"It's just high-school stuff, Chief, okay? But since you asked, that's where I was coming from."

"Why didn't you tell me that before?"

"I didn't want to get into it."

"You do realize that a woman is *dead,* and, like it or not, you're part of the *investigation,* and you owed me the truth no matter the question." He's using his full-on chief-of-police voice now and he can see from a glimpse of the kid's face in the rearview mirror that he's nervous.

"Yes," Cruz says. "But I don't want to talk about that part. It has nothing to do with anything."

"Except you were upset, yes? You were distracted? You ran a stop sign and went speeding down Surfside Road. Officer Falco almost pulled you over. And then a few minutes later, he got the call about Ms. Howe. So you can see how lying to me was a problem."

"I *did* run the stop sign and I *was* speeding," Cruz says. "I *was* upset and I *was* distracted. But I didn't hit Vivi. I found her. She was *on the ground,* bleeding from her mouth, her leg sliced open. Someone hit her and left her there, Chief, and I pulled over and called 911. The woman was *like a mother to me!*" His voice works the edge of tears and then, like a flipped switch, it turns to anger. "Why don't you just charge me with her murder? Everyone on this island thinks I did it—my friends, my coworkers, my so-called community. I'm Black, so I must be a criminal, right?"

*Sit with your discomfort,* Ed tells himself. *The kid has every right to vent his feelings.* "I'm not charging you with anything," the Chief says. "But you're all I've got, and I can't help thinking that if I can unravel exactly what was going on with you that morning, I can follow that thread to someone else." The Chief pulls into the small parking lot at the Monomoy public beach. From here, a path leads to the water. It's crowded only in the early mornings and early evenings when people are heading out in their kayaks. "Before the running shoes turned up, I could maybe have bought the theory that the driver was some summer kid—or, hell, an adult—who hit Ms. Howe, got scared, and hightailed it out of there. But the shoes turning up in your place of employment makes this something else. I know it wasn't you who hit her, okay? But someone on this island wants us to think it was you."

"I'm being framed," Cruz says. "Just like in the movies."

"Who would do that?" the Chief asks. "Do you know this guy Donald?"

"No," Cruz says. "I only work days. I know Justin, the daytime custodian. He's...kind of alternative, but a good enough guy."

The Chief drives back to the store. "What did you want to talk to Peter Bridgeman about?"

The kid shakes his head.

"If you don't tell me, I'll ask Peter."

Cruz breathes out and his nostrils flare. "He took a picture on Friday at the end of this party at Fortieth Pole and he sent it to me in the middle of the night. When I woke up and saw it, I called him but he didn't answer, so I drove over to his house."

"Was he home?"

"I didn't see his truck but I thought maybe he'd ditched it at Fortieth and gotten a ride home because he'd been drinking. He has his own apartment above his parents' garage so I went up the outdoor stairs and I knocked a bunch of times and he didn't answer, so I left. I figured he was either out somewhere or ignoring me."

"Did anyone see you there?"

"No?" Cruz says. "I don't know. His parents didn't come out or anything."

"So you left the Bridgeman house and drove straight to the Howes'?"

"Yes."

"Why?"

Cruz gives the Chief an exasperated look. "Leo is my friend. I wanted to talk to him."

"Did going over there have anything to do with this picture?"

"Yeah. I could see Leo had gotten the picture from Peter as well, so I wanted to talk to him about it. Plus, we'd had that fight..."

"When he punched you? And gave you the shiner?"

"See? You already know everything."

"Do you mind my asking what the picture was of?"

"Yes," Cruz says. "I mind." They've arrived back at the store. "Can I go, please?"

The Chief will talk to the night custodian, Donald. And also to the Bridgeman kid. "Yes," he says. "You can go."

# Amy

She comes home from work with a bottle of Cliff Lede cabernet, one of JP's favorite splurge wines, and the bourbon-marinated steak tips from the Nantucket Meat and Fish market. It's too early for local corn but this is the perfect opportunity for Amy to try a warm potato salad recipe that she found in the *New York Times* cooking column.

Amy finds JP sitting in their bedroom with the air-conditioning running on high. (Note: If she were in the bedroom alone with the AC running full blast like this, he would turn it down, saying, *This thing burns money.*)

"Hello?" she says. She's surprised to see him here. She thought he said he'd be home around eight.

He whips around as though she's caught him at something. And sure enough, in front of him on the bed is a cardboard box filled with pictures—of Vivi, of him and Vivi together, of the kids when they were little. Amy is so busy scanning the pictures that it takes her a minute to realize that JP is crying.

Amy walks out of the bedroom, closing the door behind her, and goes into the kitchen to compose herself. Wine; she needs wine. The Cliff Lede is too precious to open, but she finds half a bottle of

Whispering Angel rosé from the night before. She pours a glass and takes a sip. It wasn't pornography, she thinks, and she knows plenty of women who surprise their husbands or partners while they're in the middle of *that*. But this is maybe even worse—all those pictures of Vivi overlapping one another. It was like something pulled from Amy's nightmares.

Vivi is dead, Amy reminds herself. She is never coming back, so she is no longer competition. JP can pine for her all he wants. Lorna said, "The man should be allowed to grieve. They were married sixteen years, Pigeon. She's the mother of his children."

Does Amy have it in her to be a supportive partner right now? Yes, of course.

Holding the wine, she reenters the bedroom. She places a gentle hand on JP's back. "How're you doing?"

He shakes his head. "I can't believe she's gone. I just can't wrap my mind around it." He holds up a picture of Vivi with a red rose between her teeth. Amy wants to snatch it out of his hand and rip it in half.

Amy will not nurture this jealousy. She will let it go. "She was so pretty," Amy says. "So...alive."

JP smiles up at Amy, grateful for this compliment about his ex-wife. Amy sits on the far corner of the bed and sifts through the photographs. Where has he been hiding these? She thought she had checked out every nook and cranny of the house. This is a treasure trove of images of JP's life before Amy: Vivi and JP in front of the Christmas tree at Rockefeller Center, Vivi falling forward on ice skates, Vivi drinking hot chocolate with a dab of whipped cream on her nose. There are wedding photos—Vivi's dress was an off-the-shoulder snow-white satin gown with a nipped-in waist and a full three-quarter-length skirt poofed by tulle underneath. It's not Amy's taste at all but Vivi, of course, looks radiant with her cute pixie cut and her dramatic red lips. Savannah, her maid of honor, wore a dowdy Laura Ashley print; this must have been before Savannah made her switch to neutrals, or maybe this dress was the reason for the switch. There are pictures from various travels—a deserted beach, a hole-in-the-wall restaurant in some far-flung, dusty town, a ski slope, Big Ben, the Colosseum, the Sydney Opera House, Vivi in front of a cityscape that is either Toronto or Seattle, Amy is afraid to ask which. There are the new-baby pictures—Vivi in a bed at Nantucket Cottage Hospital with Willa, then with Carson as Willa grumpily looks on. There are Christmas pictures (one of the babies tucked under the tree like a present) and Thanksgiving (Vivi, JP, two of the kids, Savannah, Lucinda, and Penny Rosen). There are Nantucket summer photos—picnics on the beach at Fortieth Pole, striped bass on the line; Vivi lying across the bow of Lucinda's sailboat, *Arabesque;* JP and Vivi at the Galley for dinner; Vivi in a beach chair with a blanket draped over her in Lucinda's front yard as fireworks are shot off a barge in the harbor on the Fourth of July.

Amy's heart dissolves a little more with each photo; she never had to witness the home she wrecked before this moment.

Wow. It's a lot, as people say.

Of course, what JP doesn't have pictures of is Vivi being condescending or dismissive or *too busy* to properly tend to her marriage. There aren't pictures of the fight they once had when Vivi threw a glass that shattered against the tile floor and woke the children. Vivi and JP's marriage broke up for a reason, and though everyone believes that reason was Amy Van Pelt, they had been unhappy long before Amy stepped into JP's wineshop. Amy is worried. Now that Vivi is dead, that narrative might be rewritten; Vivi might be remembered as a saint whom JP wronged by falling prey to temptress Amy. She decides to play devil's advocate, see what happens.

"You two look so happy in this picture," she says, holding up a shot of Vivi and JP at Carson's christening. They're standing at the altar, the baby balanced between them, their expressions manic.

"Carson had colic," JP says. "We were up all night, every night with her. Those are two exhausted people right there."

"You two should have stayed together," Amy says frankly. "I would have quietly disappeared so you two could have given it another shot."

"Vivi didn't want to give it another shot," JP says. "She threw in the towel."

"Well, in her defense, you cheated on her."

"Yeah, but..."

"Yeah, but—what?" Amy swallows despite the rock-hard lump in her throat. "Yeah, but you didn't mean it? Yeah, but it was a mistake? *I* was a mistake? I was nothing more than a strategic move on the chessboard?" These thoughts, Amy realizes, have been lurking in the swampy depths of her mind for ten years.

"Amy, please," JP says.

"Please what?" she says. *Please don't be ridiculous* is what she wants him to say. *Our love is real, our relationship is strong, we have not been dating for ten years and living together for three just because I needed a warm body by my side.*

"Please can we not talk about this right now? We probably should have a talk at some point, but not tonight. I don't have the energy."

Amy is stopped by this. They should have a talk at some point? What does *that* mean? She thinks of the ring box in JP's dresser drawer. Maybe the talk he's referring to will include, finally, a proposal. But somehow, she doesn't think so.

"I bought a bottle of the Cliff Lede," she says. "And some nice steak tips. I have that potato salad recipe I want to try. It has a bacon dressing—"

"I won't be here for dinner," JP says.

"What?" Amy says. She takes a nice long drink of her wine, but it has no more effect than if she were drinking pink water. "Where are you going?"

"I'm having dinner on Union Street," he says. "At Savannah's. She invited me when she drove me home from Vivi's reception, and tonight was the night that worked for both of us. I should have told you this morning, I'm sorry."

Amy knows to ignore her base instincts. She smiles. "Not a problem. The steak tips can wait. I may call Lorna and see if she wants to grab a bite at the Gaslight."

"Good idea," he says. Then he adds, "Thank you for being understanding; I appreciate it. This can't be easy for you."

Amy gets into the outdoor shower where she cries hot, ugly tears and wails into the sumptuous white Turkish towels from Serena and Lily that JP insists on. She has a glass of the Cliff Lede resting on the changing bench—the steak tips could wait, but that beautiful cabernet could not—and the second she shuts the water off, she drinks lavishly. She isn't sure how to triage her pain. What hurts the worst? JP is going to Savannah's for dinner, where the two of them will talk about Vivi—memories that have nothing to do with Amy. Amy will, for the two or three hours that JP is on Union Street (at Entre Nous, a house so divine it demands envy), be erased. JP's utter devastation and his regret as he pored over the photographs is another kind of pain. And his flat declaration that they should talk is worrisome, to say the least.

Amy texts Lorna. JP informed me he's going to dinner tonight at Savannah's house.

She waits. Lorna is her best friend; there won't be any need for further explanation.

WTF????!!?!

*Exactly,* Amy thinks. She texts: Can you meet me at the Gaslight in an hour? Girls' night out!

Wish I could, Pigeon, but I'm on the boat over to Hyannis. I have the doctor bright and early.

Ugh, right. Lorna has an appointment at Cape Cod Hospital;

there was something in her mammogram that needed a second look. If JP had let Amy know his plans a little earlier, Amy would have taken the ferry over with Lorna. They could have eaten at Pain D'Avignon and shopped at the mall like regular off-island people. Amy could have been there for Lorna's appointment.

No worries! Amy says. Good luck tomorrow. Call if you need me. Now Amy needs to make a decision—stay home or go out alone?

*Go out alone,* she thinks. She pulls her sexiest dress out of the closet and lays it across the bed where JP will be sure to see it. He comes out of the bathroom in his boxers, his face slathered with shaving cream.

"You're shaving?" Amy says. "Is this a special occasion, then?"

JP shrugs and goes back into the bathroom. He doesn't even glance at the dress.

Amy drinks another glass (two) of the Cliff Lede but there's still half a bottle (a third of a bottle) left for another night. She's wearing the sexy black dress—black is so forgiving—and she feels good. It's not weird that she's going out alone, she tells herself, or that in the ten years she's lived here, she has made only one friend. She imagines herself as a character in a Vivian Howe novel—those women are always venturing out solo and finding a good time.

The Gaslight used to be a movie theater but has been reimagined as a live-music venue. It has a pressed-tin ceiling and a wall of vintage turntables and speakers; there's a stage with a hot-pink neon sign that says GASLIGHT over the drum set. The crowd at the bar is lively; the food is delicious, and the cocktails are the kind that have been created by a mixologist and include ingredients Amy has never heard of.

There's one open seat at the bar—Amy imagines this conveniently happens in Vivi's novels as well—and Amy doesn't recognize anyone, another blessing.

The bartender is a big, strapping bear of a man named Nick. He's a Nantucket celebrity. He says, "Are you waiting for someone, ma'am?"

"Yes," Amy says brightly. "My friend Lorna."

"Lorna from RJ Miller?" Nick says. "She cuts my hair. She should have texted me to let me know you were coming, I would have saved you two seats."

"May I please have a Blackout Barbie?" Amy asks. "Two, actually. I want to have one here waiting for Lorna when she arrives."

The Blackout Barbie is a cocktail made with fresh-picked strawberries from Bartlett's Farm, lemon juice, tequila, and a splash of cava; it's garnished with thyme blossoms and served with an oversize round ice cube. It's *delicious*. Amy drinks both hers and "Lorna's" in short order and after she asks Nick for a third, she says, "I guess Lorna isn't coming."

"Yeah, I texted her," Nick says. "She's off-island."

Amy isn't sure if she should act surprised or just keep rolling. She decides on the latter. "In that case, I'm ordering food. How about the cheeseburger bao buns and the poke nachos?"

Amy's cocktail comes before her food. She drinks it while studying the other people at the bar as though she's an anthropologist. The clientele is young and stunning; everyone is filled with joy and bubbly laughter, and Amy feels worse and worse about herself with every passing second. Where did she go wrong? Well, she knows where. She should never have gotten involved with a married man. She could still end things and start a new relationship with someone like Nick. Or maybe Nick is too young. He *is* too young.

Amy's food comes, but for once, Amy just isn't herself and isn't hungry. She asks Nick for to-go boxes. She would like the check, please.

"You got it," Nick says. She tries to ignore the pity in his voice. "The band starts up at ten if you want to come back then."

"Thanks," Amy says, and for a second she feels like a strong, independent woman who might be back to enjoy the band if the spirit moves her. "Maybe I'll do that."

\*    \*    \*

Out on the street, she has an idea. Then she tries to talk herself out of it.

She puts her to-go containers in the front seat of her car. *Home, she thinks. Go home.*

But she's drunk, she shouldn't drive; she should walk it off, and if her walk happens to take her down Union Street, is that a crime? She strolls along until she reaches Entre Nous. The two onion lamps, one on either side of the front door, are lit and the front windows are bright, but the rooms appear unoccupied. Amy has never been inside the house so she isn't sure of the layout, though the kids used to swim in the pool all the time back before Vivi put in her own pool at Money Pit.

Amy sees a discreet flagstone path that leads between the hedges just beyond the driveway. She checks the street—deserted. She sneaks around the side of the house to the backyard. She fears motion-detector lights will announce her trespassing, but the back is quiet. Accent lights illuminate the teal-blue rectangle of the pool.

The back of the house is all windows, and the lights are on so Amy can see, clear as day, Savannah and JP sitting at the kitchen island, a bottle of Casa Dragones tequila and a bowl of popcorn between them. Amy tiptoes to the windows so she can get a better look and try to hear what they're saying—but the windows are closed. There's air-conditioning.

Savannah has on white jeans and a black tank. She's barefoot, wears no makeup or jewelry, and her hair is piled on top of her head in a bun. She's talking, blinking rapidly, sipping tequila, and then her expression crumples and she starts to cry.

JP stands up. *Please let him be leaving,* Amy thinks. There's no sign of dinner. Maybe they've already eaten, or maybe popcorn was the most Savannah could manage. JP holds out his arms and Savannah falls into them like a woman in a movie and starts sobbing into JP's chest. He places one hand on her back and one on the back of her head and starts rocking side to side.

This is...awful. If Amy had just stayed home and imagined what was transpiring here at Entre Nous ("Between Us") it couldn't have been any more traumatizing than this.

*They're commiserating,* Amy thinks. *They lost someone important to them both and this dinner is necessary so they can talk and heal.* Amy just has to be patient.

Savannah raises her face and gazes at JP with a vulnerable expression. Are they going to kiss? Are they? How many times has JP told Amy in detail what a *bitch* he thinks Savannah is? He was so ruthless that Amy found herself defending Savannah. *She started an important charity, she saves children's lives. And she's got great style.*

The moment lingers on, the two of them seemingly suspended in the moment just before a kiss.

Amy runs out of the yard. She catches her toe on the edge of one of the flagstones and goes flying to the ground, scraping her knee. She gets to her feet. She needs to go home and check JP's top drawer to make sure her beautiful engagement ring is still there. But as she reaches the sidewalk and heads to her car, she knows she won't find it. She knows it's gone.

Her leg is bleeding, but she doesn't care. She won't get home before JP. She wants him to get home first and wonder where she is.

JP and Savannah? Impossible. Amy is sure he'll pull away and say he has to go, and all the way home he'll wonder what came over him, getting to the edge of an intimate moment like that. Amy reaches Main Street and thinks, *Club Car piano bar?* She can mix in with the mass of humanity belting out "Stop Dragging My Heart Around," and no one will realize she's by herself. But when she reaches the Club Car, there's a line out the door. No, thank you. She considers Straight Wharf (the clientele is too young) and Cru (she has spent enough money at Cru this summer). She decides to head back to the Gaslight since Nick (sort of) invited her.

She can hear the band playing before she enters. She stops at the vending machine at the entry that dispenses tiny bottles of Moët et Chandon champagne for twenty dollars a pop (as it were). It's gimmicky and exorbitant, but suddenly, Amy wants champagne to celebrate the hideous mess her life is rapidly becoming.

The champagne is delivered ice-cold. Amy drinks straight from the bottle, then wanders over to the bar, and, believe it or not, her very same stool is unoccupied. It's magical, as though novelist Vivi has been holding this seat for Amy's eventual return. But Amy's not a character. She's real. She hoists her petite bottle of Moët up to Nick in a cheers.

"Hey," the guy next to her says. "Your leg is bleeding."

Amy looks down at her leg. Yes, it's pretty gruesome; there's blood running down into her sandal.

The guy hands her a stack of cocktail napkins and she looks up at him. It's Dennis.

"Oh," Amy says. "Hey."

Dennis laughs. "We have to stop meeting like this." He peers behind her. "Where's your boyfriend?"

"Who?" Amy says, and Dennis laughs again. Dennis looks...okay. He has a tan that ends at his shirt collar and his eyes look intensely blue. There's a Cisco Whale's Tale in front of him. Is he here alone? "Are you here alone?"

"I am," he says. "Beats sitting home in an empty house."

Amy nods. Why is it fine for a man to sit at a bar alone but nothing short of pathetic for a woman? "JP is having dinner tonight with Savannah."

"Ah," Dennis says. "That must be tough on you."

"It is," Amy says, blinking against tears. Why is Dennis Letty the only person who has considered her feelings? She raises her bottle to Dennis's blue can and they both drink.

"I'll watch your seat," Dennis says. "Why don't you go clean up your leg and then we can dance."

*Dance with Dennis?* Amy thinks. One part of her rebels against hooking up with another man that Vivi got to first. The other part says, *Couldn't hurt, sounds like fun.*

"Okay," she says. "Be right back."

# Vivi

When Vivi swoops down to check on Savannah, her BFF, the godmother of her children, the person whose advice and guidance she held above all others, she finds her in the kitchen of Entre Nous being rocked back and forth in a man's arms.

*Aha!* Vivi thinks. *Who have we here?*

Then she sees it's JP.

*Plot twist!* Vivi thinks. Savannah and JP *hate* each other. For the sixteen years that Vivi and JP were married, Vivi felt like the baby pulled between her mother and father in that grisly Raymond Carver story. JP felt threatened by Savannah for reasons Vivi could never quite understand (he probably sensed that Vivi's loyalty to Savannah was stronger than her loyalty to him). Savannah, meanwhile, never thought JP was good enough. "He's damaged," Savannah used to say. "He never knew his father and he has an unhealthy relationship with his mother."

JP is running his hand up and down Savannah's back in a way that seems meant to be comforting. Savannah's breath is shuddering; she must have just finished a good cry. She lifts her face to JP's. Their mouths are inches apart. Their eyes lock.

*Kiss her!* Vivi thinks.

Or will that be weird?

Well, it will be no weirder than Vivi's novel *The Angle of Light*, about two characters who found each other after their respective spouses died. JP and Savannah have lost the same person—her!—so their bond would be even stronger. They don't have to fight over Vivi's attention anymore; there's nothing coming between them.

Literally nothing. They're hip to hip.

*Kiss her!* Vivi thinks again.

JP says, "Are you going to be okay? I should probably go home."

Savannah seems to snap back to her pragmatic self. "Yes, of course. I'm sorry I got so emotional. It's just…you're the only person who gets it."

"I know," JP says. He wipes a tear from Savannah's cheek. "Let's do this again next week. And actually eat something."

Savannah laughs. "How about a week from today? Friday-Night Sad-Sack Supper Club."

"You got it." JP releases Savannah and takes a step back.

"How is everything with Amy?" Savannah asks.

"Confusing," JP says. He sighs. "I'm going to end things. Ask her to move out."

"Whoa," Savannah says.

*Whoa!* Vivi thinks.

"Amy was a mistake," JP says.

"A ten-year mistake?" Savannah says. "Come on, JP. You must have feelings for her."

"I did," JP says. "Or I thought I did. When I met her, she was young, pretty, sweet, earnest, adoring. I was dazzled by the way she saw me. She made me feel important, and Vivi made me feel like a loser. So I started things with Amy because I wanted to feel good all the time. And I did, for years—but there were problems too. She drove a wedge between me and the kids."

*Yes,* Vivi thinks. So much time has passed that Vivi has let go of most of her resentment toward Amy. Amy was young and impressionable that first summer when she worked for JP, and he took advantage of her. She's invested ten years in him without any promise of a commitment. Surely she wants a ring? But she's settled for nothing, and now JP is tossing her out.

"She was always jealous of Vivi. She was so busy being jealous of Vivi that she never fully became her own person. Back in September, I bought her an engagement ring, but every time I looked at it, I panicked, so I returned it to the jeweler in Boston. I've lost whatever feelings I had for Amy, something I've willfully ignored for the past year or two, but now that Vivi's gone, I need to be honest with myself. I don't want to spend the rest of my days with Amy Van Pelt."

"What did she think about you coming over here?" Savannah asks. "She couldn't have been too happy."

"She's out with her friend Lorna," JP says. "She put on a vampy dress. I think she was trying to make me jealous, and maybe five years ago, or even last year, I *would* have been jealous. But now I just hope that when she goes out, she meets someone else."

"Wow," Savannah says.

"What about you?" JP asks. "Are you seeing anyone? Coach of an NBA team? CEO of Colgate-Palmolive? Head of surgery at Mass General?"

"No one right now," Savannah says. "There was the crown prince of a minor European nation, but we called it quits."

JP laughs and Savannah wheels him toward the hallway. "Go home, JP." At the front door, there's another hug, and Vivi thinks, *Kiss her! It's not too late! If you're breaking up with Amy anyway, just kiss her!*

They separate and JP disappears out the door, down the friendship stairs, and into the dark night. Savannah closes the door behind him, then leans against it and smiles.

*She likes him!* Vivi thinks. *Maybe?*

"You could have used one of your nudges, you know." Suddenly, Martha is sitting on the green velvet chaise with an Hermès scarf wrapped around her entire head like she's a fortune-teller. "It would have worked. They were close."

"I'm the novelist here," Vivi says. "Let's give it another couple of chapters."

# Willa

Summer in Wee Bit starts to take on a rhythm, a routine, and this keeps Willa from falling into a yawning hole of despair. Willa wakes up early every morning and takes her herbal tea to the back deck where she watches the sun turn the sky a pearlescent pink. She doesn't eat anything; she can't, her morning sickness hovers around her like a green miasma. She welcomes it. Has she ever been this sick before? She thinks not. She's constantly on the lookout for ways that this pregnancy is different.

Some days she drives to work, and other days, she bikes the six miles into town. The ride is picturesque, bucolic—over the simple bridge that spans the neck of Madaket Harbor, through the hamlet of Madaket, along the famed twenty-seven curves that lead past the creek and the turtling pond until she's cruising the final mile to the flagpole at Caton Circle, which marks the top of Main Street. Willa wants to avoid the cobblestones in her condition, so she bikes the long way around—New Lane to West Chester (which is, if anyone is interested in Nantucket's history, the oldest street on the island) to North Beach to the back door of the Whaling Museum.

Willa's office is air-conditioned. She does not have to guide the

VIP group tours and interact with the public until she's feeling up to it emotionally, so she sits at her desk and tends to her administrative duties—final approval of all publications, overseeing publicity and marketing, scheduling maintenance and repairs on the NHA's fourteen properties.

After work, Willa usually takes a walk on the beach. If Rip gets home early, he'll go with her and they'll hold hands for a while, then stop, then rejoin hands. Rip likes to pick up shells and horseshoe crab carcasses and dried mermaid purses. He can identify shorebirds—oystercatchers, the endangered piping plover, and, his favorite, the sanderlings.

For dinner, they either get takeout from Millie's or grill out back—burgers, steaks, chicken, thick slabs of swordfish. Protein; Willa craves it. Has she craved protein this way in the past?

Willa goes to bed early, often before it's fully dark. The exhaustion hits her like something that falls out of the sky.

This doesn't tell the whole story, of course. It skips over the seventeen times a day Willa uses the bathroom—sometimes to relieve her bladder, other times just to cry (quietly at work and then with abandon, loud and ugly, when she's in Wee Bit by herself).

Her mother is gone.

Sometimes when Willa cries at night in bed, Rip will hold her and whisper into her hair. He says he would do anything to make the pain go away; he would take it from her and endure it himself if he could. But Rip can't make things better. Nobody can make things better. Willa loved her mother so, so much, and now her mother is dead. Willa is aware that everyone loses a loved one eventually; it's part of being human. And everyone must bear the pain alone.

Willa won't say that Pamela showing up with the news that she suspects Zach of having an affair was *welcome*—but it has certainly served as a distraction. On that first day, when Pamela drove out to Wee Bit to confide in Willa, they ended up sitting at the picnic table out back. Willa said, "What, exactly, makes you think this?"

Pamela lifted her sunglasses to the top of her head and stared into the dunes. Willa noticed some strands of silver in the white-blond streak of Pamela's hair; her face was tan from playing so much tennis, and there were lines around her blue eyes. Willa couldn't recall ever being this close to her sister-in-law before because Pamela had always held herself literally at arm's length. But now the barrier was coming down.

"He's been disappearing at night," Pamela said. "Midnight, one o'clock. He claims when he has insomnia, he drives out to the beach. He says watching the waves makes him sleepy."

Willa agreed—this was suspicious behavior. "Have you checked his phone?" Willa asked.

"I can't check his account to see what calls he made," Pamela said. "His phone is issued by the FAA. They pay the bill. He can use it for personal calls too, of course, but there's no way I can access the account."

"But you could check his actual phone."

"If I knew the passcode. But I don't."

"He has a passcode?"

"Everyone has a passcode, Willa."

"I don't," Willa said. "Rip doesn't. Rip and I are in and out of each other's phones all the time."

"Well, you guys aren't normal," Pamela said.

Willa relaxed. This, at least, was a Pamela she recognized. And Willa knew that she and Rip had an unusually close relationship. She was proud of it, thank you very much. "Have you noticed anything else?" Willa asked.

"He's happy," Pamela said, and again, her eyes brimmed with tears. "And that's what makes me dead sure. He whistles. He sings."

"Couldn't his happiness be due to something else?" Willa asked.

"He has insomnia and sneaks out of the house after I'm asleep. But he's happier than I've seen him in years."

Willa had to admit, this equation had only one likely answer. "What are you going to do?" she asked.

"I'm going to find out who it is," Pamela said.

Willa is intrigued, and it pains her to have no one to share this with. She can't tell Rip. He works with Pamela every day, and though he's normally a vault when it comes to secrets, Pamela is a weak spot for him. He would break, and Willa would be deemed untrustworthy.

She misses her mother. If her mother were alive, Willa would confide in her.

Can she tell Carson? They've become closer since Vivi died. Carson texts to check in at Willa's request, and Willa has invited Carson over to Wee Bit for dinner the next time she has a night off. But Carson doesn't care for any of the Bonhams—she thinks they're cold and superior—and if Willa told her that Pamela thought Zach was having an affair, she would roll her eyes and say, *Girl, who cares?*

Willa can, maybe, tell Savannah—but Savannah is doing so much already, trying to settle Vivi's estate. Willa offered to take over the admin of the Vivian Howe Memorial Facebook page and Savannah seemed relieved.

She said, "Look at the message from someone named Brett Caspian, would you? He claims he was your mother's boyfriend in high school."

"Mom didn't have a boyfriend in high school," Willa said.

"Just look, please, Willie," Savannah said.

The Vivian Howe Memorial Facebook page has over two hundred new messages since Willa last checked. Vivi starts scrolling through the messages—so much love, so much heartbreak. One woman, Eden F., from Niagara, New York, says she can't stop crying and has personally called the Nantucket Police Department to demand justice.

This seems like a bit much. But Vivi inspired this kind of devotion. She shared unvarnished looks at her life—she would video the kitchen when there were dishes in the sink or the hallway when there was a pile of stuff at the bottom of the stairs—and her readers appreciated these details. *We all have dirty dishes, dirty laundry, stuff waiting at the bottom of the stairs, even our favorite novelist.* Vivi's readers felt like they knew her. Of course they're upset.

Willa thinks that finding the message from Brett Caspian might be a needle-in-a-haystack quest but only a few posts in, there it is—a message sent that very morning.

> I hope someone in Vivi's family will read this. I was able, with a few phone calls to the publisher, to receive an advance copy of *Golden Girl*. In high school, I wrote a song called "Golden Girl" that was inspired by Vivi. She was my girlfriend from September 1986 to August 1987. Once I read the book, I saw that she used more than just the title. She used our story. I'm going to go out on a limb and leave my phone number here in hopes that someone from the family will contact me so we can discuss this further. Thank you. Brett Caspian

Willa reads the message twice. Brett Caspian wrote a song called "Golden Girl" that was inspired by Vivi? Vivi used their story in her new novel? Willa has read only two of her mother's thirteen novels (she prefers nonfiction, biography in particular), but this is two more than Carson and Leo have read. Willa knows the premise of *Golden Girl;* it involves a high-school romance and a song called "Golden Girl," but she thought it was made up.

Willa googles *Brett Caspian* and *Golden Girl.* She gets a handful of hits about her mother's novel, and the rest are about a sitcom featuring old ladies.

Vivi never once mentioned that she'd had a boyfriend in high school. She studied and had two good friends, Stephanie and Gina, whom she sometimes talked about but wasn't in touch with, as far as Willa knew.

*You're a fraud, Brett Caspian,* Willa thinks.

And yet.

She writes his number down, because what if he's not a fraud, what if he opens a door to a part of her mother's life that Willa knew nothing about? What if Willa learns about a secret Vivi kept until her death? This is *exactly* like something that would happen in one of her mother's novels. The line between real life and fiction is becoming blurry indeed.

Even dialing the numbers feels illicit. Willa reminds herself that Savannah asked her to check this guy out and that she's merely doing her due diligence with the Vivian Howe Memorial Facebook page.

He doesn't answer and his voice mail is an automated recording. She leaves a message: "My name is Willa Bonham, I'm Vivian Howe's daughter, I saw your Facebook message and I'm calling you as requested."

She hangs up and not two seconds later, her phone rings with Brett Caspian's number on the caller ID.

Oh, boy. Willa stares at it, one hand holding the phone, one hand resting on her belly.

"Hello?" she says.

"Hello, this is Brett Caspian. You just called?"

"Yes," Willa says. The voice is appealing, she decides, strong and a little raspy. "My name is Willa. I'm Vivi Howe's daughter."

"Oh, man," Brett says. He emits a whistling breath. "I can't believe this. I'm...well, first off, I'm sorry about your mom."

"Thank you," Willa says, because although this feels awkward, it's what one is supposed to say.

"So, listen...I'm not even sure where to start. I went to high school with Vivi."

"And where was that?" Willa asks.

There's a hesitation. "Uh...Parma High School? In Parma, Ohio? You do know that's where your mother went to high school?"

Willa laughs. "Yes, I know. I just wanted to make sure that you knew. Because she never mentioned a boyfriend in high school. She said she was a nerd."

Brett chuckles at this. "Yeah, she was a nerd. She was just about the most beautiful nerd you've ever seen, always with her nose in a book or raising her hand with the right answer."

"And you were her boyfriend?"

"Senior year, yes. That was the year her father died."

*Okay,* Willa thinks, *this guy is for real.* Her legs tingle and suddenly, she has to pee. "I'm sorry, but she didn't tell me about you." Why was that? Willa wonders. Did she not want JP to be jealous? Or was it for some other reason?

"Things got complicated at the end and the breakup was hard on both of us. She went off to Duke and I moved to LA and I never saw her again. I live in Knoxville, Tennessee, now. I'm a hotel manager and I play a little guitar, but I'm not into all that Facebook stuff or social media, so I haven't kept in touch with anyone from home except the guys in my old band. Those guys held a big grudge against Vivi for reasons I can tell you about later, and we never bring her name up. Except last week, one of the guys, Roy, said he heard through his sister that Vivi had died. He told me she was a writer. So I looked her up and I saw her new book was called *Golden Girl,* which was the name of my song."

"Your song."

"The one I wrote in high school for Vivi. I just finished the book last night and, wow, so much of what she wrote was based on what really happened with us."

"I haven't read the book yet," Willa admits.

"I was hoping I could talk to you about it."

*Isn't that what we're doing now?* Willa wonders.

"I have vacation time saved up so I was thinking about driving up there, maybe week after next? I'll stay in Hyannis at the Holiday Inn, that's the company I work for. Then I'll take the ferry over to meet you."

"You want to come here?" Willa says. "To Nantucket?"

"I have pictures of your mom and me," Brett says. "I pulled them up from the depths of my trunk and...we look so young. I'd like to show them to you."

Willa isn't sure what to say to this guy. He seems legit, and maybe he *was* Vivi's boyfriend in high school in Parma, Ohio. It was a time in her life that Vivi almost never talked about. It was as though Vivi's personal history started her first week at Duke, when she met Savannah. Everything before that is, literally, *sketchy*—line drawings without any color or details filled in. "I have a place you can stay on Nantucket if you want to make it a real vacation and explore the island a bit." She clamps her mouth shut, trying to imagine what Rip will say when she tells him she's invited a *complete stranger weirdo from Vivi's Facebook page* to stay in their house on Quaker Road.

"The Holiday Inn will be fine," Brett says. "I'm used to it. So how about two weeks from tomorrow?"

"Okay," Willa says. She feels strangely excited. She's getting back a part of Vivi that she hadn't even known existed. "That sounds great. Keep me posted on your travel plans and I'll come pick you up from the boat."

"You got it," Brett Caspian says. "Thank you for calling me, Willa. It'll be such an honor to meet you. One of Vivi's kids. It said on Wikipedia that she has three?"

"Yes. I have a sister and a brother."

"I remember her saying she wanted five kids. And she was going to name them after her favorite authors." He pauses. "Are you named after an author?"

"Oh!" Willa says. "Yes, I'm named after Willa Cather. And my sister and brother are named for authors too."

"See there?" Brett says. "How could I know that if I weren't for real?"

*This is exciting,* Willa thinks. *Brett Caspian will come and he will tell me Vivi's secret history.*

# Vivi

Thank goodness she saved her nudges!

"Martha!" Vivi cries out. She goes to the green door but she's too afraid to touch it. What if Martha takes away a precious week of viewing? Vivi throws herself across the velvet chaise and stares up at the pattern of light that the Moroccan chandelier casts on the ceiling. Normally, this calms her, but not today.

A second later, Martha materializes. She picks an orange off the dwarf tree and takes a seat on the white enamel bean-shaped coffee table with her clipboard on her lap. A peek of scarf is visible at the top of her muumuu. "What is it, Vivian?"

"I can't let Brett Caspian go to Nantucket. I have to use one of my nudges."

Martha puts on her drugstore reading glasses and checks her clipboard. "I would strongly advise against that."

"Well, sorry, not sorry, I'm doing it," Vivi says.

Very slowly, Martha peels the orange; the scent is sublime and Vivi can see the juicy flesh of the orange as Martha pulls apart the segments. The color is like stained glass, like a jewel. The odd thing is that Vivi tried to eat one of the oranges herself, but when she peeled it, it was desiccated, practically dust. Martha knows how things work, and Vivi doesn't. It isn't fair.

"I'm making an executive decision on this one," Martha says. She pops a succulent orange segment into her mouth but does not offer one to Vivi. "He's coming."

Brett Caspian, coming to Nantucket? Meeting her kids? *Eeeeeeee!*

There must be a reason Martha made an executive decision. "You're going to have to learn to trust me," Martha had said at the beginning.

*Okay,* Vivi thinks with great reluctance. *I'll trust you.*

Vivi *is* flattered that Brett remembers so much about her. He remembers that she wanted to have five kids and name them after her favorite authors!

That night, while everyone is sleeping, Vivi travels back two decades.

It's February on Nantucket—raw and wet with winds that sound like a chain saw. Vivi and JP have two daughters: Willa (named for Willa Cather) and Carson (named for Carson McCullers; everyone mistakes her for a boy).

Vivi used to think that she wanted five children. She was so naive! She's hanging on to her sanity now only because Willa, at three, is so mature that she will sit in her small rocking chair along-side Vivi's bigger rocking chair and "read" her picture books while Vivi nurses the baby, and she will put headphones on and listen to her baby Spanish tapes while the baby cries.

Twenty-three hours a day, the baby is either nursing or crying.

The only hour that the baby will sleep soundly is the hour after JP comes home from work at Island Fog Real Estate. Carson's cheek hits her father's shoulder and she instantly conks out. This, at least, gives Vivi a chance to make dinner.

"We were spoiled with Willa," JP says.

Yes, Willa was a perfect baby. She slept all the time, peacefully, faceup in her bassinet and then her crib. She comforted herself without a pacifier; she nursed beautifully but never minded a bottle.

Carson, however, has both colic and reflux. She eats, she spits up, she cries. Vivi has her on the breast, gives her breast milk from a bottle, gives her formula from a bottle—there's no difference, no improvement. She's happier sleeping on her stomach, but what kind of irresponsible parent puts a baby to sleep on her stomach?

There are days Vivi cries right along with Carson, but she lets herself do that only when Willa is napping.

She tries not to think of the girls as good kid/bad kid or even as easy kid/difficult kid because what if these labels follow them into adolescence and then adulthood?

"They're just so different," Vivi says. "How did this happen?"

"Happens all the time," JP says like a man who is an expert on siblings, although he's an only child just like Vivi.

On the night that Vivi thinks might be the worst night ever— Carson is screaming bloody murder and her face is as red as a Bartlett's Farm tomato; Willa is doing this new low-key whimpering thing (which is even more grating on Vivi's nerves than the baby's crying); and JP is off-island taking the test for his real estate license, so Vivi has no backup—Vivi gets an idea for a novel about two sisters. It comes to her whole, like a neatly wrapped present. *The Dune Daughters.*

*Charlotte and Evangeline. Their father is a scalloper; he raises them by himself in a dilapidated fishing shack out in the dunes by Long Pond. One sister marries a local boy and the other marries a rich summer kid. Who will be happier?*

Willa and the baby don't fall asleep until well past midnight, but Vivi, thinking about the novel's plot, doesn't care. When they're finally quiet, she grabs a notebook and a pen and brews a cup of herbal tea (she wants coffee but there can be no caffeine while nursing).

She inhales the silence and exhales words onto the page. It is just that easy, that natural; it feels like breathing. Two hours later, like clockwork, the baby cries and Vivi's milk lets down, but she keeps writing. Miraculously, Carson stops crying on her own; the front of Vivi's nightgown is soaked, but she doesn't care. She keeps writing.

Eight months later, the first draft of *The Dune Daughters* is finished. Vivi wrote it during the girls' naptime and late at night. She learned to live with less sleep the same way people learn to live with less food during wartime.

On the night she completes the novel, she wakes JP up by sitting on the edge of the bed and kissing the crook of his neck. JP has endured one hell of a summer. As low man at Island Fog Real Estate, he was assigned the least desirable rentals, which always seemed to attract the most demanding families. JP spent twelve consecutive summer weekends meeting people with keys, chasing down plumbers to fix leaky outdoor showers, running to Yates Gas because the propane tank on the grill was empty. JP likes his boss, Eddie Pancik—everyone on the island calls him Fast Eddie—but JP knows he would be happier if he started his own business and could be his own boss.

"Don't quit," Vivi told him all summer long. "We need the money." They used the fund set up for JP by his grandparents to put a down payment on the house on Surfside and the rest went into a "contingency account," which is almost depleted. Kids are expensive. Life is expensive.

"I finished the novel," Vivi says once JP's eyes open.

He props himself up on his elbows. "You did? Just now?"

"I can't tell if it's any good," Vivi says. She has given the novel a dozen read-throughs and sometimes thinks it's inspired and other times thinks it's cheesy and clichéd, a vanity project by an overtired housewife. "I'm too close to it."

JP pulls Vivi to him and kisses the part in her hair. "Of course it's good," he says. "You wrote it."

\*   \*   \*

When Vivi tells the women in her Mommy and Me group that she has finished writing a novel, half of them are skeptical about its prospects, the other half patronizing.

JP assures her those mothers are just envious because Vivi found the time to do something for herself.

That's part of it, certainly, Vivi thinks. But it's also silly to expect people to get excited about a book that isn't published.

How will she ever get published?

Vivi has remained in touch all these years with Famous Author, the one who taught the workshop that Vivi attended in high school. In a letter, Vivi asks Famous Author what she should do with her manuscript.

He calls her, taking her completely by surprise (she included her phone number in the letter but never dreamed he'd use it).

He gives Vivi his own agent's name and address. "Send it to Jodi with a big note on top that says I referred you. I want full credit for discovering you, hear me? You're going to be successful, Vivian. I could tell that thirteen years ago. You've got something."

A week after Vivi sends the manuscript, Jodi Partridge calls to say she would be honored to represent Vivi.

"This book is so...summery. It makes me want to move to Nantucket and live my best, beachiest life."

Vivi eyes the inside of her house. There are doll clothes and Cheerios all over the floor and a juice box (not even organic) leaking onto the coffee table. Vivi had big plans of taking the girls on a walk through the moors—the foliage is changing colors and the October sun makes everything look like it's been dipped in gold—but it's two o'clock and Vivi is still in her yoga pants.

"I predict we're going to have a bunch of competing offers on this," Jodi says. "Which will drive the price up. With luck, it'll go for a pretty penny."

"A pretty penny!" Vivi tells JP the second he walks through the door. She grabs both of his hands and starts hopping up and down. "A pretty penny!"

But something is wrong. JP looks...dejected. Like his dog died. (They don't have a dog.) Or like he got fired.

"Is everything okay?" Vivi says. "Did you get fired?" It's true that JP hasn't generated a lot of income for Island Fog, but building a client list takes time.

"No," JP says.

"Then what's wrong?"

"My mother bought half of Old South Wharf is what's wrong. She bought five of those cottages along the docks to the tune of three and a half million dollars."

"What?" Vivi says.

"And she used Eddie Pancik as her broker," JP says. "Instead of me, her only son. Do you know how much commission you get for three and a half million?"

Vivi doesn't know—and at the moment, she doesn't care. Would it be rude to brag about her good news now? Probably.

"What is Lucinda going to do with five cottages on Old South Wharf?"

"Rent them out," JP says. "She told me if I came up with a business plan, she would rent one to me at a discount. So...I was thinking about a yacht-concierge business. I could cater to all the huge boats in the summer."

"You'll be right back to picking up dry cleaning," Vivi says. "And you don't want that. What about something else?"

"The other idea I had was for a boutique wineshop," JP says.

"What about something inexpensive that everyone wants?" Vivi says. "Like ice cream?"

"And compete with the Juice Bar?" JP says. "Are you high?"

It's a narrow opening, but she's going to take it. "I *am* high, actually!" Vivi says. This gets JP's attention. "I got an agent, JP! Jodi called and she likes the book and she thinks we'll get a 'bunch of competing offers,' those were her exact words. She says with luck, it'll go for a pretty penny."

JP gives Vivi a blank stare and Vivi wonders if he'll be able to put aside his own woes for a minute and celebrate Vivi.

A huge smile breaks across JP's face and he lifts Vivi off the ground. She wraps her legs around him and they kiss like they haven't kissed since before Carson was born. Carson starts to cry in the Pack 'n Play and Willa's screen time needs to come to an end, but Vivi doesn't care. She is so happy! Nothing in this world feels as good as hope.

# Carson

On Saturday night at the Oystercatcher, Carson drops a pint glass filled with Whale's Tale Pale Ale. It slips right through her fingers and shatters against the concrete floor behind the bar; no one is hurt but there are shards, and the beer splashes everywhere.

Carson is too busy to stop. "Clean that up," she barks at the barback, Jaime (girl). Carson knows that Jaime hates her, so Carson recently bought her a hundred-and-fifty-dollar gift card to Lemon Press as a thank-you for "having my back"—smoothies and acai bowls for days—but now, Carson is right back to square one.

Less than an hour later, Carson drops a tray of glasses and share plates, which makes such a loud, nerve-splintering sound that a hush comes over the entire restaurant for one moment of pristine humiliation. This time, Carson crouches down to clean the mess up herself, and when Jaime comes to help, Carson says, "Please don't. This was my screwup."

She loses precious minutes and by the time she's at her post again, there's a huge backup of orders. Jamey (boy) has been helping out by pulling drafts, but that's all he knows how to do.

*One customer at a time,* Carson thinks. That's the only way out of the weeds. The crowd will thin eventually.

Vodka cran, vodka soda, sauvignon blanc, dozen Wellfleets with extra horseradish.

Suddenly, the GM, Nikki, is behind Carson, smiling while gritting her teeth. "George wants to see you in his office after service."

"It was an accident, Nikki."

"Just passing on a message, Carson."

Carson tries to focus—so many orders, so many faces, arms waving, hands thrusting money toward her in an attempt to get her attention. She tends to wait on men first, a terrible habit she's trying hard to break, so she looks for women, and as she's doing this, she sees Pamela Bonham Bridgeman standing at the end of the bar. Carson's heart crashes to the ground just like the dropped tray because what can Carson think but that *Pamela knows* and has chosen to confront Carson at work, where it will hurt the most? Then Carson sees Willa beside Pamela and Willa is waving; she looks not exactly happy—none of them may ever look happy again—but she seems fine, normal-ish.

What are they doing here? Why are they together? Willa hates Pamela. Everyone hates Pamela.

Carson takes drink orders from every other female at the bar and then every man. When she can ignore her sister and her lover's wife no longer, she says, "Ladies! Surprise, surprise. What can I get you?"

"Chardonnay with a side of ice," Pamela says.

"Cranberry seltzer with lime," Willa says.

"You guys eating?"

"There's no room at the bar," Willa says. "They told me it's a ninety-minute wait for a table. Do you have any pull?"

*Not tonight,* Carson thinks. But she can't resist showing off in front of Pamela so she approaches the hostess stand where Nikki is busy crushing people's dreams and says, "It's my sister's first night out since my mom died. Any chance you can put her at table one?" Table one is the two-top closest to the dunes at sunset. It's the best table at the Oystercatcher.

Nikki growls. "I shouldn't, but I will. For her, though, not for you. The people are paying now. Tell her five minutes."

Carson hustles back to the bar. "Five minutes," she says, handing the chard, the ice, and the seltzer over the counter. "These drinks are on me."

"Thank you!" Willa says—but Carson doesn't care about Willa. She cares only about Pamela, who is gazing out over the beach, looking very alone among the sea of people. She accepts the chardonnay without a word and doesn't even look at Carson.

*I'm invisible to her,* Carson thinks, and although she's offended, she knows this is for the best.

After service, Carson heads down the hall, past the retail shop and the restrooms, to George's office. The door is closed. Has she been saved? Is he gone for the night? Tomorrow, her drops will be forgotten. The service industry has a short memory, especially in a place like the Oystercatcher where there is never a quiet moment for reflection.

Carson knocks.

"Enter!"

Carson swears under her breath and opens the door. George is at his desk, which is meticulously organized—invoices on the left, order forms on the right, and in the center is a weekly calendar that shows the schedule, written, always, in pencil. Pencils are sharpened, kept points up in a mason jar. The computer behind the desk displays an old-school game of Tetris.

"Please sit down," George says.

There's a folding chair, known to the staff as the Hot Seat.

Carson feels she should remain standing but she's been on her feet since three, so she gratefully collapses.

"Two drops tonight," George says.

"I know. I'm sorry. I don't have an excuse. I wasn't paying attention."

George tsks under his breath. George is universally loved at the Oystercatcher and on Nantucket. He has worked in restaurants on the island for something like forty years, managing at both the Straight Wharf and the White Elephant and then running the grill at the Miacomet Golf Club for a few years before buying the Oystercatcher. Because George has worked as a barback, bartender, busser, and server, he makes an excellent boss. He's a confirmed bachelor, a ladies' man, and loves poker and golf and clamming out on Coatue. If there's a problem with George, it's that he knows too many people, some of them famous ( Jimmy Buffett), and customers throw his name around like it's currency to get a better table or any table at all—but that's Nikki's problem, not Carson's. Carson has no complaints about George.

"What are you on?" George asks.

"Excuse me?"

"What are you *on?*" George says. His expression is inquisitive rather than angry. "You just lost your mom in a tragic accident, Carson. You know what? My sixteen-year-old sister was killed by a drunk driver when I was in college, so I get it, I've been there. And because of that, I want to know what you're taking because there's no way you can come back two weeks later to do a job that requires breakneck speed, laser focus, the patience of Mother Teresa, and a sense of humor without some kind of chemical help. Tell me the truth, please."

Tell him the truth?

Carson wakes up every day around noon, brushes her teeth, then pours Kahlua into her coffee or drinks a screwdriver. For lunch, she smokes some weed or eats a magic cookie. Before work, she drinks three shots of espresso and snorts some cocaine. Sometimes that's too much, she can feel her heartbeat in her throat and her temples and her ass cheeks, so she tempers the high with a Valium. Some days—most days—she hits productive equilibrium. She comes to work and knocks down the crowd like she's John Dillinger with a machine gun. During work, there's more espresso and a bump or two in the ladies' room. After work, the serious drinking begins—a couple of cocktails first, shots, then beer. Then weed and an Ativan or a Valium to fall asleep.

"I'm not on anything," she says. She's surprised by how convincing she sounds. "I mean, I smoke a little weed on my day off and I usually grab a drink after work…"

"But no oxy, no pills, no smack?" George says.

"No!" Carson says, sounding affronted, *feeling* affronted. "Oxy? *Smack?* Do I seem like a junkie to you, George, really?"

George takes a visible breath. He's a lot grayer now than he was when Carson started here three years ago, but Carson likes the gray. Zach has some gray at his temples, and she finds it very sexy. "I've been in this business thirty-eight years, so I have to ask. One drop, fine, accident. Two drops and I begin to think there's a problem."

"I had a bad night," Carson says. "That's allowed, isn't it?" She thinks back over her previous summers working at the Oyster-catcher. "What about when Gunner reached across the bar and jacked that guy up because of something he thought he heard? At least I didn't assault a customer."

"You're right. Gunner had a temper, which was a liability I chose to ignore because he was a big draw—handsome, charming, never forgot a drink—and because he made us so much money."

George points. "You, Carson Quinboro, have the potential to be even better at this job than Gunner was."

Carson reels back a little. This is high, and unexpected, praise. Gunner—Greg Gunn—is a living legend. He tended bar at the Oystercatcher for four years until he was "discovered" by one of their hotshot customers, who offered Gunner a job on Wall Street.

"I don't know what to say. Thank you?"

"You're gorgeous, and I say that with all due respect, and no, I'm not hitting on you. You're a little cold, a bit indifferent, you're witty and quick but not flippant, you're tough on the barbacks, and you should be, they need to shape up. I heard about the card to Lemon Press for Jaime. That was a strategic move."

Carson smiles in spite of herself. "I've been where they are," she says. "I know how to manage them."

"More than one person on the staff has come to me saying they think you're doing drugs in the bathroom," George says. "You display a marked change in temperament when you return, they tell me."

"Because I've relieved my aching bladder and gotten off my feet for thirty seconds."

"If I find out it's true or if you have another remarkably bad night like you did tonight?" Greg points a finger-gun at her. "You're fired. Consider this your warning."

Carson walks through the dark parking lot to her mother's Jeep. She's so chastened that she skips her usual post-shift Corona but not so chastened that she doesn't do a bump once she's safely in the car.

The cocaine makes her angry. George says he understands because he lost his sister, but clearly he has forgotten how challenging it is to focus when your thoughts are soaked in grief like a bar towel that has fallen into the slop bucket.

"I lost my mother!" Carson cries out. The tendons on her neck stand out, she's enraged. "Someone killed her and *drove away! I need her back!*" Now the tears come, and the snot, and the sadness, impossibly deep. Carson will never stop being sad.

The radio is playing "Stone in Love," by Journey. No way! This is the last song Vivi ever heard, one that Carson selected for her playlist because she had a long-ago memory of her mother turning it up on the radio and singing along. Carson sings now in an unhinged voice, wondering if somehow her mother is watching her. Maybe her mother had this song play on the radio to let Carson know that she's around, in the air, up above.

Carson pulls out her phone and texts Zach: Meet?

There's no response.

"Stone in Love" ends and "Everybody Wants You," by Billy Squier, begins. Carson is listening to Classic Rewind on Sirius XM because she's driving Vivi's Jeep and these are Vivi's radio stations (No Shoes Radio, the Bridge, typical old-person music). It's no great magic that Carson heard "Stone in Love" because this station plays Journey and other music from beyond the grave all the time.

She's losing her mind.

There's still no word from Zach. It's a quarter to eleven; he's probably asleep. Maybe Pamela came home from her little "night out" and they slept together. It happens occasionally, he admits, and Carson hates how much this bugs her. The agony is the price that she, and every other woman out there, must pay for falling in love with a married man. She wants to go out. She needs company, other people, even if they're nameless.

She grabs some napkins out of the center console and mops her face. She lets her hair out of the tight braids and runs her fingers through the kinks. Earlier today she bought a black paisley halter top at Erica Wilson; the shopping bag is in the back seat. She changes right there in the car. In the zippered pocket of her bag are her mother's silver Ted Muehling earrings; she takes them out and slides them through her ears. She has long coveted these earrings and on several occasions asked Vivi if she could borrow them. ("No, you'll lose them, I know you, Carson.") Carson had considered stealing them but then decided her mother was right. Now they're hers; everything is hers. She borrows Vivi's clothes, shoes, and jewelry; she sleeps in Vivi's bed. Why? Is she trying to *become* Vivi? Oh, who knows. Her mother had great taste, and the bed is comfortable. The earrings shine against Carson's dark hair. She's good to go.

The line at the front door of the Chicken Box is long but Carson, with her new cachet as head bartender at the Oystercatcher, doesn't have to wait. She walks around to the back door, where the bouncer, Jerry, who is Nikki-from-work's fiancé, lets Carson right in and gives her a cold Corona while he's at it.

The bar is packed; bodies are crushed in so tight that Carson has to turn sideways and wedge herself between people in order to get to the row in front of the stage, where there is at least room to breathe. The band, Maxxtone, is popular; they play cover tunes. The lead singer, Aaron, sees Carson and gives her a thumbs-up. He and the band came into the Oystercatcher the night before for dinner. Carson tips back her beer and tries to get lost in the song— "What I've Got," by Sublime.

When the song ends, she takes a look at the other people in the front row and sees Greg Gunn—Gunner, the legendary bartender, her predecessor—all the way in the corner. He's too dressed up for the Box—nice white shirt, seersucker pants—and he's with some smoke-show in what Carson thinks is vintage Stella McCartney.

Carson sidles her way toward them to say hi but then stops halfway because what if he doesn't remember her? It's too loud to explain who she is and she'll end up making a fool of herself, which isn't at all appealing when her night has been so bad already. She should go home. But what's at home? Nothing. She needs another beer. She heads for the bar; it's easier moving away from the stage than toward it, but when she tries to step around one guy, he moves in front of her, and when she tries to go the other way, he does too. Funny.

She bares her teeth at him.

"Carson," he says.

It's what's-his-face from the Field and Oar.

"Marshall," she says. "The Duck."

He grins. He's lovely to look at, the same way a baby or a puppy is, although here in the Box with his Cisco Brewers T-shirt and his hat on backward over his golden curls and a little scruff on his cheeks—he must have had the day off because the Field and Oar doesn't tolerate facial hair—he's more attractive than the last two times she's seen him. *Look at you, Marshall.* She thinks about having a night of good, old-fashioned fun with Marshall the Duck. They can dance, make out, drive to the Strip for a slice, go down to the Public Way by the Galley to skinny-dip and then have sex on the beach.

This would be so refreshing. So clean. So exactly the kind of night Carson should be having at the age of twenty-one.

Should she do it?

"Let me buy you a drink," she says.

"All set," he says, holding up a Miller Lite.

At that second, a little blonde in a Lilly Pulitzer shift dress grabs Marshall's hand. "Let's dance." She turns and sees Carson. "Hey, boo," she says and Carson resists the urge to smack her. "Sorry, he's mine tonight."

Marshall shrugs and lets the pipsqueak pull him through the crowd.

Carson has no right to feel rejected—Marshall asked her out; she turned him down and threw away his number—but she does. He was looking good and felt exactly like what she needed, and she lost him to a blond chew toy.

She waits a second to see if Marshall will come back. When he doesn't, she turns to leave. Some guy grabs her ass on the way out and Carson is so dejected, she can't even be bothered to hiss at him.

Back in her Jeep, she checks her phone. Nothing from Zach. He's definitely sleeping. Well, he needs to wake up. She texts again: WYD? There's no response. There isn't going to be a response; he's asleep. He won't answer his cell and she can't call the house.

She decides to do a drive-by; it's on her way home. She eases around the small rotary, on the lookout for the police. The way her night is going, she'll probably get pulled over and given a Breathalyzer. She takes Hooper Farm down to Parker and turns right off Parker onto Gray Avenue. The Bridgeman house is set back from the road about a hundred yards. It's gambrel-style and has a detached garage with a small apartment upstairs, where Zach's son, Peter, now lives. Peter is away at camp. He's been going since he was eight years old, and now he's the head counselor. Zach says that Peter fits in at the camp in a way he never fit in at Nantucket High School. Carson has heard way too much about the trials and tribulations of raising a teenager, considering that Carson is practically one herself.

She pulls over into the parking spot of the deserted horse barn across the street. From here, she has a clear view of the house, which is dark except for the porch light and a light over the garage door. Carson is tempted to knock on the front door or throw pebbles at Zach's window. She looks at her phone again. Nothing.

*The heart is a lonely hunter,* she thinks. Her namesake, Carson McCullers, had at least that much right.

She leans back in her seat and closes her eyes. What is she *doing?* And how, oh, how, did she *get* here?

The affair started the previous November. Carson enrolled in a bartending class in South Boston. She would stay in Savannah's town house in Back Bay; Savannah was doing fieldwork for her charity in Dakar, so Carson would have the place to herself. She had recently turned twenty-one and was ready for city life. She planned to run along the Charles, grab coffee from Thinking Cup, choose a museum or an outing for each afternoon, go to her bartending class, then eat out every night. She made a list of restaurants: Pammy's, Mistral, Area Four.

She was flying from Nantucket to Boston on Cape Air on a nine-person Cessna. Zach Bridgeman was also on her flight. When Carson saw him in the terminal, she waved and he waved back and smiled. She wondered if she had to go over and say hello or if she could just sit down and get lost in her music. The Bridgemans— Zach, Pamela, Peter—were now related to Carson through Willa. Seeing Zach was like seeing a distant uncle or a cousin twice removed.

She thought it was good luck when she was assigned the seat behind Zach on the plane because there would be no need for conversation. As they were boarding the plane, they exhausted their only topic of conversation—where they were going. Zach was going to an air traffic control conference at the Boston Harbor Hotel. ("Oooh," Carson said, genuinely impressed. "Fancy.") Carson told Zach that she was taking a bartending class and staying in Savannah's town house on Marlborough Street. ("I should have been a bartender at some point," Zach said. "That has always felt like something I missed.") Carson was reminded then that Zach was friendly and kind. Carson steered clear of Pamela because she could be confrontational and negative. She likely would have told Carson to go back to school, get her degree, and make something of herself.

The plane hit weather somewhere south of Boston—Plymouth, maybe. Carson always tried to pick landmarks out on the ground to mark their progress, but all she could tell before they hit the squall was that they were somewhere over Route 3. The plane bounced around and the rain sounded like gravel hitting the window. They were "in the cotton ball"—all Carson could see out the window was dense, dark cloud. The woman sitting behind the pilot reached for her barf bag. Carson was unconcerned. It was kind of fun, actually, like an amusement-park ride.

Sure enough, the plane emerged from the clouds into clear sky, the ground once more visible beneath them. Carson saw the skyline of Boston in the distance. Everyone relaxed.

The pilot turned east, out over the water.

Carson was jolted awake when the plane slammed down so hard that Carson thought they must have landed—but no, they were still in the air, back in the cotton ball. The turbulence was unlike any Carson had ever experienced. It felt like the plane was a cup of dice God was shaking. Carson's bag flew forward, the man to her left lost his file folders, the woman in the front seat puked again. The plane tipped sideways and went into a nosedive. They were plummeting and bouncing; Carson watched the pilot fight the wheel to raise the nose.

The plane was going down. They were going to die. She reached forward and, almost involuntarily, grabbed Zach's hand.

"It's okay," he said. "He'll get us down. And if I see him get in real trouble, I'll assist. I can land this plane."

Carson was only somewhat comforted by this. She bent her head forward against Zach's seat back and let a stream of profanities fly. She thought of her mother, her father, her brother, and her poor sister, who had just miscarried for the second time. They would never recover. But that was only part of Carson's anxiety. The real meat of her fear was that she was so young and would never get to do so many of the things she wanted to—live alone for three weeks in the city, eat at Pammy's, get her bartending certificate so she could be a boss at the Oystercatcher the following summer. She wanted to travel to London at Christmastime, ride a motorbike across Thailand, see Serena Williams play in the Australian Open. She wanted to earn enough money to buy a little speedboat that she could take over to Coatue whenever she wanted. She had just turned twenty-one and had a lifetime of drinks to legally buy. She wanted to fall in love. Getting married and having children and sending out an annual Christmas card with her family's names printed in script across the bottom held zero appeal, but she liked the idea that someday she would find a man to be both friend and lover. So far, her men had been either one or the other.

The plane tilted so far to the left that Carson was afraid it would start to spin.

Zach said, "We've caught the edge of a funnel cloud."

"A tornado?" Carson said. She could feel how unstable the air was around them. She was holding on to Zach's fingers so tightly that she feared she might break them, and yet she could not let go. His wedding ring, made from a dark metal, pressed into her skin.

The man who had lost his file folders was saying a prayer in Spanish.

"Fix this," Carson said to Zach. "Can you?"

The plane was rumbling like a truck over a bumpy road and bouncing not only up and down but sideways as well. The woman up front was crying. The pilot punched buttons and moved levers; Carson could see his lips moving. He was talking to the control tower in Boston.

"I think he's got it," Zach said—but just then the plane dropped and everyone was bounced out of his or her seat. Carson's head grazed the ceiling. She started crying, too, and praying. She saw her life end in fiery ruins or in a drowning when they crashed into the ocean. *Please God, let this end. I'll go back to school, I'll study, I'll contribute to society, I'll be a good person, I'll win citizenship awards.*

Suddenly the runway appeared in front of them, and the plane, although still wobbly, headed right for it. The plane lowered. They were going to land.

"He's got it," Zach said. And the plane touched down smoothly after all that.

Carson released Zach's hand. All of her muscles were coiled so tightly that relief couldn't flow like it should. But then, yes—good energy flooded into her bloodstream and she felt dizzy with it. The tension in her neck eased. She was alive. They were taxiing to their gate. She was going to put her feet on planet Earth; her plans would resume. But make no mistake—Carson was changed. She would never take anything for granted again.

The pilot removed his headset. "Sorry about the bumps," he said.

"Sorry about the *bumps?*" Carson whispered to Zach.

When they climbed the stairs to the terminal, Zach said, "I don't know about you, but I need a drink."

"Hell yeah," Carson said.

"I would suggest walking down to Legal and doing a shot, but it'll be packed. What time is your class?"

"Starts tomorrow," Carson said. "I'm free today."

"Let's have a drink at my hotel," Zach said. "My treat."

Carson thought to decline. She kind of wanted to get to Savannah's; she could go to any one of dozens of bars in Back Bay by herself. But she remembered her vow to be a contributing citizen and she wasn't sure *what* she would have done if Zach hadn't been there to calm her.

"Sounds great," she said.

They shared an Uber to the Boston Harbor Hotel, which Carson had been to once as a kid. (Vivi spoke at a luncheon, and Savannah brought Carson along to watch. Carson remembered the rotunda, the hushed elegance of the lobby, the huge floral arrangement on a central pedestal table, and the pretty soaps in the ladies' room. That was the first time Carson realized her mother was famous—a roomful of people had applauded her.)

Zach said he would check in and drop his bags off in his room. He suggested Carson leave her bag at the bell desk then go find them seats in the bar. The Rowes Wharf Bar had a lot of dark polished wood and elaborate crown molding; there was a row of low tables with plush armchairs and cozy, rounded banquettes. The room glowed with golden light and felt like the perfect spot to spend a dreary autumn afternoon. Carson sat at a banquette table in the corner and a waiter in black handed her a menu.

Carson wondered if she would ever be able to work somewhere like this. It felt like a place where things *happened*—business deals, love affairs. The prices on the menu were just south of staggering, but Zach had said he was paying so Carson ordered a glass of Veuve Clicquot.

Just then, Zach appeared. "Make it a bottle," he said.

Their server brought a selection of bar snacks that looked too pretty to eat as well as the chilled bottle, an ice bucket, and two flutes. Carson watched his elegant movements; he seemed to have four arms. The pop of the champagne cork gave her a shiver. She was alive to appreciate the pleasing sound of a champagne cork popping.

Carson and Zach raised their flutes and touched them ever so gently together.

Zach said, "We made it."

They drank.

Carson said, "Were you worried?"

"I was worried the pilot would panic and do something that would make him lose control of the plane. I would have taken copilot and gotten us down."

"You should've."

"I wasn't needed, except by you." He poured them each some more champagne and said, "I thought I was going to lose a couple of fingers."

There were no sexual or romantic feelings for Carson at first, just a sense of camaraderie, and then, as they ordered a second bottle of champagne and a burger to share with double fries, a sense of conspiracy. Carson Quinboro and Zach Bridgeman were hanging out, wasting an afternoon getting drunk in a fancy hotel bar!

Zach was easy to talk to. Carson heard about how he'd graduated from MIT with a degree in aeronautical engineering, then came to Nantucket to work for the summer before doing a master's at Rensselaer. During that summer, he worked at the Yacht Club and was "targeted" by Pamela Bonham. He was then fast-tracked into the Bonham family and a life on Nantucket.

"By 'fast-tracked,' you mean…"

"I got Pamela pregnant."

"Ah," Carson said. "You were so young."

"Yes, my friend, yes, I was. It wasn't the life I'd planned but I've made it work. I enjoy ATC. I like flying myself when I can. I love Nantucket. I'd be a jerk to complain."

Their server appeared and asked if he could bring them anything else. By that point, Carson was well on her way to being drunk and although she knew the proper thing was for her to thank Zach, collect her bag, and summon an Uber, she noticed something in Zach's expression, a crack in the friendly, confident facade. Maybe he wanted to be a jerk. Maybe he wanted to complain—and if so, Carson wanted to hear it.

She said, "I think I'm going to switch to a cocktail."

She fully expected Zach to tactfully say that they'd had enough and that he had places to be—but he didn't even hesitate. "I'll join you. A Maker's Mark on the rocks for me and…"

"Belvedere, tonic, lemon, please."


When did she realize she wanted to sleep with him? Maybe a couple of sips into her Belvedere and tonic when she excused herself to go to the ladies' room and Zach stood up (her father always did this as well, and Carson loved a man with old-fashioned manners; every boy she'd ever dated reached for his phone before she'd even left the table). Maybe it was a moment later when, sitting on the toilet, Carson considered texting Willa to say, *You are never going to believe who I'm getting drunk with right now!* Carson knew not to say anything to Willa because Willa would tell Rip and Rip would tell Pamela and what was electric about the afternoon was that Carson and Zach were forging a bond without anyone in their respective families knowing about it.

One cocktail became two. Before they ordered a third, Zach said, "I think I should send you on your way before something indiscreet happens."

Carson, emboldened by the mere suggestion that something indiscreet *might* happen, slid over on the banquette until she was close enough to feel the warmth coming off Zach's body. He was old, yes, in his *forties,* but he was kind of hot and he was so nice and smart (he had an engineering degree from MIT!) and he'd been such a hero to her on the plane, and this was the first day of Carson's new, independent adult life, and the best plot twists, as her mother would say, occurred when you least expected them. That was what made them *twists!* "I suppose you've heard I'm the black sheep of the family."

"I've always thought you were the most intriguing Quinboro. And today proved me right."

"Did it?" Carson let her hand fall lightly on Zach's thigh, which was very bad and very bold. He picked her hand up, kissed it, and said, "You're extremely beautiful, Carson. But I'm married and a father and you're half my age."

"But we nearly died," Carson said. "We should be celebrating life. I feel like something should happen now."

Zach signaled for the check. "What happens now is you go to Savannah's, and I'll see you back on Nantucket. At . . . Thanksgiving. Willa is hosting, right?"

"Right."

"We probably shouldn't tell anyone about today."

"Except we're not doing anything wrong," Carson said. "You're rejecting my advances."

Zach squeezed her hand. "Someday you'll thank me for rejecting your advances. Nothing good could come of this—not for me and not for you either."

Zach paid the bill, then escorted Carson to the lobby and waited while the bellman retrieved her bag. He took care of tipping the bellman, which was such a kind and generous thing to do that Carson fell even deeper into her infatuation.

"Shall I wait with you while your Uber comes?" he asked outside the hotel.

"Please don't," Carson said. "I'll be fine."

Zach kissed her once, gently, on the lips. It fell somewhere between a romantic kiss and an avuncular one. "Thank you. That was the best afternoon I've had in a long time."

"It could get better," Carson said.

Zach laughed and disappeared through the revolving door.

Carson waited for a few addled seconds as she tried to read that kiss. Then she canceled her Uber and dragged her bag back into the lobby. She moved straight for the elevator bank. She was grateful that some other dude (who gave her a not-so-subtle up-and-down) had a key card that made the elevator rise.

"What floor?" he asked.

"Eleven," she said. Zach's key card, still in its little cardboard jacket, had been sitting between them on the table all through lunch. Room 1112.

She rolled her bag down the thick carpet of the hallway to Zach's door. She stood quietly for a second, and, just like they say happens in the moments before death, Carson's life passed before her eyes. She saw all of the bad and naughty things she'd done in her life: slapping Willa across the face, stealing Tic Tacs from the Stop and Shop, calling her mother a bitch, telling Amy she had a fat ass, starting the bad rumor about Juliana Corty in sixth grade, vaping, smoking weed, stealing her mother's Jeep and going for a joy ride on Miacomet Golf Course, doing a beer bong at three in the morning at the Pike house and then having sex with the fraternity president in the hall coat closet, failing all but one course first semester sophomore year, generally being a smart aleck, high maintenance, a relentless attention seeker, and the squeaky wheel.

But nothing Carson had done in her twenty-one years compared to this.

She knocked. A second later, Zach answered. Did he look surprised to see her?

No.

"I watched you from the window," he said, his voice now husky.

"And?"

He stared at her for a long second, so long that Carson wondered if he was running through his own worst moments. Then he sighed and held open the door.

Carson is startled out of her memories by a pair of headlights creeping slowly down Gray Avenue. She squints. It's very late now, past one. Who is this?

She catches a glint of red and sees the outline of the Range Rover. It's Pamela. Carson is about to get busted lurking outside the Bridgeman house. How will she explain this?

She slides all the way down in her seat, fighting the urge to open the car door and vomit on the ground. She hears the Rover slowing down as it gets closer. She's every bit as scared now as she was when the plane was plummeting. She decides to act surprised to see Pamela. She'll say she didn't realize this was the Bridgemans' house. Will Pamela buy this? She'll use her mother's death as an excuse. She'll say she was on her way home from the Box, took a wrong turn, and pulled over to sober up. She'll say she has been completely lost since the accident.

The only time Carson has been to the Bridgeman home was

for Willa's bridal shower, which was one of the most unbearable afternoons of Carson's life. She remembers the squealing over monogrammed towels, the ribbons and bows taped to a paper plate that Willa was supposed to wear as a hat. Carson had slipped out to the driveway to get high—there was simply no other way to tolerate it—and when she came back inside with bleary red eyes and wolfed down half a platter of tea sandwiches that Tink Bonham had had shipped in from Le Petit Chef in Philadelphia, her mother approached her, frowning, and said, "You could have at least invited me to go with you."

The Rover seems to idle right in front of Carson's Jeep for long minutes. What is Pamela doing? Carson holds her breath, waiting for Pamela to knock on the window. It's like a horror film, and Pamela is the hatchet that will hack Carson's emotional life to bloody pieces.

The knock doesn't come and Carson can see the lights swing around into the Bridgemans' driveway. Carson lets her breath go a little at a time, and when she hears the car door slam, she pops her head up just enough to watch Pamela stumble across her front yard and into the house.

Carson counts to fifty, watching the house for lights. No lights. Carson imagines Pamela stumbling up to bed in the dark or, better still, passing out facedown on the kitchen floor.

She turns the key in the ignition and gets the hell out of there.

# The Chief

"Is this room always open?" The Chief is talking to the general manager of the Stop and Shop, a guy named Dick, from Taunton.

Dick is very protective of his employees; the Chief likes that. Turns out that Donald, the evening custodian, is nearing his eightieth birthday; he's a vet on a fixed income and is hard of hearing, and Dick would prefer he be left out of the investigation unless it's absolutely necessary.

"Yes, it's always open," Dick confirms.

"Even when the store is closed?"

"We have a cleaning crew and stockers in overnight and they use this room."

"How closely is entry to this room monitored?" the Chief asks. "Because someone put those shoes in the trash."

Dick gives the Chief a list of store employees, then admits that it would be easy for a shopper in the store to slip into the break room undetected. The break room is right next to the public bathrooms. One would only need to open the door, stuff the shoes in the trash, and close the door. Unfortunately, there are no cameras in the break room or in the hallway where the bathrooms are. "Why would we have cameras?" Dick asks. "Just in case someone pops in to dump evidence from a homicide investigation into the trash?"

The Chief leaves the store feeling dejected. It's six o'clock on a Friday night in July. Andrea is putting together a family dinner, which means that Chloe and Finn have to put their work and social lives on hold—and Ed does too.

On his way home, he calls Pamela Bonham Bridgeman and asks if he can set up a time to talk to Peter.

"About *what?*" Pamela asks. She's blunt to a fault on a good day, and usually Ed appreciates this because they all have business to attend to, and small talk can be a waste of time.

"I need his help with the Vivian Howe case," Ed says. He takes a breath to slow himself down; he's probably said too much already. "How old is Peter?"

"Nineteen," Pamela says.

"I'll speak with him directly, then," the Chief says. "Would you please give me his number?"

"He's at camp in Maine until the end of August," Pamela says. "Cell phones aren't allowed and there's no service even if they were allowed." She pauses while the Chief's spirits plummet even further. He can't get *anywhere* with this case. "Why on earth would you want to talk to Peter about Vivi's death?"

"I just have a few questions for him," the Chief says. "But clearly they'll have to wait. Thanks, Pamela."

He needs to ask for help. Investigating homicides isn't his job anyway; his job is to oversee the department. But he misses actual police work and he feels connected to this case, not only because Vivian Howe was a local (and Andrea's favorite author) but also because he wants to clear Cruz's name.

Ed calls the Greek. "The Greek" is Nicholas Diamantopoulos, a Massachusetts State Police detective.

"Nicky," the Chief says. "I could use some advice."

"I'm on vacation, Ed," the Greek says. "I'm lying on Mansion Beach on Block Island. I got here forty minutes ago and I'm not due back at the station until a week from Monday." The Chief can hear a female voice in the background. The Greek is very, very popular with the ladies. "Can this wait ten days?"

*Can* it wait ten days? Peter Bridgeman, who sent whatever photo that had Cruz so upset, is incommunicado. When the Chief called Lisa Hitt to see if she'd found anything usable on the shoes, he learned that she was on vacation as well.

"Do you have five minutes so I can run something past you?" the Chief asks.

"Five minutes," the Greek says. "Four minutes, fifty-nine seconds..."

Hit-and-run, the Chief says. Local author of some note, *New York Times* bestsellers and all that, killed running on her own street. Forensics has, so far, turned up nothing useful, but then the clothes and running shoes went missing from the hospital.

"First I thought it was just a simple mistake, they got lost or whatever, misplaced. Then the shoes show up in the trash in the employee break room at the local Stop and Shop."

"Random?" the Greek asks, and Ed can tell his interest is piqued. On vacation or no, the Greek is a professional and an unsolved homicide is catnip to him.

"No, I don't think so. The kid who called the accident in, name of Cruz DeSantis, works at the Stop and Shop. He was a friend of the deceased's son, and that morning he was driving over there to talk to the son."

"Do you think that's who hit her?"

"No," the Chief says. "Forensics found blood on his car but only on the handle, not the bumper. The woman had a gash on her leg, so it stands to reason there would be blood on the bumper."

"Don't assume," Nick says. "She could have sliced it on a rock when she hit the ground."

"He's a good kid, Nicky," the Chief says. "I know him, I know his dad, Joe. Joe's an Iraq vet—"

"That doesn't mean—"

"I think someone is trying to frame the kid," the Chief says. "The sneakers turning up at his place of employment indicate that. But who is it and why?" The Chief clears his throat. "The kid, Cruz, is Black, so it has occurred to me that race might be a factor."

"Might be," the Greek says. The Greek is Black as well—his mother is Cape Verdean. "Still, you can't discount the kid because you like him, Ed."

"I'm stuck," the Chief says. "And I'm late for dinner."

"Hit-and-run homicides are hard to solve."

"We live on an island, Nicky. Nobody can get away, that's the thing."

"You checked with the body shops?" the Greek asks.

Yes, that was Dixon's job, but he'd come up empty. All front-fender bodywork repairs since Vivian Howe was killed have corresponding accident reports. It's entirely possible that someone is just driving around with a dented fender. It's also possible that hitting Vivian Howe didn't even leave a dent. "We did, yes."

"You spoke to the son?"

"I've been saving that for last," the Chief says. "The kid lost his mother."

"Well," the Greek says. "Sounds to me like the time for that conversation has come."

# Leo

When Leo finally bumps into Cruz, it's in the place he least expects: on the docks.

Leo is working at the Nantucket Boat Basin, where he's a glorified trash collector and errand boy. He has a golf cart and a walkie-talkie and he zips around from slip to slip, bringing ice and taking people's trash. Leo likes his job, though some of the boat owners try his patience. Still, he knows he's lucky; the boats are gorgeous, the people are friendly and grateful (most of the time), and he's not only outside, he's on the water. Lots of people would kill for this job.

He has just loaded four bags of trash and one bag of recycling (glass, mostly champagne bottles) into the back of his golf cart when he sees Cruz stepping off a seventy-foot flybridge yacht called *Queen Bee*.

What?

Cruz has textbooks under his arm. He must have been tutoring a kid on that yacht. Leo thinks about throwing his cart into reverse, but that would look cowardly. Leo feels like he's being controlled by some outside force as he rolls the cart forward and stops in front of Cruz. He's not sure what to say.

Leo swallows. "Hey."

Cruz stares at Leo a second, his face unreadable. "Hey."

"Were you the one who hit my mom?" Leo asks. "Because if you were, you need to admit it, man."

"I didn't," Cruz says. "I found her on the ground. You can ask me a thousand times, and my answer isn't going to change, because that's the truth. If I'd been the one to hit Vivi, I would have told you. There's no way I could live with myself if I killed Vivi and then pretended I didn't. I have integrity."

*Integrity* might as well be Cruz's middle name, Leo knows. Adults always use that word when describing him because he's "an achiever," because he looks people in the eye, because he was nice to the kids at school that nobody liked, because he never swears and doesn't complain, because he thinks of other people before himself. And hasn't some of this rubbed off on Leo? Hasn't he tried to be a person of integrity too?

"I couldn't even keep quiet when we stole the street sign from Hulbert Avenue," Cruz says.

Leo bites his tongue; he won't give Cruz the satisfaction of smiling. The summer between seventh and eighth grade, Leo and Cruz used to sneak out in the middle of the night on their bikes. They once lit a campfire in the bamboo forest between Vivi's house and the Madaket Road and roasted hot dogs. The only reason they hadn't burned the forest down was that Cruz had thought to bring water. They skinny-dipped in the pool of some house on Cliff Road. They stole the street sign from Hulbert, home to the most expensive real estate on the island. They'd watched the sunrise a lot that summer, then went home and slept until two in the afternoon.

"I heard you ran a stop sign and were seen speeding before you got to my house," Leo says. "I think you were so upset about the photo from Bridgeman that you weren't paying attention to the road and you hit my mom. And now I think you're trading on your so-called integrity, and that's why you haven't been arrested."

"Man, f—" Cruz stops himself.

"Say it."

"Of course I was upset by the photo. I was driving over to talk to you about it."

"I want you to just admit you hit her, man. She's gone, nothing can bring her back, I get that, but you need to confess. It was an accident, obviously you didn't intend to *kill* my mother—but you were the one who hit her. The police saw you *driving recklessly, Cruz.*"

Cruz steps up, gets right in Leo's face. Leo can see the sweat on Cruz's upper lip, smell the laundry detergent that Joe uses. Cruz is his best friend in the world. His buddy since forever. Vivi had a million things she used to call them: Frick and Frack, Mutt and Jeff, Felix and Oscar, Abbott and Costello, Ben and Jerry, Beans and Rice. Vivi *loved* Cruz. She took care of him like he was another son. When Vivi cooked, Cruz always got a bigger portion than Leo. She bought special things that he liked: mangoes, cookie dough ice cream, pistachios. She lent him her books. They both read the *New York Times* and they texted each other about the articles. Cruz and Vivi were "connected intellectually" in a way that Leo and Vivi weren't. Leo could have been jealous about this, but he wasn't. He was happy they got along so well. Vivi used to say that Cruz balanced out the family—she had two girls and two boys. With an extra person, there was extra love.

Now love is dead.

"The person who needs to admit something here, Leo Quinboro, is you." Cruz pokes Leo, hard, in the chest. "You need to face your truth."

With that, Cruz strides down the dock, and Leo, not sure what to do or to think, blinks at the hot blue sky and the darker blue of Nantucket Sound and the yachts lined up in their slips like really, really expensive toys. Then his walkie-talkie rasps—slip 92 needs ice.

Leo goes home early with a "stomachache" to find the chief of police, Ed Kapenash, knocking on the front door of Money Pit.

"Hello?" Leo says. He wishes he'd stayed at work. He wishes his sister had answered the door and dealt with the Chief, but it's four o'clock. She's at the Oystercatcher.

"Hey, there," the Chief says, offering his hand. "You're Ms. Howe's son?"

"Leo," he says. "Leo Quinboro."

"Leo," the Chief says. "The lion."

"I'm named after Leo Tolstoy," Leo says. "The writer? He's Russian. He wrote *War and Peace.*"

The Chief nods. He doesn't care; nobody ever does. "You got a few minutes to chat?"

"I guess," Leo says. He pushes the door open for the Chief and they step into the kitchen. The kitchen has cathedral ceilings and a teal-blue Ilve Majestic stove with a matching hood that Vivi called "the Lambo" because it was the stove-equivalent of a Lamborghini. The kitchen was the first room in Money Pit that Vivi renovated, but no one has cleaned it since Vivi died, and it's not looking like its best self. On the counter sits the blender, half filled with a purple smoothie that has attracted fruit flies, and there are bagel crumbs and seeds all over the butcher block. The last of the sympathy flowers are dying on the table; the petals are falling, the stamens staining the white surface.

"Can I get you anything?" Leo asks. "Ginger ale?" This is what he's having. He cracks open a can and takes a sip. He really thinks he might puke. What is the chief of police doing here?

"I'm fine, thanks," the Chief says. "I have some questions for you. Do you want to sit down?"

"Uh, okay?" Leo says. The table is grimy. He could lead the Chief out to the back by the pool but Vivi's writing chaise will be there, and for this reason, Leo has been avoiding the pool. Nearly every day in summer, Vivi would lie out back, writing away in one of her notebooks. If Leo or Carson or Willa interrupted her—*Mom, would you please make me a sandwich? Can I have money for gas? Is it okay if I invite some people over?*—she would say, "I know it looks like I'm lying around in anticipation of granting your every wish and desire, but I'm working, so please step off."

They sit at the table and Leo willfully ignores the shriveled lily petals and the coat of grease from who knows what order of takeout.

"We're working on your mom's case," the Chief says. "I've gotten certain pieces of information that need clarifying. We heard about a photograph that a classmate might have sent you and Cruz DeSantis. Do you know what I'm referring to?"

Leo tenses up. The picture. The police know about the picture.

"You've seen the photo?" Leo asks.

"No, I haven't seen it. Cruz won't talk about it, and the person who sent the photo is off-island and can't be reached."

Peter can't be *reached?* Leo thinks. Where is he? *Rehab* is the first thing that comes to mind; Peter Bridgeman is addicted to his Adderall and whatever other drugs he can get his hands on. But if he'd been sent away, Leo would have heard about it from the high-school rumor mill or from Willa. Then Leo remembers that Peter goes to that camp in Maine. How did Leo not think of this before now? He figured Peter didn't send out the photo to a bunch of people because of what happened to Vivi or because he was so drug-addled he'd forgotten about it or because Cruz had managed to talk some sense into him.

Leo does some quick calculating. The police don't have access to the picture. The picture could be of anything as far as they knew.

"It's our belief that someone is trying to..." The Chief stops suddenly. "You and Cruz had a fight the night before your mother died, is that right? You gave him a black eye."

"It was self-defense," Leo says, then regrets this and tries to backpedal. "Honestly, I'm not real clear on what happened the night before my mom was killed. I don't remember getting home."

"Let me change the topic for a second," the Chief says. "Have you seen your mother's running shoes? Did you collect the shoes and clothes from the hospital?"

Leo gags. His mother's shoes. His mother's clothes.

"I'm sorry, son, I know this is difficult. But can you please just answer the question? Have you seen the clothes or shoes since your mother died?"

"No," Leo whispers. "We got the phone back. That was it."

"Okay." The Chief places a light hand on Leo's shoulder.

"I know Cruz ran a stop sign and was speeding before he got to my road." Leo meets the Chief's eye for the first time. "If he didn't hit her, then who did?"

"That's what we're trying to find out," the Chief says. "Thank you for your help. I'll be in touch."

The Chief drives away. He left his card and said if Leo had any thoughts about the shoes or the clothes to call his personal cell phone, not the station.

Leo goes up to his bedroom and closes the door. He imagines Cruz being arrested, arraigned, indicted, sentenced, jailed. He imagines the strong brick foundation that Cruz built to support his future crumbling.

He thinks of Cruz poking him hard in the chest, an imitation of Joe DeSantis when Joe wanted to get a point across. *You need to face your truth.*

*Face my truth?* Leo thinks. He's suddenly so angry that he punches the wall; his fist goes straight through the plaster. His mother would be furious about this—but his mother is dead. There's no one left to care if he punches holes in the walls.

"Mom!" he cries out. "Mama, where are you?"

He strides over to Carson's room. The door is wide open—of course, because she's not sleeping there. She's sleeping in Vivi's room. Vivi's room is at the other end of the hall, door closed tight, because Vivi alone has an air-conditioning unit.

Leo opens the door and goes over to Vivi's nightstand. He pulls out the drawer and finds what he's looking for—a sandwich baggie full of pills. He wants Ativan or something stronger; he doesn't care what. He needs to escape his head.

He shakes four of the pills into his palm. Then a fifth.

# Vivi

"I'm using one of my nudges," Vivi says. "And you can't stop me."

Martha purses her lips. She's wearing a scarf knotted around her neck, the same one she had on the first time they met. Maybe she wears them in rotation. Vivi will ask, but not right now.

"This is where a mother should step in," Vivi says. "He takes the pills, he associates the pills with feeling better, he seeks out more pills. He becomes addicted. He ends up a functioning addict, or he goes to rehab, or he dies. Is that what's going to happen? Can you check your clipboard?"

"I didn't bring my clipboard," Martha says. She closes her eyes. "I'll do it this way." Her eyes fly open. "I'm afraid you're right."

"You can see the future?" Vivi asks.

"I have some special skills," Martha says. "The mind reading, as you know. I can see potential futures, and with extra concentration, I can go back in time and follow the road not taken."

*Whaaaaa?* Vivi thinks.

"But let's not waste time," Martha says. "Use your nudge. Right now, go ahead."

"How?" Vivi asks. Leo has stepped into her bathroom and is filling her cup with water.

"Swoop down there and...nudge."

Vivi gazes down at Leo, her dear, sweet baby boy. The glass of water is full; the pills are in his palm. *Focus,* Vivi thinks. But she's distracted by the mess in the bathroom. Carson's makeup is everywhere and she has left the lid off Vivi's La Mer soft cream, which costs over three hundred dollars.

"Vivi!" Martha says.

Vivi snaps her attention back to Leo. He's bringing the pills to his mouth.

Vivi jumps off the ledge of the room. She tries to break through the membrane, but the membrane just stretches like a nylon stocking. Okay, weird. Vivi guides Leo's hand away from his mouth. Leo stares at his hand as though he realizes he's being possessed by an external agent. Then his body relaxes and seems to fall into resignation. He dumps out the water and returns the pills to the baggie.

Vivi floats back up to the greenroom, where Martha is waiting. "I should have had him flush them down the toilet," Vivi says. "Shoot."

"It's fine," Martha says. They both watch as Leo returns the baggie to the nightstand and leaves the room.

Vivi experiences what can only be described as a kind of ecstasy. She used her first nudge! She saved her son from becoming a pill addict! She feels powerful. She feels like a good mother. "I saved him!" Vivi says. "You could see the future. He would have become an addict and spent countless hours drinking coffee in church basements."

"Let's not stereotype, please, Vivian," Martha says. "He would have been okay eventually, but you spared him a struggle. He knows pills aren't the answer."

"I nipped it in the bud," Vivi says. Her self-congratulations have made her forget the other thing that's bothering her. "Why is he so angry with Cruz? Why does he think Cruz did it? There's no way Cruz did it." She pauses. "Is there?"

"I can't—"

"You can't tell me, I know." Vivi sighs. "It breaks my heart that Leo and Cruz are fighting like this."

"I think you should focus on the good you did your son."

"What if he needs me again?" Vivi asks.

"Eventually all three of them are going to have to learn to live without you," Martha says. "*All the way* without you. The summer is going to end, Vivian. Summer always ends."

Vivi can't bear to think about it—but then again, she doesn't have to yet. It's only July.

# Nantucket

Vivian Howe's last novel, *Golden Girl,* enters the world on Tuesday, July 13, and we couldn't be prouder.

Vivi's publisher, "Mr. Hooper," launches a coordinated social media effort: Facebook, Twitter, and Instagram. The company puts a full-page ad in *People* magazine, an in memoriam to its "golden girl" Vivian Howe. In the center of the ad is a beautiful picture of Vivi sitting in the dunes at Steps Beach, photographed by Nantucket's own Laurie Richards. Vivi is wearing earrings from Jessica Hicks and a soft, pale sweater woven at Nantucket Looms. The book cover is underneath. It's a bit of a tightrope walk—are the Mr. Hooper people memorializing Vivi or are they trying to sell books?

Mr. Hooper has also made a sixty-second TV commercial, a montage of Vivi talking about Nantucket and her writing. At the end of the spot is a message that reminds everyone that Vivi has passed away and if they want to own a first edition of *Golden Girl,* the last Vivian Howe novel, they'd better BUY NOW. The spot runs during all the morning shows and millions of people see it.

Savannah Hamilton called Vivi's publicist, Flor, to say that either she or JP would be willing to stand in for Vivi on *Great Morning USA* with Tanya Price. Flor nixed the JP idea right away—the country doesn't want to hear a man speaking for a woman (those days are over), and especially not her ex-husband. Savannah, as best friend, might be better but Flor intimates that the only replacement the producers would go for is one of the children. Savannah rules out Leo and Carson right away—they're both too fragile right now—and when Savannah asks Willa, she declines. She hasn't been feeling well and she doesn't want to travel. It's a busy time at the museum. This, Savannah suspects, is all a way of saying that she's terrified of going on live television in front of ten million people.

"But *I'm* not terrified," Savannah said. "I mean, I am, of course, but I'm also willing to do whatever it takes to get Vivi to the top of the list. She didn't like to say it out loud, but you and I both know, Flor, that it was her lifelong dream to get to number one."

"Sales are looking good," Flor says.

"Appearing on *Great Morning USA* would give the book a huge boost," Savannah says. "I'm willing and able to appear on the show."

"I'll check with the producers and circle back," Flor says, and Savannah, who knows every buzzword and phrase of the business world, understands that's a no.

Everyone at Mr. Hooper as well as those of us here on Nantucket are holding our collective breath on Wednesday, July 21, at 4:55 p.m., right before the following week's *New York Times* bestseller list is announced. We want Vivi to do well. The highest she has ever debuted is number two combined / number three hardcover with her previous book, *Main Street Gossip.* Can *Golden Girl* make it to number one? It's anyone's guess. The algorithm that the *Times* uses to determine where books land on the list is the biggest mystery in all of publishing.

Here on Nantucket, Savannah and JP and Willa gather around the kitchen island in Savannah's house on Union Street, watching the screen of Savannah's laptop. Flor has promised she'll e-mail the list the instant it comes in.

It's five o'clock. Savannah has champagne chilling in the fridge.

She refreshes her browser. Nothing yet.

At 5:01, JP says, "I remember the first time one of Vivi's books hit the list. It was..."

*"Along the South Shore,"* Savannah and Willa say at the same time.

"I knew that. I was working at the wine store. What number was she then?"

"Fifteen," Willa says. "I was horrified because I thought that meant she'd come in last." She shrugs. "I mean, her name *was* all the way at the bottom."

"And then *The Angle of Light* debuted at number seven," Savannah says. "I took Vivi to the Galley to dinner to celebrate."

*"Main Street Gossip* was so close," Willa says. "Number two on the combined list behind Stephen King."

"And Stephen King is the most famous writer of modern times, so he doesn't even count," Savannah says.

At 5:02, Savannah checks her e-mail. There it is, from Rivera, Flor: Bestseller List 7/25/21. Savannah clicks on the list.

*Golden Girl* is number two on both the hardcover and the combined list. Number one is a novel called *Satan's Weekend* by someone named D. K. Bolt. The description says it's the fifteenth book in the Gruesome Goth series.

"Gruesome Goth?" Savannah says. "That sounds dreadful."

Willa says, "I should have gone on *Great Morning USA*. I'm sorry. I just didn't feel up to it."

Savannah pulls the bottle of Veuve Clicquot out. "Let's drink this anyway," she says. "I know Vivi would want us to."

"You guys enjoy," Willa says. "I'm exhausted and Rip is expecting me at home."

"Oh, just have one glass in your mother's honor," JP says. "Number two in the country is nothing to sneeze at."

"I'm all set," Willa says. She picks up her canvas NHA tote bag, which is what she uses as a purse, and leaves.

"I've lost them," JP says to Savannah after they hear the front door close. "They never want to hang out with me."

"You can find them again," Savannah says. She pops the cork on the champagne. "Have you broken up with Amy yet?"

"Not yet," JP says. "I've been too busy at the Cone. But I'm taking a day off next week, I'll do it then."

Savannah brings the Waterford flutes out of the good china and crystal cabinet (which is a beaten and battered pie safe that Savannah's mother believed might fool potential burglars) and pours each of them champagne. She raises her glass. "To Vivi, number two on the list, number one in our hearts."

JP clinks Savannah's glass and drinks. "I don't know," he says. "You're putting a positive spin on this, but all I can think is that wherever Vivi is right now, she's pissed off."

# Vivi

"Number two?" she says. "I died and I *still* came in second?"

"*Satan's Weekend* sounds like the work of someone below," Martha says, chuckling. "*Way* below."

"Yes, Darla Kay Bolt," Vivi says. "I knew her at Bread Loaf. She was my *roommate!*"

"What are the *chances?*" Martha says. "The two of you battling it out years later."

"I'm glad you find this so entertaining," Vivi says. "You do realize that was my last opportunity to make it to the top? I should have used one of my nudges."

"I think we both know you didn't want to get to number one that way," Martha says.

Vivi silently concedes. She wanted to be first fair and square. Now that will never, ever happen.

"If there's one thing you learn up here," Martha says, "it's never say never. In the past few years, I've seen things happen in the world, in our country, and in individual lives that I would have said simply weren't possible. And I was proved wrong."

"So you're saying I can still get to number one?" Vivi says. "How? You have to do it in your first week. It just doesn't happen otherwise."

"Please, Vivian, stop with the hyperbole," Martha says. "I don't care for it." She strokes the scarf trailing down her shoulder like it's the tail of a beloved cat. "Just keep the faith."

# Willa

Brett Caspian arrives on Nantucket on the 10:30 ferry on Friday, July 23, and Willa, who has taken the day off work, is waiting to pick him up. He's returning to Hyannis on the 2:15, so they will have just shy of four hours to visit. Four hours seemed like the right amount of time—Willa can't believe she offered to let the man stay in her house; he's a complete stranger, and if he ends up being a sociopath or a serial killer, she's in trouble. She hasn't told anyone that Brett Caspian is coming other than Rip, and he expressed less than no interest in the fact that Willa is meeting with an old friend of Vivi's from high school.

"I hope he's legit," Rip said that morning as he wolfed down a banana slathered with peanut butter and Willa stared into her herbal tea, willing herself not to throw up at the smell. "If not, call 911, because I'll be buried."

Rip has ten claims on his desk, the most confounding of which is Marissa Lopresti's Jeep. Marissa's mother, Candace, wants to put the loss through insurance, even though there was no accident. Marissa drove the Jeep into the Bathtub out at Eel Point willfully because she was so upset about Leo breaking up with her the night before Vivi died. Rip can't make that into an accident—he's spent weeks trying to negotiate with the provider—but Candace is threatening to pull her business if he doesn't. "The woman is such a...bully. She says she's going to write a letter to the editor about our crappy customer service. How is it our fault that Marissa acted out a scene from *Risky Business*?

And it was all pointless anyway! They were back together two weeks later."

Willa pushes away her inevitable feelings of guilt. She should be paying closer attention to both Leo and Carson. She's been keeping her distance from her brother and her sister and her father and Savannah because she doesn't want them to know that she's pregnant and she doesn't want to tell them about Brett Caspian's visit.

The pregnancy is her right to keep secret. But her visit with Brett Caspian feels a little clandestine. Willa wants to talk to him alone. He'll be able to shed some light on what Vivi was like growing up—and, sorry, but Willa doesn't want to share that with anyone.

Willa has no idea what Brett Caspian looks like and yet she picks him out right away. He descends the ramp of the Hy-Line carrying a backpack and a guitar case. He's wearing a light denim shirt and darker jeans, a brown belt with a heavy silver buckle, and black high-top Chuck Taylors. If Carson were here, she would make a Justin Timberlake joke about the denim-on-denim look. Willa agrees it's awful; Brett stands out among the day-trippers in their snappy polo shirts and bright sundresses. But there's also a romantic aura about him. He drove all the way to Hyannis from Tennessee to visit the daughter of the girl he once loved.

Willa catches his eye and waves, and he comes striding over. He has longish dark hair peppered with gray and his face crinkles up when he smiles. Willa can't see his eyes behind his sunglasses but she knows instinctively that he's the type that Vivi always found handsome. He is every bit the aging rebel—part James Dean, part Steven Tyler. This stands in stark contrast to the preppy, square-jawed look of Willa's father, JP.

"I would have known you anywhere," Brett says. "You're Vivi's spitting image."

Willa's eyes well with tears. There are no words he could have said that would have endeared him to her more. It was commonly acknowledged in the family that Carson looked like JP and Willa and Leo looked like Vivi. However, Vivi's two most striking features were her pixie cut and her red lipstick. Willa wears her hair long, parted down the middle, and she doesn't wear any makeup, which Carson says is a result of her dating the same person her whole life.

"Thank you," Willa says. "You brought your guitar?"

"Thought I might sing for you," he says.

Willa feels embarrassed—whether for herself or for him, she can't tell. "I'm parked in the lot," she says, and she leads the man from her mother's past to her car.

She's nervous. She wants to jump right in and say, *Tell me everything. Tell me about my mom.* But she needs to get Brett out to the house on Smith's Point. They can sit on the back deck. Willa has the fixings for BLTs.

Her car bounces up the cobblestones and Willa slips into tour-guide mode. She points out the most impressive homes as they approach the top of Main Street. "These are the Three Bricks," she says, pointing to the trio of nearly identical mansions on the right. "Built by whaling merchant Joseph Starbuck for his three sons. Starbuck famously told his two daughters that their husbands would provide for them...which they did." Willa points next to the white mansions on the left, evocative of Greek temples, one with Ionic columns, one with Corinthian. "The sisters and their *very* successful husbands moved in across the street. All five homes were a shock, and an affront, to the Nantucket Quaker community. Starbuck built the mansions to keep up with Jared Coffin, who was building a grand red-brick home on Broad Street, and the husbands, Hadwen and Barney, built the Greek revivals to keep up with their father-in-law." Brett nods along, but Willa can see she has gone too deep into history mode.

Brett says, "So when did your mom move here?"

"After college," Willa says. "She came to visit her roommate's family and she liked it so much, she stayed."

"So that was...in '91?"

"Around then, I think."

"And she ended up graduating from Duke? She stayed all four years?"

"Yes."

Brett laughs. "I didn't even know what Duke was until your mom applied there. We were from small-town Ohio."

"My mom never talked about high school or growing up or her parents or Ohio."

Brett leans his head back against the seat. "Well," he says. "No surprise there."

Willa gives Brett the rundown on their family as they wind their way along the twenty-seven curves of the Madaket Road. Vivi married JP Quinboro, who was a summer resident. Then they decided to stay year-round. Willa's paternal grandmother, Lucinda Quinboro, is still a summer resident.

"She lives in a big house that fronts the harbor," Willa says. "You passed it on the ferry."

"So your grandmother is rich," Brett says. "Is your dad rich?"

His use of the word *rich* throws Willa off. Does anyone use that term anymore? "My grandmother's property is worth a lot," Willa says, though Lucinda is the kind of person who despises ostentation and never carries one red cent on her person. Does she even have a credit card? Willa has never actually seen her grandmother pay for anything; she just signs for things—she has an account at the dry cleaner's and at the Field and Oar Club and at the farm and at the bookstore. "My father..." Willa wants to be careful when discussing the family finances, obviously. It has occurred to Willa that maybe Brett's interest in Vivi's life on

Nantucket is financial rather than nostalgic—nostalgia doesn't pay the bills—though Willa dearly hopes not. She has told herself that if any woman is worth driving through seven states for, it's Vivi.

*Was* Vivi.

Brett says, "It's none of my business. I'm sorry I asked. Vivi never cared about money when I knew her."

Willa feels the tension in her neck ease a little, but now she urgently has to use the bathroom.

Brett whistles as they cross the bridge over Madaket Harbor. "Pretty out here."

"I should probably warn you that my house is extremely small," Willa says.

"My apartment in Knoxville is small," Brett says. "Only four hundred and fifty square feet, but it's just me. It does have a view of the river, though, so I can't complain."

Willa is now uncomfortable because Wee Bit is only her summer house.

When they pull up to the split-rail fence and Brett sees Wee Bit, he laughs. "That *is* small! I think that's one of the smallest houses I've ever seen."

"We have a deck out back with a view of the ocean," Willa says. "Why don't you go around the side? I just have to use the bathroom."

When Willa comes out onto the deck, Brett is gazing over the dunes at the water.

"I like thinking your mom ended up somewhere so beautiful," he says. "Your mom was special."

"Tell me about when you knew her."

Brett is a good storyteller, maybe as good as Vivi. He tells Willa that he and Vivi met while he was in detention and she was making up a quiz in calculus.

"She was a very smart kid and I was a very bad kid," Brett says.

"I used to smoke in the bathrooms and in the breezeway; I was into my music. I played in this band called Escape from Ohio."

Willa barks out a laugh.

"I knew who your mom was. She wasn't popular but she was very, very pretty and our freshman year, my locker was right across the hall from hers so I'd see your mom every day. She had long hair like yours and she'd braid it or put it in a ponytail or she'd wear it in a headband. I checked every day to see how your mom fixed her hair. Then I sort of forgot about her for a couple of years until she turned up in my detention. And I thought, *This is my chance and I'm not going to blow it.* So I asked if I could give her a ride home."

"What did she say?"

"She said okay. Honestly, Willa, that surprised the hell out of me because socially, there was a very wide gulf between your mom and me. She was a goody-goody, a nerd, like you said on the phone, and I was a druggie. All I ever did was smoke cigarettes—and weed if it was offered to me. But you know what your mom and I did? We built a bridge. I started paying more attention to school. I played guitar in the pit orchestra for the high-school musical, and your mom loosened up a little, she bought some cute jeans and a pair of Chucks. She got the top of her ear pierced, and she came to my band practices in my buddy Wayne's garage."

"Did you know her parents? My grandparents?" Grandparents are something of a mystery to Willa. She has only ever had one: Lucinda. Lucinda is fine, though she has her own busy life both here on Nantucket and back in Manhattan, and she has never really paid attention to her grandchildren except as something to present to her friends at the Field and Oar Club. Willa longs for a kindly, white-haired grandfather who smokes a pipe and pulls nickels out of his ears.

"I knew Nancy a little," Brett says, shaking his head. "Tough woman. And I met Frank once before he died."

"You did? You met my grandfather?" Of Willa's three dead grandparents, the one she's most curious about is Vivi's father, Frank Howe. The one who killed himself.

"He and Vivi had a standing breakfast date. Every Saturday, they went to the Perkins in Middleburg Heights. They never missed a week. So when Vivi and I started dating, I asked if I could join them. At first Vivi said no, it was their thing. Then she changed her mind and decided she wanted me to meet her dad without her mom around. I hadn't met Nancy yet at that point. I used to pick your mom up and drop her off at the corner down from her house. It was pretty clear she hadn't told her parents we were dating, but that didn't bother me, I knew she was out of my league. I was just happy she liked me back."

"So you went to breakfast?"

"Yep, I can remember it like it was yesterday. Your mom and grandpa always sat in the same booth and had the same waitress, and they'd order everything on the menu: French toast and omelets and sides of bacon and sausage. I remember I had the chocolate chip pancakes with a side of hash browns. Her dad asked me about my music. He sang in a barbershop quartet."

"He did?"

"I never heard him sing. I was just happy he didn't think my music was a waste of time."

"Did he seem sad?" Willa asks. "Troubled?"

"No," Brett says. "He seemed like a regular hardworking guy who loved his daughter. When Vivi went to the restroom, I remember he said, 'Always be good to her.' And I said, 'Yeah, of course.' I didn't find it strange at the time; it just sounded like a dad-thing to say, like he wanted to be sure I wouldn't leave Vivi at the football game to go out with my friends or pressure her into having sex. But then, a few months later when he killed himself, I thought about him saying that."

Willa feels herself growing misty. "I'm starving. Do you mind if I make us some lunch?"

Brett laughs; he wipes at the corners of his eyes. "I'd love it, thanks."

Over the BLTs and potato chips and peaches that are so juicy they drip and make an embarrassing mess, Brett talks about the stuff he and Vivi did in high school. They walked around the Parmatown Mall, they went bowling at Maple Lanes, they went to teen night at the Mining Company, they went to football games and then to Antonio's for pizza. Vivi used to study on a brown sofa in Wayne Curtis's garage while Brett practiced with his band. They did a fair amount of "driving around"—to the canal of the Cuyahoga River and along State Hill Road. They used to go to Sheetz to get Cheetos and hand pies and bottles of root beer. When the weather got warmer in the spring, they drove to Lake Erie and sat on the beach at Edgewater Park.

Willa feels like he's building toward something. By now, they've finished their lunch and Willa has cleared their plates and gone to the bathroom twice. It's twelve thirty and suddenly sand seems to be slipping through the hourglass faster than Willa wants it to. They have to leave for the ferry dock in an hour.

Why had she not insisted Brett spend the night? He hasn't even set foot on the beach yet, although in jeans and Chucks, he isn't dressed for it.

"I brought you pictures," Brett says, reaching for his backpack. "I had copies made so you can keep these." He pulls a packet of photographs out and flips through them for Willa.

Vivi in a pink Fair Isle sweater and a forest-green down vest sitting in the bleachers at a high-school football game next to Brett, who's wearing jeans and a jean jacket and flipping off the guy behind the camera.

"This was early in our relationship," Brett says. "Your mom still has her headband. But then..." He flips to the next picture, where Vivi is wearing tight jeans, a pair of Chucks, and an REO

Speedwagon T-shirt. Her eyes are rimmed with black eyeliner and she's wearing a black lace choker. Brett is still in his jeans jacket. They're on a bench at a mall; there's an Orange Julius cup resting between them.

"Then the Christmas formal," Brett says. The picture is the two of them posing together in front of a silk-screened winter wonderland. Vivi is wearing a black dress with thin straps, and Brett is in a gray pin-striped suit with a purple shirt and purple tie. His hair has been shaved at the sides to leave an impressive mullet.

What strikes Willa about her mother in all three pictures is how young she is, and how unknowable. This is Vivi before she was married, before she had kids, before she set foot on Nantucket or maybe even knew what Nantucket was. This Vivian Howe is real; it's her mother, but she's a stranger.

"Then the end of the school year came and we were graduating. Your mom had gotten into Duke with a scholarship. I didn't have any firm plans but my band was starting to get some paying gigs. We were hired to play a bar mitzvah at the Holiday Inn in Independence." He stops, nods. "That's when everything happened."

"What?" Willa says. "What happened?" What, she wonders, could possibly happen at a bar mitzvah at a Holiday Inn in Independence, Ohio?

"One of the guests at the bar mitzvah, the kid's uncle, liked our sound. Turns out the uncle was John Zubow, vice president of Century Records in Los Angeles."

"No way!" Willa says. "So you were discovered?"

"John asked if we had any original material. We had two songs. One was called 'Parmatown Blues,' written by our drummer, Roy. The other was 'Golden Girl,' which was a song I wrote for your mom after her father died. When Frank killed himself, she was...devastated." Brett bows his head. "I guess you know exactly how she felt. That profound loss. The sense that nothing is ever going to be right again."

"I do," Willa whispers.

"I wanted to make her feel better. I would hold her while she cried and I supported her when she fought with her mom, but that wasn't enough. So I asked myself, *What do I know how to do?* All I knew was music. And I wrote Vivi this song."

"Gah!" Willa says. She can't believe this!

Brett lifts his guitar out of its case. Willa knows nothing about guitars but she can tell this one is special. It's dark wood with a mother-of-pearl pick guard, and the strap that goes over Brett's head is embroidered. When he strums the first chord, Willa gets chills. She's a person who has spent her entire life planning for some imaginary point in the future when she would achieve...perfect happiness. There's a way in which Vivi's death has freed her from this quest. Nothing will ever be perfect again because Vivi won't be there to share it with her. Even if Willa lives to be a hundred and is surrounded by children and grandchildren and great-grand-children, she will still miss her mother. So all she can hope for are unexpected moments of grace. Like now. Willa has met Vivi's high-school boyfriend. She has seen pictures of her mother wearing liquid eyeliner and jeans that fit her like the skin on a grape.

Brett will now sing the song he wrote for Vivi.

"When we started going out, our song was 'Stone in Love,' by Journey," Brett says. He pauses. "Have you ever heard of Journey?"

Willa takes a stab at it. "'Don't Stop Believin''?"

"Yes. 'Stone in Love' is another song of theirs. We used to listen to it in the cassette deck of my Skylark, and Vivi would rewind it over and over again and we'd turn the stereo up and put the windows down and belt out the lyrics. That song came to define high school for me." He strums another chord. "Do you have a song like that?"

"'Castle on the Hill,'" Willa says. "By Ed Sheeran." She feels like Brett might find Ed Sheeran silly, but his face lights up.

"Right, exactly, that's another song about being a teenager in love, so it makes sense that it would appeal to teenagers in love."

Yes; it's one of Willa and Rip's songs. They danced to it at their wedding.

"To be honest, Vivi and I were never exactly sure what 'stone in love' even meant. We thought it meant the purest, best kind of love a person could experience, and that's your first love."

Willa nods emphatically. She agrees. Rip, her one and only!

"There's a line at the end of the song that goes 'Golden girl, I'll keep you forever.' And that was the jumping-off point for my own song. Vivi was my golden girl. She was the one I would hold above all others." He looks at Willa. "To this day, that's true."

"Will you play it?" Willa whispers.

Brett slaps the front of the guitar for rhythm, then launches into the song. It's immediately catchy, a little bluesy, a little folksy, but with a rock beat. Brett's voice is…sexy. This isn't a word Willa wants to use, but it's true. His voice has strength, tenderness, and a little bit of a rough edge. *You're my sunshine and my light, my treasure, my prize; you're the fire in my eyes…my golden girl, my girl so bold, your path I'll clear, your heart I'll hold.*

Willa can't believe how good the song is. It's every bit as good as Ed Sheeran. As soon as Brett finishes, Willa claps like crazy and says, "Play it again, please? I want to take a video of you singing so I have it."

She thinks he might balk at the idea of being taped, but instead he smiles and sits up straighter. The sun is on his face, and the dunes and a thin blue ribbon of the ocean beckon beyond him. The song is even better the second time. Willa's heart aches with the lyrics, and although she has never been to Ohio, she is suddenly there as her mother would have been, way back in the 1980s, her feet on the dashboard of Brett's car, which thrums with the bass line of the stereo, wind rushing in through the windows, bringing the smell of fresh-cut grass, her heart filled with passion, restlessness. But if love doesn't get any sweeter than this, then what is Vivi looking for?

Willa is envious that someone loved Vivi enough to write this song for her. And confounded that her mother never mentioned it. To anyone.

When Brett finishes, Willa says, "I can't believe you're not famous."

"Well," he says. "That's the rest of the story."

The rest of the story. His tone of voice—and the fact that he's now managing a Holiday Inn in Knoxville, Tennessee—means the story doesn't end the way it should.

"You read your mom's book?" Brett says.

Willa nods reluctantly. She started *Golden Girl* right after their phone conversation but she's only on chapter three. She's so tired at night that she sometimes falls asleep before she can make it through even one page.

"My band flew to LA to meet with executives at Century Records."

"Did they not like the song?"

"They didn't like 'Parmatown Blues'; they said it was too regional. And it was. But they liked 'Golden Girl.' They let us make a demo in their studio and then they talked about us staying in LA permanently. We could write some more songs, play some bigger venues, try to get some exposure while we worked on an album." Brett stops. "Then your mom called to say she was pregnant."

"What?" Willa says. She's up on her feet, and instantly, she has to pee. "Wait, I'll be right back. Two seconds."

Willa races to the bathroom, thinking, *I have a sibling!* Willa has heard some crazy stories from Facebook friends about the surprises they've found in their genealogy studies, and honestly, Willa thought these stories strained credulity. But now! Willa has an older brother or sister, and *that* is why Brett Caspian drove through seven states to get here.

But as Willa washes her hands at the sink, she studies herself in the mirror and thinks, *No, that's not what he's going to tell me. He's going to tell me something else.*

She curses herself for not getting farther along in the book.

When Willa retakes her place at the table, Brett looks extremely uncomfortable. "I gather Vivi never told you she got pregnant in high school?"

"No," Willa says.

"Well," Brett says. He seems hesitant to continue. "She called me in California to tell me she was pregnant, and I flew home."

Willa feels the BLT shifting in her stomach. What is he going to say next?

"The second half of that summer was a confusing time," Brett says. "I can see that more clearly now, from a distance. We were just kids. We weren't sure what to do. One minute, Vivi would say she wanted to keep the baby, the next minute she said she thought we were too young to be parents. She didn't know what to do about Duke. We wanted to have the baby and stay together, but we also wanted to have a future."

"Did my mom have an abortion?" Willa says.

"We never had to make that decision," Brett says. "She showed up at my house early one morning to tell me she'd miscarried."

Willa is speechless. Her mother lied to her! Lied right to her face! "She had a miscarriage? She lost the baby?"

"Yes," Brett says. "I was pretty upset, but your mom was relieved, I think. It saved us from having to make a decision, anyway."

"So then what happened?"

"Then...I flew back to California. Vivi ended up going to Duke, and that was the last I saw of her."

"What about your music?"

"It never took off," Brett says. "I was only gone a couple weeks but by the time I got back, John Zubow was working on another project. My bandmates, Wayne and Roy, blamed me for leaving, but the truth was, we had no money and they missed Parma and wanted to go home. I pushed to have 'Golden Girl' released as a single, but Zubow wasn't a one-hit-wonder kind of guy. He wanted to put his money behind a band that would have longevity. He was looking for the next Aerosmith."

Willa says, "The song is so good. And it just died on the vine? No one ever heard it?"

"Zubow wanted to sell it to someone else to record. John Hiatt was interested. But I didn't want to sell the song. I didn't want to hear John Hiatt or John Fogerty sing a song I'd written for Vivi." Brett laughs. "In addition to managing the Holiday Inn, I play guitar on Friday nights in the bar there during happy hour. It gets pretty rowdy on football weekends with all the Vols fans. I play cover songs mostly, but I always slip in 'Golden Girl,' and some folks think they've heard it before and are shocked when I tell them I wrote it. I made CDs of it that I sell out of a box for three bucks apiece. I've sold six hundred and twenty-four copies to date. I tell myself one of these days, it's going to get into the right hands."

"Do you resent my mother for ruining your big chance?" Willa says.

"Aw, gosh, I didn't back then. I figured she didn't get pregnant by herself," Brett says. "And now? Listen, I've always believed things work out the way they're supposed to. If I was meant to be a big rock star, someone else would have discovered me along the way. Tennessee is filled with music people, even Knoxville." He shakes his head. "Please don't feel sorry for me, if that's what you're doing. I have a good life, Willa, and very few regrets." He puts his guitar away like he's tucking a child into bed. "I do wish I'd gotten to see your mom again." He smiles at Willa. "But meeting you has been a sweet surprise."

They drive back to town in silence. If Willa were her normal self, she would be bright and clever, asking about life in Knoxville or some other safe topic. But she's completely preoccupied with the news that Vivi got pregnant as a teenager and then miscarried.

Brett seems to notice something is wrong. He says, "Are you okay? Did I throw your world into a tailspin by showing up?"

"That's not it," Willa says. "It's just that...I've miscarried three times."

"Oh, hey, Willa, I'm so sorry."

"I'm pregnant now." Willa presses her lips together. Did she just say that out loud? Did she tell Brett Caspian, a man she's known for four hours, that she's pregnant before telling her own family?

"Congratulations," Brett says cautiously. "How far along?"

"Eleven weeks," Willa says. "So I'm still not out of the woods. I've been as far along as fifteen weeks and then..."

"Oh, Willa."

"When I miscarried the first time, I asked my mother if she'd ever been through it," Willa says. "And she told me no."

"Ah," Brett says.

"I was looking for commiseration, of course," Willa says. "But I was also looking for a *reason*. Was there a family history of spontaneous miscarriages? My mother lied. She told me no. When the answer was yes." They've arrived at the ferry. Willa parks in the lot; there's still a little time before Brett has to go.

"Well," Brett says. He sighs and Willa feels bad for plopping him right in the middle of their family drama just as he's about to leave. "One of the things that crossed my mind when I read your mom's book..."

Willa winces.

"You didn't read the book, did you?" Brett says.

"I'm only on page thirty-eight," Willa admits.

Brett inhales. "Well, in the book, the situation is the same as it was with your mom and me." He laughs. "It's definitely me, I'm Stott Macklemore to a T. But anyway, in the book, the girl, Alison, calls Stott out in California to say she's pregnant—and she's lying. She's...faking it because she's afraid she's going to lose Stott to the rock-and-roll life. So he flies home from California, and a week or two later, she tells him she's miscarried."

Willa gasps. "So you think my mom was...faking it? She wasn't pregnant at all? She didn't miscarry? She lied to you?"

Brett moves his palms like he's weighing something on a scale. "I'm not sure what to think. Looking back, I think she *could have* lied about being pregnant. She was still emotionally raw from losing her dad, and then suddenly I was off starting a new life without her, and she was lonely and sad and...desperate, just like Alison in the book." Brett looks out the window and shakes his head. "And just like Alison, as soon as I flew home, she lost interest—and off to college she went, without ever looking back."

Willa is gutted by this. "I don't think my mom would do that. She was a good person. And also a really strong person, self-aware, self-confident."

"I'm sure she was as a grown-up," Brett says. "But when she was seventeen, she was battling some pretty serious demons. The way she described Alison in the book sounded exactly like the Vivi I knew."

"She probably had Alison lie about the pregnancy because that made for a better story," Willa says. "She liked a lot of drama in her fiction."

Brett sighs. "The only person who knows the truth is your mom, and sadly, she's not here to tell us." He opens the car door and leans over to kiss Willa on the cheek. "Your mom was a human being, Willa, just like the rest of us." With that, Brett gets out of the car, shuts the door, and waves through the open window. "Thank you for today. Let's stay in touch."

"Okay," Willa says. She wants to assure him that her mother didn't lie to him and didn't sabotage his big chance because she was lonely and insecure back in Ohio—but then Willa realizes that what Brett said is true: The only person who knows the truth is Vivi. What if Vivi *did* lie about the pregnancy? That could be a reason why she never breathed a word to anyone about Brett Caspian or their romance or the song. She might have been too ashamed. And this would also explain why Vivi told Willa she had never miscarried—because she *hadn't.*

*Mom!* Willa thinks. *What did you do?*

Willa feels like she needs to apologize to Brett, make amends in some way.

When she gets back to Wee Bit, she forwards the video of Brett singing "Golden Girl" to her mother's publicist, Flor; maybe Flor knows someone in the music business, maybe this can be the first step toward getting Brett an agent.

Then Willa watches the video again herself. Three more times.

# Vivi

*The only person who knows the truth is your mom, and sadly, she's not here to tell us.*

*I'm here!* Vivi thinks. *Up here!*

*Your mom was a human being...just like the rest of us.*

*Brett!* Vivi thinks. She's not sure she deserves his kindness.

That night, while everyone sleeps, Vivi can't help herself. She goes back to the summer of 1987.

Brett tells Vivi that his band, Escape from Ohio, has an actual paying gig, a bar mitzvah at the Holiday Inn in Independence.

"Six hundred bucks!" he says. "Two hundred apiece! For one night of work!"

"Can I come watch?" Vivi asks.

Brett looks uncomfortable. "You'd better not," he says. "It's a private function, they're probably getting charged by the head..."

"I'm not going to *eat* anything!" Vivi says. "I just want to hear you."

"I'll meet you after," he says. "We'll drive to the lake, how about that?"

Vivi agrees, even though she feels shut out. She spends the hours when Brett is playing the bar mitzvah going through her drawers and closet. She leaves for Duke in six weeks. She and Brett haven't talked about what will happen after Vivi leaves because it's a topic that upsets them both. Vivi has been thinking of not going to Duke at all; she has been thinking of going to Denison, where she was offered a free ride as well. It's a good school and it's only two hours away. Brett could come every weekend. If she were assigned a single, he might be able to live in her dorm.

Brett is an hour late picking Vivi up after the gig, but instead of apologizing, he's bursting with news. There was a guest at the bar mitzvah, the kid's uncle, John Zubow, who's a bigwig at Century Records and who likes their sound! He wants them to come to LA!

Vivi holds Brett's hands and jumps up and down. She can feel her heart shattering into jagged pieces.

John Zubow buys Brett, Wayne, and Roy plane tickets to LA. Vivi and Brett's summer together is being shortened by six weeks. Brett is leaving Ohio, and Vivi is staying behind. It was supposed to be the other way around.

Vivi drives Brett to the airport. She's in shock. This all happened so fast; she isn't ready, she doesn't want Brett to leave, and if she were very honest, she would admit that she doesn't want Brett to become a rock star. All Vivi can think of is Brett dripping with pretty girls the way that Zsa Zsa Gabor drips with diamonds. But she has to pretend to feel enthusiastic, optimistic.

"This is going to happen for you," she says. "The song is terrific."

"It's your song," Brett says.

"It's *your* song," Vivi says. She swallows against the sore, gumball-size lump in her throat. "Do you think you'll be back before I leave?"

"I'm not sure," he says, stroking her hand with his thumb. Vivi has a memory of him stroking her hand the same way at her father's funeral. "I hope so."

Vivi knows he's lying—he hopes for the opposite. He hopes the band is a success and that they can start a life in Los Angeles.

"Maybe I should forget Duke," she says, "and go to college in LA instead."

"Vivi, no. You have a future."

She starts to cry. "I don't care about my future. I want to be with you."

Very softly, Brett starts singing the song, and Vivi cries so hard that she has to pull over on 480 and let Brett take the wheel. Vivi chastises herself for falling so deeply in love. What if she had said *No, thank you,* when Brett asked if she wanted a ride home after his detention? What if she'd said, *I'll take the sports bus?* What if she had stayed focused on her schoolwork? She might have heard that the band Escape from Ohio had been discovered by a record company and she would have thought, *Oh, that's cool,* but she wouldn't be left empty and aching.

Outside the departures terminal, Vivi and Brett kiss long and deep, and Vivi says, "You're going to be great. I love you."

Brett grins. Excitement is dancing all over his face. "I love you too."

"Call me," she says. "When you can."

He pulls his duffel bag and his guitar out of the back seat. Wayne and Roy are waiting for him by the entrance. "Let's go, Caspian!" Roy calls out.

Brett gives Vivi one more kiss but he misses her mouth. He's already gone, she thinks. She watches as he hops the curb and strides over to Wayne and Roy. He disappears into the terminal without even turning around to wave. The automatic doors close behind him and Vivi thinks, *I need to find a way to get him back.*

She can't keep food down. She can't sleep. Her mother extends a rare offer of sympathy. "I'm sure it's difficult, letting him go. But you know what they say, if it's meant to be, he'll come back to you."

Vivi types out this saying, cribbed from Kahlil Gibran, and tapes it to her bathroom mirror, but reading it doesn't help.

The Parma Tavern, where Vivi is waiting tables that summer, has a beer-sticky floor and smells like buffalo wings. It's subject to erratic strobe lighting cast by the pinball machines. The soundtrack is Van Halen, Howard Jones, Run-DMC. After Brett leaves, Vivi goes on autopilot. She takes orders without listening. She has to remind herself to smile—her tips depend on a smile—and she tries to flirt with the men who come in after their company softball game, but it all feels fake and dirty.

A week passes with no word from Brett. Vivi knows he's at a hotel; she realizes he can't call her long distance from the room. She checks the mailbox. Has he written like he said he would? How long would it take a letter to get from California to Parma?

She loses three pounds. Her mother says she's "skin and bones" and actually brings home treats—bratwursts, pierogis, a box of Jack Frost doughnuts. Vivi doesn't want any of it.

On July 20, Peter Wolf of the J. Geils Band is playing at the Blossom, and Vivi and Brett had gotten tickets. Brett left them with Vivi, telling her she should take someone else, but who else would Vivi go with? She gives the tickets to a girl at work named

Tami. Tami says, "Are you sure?" When Vivi nods, Tami gives her a one-armed neck hug. This is the only person to touch Vivi since Brett left.

A postcard comes in the mail the next day. On the front is a picture of the Hollywood sign. The back says: *We're staying at the Marriott in Burbank, room 331. Call if you can. We are recording a demo of "GG."* I miss you! Love, Brett

*I miss you! Love, Brett.* Vivi reads this fourteen times, willing it to say, *I love you.* Why didn't he write *I love you?*

She has the phone number now. She can call him.

That night at the Parma Tavern, one beautiful couple stands out—they're young and fresh and look as though they've been clipped out of a magazine. They're wearing the same shade of light blue. They take an interest in Vivi, ask how long she's lived in Parma. She says, "My whole life," but adds that she's leaving for college at the end of August.

The woman, who is blond and wearing a seersucker sundress with a matching headband, asks where Vivi is going to school.

"Duke University," she says.

The man, in a light blue polo, says Vivi must be smart. Duke is a great school!

The woman orders the cabbage and noodles. "I've had the strangest cravings since I got pregnant," she says.

Vivi blinks. "You're *pregnant?*" The woman is slim; Vivi never would have known.

"Just twelve weeks," she says. "My morning sickness was really bad, and then as soon as I could keep food down, all I wanted were the weirdest combinations."

"Like cabbage and noodles!" the man says.

When Vivi gets home from work, she calls the hotel room in Burbank. There's no answer. It's nine thirty in Parma, six thirty on the West Coast. Brett must be at dinner. Vivi wonders if he and

Wayne and Roy eat at McDonald's every night or if John Zubow has been taking them to Spago and the Ivy and other restaurants that you read about in magazines. Vivi calls again two hours later, after her mother has gone to bed. She tiptoes down to the kitchen and whispers when she asks the front-desk clerk for room 331.

There's no answer in the room.

It's only eight thirty in LA, she reasons. Lots of times this summer, Brett would pick Vivi *up* at eight thirty.

She goes back to bed and dreams of the woman in the blue sundress with the matching headband. That couple will have a little boy; she can feel it.

Vivi wakes up again at a quarter to four. It's a quarter to one in LA. Brett will definitely be home. Vivi slips back downstairs to use the phone.

The desk clerk connects her to room 331. There's no answer.

He's not home at a quarter to one. He's out...partying? Vivi thinks about what she knows of Los Angeles: Hollywood, Beverly Hills, Mulholland Drive, Malibu. He's at a party with record-company people, which means models with teased hair and sparkly purple eyeshadow wearing tight leather skirts and high heels. Vivi has watched thousands of hours of MTV; she knows about life backstage.

She sits in the dark kitchen and realizes why Brett didn't say he loved her on the postcard. He's outgrown her; he's moving on.

She calls the hotel again. No answer. Her mother is going to hyperventilate when she gets the phone bill. Every time someone answers in California, there will be a separate charge.

Things were better when Vivi didn't have Brett's number because then she didn't know for sure that he wasn't home at one in the morning.

She falls asleep at the kitchen table and wakes up with the pearly-pink light of dawn and the neighbor's dog barking. It's twenty past five, two twenty in California. Vivi looks at the phone.

*Don't call,* she thinks. It's better not to know. She should wait until right before she leaves for work at eleven thirty. She might wake Brett up but at least he'll be home. If she calls now and he's not home, her world will collapse. She's delirious from lack of sleep as it is.

*Don't call,* she tells herself. Maybe she should wait until tomorrow, or the day after tomorrow. He can wonder what *she's* up to.

Yes, this is what Vivi should do. Wait.

But...she's consumed with love and rage and panic. She feels like Brett has dropped down into a hole. What if something *happened* to him? What if he's in the hospital or in jail?

Her father has been dead for exactly six months but Vivi can't mention this to her mother. Vivi doesn't ask if there will be a Mass said in her father's name. She knows the answer is no—because killing yourself is a sin. Vivi has lost her father's love; it vanished when he died. Brett tried to make up for that loss. He tried to love Vivi enough for two people. She *can't* lose him.

She picks up the phone and dials; she has the number memorized by now.

Two rings in, Brett answers. "Hello?"

Vivi is so overcome by hearing his voice that she starts to cry.

"Vivi?" he says. "Vivi, is that you? Why are you crying?"

"I'm pregnant," she says.

Brett flies home at the end of the week, and on Saturday night, they're in the back seat of his Buick Skylark, making love. Vivi is simultaneously ecstatic and devastated. She has told a...monstrous lie, and now she has to deal with the consequences.

Brett wants to keep the baby. His parents had him when they were just out of high school and they're still together, still happy.

*Still in Parma,* Vivi thinks. *In a bowling league with Mr. Emery, the calculus teacher.* Somehow the idea of staying in Parma, which she gladly would have accepted as her fate when she was dropping Brett off at the airport, has lost its luster.

"What about your big chance?" Vivi says. "The record deal?"

"It's not a sure thing, Viv." Brett has told Vivi what his time in LA was like. They recorded the song, they played for the owners of some clubs, they were told the next step was to write enough songs for an album. But, Brett says, the songs weren't flowing. He squeezed her and said, "My inspiration was missing."

Vivi says she doesn't know what she wants to do about the baby. She needs time to think.

Vivi is caught in a vipers' nest of lies. She pretends to feel sick; she pretends to feel dizzy. She rests her hand on her belly and agrees when Brett says they should call the baby "Bubby" for now.

They have sex often, without protection. Vivi can't exactly ask Brett to wear a condom or even pull out when she's already "pregnant." The result, she's sure, is that she will end up pregnant, which is the most devastating karma she can imagine.

She'll pretend to lose the baby. She goes to Kmart in search of fake blood, but the salesclerk says they don't put out the Hallow-een merchandise until after Labor Day. Vivi decides she'll do it without fake blood. She has a sense that Brett—and maybe men in general—don't understand how a woman's body works.

She waits another week because she likes the way things are between them. Brett is extra-loving, gentle, solicitous. She has become his queen; she's the mother of his unborn child.

During that week, two things happen. The first is that Wayne and Roy call and ask Brett when he's coming back to LA.

"What did you tell them?" Vivi asks. She has tried to ignore that she is messing with more than just Brett's fate. Wayne and Roy have been left to twist in the wind.

Brett grins. "I told them I was looking at rings."

These words don't produce the kind of elation Vivi would have predicted.

The second thing that happens is a packet from Duke arrives in the mail. Inside is Vivi's class schedule, a timeline for freshman orientation, and her dorm assignment: Craven Quad on West Campus. Her move-in date is August 31. Suddenly, Vivi can see the future like a bright doorway in front of her. All she has to do is step through. But first, she has to fix things. She can't *believe* how impetuous, how shortsighted, and, most of all, how *selfish* it was to lie. Her mother brought a self-help book home from the Cuyahoga Library called *When Good People Do Bad Things*. Vivi knows her mother is still struggling with her father's suicide, but the title of the book speaks to Vivi. *She* is the good person who has done a bad thing. It's *her*.

The next morning at seven thirty, Vivi heads over to Brett's house because she knows that Brett's parents leave for work at a quarter to seven. She also knows Brett is asleep, so she sneaks inside the house, creeps up the stairs, climbs into bed with him, and presses her face between his shoulder blades. He's so warm and he smells like himself. Vivi loves him in a way she knows she'll never love anyone else.

"Brett," she whispers.

He startles awake and flips over, and when he understands that it's her, he gathers her up in his arms. "What are you doing here, Viv? Did my parents leave for work?"

"Yes," she says, and she starts to cry. "I lost the baby."

"What?" Brett says. He sits up and clutches his head. "What? No! No, Vivi, no!" His torso starts to shake; it's awful to witness. He is *really* upset, as upset as she's ever seen him, all because she was insecure and foolish and cruel. This makes Vivi cry harder. Her guilt is so overwhelming that she almost comes clean. But no, that will make things worse.

She says, "I'm sorry, Brett. I feel like I failed. I feel like this is all my fault."

He asks if she's sure the baby is gone; he thinks they should see a doctor. She says yes, she's sure. She also says she can't afford a doctor, and she can't see a doctor using her family's insurance. He asks if she should take a pregnancy test. With a deep sigh, she says yes.

They head out into the summer morning and buy a pregnancy test at a pharmacy in Middleburg Heights, not Parma, so they won't see anyone they know. The pharmacy is near the Perkins, and Brett asks Vivi if she wants to go for breakfast.

Vivi is starving but she can't bear to enter that Perkins or any other—she hasn't been inside one since her father died—and she doesn't want to risk seeing Cindy. She thinks about how disappointed her father and Cindy would be if they knew what she'd done. She was such a good kid, ordering French toast and hash browns and crispy bacon, drinking coffee, reading the movie reviews in the *Plain Dealer,* then checking her horoscope.

She remembers the hope with which she used to unfurl those tiny, tight scrolls and read what was in store for her as a Capricorn. Nothing in them ever led her to believe that she would create a tumultuous situation like this one.

"I just want to go home," Vivi says. "Your home."

Back at Brett's, Vivi takes the test—negative.

Brett and Vivi climb back into Brett's bed for a nap. Brett kisses the top of Vivi's head and says, "We can still get married."

The next few days are tense. Vivi wants Brett to fly back to LA—she even offers to pay for his ticket out of what she's saved waiting tables—but Brett says he doesn't want to leave until she's "one hundred percent recovered." She assures him she's recovered.

"You need to go *back*," Vivi says. "Wayne and Roy are waiting for you."

"Come with me," he says. "You're my muse." He runs his hands over her face like he's trying to read Braille. "I can't write songs without you. I tried and I can't, Vivi."

"But I have college," she says.

"You said you might want to go to college in LA. There's UCLA, USC."

She did say that—and at the time, she'd meant it. She can't believe how different she feels now; it's like she and Brett have switched places. "I'm going to Duke." She hugs him. "I'm sorry, I just think I should stick to my plan."

"Fine," he says. "I'll go back to LA, then. And we'll put off getting married." He speaks the words like a threat, but the thing is, Vivi is relieved.

The following week, she takes Brett to the airport. "You're going to do great," she says. "I love you."

Brett slouches toward the airport doors. He turns back to wave and then disappears inside.

This is the last time Vivi sees Brett Caspian. She calls him at the hotel the night before she leaves for Duke and breaks his heart.

"Martha?" Vivi whispers with her eyes closed. She's lying on the green velvet chaise, still in a dream state. She raises her voice a little. "Martha?"

There's a rustling. When Vivi opens her eyes, Martha is sitting on the white enamel bean-shaped coffee table, facing her. "Yes, Vivian, I'm here." Martha's scarf is wound around her wrist and forearm, looking like a cross between a cuff bracelet and a very chic bandage.

Vivi's eyes flutter closed again. The phrase *I'll sleep when I'm dead* drifts through her mind. "I want to use my second nudge," Vivi murmurs. "I need to let Brett know that I'm sorry."

"He knows you're sorry," Martha says. "It's all right there in your book."

249

"Will everything be okay, then?" Vivi says. "My secret won't come out?"

There's no answer. Vivi rouses herself and turns to see the tail end of Martha's muumuu disappearing through the green door.

"It had better be okay!" Vivi calls after her, wide awake now. "You made an executive decision!"

Brett could still tell people. Vivi is number two on the bestseller list; his revelation might be newsworthy, if only because his story so perfectly mirrors the plot of the book. The internet might blow up. Vivi's secret might come out and go viral. Aren't readers always looking for the story behind the story? And what if Willa tells Carson, Leo, Savannah, JP? What will they think? Will they think she was just a human being like the rest of them? Or will they think something worse?

When Vivi wrote the book, she knew there was a slim possibility that Brett would find out about it and an even slimmer chance that he would read it. A surprising thought crosses her mind: Maybe a teensy part of her, lurking in the dark chamber where she's been hiding this secret all of these years, *wanted* Brett to know the truth. Maybe she wanted to confess.

She stares up at the ceiling and runs her hand along the soft velvet of the chaise. She can't deny it—she feels lighter, nearly unburdened.


# Amy


JP takes Monday off so he and Amy can go to the beach together. Amy puts on the new black bikini she optimistically bought on

January 8, a week into her new year's diet, and studies herself from every angle. She has bulges of fat at her middle that are threatening to turn into actual rolls; she'll have to be careful how she sits. Her backside has filled out, but Amy thinks maybe the world likes this look now. (Sometimes at work, Lorna will grab Amy's ass and say, "Dummy thicc," which is apparently a compliment.) Amy puts on a diaphanous white cover-up and applies her expensive sunscreen and wishes she'd gotten a pedicure—she works at a salon!—but JP announced his intention to take a day off only the night before. It's a spontaneous decision to spend quality time with the woman he loves...but it might also be a chance for them to have the "talk" he mentioned, something Amy has been studiously avoiding.

The ring is no longer in the top drawer. JP either returned it...or moved it. It might be in his truck. Is she grasping at straws? Oh, hell, probably—but it stands to reason that any proposal JP had planned would have been pushed back by Vivi's death. It's not *impossible* that he's going to propose today.

JP is in charge of the food. Amy is hoping they can go to the Nickel for sandwiches but JP feels awkward about seeing Joe DeSantis because apparently Leo and Cruz aren't speaking. JP makes ham and Swiss with thin slices of ripe fig and a combination of mayo and Dijon on toasted sourdough that he got at Born and Bread. He packs a bag of dill-pickle-flavored potato chips (Amy's favorite, a nice touch), some cold grapes, and several bottles of water.

Amy notices there's no alcohol—no bottle of Whispering Angel rosé, no champagne, not even a beer. She nearly says something, but the picnic is JP's department and she won't interfere.

She's deluding herself about the proposal. Nobody proposes without champagne.

As Amy wanders into the mudroom for towels, her expectations pop like so many party balloons. The best-case scenario now is that she and JP will have a nice, quiet, relaxing day at the beach. She grabs their striped beach umbrella, two chairs, the book she's been reading since Christmas, and the book JP is reading, which is *Golden Girl*. Amy considers leaving it behind. Would it be too much to ask to have a beach day without bringing Vivi along?

Vivi is dead, Amy reminds herself. Her continued jealousy is childish and absurd. She tucks the novel into her bag.

When they're finally ensconced in the front seat of JP's pickup, she says, "So where are we going?"

"Fat Ladies," he says.

"It's just Ladies," Amy corrects him.

"It was always Fat Ladies when I was growing up."

"Well, it's no longer appropriate to use that name. It's body-shaming."

JP scoffs.

"It'll be crowded at Ladies," Amy says. "What about Great Point?"

"Too far," JP says, and Amy's last hope is quashed. Daytime proposals always take place at Great Point; evening proposals on Steps Beach as the sun sets. "But you're right. Ladies will be crowded. Let's go to Ram Pasture."

Amy doesn't have the heart to say no but she hates Ram Pasture because that's the beach where JP and Vivi went on their first date. JP has told Amy the story about how he met Vivi at the dry cleaner's, asked her out, and took her to the beach for the day, *which turned into a full-fledged summer romance, which led to us getting married.* JP told Amy this story during her first week of work at the Cork, and at the time, Amy thought it was cute and romantic. She also thought JP and Vivi were happily married, a notion that eroded like a sandcastle in the surf over the course of the summer.

Maybe JP doesn't associate that beach with Vivi any longer, but it's undeniable that certain places remind you of certain people. Subconsciously, JP must be thinking of Vivi.

Well, Amy and JP will just have to make their own memories at Ram Pasture—ones that are more powerful.

Amy cranks up the music—Pearl Jam, because it's a band they both like—puts her bare feet up on the dash, then takes them down because of the state of her toes. She reaches for JP's hand. This is going to be fun. Relaxing. A much-needed reconnection. It's a beautiful day with a scrubbed-clean sky, no humidity, a light breeze. The low vegetation and open land on the way out to Ram Pasture remind Amy of pictures she's seen of the African savanna—but then, on the horizon, a thin blue ribbon appears. To the left, she catches the first glimpse of Little Ram Pasture Pond, which is ringed with rugosa roses in full pink and white blossom. Amy spends so many long hours in the salon that she forgets the rest of the island is outside showing off like this.

"You were right," she says. "Paradise."

They set up chairs and their blanket, place the cooler in the shade of the umbrella. JP peels off his T-shirt and Amy studies him. They haven't had sex for weeks—not since a few days before Vivi was killed—and it looks like he's lost some of the weight that he put on when he first opened the Cone for the season (too much peach cobbler ice cream). Still, his body is nothing remarkable, although Amy doesn't care what he looks like. She loves *him*. She *loves* him. Has the magic worn off a little, has her infatuation settled into something less urgent? Yeah, sure. That's what happens. But there's still a surge there, an energy.

She puts a hand on his back and tries to turn him for a kiss but he goes charging into the water. He's an exuberant and fearless swimmer; it doesn't matter to him how big the waves are or how cold the water is. Over the years, Amy has conquered most of her fears, but the fact remains that she didn't grow up near an ocean. She went to the beach infrequently and when she did it was the decidedly calmer and warmer Gulf.

Beyond JP, she sees the dark, sleek head of a seal, and although there's a certain delight in seeing animals in their natural habitat, she knows that seals can mean sharks. She walks to the water's edge and lets the foamy waves nip her feet, but she's not going in.

She repairs back to their camp and decides to stretch out on the blanket rather than sit in a chair. Half-heartedly, she opens her book. It's been so long since she's looked at it that she should probably start at the beginning.

When JP comes back, he rubs a towel over his head and says, "Do you want to take a walk?"

"I just got settled."

"Oh," he says. "Okay." Instead of sitting in his chair, he plops next to her on the blanket. "Amy?"

She props herself up on her elbows and sucks in her stomach and tenses her thighs. "JP?"

He's silent for a second and Amy realizes that the moment she's been dreading is upon her. *We probably should have a talk at some point.*

"I know that things haven't been easy for you since Vivi died," he says.

Understatement.

"Don't worry about me," Amy says. "I'm worried about you. And the kids."

"I worry about the kids too," JP says. "I need to make them my focus."

"Of course," Amy says. She has kind of stalled where the kids are concerned. She hasn't seen any of them since Vivi died. "Maybe we should invite them over for dinner?" This sounds like a solid starting point, but dinner for their family is a pipe dream. JP works at the Cone every night until ten, Willa lives in married bliss with Rip, Leo is leaving for college in another month, and Carson also works at night, plus, sorry, she's not the family-dinner type.

"Amy," JP says. "I want to take a break. No, that's misleading. I want to break up. I want you to move out. I want us to go our separate ways."

The words hit Amy like pellets, and her jaw drops in increments until her mouth is hanging fully open. She knows she must look shocked. But she's *not* shocked. If she were very honest, she would admit that the second she let JP Quinboro kiss her in the wineshop after drinking two and a half bottles of Cristal, she knew this was one way it could end—with JP cutting the line, deciding that she wasn't a keeper.

"I'm sorry," JP says, but Amy can hear in his voice that he's not sorry, he's relieved. The death blow has been landed. The ten years that Amy has invested in this relationship has been dissolved with a few sentences. "You're a wonderful girl—"

"Stop," Amy says. "There will be no patronizing, please." Her voice is surprisingly clear and firm, a welcome change from the singsongy tone she typically uses with JP in an attempt to sound charming, cute, lighthearted. "Does this have anything to do with Vivi's death?"

"Kind of," JP says. "I've taken a self-inventory. I don't have the right feelings for you. You deserve to be loved and adored."

"And you don't love me? You don't adore me?"

"No."

There's no hedging, no gray area, no room for any interpretation except one, and for this, Amy is grateful. JP is sparing her from believing there's hope. And without hope, Amy is free to be honest.

"I should never have let you kiss me in the wineshop," she says. "I knew it was wrong, I knew you were just unhappy in your marriage and looking for validation from an attractive female."

"You were the answer to my prayers," JP says. "Every day that summer, I was happy. I looked forward to waking up and going to work. You were the sun."

"I was blinded by my feelings for you. You were older, you were sophisticated, so handsome, so...forbidden." That was part of the allure, Amy knows—JP belonged to someone else.

"I wanted it to work, Amy. I gave it my best shot. I think when you moved in..."

Yes, three years ago when Amy moved in with JP, things became stressful, and that stress eroded the romance. The kids were older; they had opinions and allegiances. But Amy had needed a place to live, and she and JP had been together nearly seven years—it made sense. But she should have maintained her independence. She should have rented, or even purchased, her own place.

"I was always jealous of Vivi," Amy says. "You were divorced, but the two of you were still codependent. Even after we'd been together for years, she was still the most important woman in your life. It was never me, it was always Vivi." She expects JP to refute this, but he says nothing. "You used to tease me about being jealous of her. You said it was absurd, that I was insecure. But I was only reacting to always coming in second." Now the anger surfaces. It feels like acid she wants to throw on him. "I shouldn't have believed a word you said. I should have left years ago. You stole the best years of my life."

"You're only thirty-three. There's still plenty of time for you to meet someone else and have a baby."

He's right. Now that Amy is free, she can meet someone and get pregnant, whereas with JP, that avenue was closed. He'd had a vasectomy after Leo was born.

"Do you remember the night you went to Savannah's for dinner?" she says. "I spied on you through the back window of her house."

"You did not." He holds her gaze. "You *did?* Wow, that's a new low for you, Aim. You do realize that Savannah and I are just friends—"

"You weren't friends before. You hated her before."

JP concedes this with a dip of his head. "Our relationship is complicated. Lots of history. I've known Savannah my whole life. Long before Vivi."

Amy has heard it all before. JP and Savannah grew up together at the Field and Oar Club, two children of extreme privilege with shared memories of this tennis match, that sailing race, their parents laughing and drinking gin and tonics together on the patio. "You looked pretty cozy."

"We were grieving."

"Well," Amy says. "When I left Union Street, I went to the Gaslight and bumped into Dennis."

"Ugh," JP says. "Poor you."

"He asked me to dance," Amy says. "We ended up making out in the front seat of his truck."

JP recoils. Is he bothered by this? Jealous? Amy never planned on telling JP about this indiscretion, though she's revisited the moment many times since it happened. Dennis had been sur-prisingly gentlemanly with Amy—respectful, kind, generous (he bought all her drinks)—and he'd also been insightful, funny, and honest. "Don't stay with JP," Dennis said. "He's not good enough for you. Even Vivi used to say that you deserved someone younger, with more energy."

And then, later in the night, while they were making out pretty heavily in his car, he whispered, "I've always thought you were so hot. I mean, *so* hot."

Amy had leaned into these words because what woman wouldn't relish hearing this? Amy had never found Dennis particularly attractive, although the size of the bulge in his jeans that night was intriguing. (She's not vengeful enough to mention this detail to JP.)

"You made out with Dennis," JP says, his voice flat. "Forget what I said earlier about a new low."

"We were grieving," Amy deadpans. She brushes sand off her shins. "We should probably go. I have to pack my stuff."

"You don't have to move out today," JP says.

"Oh, but I do," Amy says. She can already predict what Lorna will say: *Of course you can stay with me, Pigeon. Stay as long as you like.*

"It's such a pretty day," JP says.

"If you wanted to enjoy the beach, you should have strung me along until the end of the afternoon," Amy says. "After ten years, what's a few more hours?"

JP hangs his head, and in spite of herself, Amy feels sorry for him. He has worked every single day of the summer except for the day of his ex-wife's memorial, which ended with Dennis punching him in the face. "You stay," she says. "I'll take the truck home, pack up my things, come back in a few hours to get you, and you can drop me off at Lorna's."

He flops back on the blanket. "Thank you. I don't deserve that."

He *doesn't* deserve that. He deserves sand kicked in his face. He deserves to call an Uber to get home, and if he has no cell signal, too bad, he can walk. Amy puts on her cover-up and strides off the beach, thinking that although the pain is fresh and she's likely in some kind of emotional shock that will wear off and she will realize that her heart has been exposed bare, she will survive this. She will grow from it. Relationships end all the time, every single day. Amy isn't special.

She considers texting Dennis and telling him she's now a free woman, that JP has given her the boot, but she figures he'll find out soon enough through the Nantucket grapevine. Some people, no doubt, will say that Amy got what was coming to her. However, other people might feel sorry for Amy and decide that they judged her too harshly and should maybe give her a second chance.

And Amy will be *so there* for it!

# Vivi

"Good for Amy," Vivi says—to no one. Martha isn't around. Vivi must not need her.

Vivi checks on JP on the beach. This couldn't have been easy for him, ending a ten-year relationship.

JP has fallen asleep.

That night, Vivi goes back.

It is, once again, her first summer on Nantucket. She has left the Hamilton house on Union Street. After three nights of sleeping in the hostel out in Surfside, she found a room for rent in a house on Fairgrounds Road and she scores a job working the front desk at Fair Isle Dry Cleaning.

The dry-cleaning job pays nicely but it's *hot*. There's no air-conditioning and even though there's a cross breeze from leaving the side door and front door open, sweat drips down Vivi's temples, between her breasts, and down her back throughout her shift. (She once goes so far as to blot her forehead with a cotton dress she pulls out of a drop-off bag.) Her long dark hair feels like a furry animal, a raccoon or a mink, that's gone to sleep on her head. After her first week, she goes to RJ Miller and tells the stylist to cut it all off.

"Give me a pixie cut," she says. "Like Demi Moore in *Ghost*." *Then let me meet my Patrick Swayze,* she thinks.

JP comes in to pick up clothes for his mother, Lucinda Quinboro. He's wearing athletic shorts, a Chicken Box T-shirt, and flip-flops.

His hair is a mess. He looks like he just woke up. Vivi checks the clock—it's half past twelve.

Vivi has gone back over the details of their meeting thousands of times in recent years as a way of chastising herself. Why did she not see the warning signs? He had just woken up in the middle of the day, he was picking up dry cleaning for his mother. What about this made Vivi think, *I want to marry this guy and have kids?*

Well, Vivi isn't thinking in the long term when she meets JP. She's thinking: *Ninety-nine percent of the people who walk through that door are either housewives or household staff. Here, finally, is a cute guy my age.*

She flexes her flirting muscles, which she's been toning when she goes out to the Muse and the Chicken Box at night with Savannah. Vivi has met boys and even kissed a few, but she has not yet embarked on a summer romance.

"Here you go, Lucinda," Vivi says, handing JP a clutch of dresses and blouses sheathed in plastic.

"I'm Lucinda's errand boy," he says, laughing. "JP Quinboro."

"I'm Vivian Howe—everyone calls me Vivi. So, what does JP stand for? No, don't tell me, let me guess." She assesses him. He's WASPy; he will have the name of a British monarch. "James Peter."

"Nope. Want to try again?"

"John Paul?"

"You got Peter and Paul right, but you forgot Mary."

"Excuse me?"

"My real name is Edward William Quinboro," JP says and Vivi nearly laughs out loud because she was so right about the British monarch. "But my mother is a big fan of Peter, Paul, and Mary and her favorite song is 'Puff the Magic Dragon,' so she called me Jackie Paper growing up. Shortened to JP."

Vivi loves this story so much she considers ripping up the ticket and giving him the clothes free of charge. "That is *so* cute."

"It's the only cute thing about my mother," JP says. "Trust me. You'll put these on her account?"

"I will." Vivi winks at him. "See you later, Jackie Paper."

JP walks out and Vivi watches him lay the clothes across the back seat of a convertible Chevy Blazer. The clothes will slide to the floor of the car the second he reverses. His mother should find another errand boy.

Instead of driving off, JP comes strolling back into the dry cleaner's. "Want to go out sometime?" he asks. "When's your next day off?"

"Sunday," she says.

"Beach on Sunday?" JP says. "I'll take care of everything."

Vivi tells Savannah that she has a beach date on Sunday with a cute guy she met at work, and Savannah is both excited and jealous. "I never meet men at work," she says. "The perils of working at a needlepoint shop. I should have gotten a job on a fishing boat or at the golf course. What's this guy's name?"

"JP Quinboro," Vivi says. "You'll never guess what JP stands for."

Savannah groans. "Jackie Paper."

"Wait," Vivi says. "You know him?"

"Unfortunately, yes," she says. "Since forever."

"Did you date him?"

"God, no."

"What's wrong with him?" Vivi says.

"I'll let you find that out for yourself," Savannah says.

Is Vivi deflated that JP is, apparently, flawed in some way? No—Savannah has unrealistic expectations when it comes to men, whereas Vivi is just fine with a mere mortal.

JP picks Vivi up in the Blazer. He's wearing only board shorts, flip-flops, and a visor, so Vivi gets a good look at his smooth tan torso. She's wearing a yellow sundress over a yellow bikini. JP asks the appropriate first questions—how long has Vivi been here, where did she come from—and Vivi says that she was Savannah Hamilton's roommate at Duke and that Savannah invited her to Nantucket for the summer without asking her parents, and the parents kicked Vivi out after a week, so she had to cobble together a summer on her own.

"You went to Duke with Savannah?" JP says. "I've known her forever. She's great."

"That's exactly what she told me about you!" Vivi says with a grin.

Vivi thinks maybe JP will take her to Surfside or Nobadeer or Madequecham, which is where people their age hang out, but instead he drives her down a long sandy road to a beach that is completely deserted. It feels like a secret.

"Is this where you bring all of your unsuspecting victims?" Vivi says, because it would be easy enough for JP to kill her here and send her floating out to sea. (She wonders if this would make a compelling short story, something in the vein of Joyce Carol Oates's darker work. "Beach Date," she could call it.)

JP says, "My friends hang out at Nobadeer but I wanted to come here because it's quiet and we can talk."

JP plants an umbrella in the sand with great seriousness and intention while Vivi admires the rippling muscles in his arms and back. She slips her sundress over her head and feels JP's eyes lingering on her body. His gaze is so intense, it's as if he's resting his hands on her waist.

It's like they're in a Harlequin romance novel, she thinks. Except it's real.

JP asks if she wants to go for a walk and when she says yes, he reaches for her hand. It's the first time he's touched her and it's…electric. There's chemistry. Vivi hasn't held hands with a boy since Brett Caspian in high school, but she doesn't want to think about Brett right now.

She asks JP about himself. He grew up with his mother and grandparents in Manhattan, went to the Trinity School and then to Bucknell, where he majored in fraternity. (When Vivi laughs, he says, "No, really, I was president of DKE and it took up *all* my time.") He, like Vivi, just graduated and needs to figure out what to do with his life—but before he worries about that, he wants to squeeze every last drop of juice out of the summer.

"I'd rather be in Nantucket than anywhere else," he says. "And I'm aware that real life does not take a break for the summer, so this is probably my last chance to be free and irresponsible."

"Couldn't you just stay here?" Vivi asks.

JP laughs. "Spoken like someone who has never seen this island in the middle of January."

Vivi would like to see Nantucket in January—quiet and blanketed in snow or even gray with a howling wind. She doesn't care. She loves it and that love is starting to feel unconditional. She can easily see working at the dry cleaner's year-round and maybe finding a nicer rental. There would be lots of time to write. "What about your dad?" Vivi asks. "Are your parents divorced?"

"He was killed in a Chinook crash in Vietnam while my mother was pregnant with me," JP says. "So I never knew him."

Vivi envies the insouciance with which JP announces this. He could have been telling her he grew up on the ninth floor of his apartment building. "I'm so sorry."

"Can't miss what you never had," JP says, and this time Vivi detects a hint of bravado. It couldn't have been easy for him to grow up without a father.

Vivi shocks herself by saying, "My father is dead too." She knows JP's next question will be *What happened?* and she nearly heads him off by telling him what she always tells people when they ask, which is *car accident.* But instead, she says, "He killed himself in the garage. Carbon monoxide poisoning." Her voice sounds calm and emotionless, and for the first time in her life, Vivi feels like an adult. Since she left Parma, she has kept the truth about her father private from everyone except Savannah. She feels ashamed because of both how her father died and the fact that he's dead. In a world where people are meant to have two parents, she feels lopsided, defective.

JP squeezes her hand. "Were you close to your dad?"

"Yes."

"What about your mom? Are you close to her?"

"No."

"But she's still alive?"

"Yes. She lives in my hometown."

"Where's that?"

"Parma, Ohio." Vivi takes a deep breath of the salt air. She's starting this relationship off on the right foot by talking about that which she normally keeps secret. At Duke, she often just told people she was from Cleveland.

When they turn around to head back, JP takes Vivi's face in his hands and kisses her. She is worlds away from Parma.

Things get serious quickly. For their second date, JP reserves a table at 21 Federal; it's an elegant restaurant in one of downtown's "antique" homes. The place is legendary; the Hamiltons talk about it all the time—the famous people who eat here, the infamous locals who populate the sometimes-rowdy bar scene. The maître d' greets JP with a bear hug, then leads him and Vivi up the creaky back stairs to a cozy, wood-paneled room with one candlelit table at a window overlooking charming cobblestoned Oak Street.

"You arranged for this?" Vivi says.

"Mattie owes me a favor," JP says. "I helped him dig his Jeep out at Great Point earlier this summer."

Vivi closes her eyes. This is a quintessential Nantucket moment. JP moves his chair so it's next to hers and holds her hand. He orders champagne. They eat the most delicious food Vivi has ever tasted in her life—a roasted portobello mushroom over parmesan "pudding," a wood-fire-grilled sirloin, a peach and blueberry cobbler that comes in a tiny cast-iron skillet and has a scoop of homemade ginger ice cream melting on top.

When Mattie comes up to check on how everything was, JP says, "Thank you for everything, man. You've made me look good in front of my girlfriend."

"I'm your girlfriend?" Vivi says. "This is only our second date."

"I've never heard him utter the word *girlfriend* before," Mattie says.

"Date number three, I'm proposing," JP says. He looks at Mattie. "Know any good jewelers?"

"What have you done with my friend?" Mattie asks Vivi.

JP keeps swinging by the dry cleaner's with treats—one day it's a sandwich from Something Natural, the next day it's a bouquet from the truck that sells wildflowers on Main Street. He picks her up and drives her out to Madaket to see the sunset. They go to the movies at the Dreamland Theater. On her days off, he takes her to far-flung beaches—Smith's Point, Quidnet, Coatue.

"I think I'm in love with JP," Vivi tells Savannah. They're sitting by Savannah's pool with margaritas made by Mr. Hamilton.

"Lord help us," Savannah says. "Listen, I like JP. He's essentially a good guy and I've been impressed with him this summer because he's treated you beautifully. But he's soft, Vivi. He gets everything handed to him by his mother. He's never held a real job and has no plan for the future, no ambition, no drive."

"I'm not you," Vivi says. "I don't need those things." She doesn't tell Savannah that she and JP have already talked about spending the winter on Nantucket together. They might get a rental—JP says he's keeping an ear to the ground—or Vivi might stay where she is and JP might stay in his mother's house. The house isn't winterized so it'll be months of fires in the hearth and space heaters, but it sounds heavenly to Vivi, the two of them bundled up in a big old house that overlooks the harbor.

Vivi doesn't share this vision with Savannah, but if she had, Savannah would have pointed out that Vivi hadn't yet cleared the biggest hurdle to the relationship—she hadn't met Lucinda.

JP invites Vivi to be his date for the Anchor Ball, held on the Saturday of Labor Day weekend at the Field and Oar Club. Vivi doesn't have anything to wear, so Savannah lends her a pale pink sleeveless dress with a full skirt that makes Vivi feel like Audrey Hepburn. She borrows Savannah's pearl necklace and earrings.

"Are you sure you don't want to wear these yourself?" Vivi asks.

"I'm not going to the Anchor," Savannah says. "You could not pay me enough money."

"Why not?" Vivi says. She would feel more comfortable if Savannah was there. According to JP, nearly the entire club shows up for the Anchor. It's a bastion of old-fashioned elegance. There's a cocktail hour on the lawn where everyone gets pleasantly buzzed, then a sit-down dinner, then dancing all night to an orchestra. It sounds divine to Vivi—except for the part where she'll finally meet Lucinda.

Lucinda won't like her. Vivi comes from nowhere and no one. The Hamiltons and the Quinboros move in the same social circles, and the Hamiltons find Vivi pleasant and amusing, but their accepting Vivi as Savannah's best friend is different from Lucinda accepting Vivi as JP's girlfriend.

Or maybe it's exactly the same, Vivi thinks. Maybe she can charm Lucinda with her intelligence, wit, self-sufficiency. She's plucky! She's a go-getter! Already she has been promoted to assistant manager at the dry cleaner's and she's in charge of training all the new staff. Besides this, she has a degree from Duke! She won the creative-writing award!

Vivi thinks back on all the hours she spent in the front seat of Brett Caspian's Skylark driving around Parma, listening to the same songs over and over again. "Stone in Love," "Jungleland," "Fly Like an Eagle." What a waste of time! She should have been reading Steinbeck or learning French or taking a ballroom-dancing class. She should have been improving herself, preparing for her eventual attendance at the Anchor Ball on Nantucket as the date of JP Quinboro.

Vivi and JP are ushered forward to shake hands with the commodore and rising commodore of the club before they officially enter the ball. Vivi tucks her cute pink velvet clutch (also Savannah's) under her arm in a way she hopes seems elegant and Holly Golightly–like and offers her hand to the commodore. His name is Walter Rosen. His wife, Penny, is Lucinda's best friend.

"Vivian Howe. Pleasure to meet you."

Walter winks at Vivi and squeezes her hand warmly. "We've heard a hundred wonderful things about you," he says. "Someone has finally captured the heart of our JP. Welcome, Vivi. My wife will be extremely jealous that I met you first."

The rising commodore's name is Chas Bonham. He's only about ten years older than Vivi and JP, and though he's more reserved than Walter, he's very kind.

Receiving line completed, JP guides Vivi with a hand on her back to a server holding a tray of champagne flutes. He gives one to Vivi and takes two for himself. "Let's get this over with."

They find Lucinda standing in a circle of people out on the lawn. Vivi wore ballet flats at Savannah's suggestion and now she's grateful. She glides over the grass and stands at Lucinda's elbow, waiting to be introduced. Lucinda no doubt notices her son and his date lingering but she's in a conversation with the woman to her left about a disagreement she had in the A and P parking lot that morning. A man heading to the ferry had pulled his suitcase over Lucinda's espadrille.

"Mother," JP says.

"Jackie!" she says. She turns. "And you must be Vivian. JP hasn't stopped talking about you and now I can see why. Aren't you enchanting!"

Vivi offers her hand but her voice has left her.

"We'll see you at dinner," JP says. He wheels Vivi back inside to the bar and Vivi thinks, *That's it? It's over?* It was the blink of an eye. Vivi hadn't uttered a single word.

She wonders if she'll be seated next to Lucinda at dinner—but no, proper placement is boy-girl-boy-girl, and Vivi finds herself between JP and Walter Rosen. Lucinda is all the way across the table, so there's no opportunity for conversation. Initially, Vivi is dismayed by this. Her main goal of the evening was to impress Lucinda, and her first chance was squandered. She might have looked enchanting but she stood there like a lamppost.

Vivi needs to *be* enchanting. She won't fret about Lucinda; she'll be present in the moment. There's wine at dinner and warm rolls with pats of butter that look like roses. Walter asks Vivi about her time at Duke. He's a basketball fan, so she throws around the names of the players she says she used to drink with at the Hideaway—Laettner, Hurley, Hill—and Walter laps it up like a kitten with cream. (It's only a bit of an exaggeration; they were at the next table.)

Before dinner is served, the orchestra starts to play. Walter offers Vivi his hand. "Dance?"

*Now?* Vivi thinks. Yes—there are already couples out on the dance floor, and Vivi and Walter Rosen, commodore of the Field and Oar Club, join them. Walter is in his late fifties, Vivi guesses, and he's a skillful dancer; all she has to do is let him lead. She feels light as a feather; the skirt of her dress twirls, and she smiles at Walter, smiles at the bandleader who is snapping his fingers as he sings "Mack the Knife," smiles at the other couples on the dance floor and the guests who are still seated. She sees Bob and

Mary Catherine Hamilton. Mary Catherine waves to Vivi and gives her the thumbs-up, which is very unlike her. An outward sign of approval!

The song ends. Vivi claps politely, then Walter offers Vivi his arm and escorts her back to the table.

JP leans over and whispers in Vivi's ear, "You were dazzling. Luminous. I couldn't take my eyes off you. Nobody could."

Vivi glances across the table. Lucinda is deep in conversation with Penny Rosen.

There are other things Vivi remembers about that evening: The classic filet mignon and jacket potato dinner with a side of asparagus and grilled tomato. The baked Alaska for dessert. Twirling in JP's arms until Bob Hamilton cuts in for a dance.

"You're the belle of the ball, Vivi," Bob says. "Mary Catherine and I are proud of how you've created your own summer here. Though, frankly, I would have preferred it if you'd stayed with us. Savannah still isn't speaking to me."

"It was for the best," Vivi says. "I'm happy I made it work."

When the band takes a break, JP heads to the bar to freshen their cocktails and Vivi goes to the ladies' room to powder her nose.

There are two stalls occupied. A voice from one says, "I wasn't sure what to expect but she's lovely."

"A breath of fresh air," the voice in the other stall says. "This club can feel so…inbred at times, everyone's children marrying one another. We need new blood. Do you think it's serious?"

"It's a summer romance," the voice in the first stall says. Vivi has by now figured out that it's Lucinda and Penny Rosen behind the doors. She should leave immediately—they're talking about her; how awkward!—but she wants to hear the rest of the conversation.

"Summer romances are the best kind of romances," Penny says. "Remember the Teabury brothers, Lucy?"

"Who could forget the Teabury brothers," Lucinda says. "The only problem is that these summer romances don't last. There's no point getting to know this girl, whoever she is, because she'll be gone by the end of September. Next summer we won't even remember her name."

When fall arrives, both Vivi and JP stay on Nantucket. JP lives in the icebox that is Lucinda's house, though it's so inhospitably cold and the water heater so unreliable that most nights, they sleep in Vivi's drab (but warm) rental on Fairgrounds Road. Fall becomes winter. Everything closes down; people go inside; the only places with full parking lots are the high school during basketball games, Marine Home Center, and Nantucket Wine and Spirits. JP and Vivi eat a lot of ramen, a lot of scrambled eggs and toast. They drive out to Fortieth Pole on Friday afternoons and look for seals off the coast. On Saturday nights, they go out to dinner at the Atlantic Café or the Brotherhood and sometimes to a movie at the Starlight.

March feels like it's eight weeks long; it's bitterly cold with a ferocious northeast wind. There's no sign of spring—no crocuses, no bunnies, no mild sunshine. The writing that Vivi promised herself she'd do hasn't happened. She rewrites the story she's been working on since high school, "Coney Island Baby," about a woman who thinks her husband is having an affair but discovers he's singing in a barbershop quartet.

On St. Patrick's Day, Vivi and JP go to the Muse to shoot pool and drink green beer and dance to Celtic music, and while it's not exactly the Anchor Ball at the Field and Oar Club on a starry summer night, it's still fun. Everywhere with JP is fun, Vivi decides.

She drinks too much and passes out in her clothes without brushing her teeth. When she stumbles into the bathroom in the morning, she blinks.

Taped to the mirror is a note: *Will you marry me?*

"What?" Vivi says. She turns; JP is sitting on the side of the bathtub with a ring box open in his hand.

"Vivi," he says. "Will you please be my wife?"

# The Chief

The bad thing about there being no breakthroughs in the Vivian Howe case is that there are no breakthroughs. The good thing about that is that Cruz DeSantis is out of the hot seat for the time being, and one afternoon in July, the Chief feels like he can finally return to the Nickel to grab lunch. When he leaves the station, he sees Officer Pitcher leaning against Alexis Lopresti's car, chatting her up. The Chief waves; they end their conversation and Pitcher heads inside. There's nothing wrong with Pitcher and Alexis dating—until they break up. Then, unless they handle themselves like adults (and how can they? They're so young), everyone will suffer.

The Chief gets to the Nickel at a quarter past two. There's a cheerful-looking couple dressed for the beach picking up their order. When Joe DeSantis sees the Chief, his eyebrows shoot up, but he doesn't smile.

It's a Thursday, so the Chief decides to get the blackened shrimp po'boy with homemade spicy slaw. As soon as the happy couple leaves, the Chief says, "How're you doing, Joe? The special for me, please."

Joe turns to the griddle and throws on the shrimp. "Business is down eight percent, Ed." There's an accusatory note in his voice.

"You don't think it's because—"

"Because people in town, the locals, think my kid might have killed Vivi Howe? Because your department can't seem to figure out who did it?" The shrimp sizzle and the smell is enough to make Ed weak in the knees, but he can't let the food distract him. "I vote to increase your budget every time it comes up in town meeting. Your department has plenty of resources. Why can't you do your job?"

Joe is angrier than Ed had anticipated. And he's not wrong. "Hit-and-runs are hard to solve, Joe. Here's what I can tell you. We've checked with the insurance companies and the body shops on-island to see if anyone has come in with a dented bumper but no accident report. We struck out there. We asked every land-scaper and contractor who's doing work on Kingsley Road to see if they sent crews early Saturday morning. Falco interviewed all the neighbors to see if anyone noticed a car turning around in the driveway or any strange car, period, early on Saturday morning. I tried to track down the Bridgeman kid but he's up in Maine. I came in here for a sandwich and to say hello, but since we're on the topic, can you give me the names of some of Cruz's other friends so that I can ask them about the party the night before Vivian Howe was killed?"

Joe swings around. "Why are you worrying about high-school stuff? That's not where the answer is. My boy didn't kill Vivian Howe." Joe makes the Chief's sandwich, wraps it in white butcher paper, and slams it down on the counter. "You're ruining my kid's life, Ed. He doesn't hang out with his friends anymore. Now, I realize he's off to college in six weeks and he'll start the next chapter of his life at Dartmouth. But I worked hard to build the kid a community here and it feels like the community has turned on him." Joe pauses. "And on me."

The Chief stares down at the sandwich, though he's rapidly losing his appetite. "I'm sorry, Joe. Cruz had the misfortune of being the one who found Ms. Howe, and we had to proceed with the investigation the way we did. If it makes you feel any better, I know Cruz is innocent."

Joe says, "The sandwich is twelve-fifty."

The Chief hands Joe fifteen dollars and stuffs the change Joe gives him into the tip jar. There isn't another word he can offer that won't make him sound patronizing or insensitive, so the Chief raises a hand to say goodbye and heads for the door.

"Jasmine Kelly," Joe says before the Chief steps outside. "She's Cruz's girlfriend. If anything noteworthy happened at the party the night before the accident, she'll know about it."

The Chief nods, the bell on the door rings, and the Chief leaves, sandwich warm in his hand.

Jasmine Kelly. The Chief thinks this is Sharifa Kelly's daughter. Sharifa works in the Town Building, at the Registry of Deeds. The Chief gives Sharifa a call.

"Jasmine's a lifeguard this summer, Ed," Sharifa says. "If you can manage to track her down, God bless you. I only see her in a blur, coming and going, which makes me sad. She leaves for Vanderbilt on August tenth. Southern schools start early."

"Thank you, Sharifa, I appreciate this more than you know," Ed says. He can call Rocky Moore, who oversees the lifeguards, and ask to speak to Jasmine one morning before the guards do their training drills. He thinks about Joe's words and wonders if he *is* wasting his time with the high-school stuff. Somehow, he doesn't think so. Planting the shoes—who would do that? Someone who wanted to see Cruz blamed, someone who knew Cruz worked at the Stop and Shop. It has an unsophisticated, Hail Mary feel to it—*Let's dump the shoes in the trash where Cruz works and see if that gets him in trouble.*

This is starting to feel like an episode of *Gossip Girl* or whatever show it was that Kacy used to watch growing up. Every show on TV is either police, hospital, or teenagers because that's where the drama is.

*     *     *

The Chief gets back to the station and has just sat down to unwrap his po'boy when his cell phone rings.

It's Dick, from the Stop and Shop.

"I just had a very interesting conversation with the daytime custodian, kid named Justin," Dick says. "He confessed to planting the shoes."

"What?" Ed shoots up out of his chair and starts pacing his office.

"He's here," Dick says, "if you want to talk to him yourself."

Justin is in his early twenties and looks like a skateboarder, although Ed might be stereotyping—he has a lot of tattoos and piercings and blond bangs that he's keeping off his face with a little girl's barrette. He's sitting up straight and seems clear-eyed and alert when he tells the Chief that some "uptight dude with a very hot chick" offered him two hundred and fifty bucks to put the shoes in the break-room trash.

"I thought it was weird," Justin says. "Sketchy, you know. But I needed the cash and it didn't seem like it was hurting anyone, so I did it."

"Can you describe the two people?" the Chief says. "Did you recognize them?"

"Nah," Justin says. "They seemed like normal establishment— straight or clean-cut or whatever. She had dark hair and beautiful legs. Honestly, I don't remember what the dude looked like at all except he had military-grade posture."

"Were they driving a car?"

"Didn't notice. They were just standing outside the break-room door when I left work."

The Chief stares at the kid. He sounds legit, and this all but clears Cruz's name—unless Cruz has somehow put the boy up to this?

"Why did you decide to come forward now?" the Chief asks.

Justin shakes his head slowly. "I heard through the grapevine that Donald was maybe getting in trouble for it. That guy is like a grandpa to me and I couldn't let him take any kind of heat." Justin shrugs. "I just thought it was a quick, easy way to make some jack. I didn't realize the shoes were...evidence or whatever. Sorry."

The conversation with Justin feels like a breakthrough—but is it?

The Chief decides to call the Greek later and give him an update. Maybe he'll have some ideas. Meanwhile, the Chief will talk to Jasmine Kelly and see if she can shed some light on who might want to frame Cruz. It's all he's got.

# Carson

We have to stop, cold turkey, right now. I'm sorry.

The text from Zach comes in while Carson is driving to work and she reads it in the parking lot. No big deal. One or the other of them has a crisis of conscience every week.

She texts back: K.

Immediate response: Please don't text me again.

Carson sighs. It's ten minutes to three; her head is vibrating like a tuning fork from the two shots of espresso she did at home. She considers taking an Ativan real quick but worries it will soften her edge, and at the beginning of a seven-hour shift, she needs her edge.

She calls Zach at work. He's the boss, so he has his own line and an office with a door that locks. He always answers because he doesn't want Carson leaving a voice mail on his work phone.

"Hello, Zachary Bridgeman."

"It's me."

There's a pause, during which she can tell he's thinking about hanging up, but if he hangs up, she'll call back. He knows she'll call back. "I can't talk."

"Did something happen?"

"Yes."

"She got your phone?" Carson feels the black syrup of dread drip through her veins.

"No."

"What, then?"

"She saw you parked across the street from our house in the middle of the night," Zach says. "She didn't know it was you then, but she took down the license plate and ran it at work, so now she knows."

"Shit," Carson says. Stalking Zach's house, stalking *anyone's* house, is always a bad idea. Now, in the bright light of midafternoon with the intense clarity brought on by mainlining caffeine, Carson can't fathom *what* she'd been thinking. Was she thinking Zach would come out to play? Was she thinking she'd be invited inside? "What did she say?"

"She said she thought you were waiting for your drug dealer."

Carson laughs for the first time since her mother died. "So my bad reputation saved us?"

"It didn't save us. Pamela isn't suspicious of you in particular, but she's suspicious in general. She watches me, Carson. I see her eyeing my phone, and every time I get a text at home, she hovers over my shoulder. I can tell that she looked up our credit card statement online. When I got to work, I checked my car for a tracking device."

"You're overreacting."

"You're underreacting."

"She thinks I was meeting my drug dealer."

"She thinks that *now*. But if you appear unexpectedly again or something else brings you to her attention, we're doomed. I promise you the only reason she hasn't put two and two together is that the idea of you and me is so preposterous."

"I thought we were going to run away," Carson says. "But instead, you're breaking up with me."

"I'm sorry, Carson. I should never have talked about Paris or Alaska. I was caught up."

"That was your heart talking."

"I think the world of you."

"So we've gone from you being madly in love with me to you thinking the world of me. Do you want to write me a letter of recommendation for my next inappropriate lover? List my attributes? Rave about my performance?"

"I knew this would happen."

Carson can't handle his tone. "You knew *what* would happen? That I'd fall in love with you because I'm so young and impressionable and you're such a lady-slayer?"

"I knew things would end badly," Zach says. "But you have to believe me when I tell you that they aren't ending as badly as they could have."

"I wish I could tape you," Carson says, "and then play you back to yourself when you're begging to see me in three days."

"That's not going to happen, Carson. Pamela and I are driving up to Maine this weekend to see Peter. I'm going to use that as a chance to reconnect with my wife."

Gah! Did he really just say that? Carson thinks. *Reconnect with my wife?*

"Did you find a room at some cute little bed-and-breakfast with lots of chintz and a house cat named Mittens and popovers and fresh-squeezed juice in the common room starting at eight sharp?"

"Yes," Zach says, a hint of misery creeping into his voice. "I did."

"Tell me you love me," Carson says.

"I can't."

"Tell me you love me!" Carson says, so loudly that a mother packing up her kids after a day at Jetties Beach turns around to stare. Carson flips her off.

"I can't, Carson. I'm sorry. Please don't call me again. Good-bye." Zach hangs up.

Carson throws her phone at the dashboard; the screen cracks down the middle, just like her heart. She stares out the windshield at the Oystercatcher. She can't work; she'll have to call in sick. It's three o'clock on the nose. If she calls in, she'll be leaving them in the lurch, big-time. She has nothing left but this job.

She opens her door, climbs out, and somehow puts one foot in front of the other.

But oh, she's in a mood.

Jaime (girl) is as chipper as a Girl Scout on the first day of the cookie sale. "Thank you for the gift card," she says. "I love Lemon Press."

Carson stares at her. "I know I should say you're welcome, but you're not welcome." She steps a little closer to Jaime and notices that she has a new nose piercing, a diamond chip embedded in the side of her nostril surrounded by sore-looking pink skin. "I resent having to *pay you off* to ensure that you'll help me out. Girl, do you think Gunner ever bought me so much as a freaking latte? He did not, but I still worked my ass off for him. And why? Because I'm a team player, that's why." Carson sniffs. "I know you think you're taking over my job when I move on, but you're not, Jaime." Carson waits a beat. "Because you're not hot enough."

This lands hard because it happens to be kind of true, and Jaime knows it. She's not beautiful like Carson. It isn't fair, but if Carson can teach anyone a lesson, it's that life isn't fair.

\*     \*     \*

A dozen Island Creeks, a dozen Wellfleets, two dozen cherrystones, and a round of kamikaze shots. Carson glances up at that—yep, the guy ordering is in his fifties. Nobody young orders kamikaze shots or even knows what they are.

"And pour one for yourself," he says, leering at Carson. He's suntanned and wearing a tailored shirt. Breitling watch. He's with a bunch of other guys his age, all of them with slicked-back hair and needlepoint belts and horn-rimmed glasses, half of them staring at their phones, the other half watching him trying to flirt with Carson. The guy ordering (and paying, she assumes) isn't wearing a ring.

She pours the shots, including the one for herself, which she throws back quickly. Technically, it's not allowed, but every bartender in America does it.

The guy plops his neon-orange American Express down; this must be a new color to announce one's douchebag level of wealth. Brock Sheltingham—a name straight out of a Vivian Howe novel.

"Keep it open, please," Brock Sheltingham says.

The shot goes to Carson's head. It doesn't help that she made the kamikazes with tequila, her nemesis. Not only does Carson hate the taste but it reminds her of her mother. It also doesn't help that the gentlemen want to do a second round of kamikaze shots. Fine; Carson makes them strong, thinking that when these guys leave her a ten-thousand-dollar tip, she'll be internet-famous.

If that happens, Carson will give a thousand to Jaime to make up for the horrible thing she said.

Carson does the second kamikaze shot as well; to decline seems rude.

Two chards, a sauvignon blanc, a martini, no olives (why even bother having a martini?), two Whale's Tales, a dozen cherrystones, and an order of calamari. *Reconnect with my wife.* Carson has no one but herself to blame. She was the one who canceled her Uber and sneaked onto the elevator and up to the eleventh floor of the Boston Harbor Hotel. She's young, but she knew what she was doing was wrong. She could have left it as a onetime fling, but no, she had stayed at the Boston Harbor Hotel for the entire three-day conference, ordering up room service like Eloise at the Plaza, leaving only to attend her bartending class and then going right back to Zach's bed. It could have ended *there;* it could have been a conference affair—this seemed like a thing that must happen all the time between consenting adults—but Carson gave Zach Savannah's address and he returned to Boston the following week. For an additional two and a half days, they had lived together in Savannah's beautiful town house. Zach had cooked for her—pasta carbonara and Caesar salad with homemade dressing and a simple chocolate mousse—and by the end of his stay, they were in love. The rest of the relationship has been texts, phone calls, surreptitious meetings at the end of Kingsley Road, the naughty, delicious buzz that arrived over the holidays when they were both seated at Willa's dining-room table at Thanksgiving and Christmas Eve.

Jaime bumps into Carson from behind in a way that feels aggressive. Carson once told Willa she wasn't pretty and Willa had gotten the same expression on her face that Jaime has now—shock, hurt, resignation. With Willa, it wasn't quite as bad. Willa was pretty, just not as pretty as Carson. This, maybe, had been at the heart of their sister conflict. At one Christmas Stroll when Willa and Carson were twelve and nine, a group of women in full-length fur coats had approached them, exclaiming about how *gorgeous* Carson was. *Exquisite. Pretty enough to model. Someone get this kid an agent!* Carson had loved the compliments, but she'd been self-conscious about Willa. Why hadn't the women said anything about Willa? Once the ladies moved on, Carson turned to Willa and said, "You're pretty too." Willa had slapped Carson right across the face, sending Carson's cocoa flying out of her hand; it landed on the brick sidewalk and detonated in a hot-chocolate-and-whipped-cream explosion. Carson just picked the cup up and threw it away. She knew, somehow, that she'd deserved it.

The gentlemen order a third round of kamikaze shots—they're on an actual kamikaze mission, it seems—and then a fourth. Although four shots is where Carson should draw the line with herself, if not with them, she throws hers back. Then Brock Sheltingham asks for the check and when she slaps it down, he says, "How about a kiss?"

The question is outrageous. Has this dude not heard of #MeToo? Does he not know that women are no longer to be messed with? Carson can see the other so-called gentlemen watching Brock with barely suppressed alarm and maybe also delight. He's showing off. *Okay, then,* Carson thinks. She pulls Brock forward by the front of his beautiful, expensive shirt and lays on one hell of a kiss with tongue, a kiss old Brock can't handle; he'll be tenting the front of his trousers when she's done with him. The gentlemen are cheering and Carson guesses that the rest of the bar is starting to take notice and that probably a few phones are out. She milks it for another second or two, sending a psychic message to Zach: *At least someone wants to kiss me!* Carson could easily take this guy as a sugar daddy; she could wear Balenciaga and travel in private jets. No more Cape Air flights for Carson!

She lets Brock go. The gentlemen cheer, and she runs the card.

Jamey (boy) comes over and says, "Do you know that guy? Is he your boyfriend or something?"

"My uncle," she says.

The look on Jamey's face is priceless but Carson can't maintain a straight face. "Kidding. He's just a customer."

Four kamikaze shots have gotten her seriously buzzed.

Two Whale's Tales, vodka soda, vodka tonic, Mount Gay and tonic, Diet Coke (Carson looks up to make sure that isn't Pamela), margarita, no salt. Carson handles the orders but her head is swimming; she's sloppy with the soda gun. Bartending isn't a job that can be done well while intoxicated.

She lassos Jamey (boy) and says, "Cover me for a minute, please, bruh. I'll be right back."

She's not *drunk,* but she's not sober. She neglected to eat today—no smoothie, no bagel—which was why the espresso hit so hard and why she's spinning now. She needs to clear her head and make it through her shift, then she can go home and rage against the machine, the machine being love.

She's not quite all the way in the bathroom stall when she pulls out her vial of cocaine. She sits on the toilet and bumps, then bumps again, not realizing that the stall door is hanging open and that someone is watching her and that the someone is Jaime until it's too late.

Jaime walks out of the ladies' room without a word. Carson stuffs the cocaine down into her purse—no, that's not good enough, she needs to throw it away, but she can't bring herself to throw it away. Jaime won't tell, she's too chickenshit, and even if she does tell, it's Jaime's word against Carson's.

Carson strides out to the bar, shoulders back, beaming. Jamey looks relieved to see her. He says, "There's stuff on your nose."

"Thanks, now piss off," Carson says, and she runs the back of her hand under her nostrils.

Vodka tonic, planter's punch, sauvignon blanc. Carson is pulling a fresh bottle of Matua from the minifridge when she sees a pair of legs. Carson's eyes travel up. It's Nikki.

"George wants to see you in his office," she says.

"Now?" Carson says. "I'm busy."

"Now," Nikki says.

*It's not true Jaime is holding a grudge about something I said earlier, my boyfriend broke up with me, my mother is dead, it will never happen again, I'll do whatever you want me to do, I'll go to a program, see a therapist, just please don't fire me.*

"I'm sorry, Carson," George says. "You were warned. I knew you were lying to me when we talked last time. And, frankly, the nonsense with Brock Sheltingham didn't help."

"He asked me for a kiss."

"I'm sure he did, but you should have ignored the guy instead of turning it into a public spectacle. This isn't Vegas, Carson. This isn't Coyote Ugly. It's a family restaurant."

"Don't be grandiose. It's a beach bar."

"There are children around and those children have parents and your behavior was inappropriate and doing four shots in a row with customers is obviously unacceptable. I could maybe have looked the other way on that stuff in the name of fun and you showing Sheltingham who's boss. But drugs on your shift? No. I told you I would fire you and I'm firing you."

Carson nods to let George know she heard him, but she can't accept this outcome. "I need this job, George."

"Take some time, properly grieve your mother, clean up your act or tone it down, do what you need to do. I'll give you a glowing recommendation in the fall and you'll be able to work anywhere on Nantucket that you want, or you can go off-island. But you have to get your head on straight." He sighs. "I like you, Carson. I want what's best for my business but I also want what's best for you."

Carson stands up. She's getting a hangover, and the coke has made her jittery. There's a mounting wave of destructive energy inside of her that is telling her to burn this bridge. George says he gets it, but he doesn't.

"I understand," Carson says. "You should give my job to Jaime. She'd be great." With that, Carson leaves the office and walks out of the Oystercatcher, swiping a bottle of Triple Eight vodka as she goes.

\*     \*     \*

In her car, she checks her phone. Nothing from Zach. She sends him a text: Got fired.

Fired. She got *fired*. It's so humiliating—and yet, she full-on deserved it. Only two hours earlier, she had considered calling in sick and thought *that* was the worst thing she could do.

Ha. Not even close.

Zach doesn't respond so she takes a swig of the vodka, coughs, then calls Zach's cell. She's sent straight to voice mail. He's blocked her. She'll have to go over there.

It's five thirty; he'll be home from work but Pamela might be getting home soon. She works erratic hours—sometimes she stays late, sometimes she goes back to the office after dinner and works until midnight.

Can Carson reasonably go over there?

She drives down North Beach Street, one hand on the wheel, one hand on the neck of the vodka bottle, which she has nestled in the cupholder. Stalking is always a bad idea, she reminds herself.

She can't believe she's been fired. It doesn't feel real. But yes, it is real, she's out driving around at five thirty in the evening instead of taking drink orders, making people happy, ringing the dorky bell. Her identity is rapidly evaporating. She has lost her mother, lost her lover, lost her job. Who even is she?

She sees people walking into town with strollers, dogs, little kids, teenage kids. These are people who have their lives together enough to take a vacation. Carson feels tears welling, so she plays a game called What Could Be Worse? Well, she could be pulled over right now for driving under the influence, lose her license, go to jail—that would be worse. She needs to eat something! She can sign for food at the snack bar at the Field and Oar Club, get a grilled cheese, a hot dog, a peanut butter and jelly. She can pretend she's ten years old and has just survived a sailing lesson.

When she pulls in to the club, she sees Pamela's red Range Rover in the parking lot. *She's here,* Carson thinks, *probably playing tennis.* Which means Zach will be at home alone.

Carson pulls out and leaves the Field and Oar behind.

She won't park across the street at the horse barn; she's at least that smart. Instead, she parks beyond Zach's house at the far end of Gray Avenue. She runs back to Zach's house and knocks on the front door, then decides she doesn't need to knock so she swings the door open and calls out, "Zach!"

He comes shooting down the stairs. "What the hell are you *doing* here?"

"I saw Pamela's car at the club," Carson says.

"Yes, she's playing tennis with her mother. Why are you not at work?"

"I got fired," Carson says and she starts to sob. She is so, so sad, so wounded, so adrift. The driver in the hit-and-run didn't kill just Vivi. He killed their whole family.

Zach reaches out and takes Carson in his arms and rocks her back and forth, shushing her. "I'm so sorry, baby. But you can't stay here. You have to go."

Carson raises her face and they start kissing. Carson feels Zach's entire body leap to life; he's helpless when they're together. How can he possibly think he could break up with her?

He runs his hand up her T-shirt and unbuttons her skirt.

# Vivi

She has been watching closely because she's worried Carson is going to do something stupid—hurt herself or someone else. Vivi should have used a nudge to close the bathroom door so Jaime—poor, sweet Jaime—didn't see Carson, and Carson didn't get fired. Or, better still, she should have had Carson drop the cocaine into the toilet. George is right—Carson needs help. She's on a path to self-destruction.

What can Vivi do?

At that instant, the green door swings open and Martha enters. She has tied a brilliant blue Hermès scarf at the corners, slipped her arms through the holes, and is wearing it as a little shrug.

"Now, that," Vivi says, "is the cutest look yet." Then she remembers herself. "What are you doing here? Do I need you?"

"Pull back your scope," Martha says.

"Gladly," Vivi says. She was about to leave Carson and Zach anyway, for obvious reasons. She would very much like to nudge them far, far away from each other, but any fool can see that they are beyond the point of a nudge.

Vivi widens her scope—and gasps. Pamela's red Range Rover is rolling down Hooper Farm toward Parker Lane. She'll be home in two minutes.

"Carson!" Vivi shouts.

"She can't hear you."

Vivi stops herself from swearing out loud, but of course it doesn't matter; Martha reads minds. "What can I do?" Vivi asks.

The Range Rover turns onto Parker and before Vivi can say one more word, it turns onto Gray Avenue.

Carson and Zach are going to get caught. Vivi tries to predict what this will mean. Carson will be vilified by Pamela and by the elder Bonhams—who is Vivi kidding? She'll be vilified by the entire community. Nantucket will blame Carson instead of Zach. Carson is wild, they'll say. She gets fired one minute and is revealed to be a homewrecker the next. Vivi thinks about Peter Bridgeman. He's an odd duck but Vivi would never want to see him hurt. However, Vivi's main concern is Willa. Poor Willa will be caught in a firestorm. She will take Pamela's side over her own sister's because Willa has an intractable sense of right and wrong; she doesn't even like *reading* about infidelity. (She didn't care for *Along the South Shore* for this reason, she told Vivi.)

Everyone in Vivi's family has been through enough without piling this on top. Getting fired will, Vivi suspects, be good for Carson in the end. But this—no. The affair with Zachary Bridgeman needs to stop, obviously. But not like this.

"Is there a way for Carson to realize she has almost been caught but not be caught?" Vivi asks. "Can we scare her straight?"

"Use a nudge," Martha says. "Pronto."

Carson and Zach are going at it on the living-room sofa. Carson's clothes are scattered across the floor of both the living room and the hallway. When Pamela pulls into the driveway, there's a three-tone chime that sounds throughout the house. It's an alarm, Vivi realizes, to let the occupants know someone has arrived. An alarm for this reason feels like overkill—they're on Nantucket!—but of course, Pamela works in insurance. Possibly the alarm company offered it to Pamela free of charge. The alarm is worth its weight in gold in this situation.

Zach leaps to his feet, pushing Carson off him and into the coffee table, where she knocks over a pair of candlesticks.

"She's home," Zach says. "Go out the back."

Carson is naked. "I need my clothes."

She and Zach snatch up Carson's clothes. Pamela, meanwhile, turns off the ignition and reaches into the back seat for her sports duffel and her racket.

"I can't find my thong," Carson says. "What did you do with it?"

Zach runs a frantic hand around the cushions of the sofa. "Just take what clothes you have and go."

Pamela reaches for the car door.

"Nudge," Martha prompts. "She isn't going to make it out of the house in time. Nudge right now."

"How?" Vivi says.

"Call Pamela," Martha says.

"*Call* her? On her cell? How can I call her? I'm dead."

"Who will she pick up the phone for?" Martha asks.

"Work?" Vivi says. "Rip? Her parents?" Vivi feels the answer like someone kicked her in the rear. "Peter."

"Yes," Martha says. "Do it now."

Vivi peers down into Pamela's purse and thinks, *Call from Peter, call from Peter!* Pamela's phone lights up and starts to play the marimba ringtone, which was also Vivi's cell's ringtone. She feels a sad nostalgia even though she hated when her phone rang and tried never to answer.

The screen says, Son Peter.

Pamela ignores the ringing. Arrrrgh! Vivi watches with horror as Pamela puts one foot out of the car.

Carson is struggling with her T-shirt and finally gets it on, inside out and backward. She hurries down the hall, naked below the waist. Her skirt is in one hand, shoes in the other.

*Answer the phone!* Vivi thinks. She reaches down through the stretchy membrane and turns the phone so that when Pamela glances at it, she sees a picture of Peter's face lighting up the screen.

"Ah!" Pamela says. She snaps up the phone. "Darling? Is everything all right?" There's a pause. "Darling? Peter? Peter, it's Mama, can you hear me? Your reception is terrible. Hello? Peter? Well, if you can hear me, just know that Daddy and I will be there around two on Saturday afternoon." Pamela holds up the screen, checks to see if the call is still connected. Improbably, it is. "Okay, honey, love you. We'll see you Saturday."

Carson steps out the back door, hides between two hydrangea bushes, and wriggles into her skirt. Her breathing is shallow, and her heart is beating like the heart of a small, scared animal that narrowly escaped becoming part of the food chain; Vivi can hear the thumping even from up here. Zach finds a red Hanky Panky thong under the sofa and stuffs it into his pants pocket. He straightens the cushions, stands the candlesticks upright. Through the living-room window, he watches Carson slip through the border of lacecap hydrangeas into the neighbors' yard. He's exhaling his relief as the front door opens. Pamela walks inside, staring at her phone.

"I just got a call from Peter," she says. "But I couldn't hear a word. The service up there is nonexistent. I hope everything is okay."

"I'm sure everything is fine," Zach says. His voice is tight and high but Pamela doesn't seem to notice. "He probably wants us to bring up junk food. He likes those white cheddar Doritos. How was tennis?"

Only then does Pamela give her husband the briefest of glances. "Fine," she says. "I won in two sets, but, I mean, that's nothing to brag about, my mother is nearly seventy. I'm going to shower."

"Okay," Zach says.

Pamela disappears up the stairs and Zach collapses onto the sofa. His head lolls back, exposing his Adam's apple, which moves with shudders of relief.

Carson runs down Gray Avenue in her bare feet and climbs into her car. When she's back on Hooper Farm Road, she says, "Thank you, God."

"It was me, honey!" Vivi calls out.

Martha shakes her head. "Oh, Vivian," she says.

\*   \*   \*

Carson drives home, orders Lola Burger for herself and her brother, and goes to bed at ten o'clock without the aid of so much as a sleeping pill.

After Carson has safely fallen asleep, Vivi goes back.

It's 2011, the third summer of the wineshop. The Cork is hemorrhaging cash, and JP is late with the rent to his mother; he's asked Vivi nicely if he can pay Lucinda out of their joint savings account and Vivi has said she'll think about it. She doesn't want to give in to JP on this, but what choice does she have? Lucinda is a tough landlord; she won't let him slide. Vivi wishes Lucinda would just evict him and then, as his mother, tell him what Vivi herself is too afraid to say: JP doesn't have a head for business. He should close the shop for good at the end of the summer and do something else. Vivi is now making enough money that JP could simply stay home and be a full-time dad, take some of the parenting duties off Vivi's plate.

One night in the final, honey-gold week of August, JP comes home from the Cork visibly drunk. This isn't the first time he's come home drunk and Vivi suspects part of the reason the Cork is failing is that JP is imbibing the profits.

He says, "There's something I need to talk to you about."

*Hallelujah,* Vivi thinks. He's reached the decision on his own—this will be the last summer for the wineshop.

"What is it?" Despite how badly Vivi wants to hear the words come out of his mouth, she's also busy. She has spent all summer driving the kids around. Willa, at age fourteen, has stopped going to the beach with Vivi—she and Rip ride their bikes to meet up with their group of friends—but Vivi still has Carson, Leo, and Cruz to cart around. Cruz's father, Joe, has just moved his sandwich business from his home kitchen to a bona fide storefront downtown. The shop is called the Nickel and it's going to be a runaway success, Vivi knows, but Joe needs help with Cruz, and Vivi is happy to pitch in. Cruz is always grateful for Vivi's efforts, whereas the other kids just expect the homemade lunches and clean beach towels and boogie boards and umbrella packed neatly in the back of the Jeep. Vivi has just dropped Cruz at home and is trying to get dinner on the table.

"We need to talk in the bedroom," JP says.

"I'm in the middle of shucking corn," Vivi says.

"Leave the corn." JP heads down the hall to their bedroom and Vivi, sensing something is wrong, something more than a failed business, follows him.

JP tells Vivi that he has "fallen for" his employee Amy Van Pelt.

"What does that mean?" Vivi says. She has never met Miss Van Pelt, though JP waxes rhapsodic about her all the time—she's "sweet" and "cute," an Alabama sorority girl with an abundance of "Southern charm." "You're in love with her?"

"I wouldn't say that. Yet. But I want to be with her. I'm leaving you, Vivi."

Vivi laughs. "You're *leaving* me? For your twenty-three-year-old shopgirl?"

"Yes," he says. "I'm sorry."

It feels like a ploy. JP seems like a disgruntled child who packs a pillowcase full of clothes and heads out to the end of the driveway to "run away." But JP is resolute: He wants to pursue a future with Amy. He wants to break up the family, burn down their hopes and dreams.

Anger, confusion, anger, fury, anger, sadness, rejection, anger—and, finally, more anger.

They schedule an emergency session with their therapist, Brie. ("Cheese therapy," they call it when they're in a light mood, which they are not today.) Brie astonishes Vivi by announcing that affairs are the responsibility of both parties.

"If you, Vivi, had made JP feel more treasured, more loved, more central in your life, then he wouldn't have gone outside the marriage to find affirmation. I've been seeing you both for eighteen months. JP has been clear and vocal that his emotional needs aren't being met but you've made no changes. Frankly, I'm not surprised this happened."

"Wait a minute," Vivi says. "You're blaming *me?*"

"You're both at fault," Brie says.

Initially, Vivi wants to reject this. But if she honestly examined her feelings, the ones that she has done her best to sublimate and ignore, she'd have to admit that, over the years, she has lost respect for JP. She has placed him in the same category as the kids. He's someone she has to support, someone she has to guide. In previous therapy sessions, JP articulated that he didn't feel important to Vivi—not as important as the kids, not as important as her writing, not as important as her running. Is he wrong? Wouldn't Vivi choose all of these things (even her running) over JP? Hasn't she thought, at times, of leaving *him?* She has stayed because they have a whole huge life—the kids, the house, their friends, their routine. They have stability. Their household is happy, often joyous—which is different from how Vivi and JP grew up.

But now—Amy?

It's reasonable for Vivi to ask JP to move out; after all, he's the one who's ending the marriage. But incredibly, he refuses to go anywhere. He wants to stay in the house; he wants them *both* to stay in the house while he pursues a new relationship with Amy. It'll be better for the kids, he says.

"Who do you think you are, François Mitterrand?" Vivi says, a question that sails right over JP's head.

Vivi is *not* going to live in the same house with JP while he sleeps with his twenty-three-year-old employee. Sorry. They have a lot of whisper-fights in Vivi's home office, which is the room farthest from the den, where the kids watch TV. Vivi realizes that JP has always been handed exactly what he wants without any accountability—but not this time.

"You stay," Vivi says. "I'll go." Her novel *Along the South Shore* has sold well over the course of the summer, even though Vivi refused to go on tour. The kids are young and she's needed at home (besides which, she waits all year long for summer on Nantucket and the last thing she wants to do is leave). What if she were to go on tour now, at the end of August, beginning of September? She runs it past her publicist, Flor.

"I have dozens of requests for you," Flor says. "You've created a bit of a mystique by not going on the road before now. Let me see what I can pull together. How long do you want to go for?"

"A month?" Vivi says. "Two months?"

Flor puts together a twenty-nine-stop tour that's spread out over seven weeks; it's a systematic march across the country. Vivi spends Labor Day weekend at Browseabout Books and Bethany Beach Books at the Delaware shore. She hits Politics and Prose in DC, then Fountain Books in Richmond. She heads to North Carolina: Quail Ridge Books in Raleigh, Malaprops in Asheville. Then it's down to Fox Tale in Woodstock, Georgia, and Page and Palette in Fairhope, Alabama.

She goes to Oxford, Mississippi; New Orleans; Houston; Dallas; San Antonio; Phoenix; Wichita; Edmond, Oklahoma; and the legendary Tattered Cover in Denver.

She misses the kids' first day of school. It has been a Quinboro tradition to take a picture of all three kids on the back deck. When Vivi asks JP to send the picture, she gets no response. She later sees the picture posted on Facebook, because for some reason Vivi and JP are still Facebook friends. Vivi copies the picture and makes it her screen saver, which she shows to any reader who asks. In the picture, Carson is wearing a sweater with a hole in the shoulder seam. Leo has a cowlick. Willa's scowl seems to be an indictment of Vivi's absence.

*This isn't my fault!* Vivi wants to tell the kids. But Brie has been crystal clear that this isn't allowed—and apparently, it *is* partially her fault.

Turnout at Vivi's events varies from place to place. Sometimes there are sixty people in attendance, sometimes six. But Vivi's readers are always enthusiastic. One woman packed up her two little kids and a baby she was still breastfeeding and drove three and a half hours from Kansas City to Wichita. Another woman took the day off work and drove from New Mexico to see Vivi at the Poisoned Pen in Scottsdale.

Vivi calls the kids every night. They cry. Carson, especially, is having a hard time. She wants to know if Vivi will be home in time for her eleventh birthday. The answer is no; Vivi will be in San Francisco doing a signing at Book Passage.

"I'm sorry, sweetheart," Vivi says. "I'm sending presents." What Vivi does not say is that she was the one who ordered the cake from the Juice Bar and she texted JP the contact info for the parents of Carson's friends so he could send out the invites for the sleepover.

By the time Vivi gets to California, she understands why rock stars are so often drug addicts. Life on the road is brutal. Vivi's agent, Jodi, has negotiated the best tour package possible—Vivi has car service wherever she goes and stays at hotels with twenty-four-hour room service, and Mr. Hooper picks up the tab. When Vivi started out, there was wonder, relief, and excitement in dialing a number and soon after having a club sandwich, French fries, coleslaw, chicken noodle soup, vanilla crème brûlée, and a bottle of wine appear on a tray at the door, and then an hour later having that tray whisked away and replaced in the morning by freshly percolated coffee and a pitcher of real cream. Vivi's suitcase grows fat with pilfered bars of soap, tiny bottles of shampoo and body lotion, notepads with the hotel's name and logo at the top (perfect for grocery lists), pens, and individually wrapped artisanal chocolates.

But there are just as many (too many) trips to Hudson News for a Coke Zero and a prepackaged sandwich (Vivi chose tuna once and only once). There are days she has to fly early and misses her run; there's the never-ending quest for a place to charge her phone. There is a yawning loneliness and too much time for reflection. What breaks Vivi's heart is the memory of JP sitting on the edge of the tub holding out the ring, asking her to be his wife, and of how much she loved him in that moment and how lucky, how truly and incredibly blessed she felt to be marrying Edward William Quinboro. At that time, she thought he was better than her. But Vivi has learned that where a person comes from means far less than what she makes of herself.

In Seattle, Vivi gets on the elevator, and although she knows she's staying on the fifth floor, she can't recall her room number. There have been so many: 1246, 818, 323. She has her key, but that's no help; the cardboard sheath with the number written on it is sitting on the bureau in front of the TV in the room. Vivi heads back down to the front desk and while she's waiting in line, she checks the Facebook app on her iPhone, and there, in JP's feed, are pictures of Carson's birthday party.

Vivi waits until she's back up in her room (547) to cry. When she's finished sobbing but still hiccup-y, she calls Savannah.

Savannah is home in Boston for most of the fall (she's dating a part owner of the Celtics and things are getting serious) but she understands how soul-shredding traveling for work can be. Savannah spends weeks, sometimes months, in places like Mali, Paraguay, and Bangalore, but Vivi thinks traveling might be easier for Savannah because Savannah doesn't have children.

"Where do you go next?" Savannah asks. "Cleveland?"

Vivi shivers. She isn't going to Cleveland. If she ends up going on tour every year from now until she retires, she will not go to Cleveland. That's where the ghosts are.

"Minneapolis, Madison, Petoskey, Chicago, Indy, and Pittsburgh."

"For the love of Pete," Savannah says. "Skip those places and go home."

"I want to," Vivi says—oh, does she want to! "But I can't."

"Will you get fired?" Savannah asks. "No. This tour is something you took on voluntarily, Vivi."

"I agreed to it," Vivi says. "And you know how I am." Vivi sticks it out; she isn't a quitter. She does what she says she's going to do. Even if there were only ten people, three people, *one person* at each of her events in this final stretch, she would still show up. Because that one person has expectations—maybe she, like some of the others Vivi has met, traveled a long distance to get there. Maybe she has been looking forward to the event for weeks. Maybe it's her dream to meet a real author and get a book signed. Vivi isn't going to let her down.

At this point, Vivi thinks, the readers are her family.

A week later, Vivi steps off the elevator at the Drake Hotel in Chicago to see Savannah standing in the lobby. Savannah links her arm through Vivi's and says, "I'm coming to your event and then we have a nine-thirty impossible-to-get reservation at Topolobampo. Mr. Celtics is friends with Rick Bayless."

Vivi gets home on the fourteenth of October and moves directly into a tiny cottage on Lily Street. It has one closet-size bedroom for Leo and a loft where she sticks the girls. Vivi sleeps on a futon in the back TV room. They eat dinner around the coffee table in the living room. There's one bathroom with a shower stall. They're right on top of one another and Vivi loves it.

But...the kids are different. JP has been spinning a wild tale of Vivi's "abandonment." He refused to confirm the date that Vivi was coming back or even *if* she was coming back and the kids bought into this despite Vivi's daily assurances that she would be back on Nantucket on October 14, long before Halloween. The kids alternately cling to her and mouth off (Carson), calling her an "absentee parent."

She meets Amy for the first time at Leo's football game at the Nantucket Boys and Girls Club. It's the first week of November on a bright, crisp autumn day and Vivi is tucked in among her sports-parents friends in the bleachers like an apple in a barrel. She has regained her equilibrium; all the loneliness she suffered through on the road has been forgotten like the pain of childbirth.

Watching eight- and nine-year-olds play football is two steps forward, one step back. It's easy to get distracted, and Candace Lopresti says brightly, "Hey, is that JP's new girlfriend?"

Vivi turns to see JP, wearing his obnoxiously preppy Ralph Lauren green suede barn jacket, walking up the sidelines of the game. He's holding hands with a blonde wearing a cute tartan miniskirt, navy tights, and navy ballet flats. JP must have misrepresented the pee-wee football game as something Amy needed to dress up for. Vivi sighs. Amy is as blandly pretty as Vivi expected; the inappropriate outfit choice serves to make her a tad more likable. Vivi climbs over Candace, Joe DeSantis, and her other friends to go introduce herself. She has always preferred the high road. Besides, she's with her people and she knows she looks good. She's wearing her best jeans, her cutest warm boots, a creamy sweater, a down vest, a pom-pom hat, cashmere fingerless gloves, and round Tom Ford sunglasses purchased for her by Savannah on the Miracle Mile.

"Hey, guys," she says. She makes sure her voice is friendly and warm. She smiles and extends a hand. "You must be Amy. I'm Vivian Howe—it's nice to meet you."

Amy's hand is cold and limp. She's in a peacoat, no hat, no gloves.

"Hi," she says. She's studying Vivi behind the lenses of her aviators, that much is clear, and Vivi gets the feeling she was expecting someone else—someone bitchy and monstrous. Oh, well.

"Do you want to come sit, Amy? I can introduce you around."

"No, thank you," Amy says. She looks up at JP.

"We aren't staying," JP says. "We're going out to lunch at the Brotherhood."

*Must be nice!* Vivi thinks. "Well, it was kind of you to stop by."

"I love football," Amy says. "I graduated from Auburn, where game days were huge. The fraternity guys used to wear coats and ties, and some of the tailgates had crystal and china and candelabras." She pauses, seemingly caught in a reverie. "Nobody does football like the SEC."

"Yeah, our tailgating scene here is sadly lacking," Vivi says. "No candelabras." She lowers her voice to a whisper. "Though some of the moms put Kahlua in their coffee."

JP clears his throat, his signal for *That's enough.* "How's Leo doing?"

"He's carried the ball four times, fumbled three times," Vivi says.

JP groans. "Are you serious?"

"He's still Mr. Butterfingers," Vivi says. "But at least he's smiling."

"Leo always smiles," JP says. "He was smiling the day we brought him home from the hospital, remember?"

"That was gas, honey," Vivi says and she and JP laugh. Amy stares at the field and then gives an exaggerated shiver. Or maybe she's not exaggerating; it's pretty chilly.

"I'm going to wait in the car," she says, "while you two reminisce or whatever." She heads for the parking lot.

"I tried," Vivi says.

"She's insecure," JP says. "She was afraid to meet you."

"She should have been afraid. She firebombed our family."

"*She* did nothing of the sort."

"Fine. You firebombed the family and she was complicit." Vivi can feel the eyes of three dozen parents on her back. "But I don't want to fight. She seems like a perfectly nice girl."

"Thank you for being civil. I appreciate it."

"I'm going to heaven," Vivi says.

"I don't know about all that," JP says. He takes a quick peek over his shoulder at the parking lot. "But you were nice, so I'm not sure what her issue is."

"Her issue is that we have eighteen years of history that doesn't include her. She's jealous."

JP sighs. "Off to do damage control."

"Have fun at lunch," Vivi says. "I'll just stay here and watch our son fumble like the absentee parent that I am."

JP laughs and Vivi would like to kick him in the nuts. But as she watches him walk away, she has to admit, she feels sorry for him. He made a large mistake in leaving her, but he will realize this only with time.

The holidays are dismal. Vivi "has" the kids for Thanksgiving, but she doesn't have enough space in her cottage to do a proper dinner so they go to Savannah's and eat with the elder Hamiltons. Savannah has bought everything premade from Whole Foods and transported it from Boston; the only exceptions are the corn pudding, which Vivi brings, and the pies, which come from the Nantucket Bake Shop. Mary Catherine has just been diagnosed with Alzheimer's. She gets confused and starts weeping halfway through dinner about her brother Patrick (he of the blended family, brood of six) who was killed in a car accident on New Year's Eve 1999. Bob Hamilton is at a loss for what to do about Mary Catherine so he ignores her crying and pretends everything is just fine. He asks Vivi's kids about school but then he's too distracted by his wife to listen to their answers.

The kids are antsy and impatient to leave, and Vivi suspects Savannah would just as soon have them gone so she can tend to her mother and stop playing hostess. It pains Vivi to have the day end prematurely—the kids have informed Vivi that JP and Amy are having a romantic dinner for two at the Ships Inn because Lucinda went to Boca to spend Thanksgiving with Penny Rosen—but she can see no alternative, so she packs up four pieces of pie to go.

In the car on the way home, Willa says, "I should have eaten with the Bonhams."

"Everything is always better at the Bonhams," Vivi sings out.

"It is, actually," Willa says.

"The Cowboys are playing at eight," Leo says. "I want to watch."

But Vivi has only the basic cable package, which somehow doesn't include the channel broadcasting the Cowboys game, and Leo starts crying and saying he wants to go to his father's house, and Carson piles on—why not?—asking why Vivi can't buy a real house like their dad's, one where they all have their own rooms so she doesn't have to sleep in a bed with stinky Willa. Willa tells Carson she doesn't enjoy it any more than Carson does, and things escalate from there. Everyone is in a state when they pull up in front of the cottage, and once they get inside, Vivi screams, "Pack up, kids! I'm taking you back to your father's!" This makes her cry because she's supposed to have them all weekend. She makes a big production of throwing the pie in the trash and this silences the kids. Willa apologizes first, then Leo, then Carson, and they all curl up on Vivi's bed and watch *A Christmas Story,* which makes Vivi irate because it isn't Christmas yet, it's still Thanksgiving, but also happy because apparently her cable package isn't a total loss after all.

A full-blown Thanksgiving crisis is averted. But it's not great being a single mom at the holidays. It's just not.

JP has the kids for Christmas. He won't let Vivi see them on Christmas Eve—they're busy, he says, with church and the party at the Field and Oar Club. Vivi stays home alone, makes a grilled cheese, and wraps presents for the kids (she has intentionally saved her wrapping for tonight, fearing she would end up with nothing else to do). She puts on the Vienna Boys' Choir, opens a split of Veuve Clicquot, and toasts her tiny, bedraggled Charlie Brown tree. She admits to herself that she went overboard on gifts, just like a stereotypical "absentee parent."

It feels *profoundly* unfair that JP had an affair and Vivi is the one who has been cast out.

As she drinks her champagne and stacks the gifts in three piles—the children will be over tomorrow afternoon to open gifts, then it's back to JP's by six because they're having a "big Christmas dinner"—she makes some promises to herself. She will not succumb to self-pity, tempting as that may be. She will not bad-mouth JP or Amy. She will buy a big house and spend whatever it takes to make it even warmer and cozier than the one she left. She will be resilient; she will bounce back. She will be happier than ever before.

# Willa

Vivi's publicist, Flor, calls Willa.

"I shared the video of Brett Caspian singing 'Golden Girl' with the producers of *Great Morning USA,*" she says. "Tanya Price wants him on the show next week. Would you forward me his contact info?"

"Oh!" Willa says. "*Great Morning USA?* Really? Wow...um, I should probably...check with him first? He's a private person."

"Of course," Flor says. "I hope he agrees. This could be huge for the book."

"Would he just be singing the song?" Willa asks. "Or would he be talking with Tanya about his relationship with my mom?"

"A little of both, I imagine," Flor says.

That's what Willa is afraid of. *Golden Girl,* which the entire country is buying and *loving*—the Facebook messages gushing over the novel number in the thousands—will be exposed as containing Vivi's own secret within it, a secret so guarded, Vivi didn't even tell her own children, her husband, her best friend.

Willa considers calling Flor and saying that she checked with Brett and he'd rather not appear on the show.

But Willa can't lie like that. She's a rule follower. She likes to do the right thing, not the easy thing. Calling Brett isn't easy, but she has to do it.

She tells Brett that she sent the video of him singing "Golden Girl" to Vivi's publicist. (Did she overstep in doing this without his express permission? Probably.) The publicist then forwarded the video to the producers of *Great Morning USA,* who showed it to Tanya Price, and now Tanya Price wants Brett to sing on the show.

Brett laughs. "That's crazy," he says. "We put *Great Morning USA* on in our lobby every day. And you're saying she wants me on to sing?"

"You may have to talk a little bit about your relationship with my mom," Willa says. "But…if you do that, I think you should exercise discretion."

Brett is quiet. Willa needs to make herself crystal clear.

"I'm not sure you should tell the nation that my mom got pregnant in high school. Or that she *told* you she got pregnant."

"Willa," Brett says. "I would never do that. I'll just stick to talking about our romance and the song."

Willa exhales. "Thank you." She wonders if she can trust him. Willa has watched Tanya Price enough to know that she's a serious journalist who finds the heart of every story like a heat-seeking missile, and although Brett seemed pretty sanguine about the whole Vivi-maybe-probably-lying situation, if he wanted to get revenge, this would be the way to do it. "Can I trust you?"

"Willa," he says, and she feels bad for even asking.

*     *     *

Brett is scheduled to appear on *Great Morning USA* the following Monday at eight thirty. Willa realizes she has to tell her siblings, her father, and Savannah. She would prefer just not to mention it; Carson and Leo don't watch TV, JP is busy at the Cone in the morning making ice cream, and Savannah is so busy running her nonprofit and caring for her parents that she has even less free time than JP. Brett could appear, sing his song, and tell the story about dating Vivi, and none of them would ever know.

Lucinda watches *Great Morning USA*. Penny Rosen too. Probably a lot more people watch than Willa realizes—ten million people. There's no way to keep this quiet.

Willa sends a text to her siblings: FYI, turns out Mom had a boyfriend in high school back in Ohio named Brett Caspian and he's going on Great Morning USA to play the song he wrote for Mom at 8:30 a.m. Monday.

There's no response from either Carson or Leo—no surprise there. They're absorbed in their jobs, their friends, plus Leo has Marissa, and Carson has her controlled substances. Willa thinks she should check on them tomorrow but then she reasons that they're both adults, and if they need her, they'll let her know.

She wonders if she should tell her father or Savannah next and easily decides on Savannah. Since Savannah's house is only two blocks away from the Whaling Museum, Willa stops by after work.

She sees Savannah's car in the driveway so she knows she's home, but nobody answers when Willa knocks. Willa opens the door. "Hello? Savannah, it's Willa!" She hears vague people noises coming from the back, so after a quick pit stop in the powder room (the walls are covered in photographs, including some of Willa, Carson, and Leo when they were growing up and some of Vivi and JP when they were still married), she heads to the kitchen. Through the window, she can see Savannah's back. She's sitting on the edge of the pool.

Willa pops outside. "Hey!"

Savannah whips around. "Willie! Willie, hi." Her voice sounds strange, strained, and Willa realizes that Savannah has company. There's a man in the pool; Willa can see his form underwater.

Before Willa can even think, *Oops, I interrupted something,* the man surfaces. It's JP.

"Dad?" Willa says. "What are you doing here?"

"Came for a swim," JP says. "Before the mad after-dinner rush at the shop."

"Oh," Willa says. She tries to process this. It makes sense, sort of. Savannah's house is even closer to the Cone than it is to the Whaling Museum, and Willa knows that her father and Savannah have bonded since Vivi died. But this feels like a thing. Is this a thing?

"How are you?" Willa asks. "How's Amy?"

"Amy and I broke up last week," JP says. He clears his throat. "I'm sorry. I should have told you."

"You...what do you mean, you broke *up?* Did she move *out?*"

"She did," JP says. "She's living at Lorna's."

Willa blinks. "Wow. Okay."

"I apologize, honey. I honestly didn't think you'd care."

"I mean, I don't *care,*" Willa says. "But also, it feels weird that we're all living on this island and major things are happening and nobody is talking to one another and we're supposed to be a family."

"You're right," JP says. "I planned on killing three birds with one stone and telling you all at Grammy's birthday dinner a week from Tuesday."

*Ugh!* Willa thinks. August is moving way too fast, as it always does. She has completely spaced about Lucinda's birthday dinner at the club. Now she'll spend the next ten days dreading it.

"Did you stop by for a reason, Angel Bear?" Savannah asks. "Do you want to talk? Can I get you a glass of wine?"

"I'm all set, thanks," Willa says. She has to decide if she wants to tell Savannah and her father about Brett Caspian together now or wait and tell only Savannah. She decides to just come out with it. "So, listen, this completely bizarre thing happened. I found that guy you were talking about on Mom's memorial Facebook page, the one who said he was Mom's boyfriend in high school."

"Your mother didn't have a boyfriend in high school," JP says.

"Did you contact him?" Savannah asks.

"I did." Willa should have told Savannah sooner, she realizes. She should have told her right away. "He's legit."

"He...what?" Savannah says.

"Your mother did not have a boyfriend in high school," JP says. He lifts himself out of the pool and dries off. "You know there are crackpots out there, sweetie."

"I invited him to come to Nantucket for the day," Willa says. She swallows. "He had all these pictures of him and Mom back in Parma, hanging out at the mall and at the Christmas formal. He told me stories about her father..."

*"What?"* JP says.

"And he played me this song he wrote for Mom," Willa says. "'Golden Girl.' It's a really, really good song." Willa stops there. She isn't going to say a word about the fake pregnancy to anyone, not Savannah, not even Rip.

"What's the guy's name?" JP asks.

"Brett Caspian," Willa says. "He's going on *Great Morning USA* on Monday to play the song and talk about Mom. Tanya Price is interviewing him."

"What?" Savannah and JP say together.

# Nantucket

We've been keeping an eye on the *New York Times* bestseller list and the top two spots on Hardcover Fiction have remained the same: *Satan's Weekend* by D. K. Bolt at number one and *Golden Girl* by Vivian Howe at number two. Number three has been something of a revolving door, though one of our favorite Low Country writers, Dorothea Benton Frank, camps out at number three for two weeks. Everyone loves Dottie!

A rumor goes around that a man from Vivian Howe's past has emerged from the woodwork and will be appearing on *Great Morning USA* to play a song he wrote for Vivi. None of us want to miss that.

At precisely 8:40 on Monday morning, Tanya Price, our very favorite of all the morning-show hosts, introduces the segment.

"On Saturday, June nineteenth, at approximately seven fifteen a.m., bestselling novelist Vivian Howe was out for her morning run when she was struck by a car and killed. The identity of the driver is still unknown, and the island of Nantucket, located thirty miles off the coast of Cape Cod in Massachusetts, mourns one of its most celebrated locals. Vivian Howe leaves behind three children and thirteen novels about her island home, the most recent of which, *Golden Girl,* is presently at number two on the *New York Times* bestseller list.

"The novel begins with a high-school romance between characters Alison Revere and Stott Macklemore. I can't say much else without spoilers, but what I can tell you is that Stott Macklemore is a budding musician who, in the book, writes a song for Alison called 'Golden Girl.' Turns out, Vivian Howe enjoyed her own high-school romance with our next guest, Brett Caspian. He wrote a real song entitled 'Golden Girl' over thirty years ago. He's here to play it for us now."

The spotlight shifts to the stage, where Brett Caspian sits on a high stool in front of a microphone. Some of us are nervous—who is this guy? Is he talented enough to play for a national audience or will he make a fool of himself?—but when he starts to sing, we are instantly mesmerized. The song is a love ballad with a rock beat. *You're the fire in my eyes.* Brett Caspian looks like someone who might have been a heartthrob in the 1980s. Pamela Bonham Bridgeman, who is watching the segment on the office computer with her brother, Rip, thinks Brett's attire—a white T-shirt and jeans—is meant to be reminiscent of a Bryan Adams album cover. Brett has longish dark but graying hair that flops in his eyes and a soulful, yearning voice with a bit of a rough edge. It's safe to say that every straight woman on Nantucket—maybe even across the country—instantly develops a crush on him.

When the song is over, many of us applaud in our own kitchens, our own living rooms. Woo-hoo! He did it! What a tribute to Vivi!

Brett strides across the stage to sit down with Tanya Price.

"That was *incredible.*" Tanya Price is beaming. She looks pretty smitten herself. "So that's a song you wrote thirty-four years ago for your girlfriend at the time, Vivian Howe. And Vivian made this song central in her novel *Golden Girl.*" Tanya leans in. "Is the character of Stott Macklemore based on *you,* Brett? Did Vivian Howe borrow more than just the title of the song from her real-life experience?"

Brett smiles shyly. "The character in the book and I have a lot in common, but it's not *me.* I think what Vivi did in this novel was to take the emotions she felt while we were together and use them in the story. We were together our entire senior year of high school and there were a lot of intense feelings. We were growing up in small-town Middle America. It's the stuff rock and roll is made of—so many classic rock anthems use the tumultuous teenage years as their emotional touchstone."

On the screen behind Tanya and Brett is a photograph of a young Brett and a young Vivi on a bench at the mall sharing an Orange Julius. Those of us who knew Vivian Howe on Nantucket gasp. It's undeniably her but she looks so different. Her hair is so long, her makeup so heavy; she looks like a young Joan Jett.

"In the novel, the character of Stott Macklemore is discovered by a record executive, and 'Golden Girl' becomes a big hit." Tanya pauses. "What happened in your case?"

"My band, Escape from Ohio, had a record company interested in us. They flew us to LA. They really liked the song 'Golden Girl.' " Brett smiles directly into the camera. "But that was before the age of iTunes and online music. If you wanted to make it big back then, you had to have an album in you." He shrugs. "And we didn't."

On the screen now is a photograph of Vivian Howe in cutoff jeans eating an ice cream cone while sitting on the hood of a silver 1976 Buick Skylark. She looks for all the world like a character plucked from a Bruce Springsteen song. Who knew that this was how Vivian Howe grew up? She always seemed like the quintessential mermaid to us—raised by the ocean, sun on her face, salt in her hair, sand between her toes.

There's a beat of silence. Tanya Price is the queen of the grand finale, so we all move a little closer to the screen and turn up the volume.

"When was the last time you saw Vivian Howe?" she asks.

"August 1987," Brett says.

On the screen is a picture of Vivi and Brett standing side by side in their caps and gowns outside Parma High School. Brett holds two fingers up in a *V* over Vivi's shoulder. *V* for victory because he managed to graduate? *V* for Vivi? Or peace out—was that a thing in the eighties?

"And you weren't in touch all these years?"

Brett shakes his head. "I figured she had a happy life somewhere else. I didn't even know she was a writer." He smiles ruefully. "I don't read much."

"And then you heard she'd passed away."

"Yes, through the sister of a friend," Brett says. "I read her new book and I saw bits of myself in it, so I reached out to her family."

"If you could tell Vivian Howe something now," Tanya says, "what would it be?"

"Well, Tanya, you never forget your first love. It's a feeling like no other. So I guess I would tell Vivi: You always were and forever will be...my golden girl."

Tanya holds out showcase hands. "Brett Caspian, thank you for joining us!"

The broadcast cuts to a commercial.

JP and Savannah stare at the television.

"You swear she never told you about this guy?" JP asks.

"No!" Savannah says. "But he's telling the truth. Could you believe those pictures? The eyeliner! She'd abandoned the Wednesday Addams look by the time she got to Duke, thank goodness."

"Don't you think it's weird that she never told either of us about Brett Caspian?" JP says.

"Maybe he broke her heart and she didn't want to think about it after she left Parma," Savannah says.

"Or maybe she broke his," JP says.

Amy claims she doesn't want to watch the segment but it's Lorna's apartment and there's no way Lorna is going to miss it. They don't have to be at the salon until ten. There's plenty of time to pour coffee, settle down on the sofa with Lorna's Weimaraner, Cupid, at their feet, and watch *Great Morning USA.*

Amy is pretending like she needs extra time in the bathroom but Lorna isn't buying it.

"Just come out and watch, Pigeon. You know you want to."

Amy slinks around the corner, arms locked across her chest. She has a big purple hickey on her neck that she got from Dennis and she has done an inadequate job of covering it with foundation.

"I don't need another morning of my life to be about Vivian Howe," Amy says.

"Is Dennis watching, do you think?" Lorna asks.

"No," Amy says. "He's at work."

As Lorna rubs Cupid between the ears, she predicts Dennis is sitting in his van, watching on his phone.

When Brett Caspian sings, Lorna says, "Damn, but he's hot. Why did Vivi get all the hot guys?"

"Do you expect me to answer that?"

Lorna turns up the volume and sings along. *"You're the fire in my eyes!"* Cupid barks.

Amy disappears—back into the bathroom, Lorna supposes, to do something more about the hickey. "Use concealer!" she calls out.


# Vivi


She's overcome.

She's *so* overcome that Martha appears. Her scarf is twisted into a tight rope and secured around her neck in a way that looks painful.

"It's not," Martha says. "I'm fine."

"Did you see Brett?" Vivi asks. "Did you hear what he said?"

"I heard what he *didn't* say." Martha clears her throat. "Brett kept your secret. Nobody knows what happened between you two, and nobody knows how much of your book is true. So, you see…there was no need to use a nudge."

Martha is right; Vivi's secret is safe. Willa hasn't told anyone, not even Rip—and Vivi suspects she won't.

*Thank you, Willie,* Vivi thinks. *I love you and please forgive me.*

Martha says, "Have you checked your ranking on Amazon?"

"No," Vivi says. "Should I?"

Martha shrugs.

Vivi swoops down to the Manhattan offices of Mr. Hooper, where Flor and her assistant, Jenny, are jumping up and down in front of Flor's computer.

*Golden Girl* is number one on Amazon! Number one!

Flor clicks on BN.com. *Golden Girl* is at number one!

"I just checked Twitter," Jenny says. "People are clamoring for Brett Caspian's 'Golden Girl' to be released as a single on iTunes. The YouTube video has seven hundred thousand views so far."

"This is the kind of publicity I've waited my entire career for," Flor says. She raises her eyes to the office ceiling. "We're going to do it, Vivi. We're going to get you to number one!"

"I'm not getting my hopes up," Vivi says.

Martha starts humming; this is something new. Vivi listens closely. She's humming "You Can't Always Get What You Want," by the Rolling Stones.

"Are you trying to tell me something?"

"Not really," Martha says. "I was just at choir practice and the song got stuck in my head."

"The choir of angels sings the Stones?" Vivi says.

Martha laughs. "Oh, Vivian!"

*Oh, Vivian—what?* she thinks.

"'If you try sometimes, you'll find you get what you need,'" Martha says.

Vivi isn't sure she *needs* anything other than for her children to be healthy and happy, but at five p.m. on Wednesday, August 11, when the *New York Times* bestseller list is announced, D. K. Bolt's *Satan's Weekend* is at number three, the Dorothea Benton Frank book is at number two, and...

*Golden Girl,* by Vivian Howe, is at number one.

"I'm number one!" Vivi shouts, and she dances around a bit with her hands in the air. She's certain this kind of behavior is frowned upon up here—pride is a deadly sin and all that. But she can't help herself! She is so excited! She has the number-one novel in the country and she did it without using any of her nudges!

She half expects Martha to appear, but Martha doesn't. Vivi doesn't need her. This moment is for Vivi to celebrate on her own.

*Thank you, Brett,* she thinks.

# Willa, Carson, Leo, and Rip

Lucinda's birthday is August 17, and every year, the Quinboros celebrate with a family dinner at the Field and Oar Club. Lucinda reserves the round table in the center of the dining room so that everyone she knows can come bestow his or her warm wishes.

This year, JP brings Savannah as his guest, which would have been completely unthinkable in previous years but, with the event of Vivi's death, now feels just right. Willa and Rip are there; Leo has brought Marissa, and Lucinda invited Penny Rosen. Carson is alone.

Normally, Carson would show up high or already drunk, but she seems straight to both Willa and Leo. It's only a matter of time, they suppose, until she orders a Mind Eraser and says something outrageous. Carson's theatrics bore them, but on the occasions of their grandmother's birthday dinners, they count on her for entertainment.

Their grandmother's favorite server, Dixie, comes to take their drink orders. Willa is afraid that if she orders seltzer, someone will ask if she's pregnant again, so she orders a chenin blanc and squeezes Rip's hand to signal him not to say anything. Leo and Marissa order Cokes. Carson orders a ginger ale.

"Feeling okay, sweetie?" JP asks.

"Fine," Carson says. "Just taking it easy tonight."

This is *highly, highly* unusual but nobody says anything. Penny Rosen starts the conversation by asking Marissa where she's going to college.

Marissa says, "Salve Regina, in Newport."

"Leo is heading to Boulder," Penny says (which is impressive, Carson and Willa think. Their own grandmother might not even remember this), "so I suppose it'll be a teary farewell in a few weeks, with you two being so far apart."

"We're committed," Marissa says. She raises her voice so the whole table can hear her. "Leo and I have set a date for our wedding. June twenty-second, 2024."

"Wow," Carson says. "Have you booked a venue?"

Leo knows his sister is baiting Marissa and he also knows it will work. "Stop it, Carson."

"We haven't *booked it,* booked it," Marissa says. "But we've decided. The ceremony will be at St. Mary's and the reception will be here."

"Here?" Lucinda says. "Are your parents members?"

"No," Marissa says. "My mother applied in 2016 but she's still on the waitlist."

"It's a very exclusive club," Lucinda says. "Especially for a single parent."

"But you belong, Grammy," Carson says. "And you're single."

"Yes, well, my father..." Lucinda says.

"We're going to use Leo's membership," Marissa says. "If my mother doesn't get in."

JP clears his throat.

Lucinda says, "I don't think we need to be discussing an event so far in the future that may or may not ever take place."

*Ouch,* Willa thinks. She feels empathy for Marissa, maybe for the first time since she's known her. Mr. and Mrs. Bonham expressed this same cynicism when Willa and Rip said they wanted to get married.

Penny says, "College is about opening yourself up to new people and new ideas. It's best to embark on that voyage with a clean slate."

Marissa bows her head over the menu.

Carson says, "I hear the rabbit is delicious."

Willa tries not to gag. The Field and Oar does offer a rabbit dish on the menu, and all three of the Quinboro children have joked about it for years. Willa breathes in through her nose, out through her mouth. The drinks arrive and JP raises his glass.

"Happy birthday, Mother," he says. "You look wonderful."

"Lucy never ages," Penny says. "It's irritating."

They all touch glasses over the center of the table. Willa brings her wine under her nose and the smell further unsettles her stomach. She sets the glass down and picks up her water.

"Just so no one has any doubts, Leo and I *are* getting married, and we're going to be happy. Just like Willa and Rip," Marissa tells everyone.

Savannah says, "They're certainly setting a wonderful example."

"Can we please change the subject?" Leo says.

"What's wrong, bruh?" Carson says. "Getting cold feet already? It's only 2021."

Marissa narrows her eyes. "Do you know why nobody likes you?" she says to Carson. "Because you try to be funny and, I don't know, *clever,* but you're just mean."

Carson laughs. "Am *I* the one nobody likes?"

Marissa stands up, throwing her napkin on her plate. They all get a gander at just how short the dress she's wearing is. It's short enough to break every rule at the Field and Oar.

Marissa storms off.

Leo sighs. "We aren't getting married."

"Thank God," Carson says.

"Thank God," Lucinda says. "I hate to say it but her mother is never getting into this club. Gordy Hastings finds her brash."

"You're far too young to be talking about marriage," JP says. "My advice is to wait as long as you can. There's no reason to marry your high-school sweetheart. I'm sure Marissa is just the first of many girls for you."

Willa can't believe her father just said that! She kicks Rip under the table. "I'm getting the chicken," she says to no one.

"Are you going to check on her?" Savannah asks Leo. "Or would you like me to do it?"

"She's fine," Leo says. He reaches for a dinner roll. "She does this all the time."

She does this all the time, but this is the last time, Leo thinks. After dinner he's going to drive Marissa home and end things. For good.

Marissa does come back, her nose pink and her eyes moist, and Dixie appears like someone heaven sent to take their order, so no one has to ask Marissa if she's okay.

Willa needs air, so after she asks for the Statler chicken and Rip requests the sirloin, medium (he's been ordering this for dinner at the club since he was five years old and can't be persuaded to try anything new, but Willa views this as a sign of his innate loyalty), Willa says, "We're walking to the water. Be right back."

"I'm coming with you," Carson says.

"Stay put," JP directs, and Leo feels his airway constrict because he wanted to go with Willa and Rip too. The atmosphere at the table is stifling.

Willa and Rip stroll hand in hand over the clipped green lawn, past the flagpole and the cannon—shot off each night at sunset—to the water's edge. Willa has a vision of them a year from now at this same dinner, only they'll be parents. Right? This pregnancy is going to thrive. It has to.

"I ordered wine because—"

"I know why," Rip says. "It was a good idea."

"Drink some of it for me when we go back."

"I will," Rip says. They gaze across the harbor, listening to the piano music coming from inside the clubhouse—"Falling in Love Again"—and admiring the soft blue and gold sky, the sailboats bobbing on the water.

"I miss her," Willa says.

"I know."

"It's fun to have Savannah here," Willa says. "But do you think there's something going on between her and my dad?"

"Would that be so bad?"

"I just can't wrap my mind around it," Willa says. "Savannah belonged to my mother."

"I'll point out the obvious," Rip says. "People don't belong to other people."

"Tell that to Marissa," Willa says.

*Marissa,* Rip thinks. She's having a tough night and it's about to get tougher. Rip has some bad news about the claim her mother is trying to file with Marissa's Jeep.

They turn around and walk back to the table. Rip waves to someone over Willa's head. When she turns, she sees Pamela and Zach on the tennis court.

"That's nice. Your sister and Zach are playing tennis together," Willa says, the wheels in her mind turning.

"I'm sure she's eating him alive," Rip says. "He has no serve."

Willa and Rip have just returned to their seats when the bartender appears at the table.

"I just wanted to say congratulations," he says.

"Why, thank you," Lucinda says.

The bartender looks confused. "I mean, because I saw that *Golden Girl* went to number one on the *New York Times* bestseller list." He seems to be speaking specifically to Carson. "You must be proud."

Carson is impressed. Marshall brushed up on his bestsellers *and* he had the guts to approach Lucinda's table unsolicited.

"We're so proud," Carson says. "Thank you for acknowledging it."

"I don't know what the young man is talking about," Lucinda says.

"Oh, you do so, Lucy," Penny Rosen says. "We went over this on Sunday. Vivi's new book went to number one."

Marshall hovers at Carson's place. "I went to the Oystercatcher to see you last night. Must have been your night off?"

Carson can't let him go any further. She hasn't told anyone in her family that she's been fired, and now, over two weeks later, no one has asked, not even Leo, who lives with her. The only person who paid attention to Carson's comings and goings is dead.

"I'll swing by to chat after we've finished," Carson says.

"I'd love it. Until then, I'll be admiring you from afar." He touches her shoulder, then turns and says, "Happy birthday, Mrs. Quinboro."

"Thank you," Lucinda says. Then to Penny: "That's more like it."

\*    \*    \*

A moment later, Pamela and Zach Bridgeman stop by, sweaty in their tennis whites.

"Happy birthday, Mrs. Quinboro," Pamela says.

"We don't mean to interrupt your dinner," Zach says. His expression, Carson can see, is strained, but his agony can be nothing compared to her own. The inside of her mouth becomes chalky; there's a bright, piercing pain in her chest. They were playing *tennis* together? This is hard evidence of their reconnecting, she supposes.

"Who won?" Carson asks.

"I killed him," Pamela says.

"I have no serve," Zach says. "I'm fat and out of shape."

"Me too," JP says.

"Me three," Savannah says. "Kudos to you, though, Zach, getting out on the court."

"You look good to me!" Carson sings out. She winks at him and everyone at the table chuckles. She can't believe her own audacity—and she's completely sober. But she isn't going to let him appear at her family dinner as though everything is just fine.

He doesn't even look at her; he simply steps back with a raised hand, and Pamela takes the hint. They both head over to the bar and plop themselves in front of Marshall.

Carson needs a drink. Badly. But she won't let Zach break her. She's stronger than that.

Their entrées arrive; they chat about the food and how it hasn't changed in fifty years; they discuss how busy it's been at the Cone and talk about Savannah's upcoming trip to Brazil.

"You should go along," Lucinda says, nudging JP's elbow. "I always wished the two of you would get together when you were younger, but it never happened."

"That's right," JP says. "I married Vivi."

"And had us," Carson says. "Your beloved grandchildren. If Dad had married Savannah, we wouldn't be here, Grammy."

The silence that follows seems interminable.

Leo gets up to use the restroom, then Carson and Willa disappear as well. Seeing his chance, Rip slides over next to Marissa. "I hate to talk business at dinner," he says in a low voice. "But I need to give you a heads-up that insurance isn't going to cover your Jeep at all, not one penny."

Marissa shrugs. "I didn't think it would."

"Does your mother know that? Because she's threatening to sue our agency."

"She's just blowing smoke."

"She doesn't have a leg to stand on; the coverage is spelled out. But it looks bad—for us, for your mom—and we pride ourselves on being an island business with excellent customer service. Having your mom going around complaining about how poorly she's being treated is unfair."

Marissa turns to Rip with an expression halfway between a smile and a snarl. "I just want to move on. My mom has plenty of money. She bought me a new Jeep, and the incident is ancient history. I apologized."

"You apologized for intentionally trashing your perfectly good Jeep."

"Yes. She knows I was upset because Leo broke up with me. She understands."

"She understands. That's good for you, I guess. And the thing is, it's not a total loss in the end; she can still sell it. The engine wasn't as corroded as you'd expect for a car that sat in the Bathtub overnight. The mechanic said it looked like the Jeep had been in the water for an hour, tops. But you drove it into the Bathtub Friday night, right? And called the tow truck on Saturday?"

Marissa swallows and casts her gaze down at her butter plate. "Right."

*She's lying,* Rip thinks. But what else is new? He's in claims. People lie to him every day.

Willa and Carson use the "secret" bathroom on the second floor, across from the Commodore Room, which is for private functions only. This was at Willa's suggestion.

"I have something to tell you," she says. "But you can't repeat it."

"You're in luck," Carson says. "I have no friends and barely any acquaintances." Normally, Carson would guess that Willa is pregnant, but she ordered wine at dinner, so that's not it. "Does it have something to do with Brett Caspian?" Carson asks. "Because he said on TV that he's been in touch with 'Vivi's family,' except it wasn't me and we both know it wasn't Leo."

"I told you I heard from this guy," Willa says.

"You didn't."

"I sent a group text to you and Leo telling you about the segment. You didn't respond."

*That's right,* Carson thinks. She saw the group text come in from Willa and deleted it without reading it. "I've had a rough couple of weeks."

"Why?" Willa says. "What happened?"

"Nothing."

"Just tell me, Carson. I know I've been self-absorbed—"

"Yes, you have been, but that's okay."

"What happened?" Willa reaches out and touches Carson's hair. She used a curling iron tonight and her hair falls in long barrel curls; it looks very extra. Willa can't believe she made such an effort for Lucinda's birthday. And what is up with her drinking ginger ale? "You can tell me."

Carson wishes that were true. She's always wanted Willa to be the kind of big sister she could confide in and conspire with. But

Willa is sanctimonious and judgmental. She thinks she's better than Carson, morally. And, okay, maybe she *is,* but she doesn't have any compassion for people who are flawed.

"You brought *me* up here to tell *me* something," Carson says. It's nice being sober and having a clear head. "I'm ready."

Willa takes a breath. "Okay." She glances at the door and lowers her voice to a whisper. "Pamela thinks Zach is having an affair."

Carson gasps—which is good because Willa interprets this as *Carson is shocked because this is such juicy and unexpected gossip* rather than *Carson is shocked because she's been caught, or nearly.* Carson wonders if this has anything to do with the night last week when she and Zach had sex in the Bridgemans' living room. Carson won't lie; she was so deeply spooked that she hasn't had a drink since that night and she hasn't contacted Zach at all.

"I know, right?" Willa says. Her eyes shine with prurient excitement.

Carson wants to be careful about how she proceeds. "He doesn't seem like the cheating type, does he?"

"No!" Willa says. "But Pamela is so..."

*Bitchy,* Carson thinks. *Controlling. Unpleasant.* "Merciless?" Carson says. "She clearly enjoyed beating the crap out of him at tennis."

Willa rolls her eyes.

"Does she think she knows who it is?" Carson asks lightly. "Any leads?"

"Not yet," Willa says. "She can't access his phone records because it's issued through ATC. But she texted me this morning to say she needs to talk to me ASAP, so there might be a new development."

Carson feels like she's riding a mechanical bull at the moment before she gets flung to the ground. "Well, it's nice that she's made you her confidante."

Willa laughs, then disappears into one of the stalls. "It is nice," she says. "Twisted, but nice."

Willa, Carson, and Leo all return to the table just in time for cake—a yellow cake with chocolate frosting, yellow sugar roses, and *Happy Birthday, Lucy* written in the middle.

*Lucy?* Willa thinks. Penny Rosen must have been the one to talk to the pastry chef.

Lucinda blows out the candles, then winks at JP and Savannah. "You'll never guess what I wished for."

"Mother, please," JP says.

Willa and Rip are the first to leave; Willa is tired—*quelle surprise*—she likes to be in bed by nine and it's an hour past that. Leo and Marissa leave next; Marissa is mopey and barely manages to say thank you and goodbye. JP and Savannah wait ten minutes before they excuse themselves. Are they leaving together? Carson suspects their relationship is platonic; they probably sit around and talk about how much they miss Vivi.

This leaves Carson, Lucinda, and Penny Rosen.

Carson says, "I'm going to go flirt with the bartender."

"Excellent idea," Lucinda says. "Penny and I will join you."

"No, Lucy," Penny says. "I'm driving you home."

"Happy birthday, Grammy," Carson says, and she kisses Lucinda's cheek.

"Thank you, darling," Lucinda says. "You were very well behaved tonight. I was surprised."

"And *I* was disappointed," Penny Rosen says with a wink.

Carson takes a seat at the bar. Zach and Pamela are long gone—off for an evening of Zach's carbonara and Netflix. They'll chill, maybe have a little wine; maybe they'll make love. Carson tries not to care.

*Pamela thinks Zach is having an affair.*

*Not any longer,* Carson thinks. It's over, there's nothing to worry about, and Pamela can't access Zach's phone, so Carson is safe. She's not sure why her heart is beating so fast. Maybe it's because of Marshall.

"What can I get you?" Marshall asks.

"Ginger ale," Carson says. "What the hell, make it a Shirley Temple."

Marshall nods and cashes out the only other member at the bar, Dr. Flutie, who must be a hundred years old. He used to play Santa Claus at the club Christmas party when Carson was a kid.

"Shirley Temple seems a little strong for you," Marshall says. "Did something happen?"

The club is a good place for Marshall to work, Carson decides, because he takes a genuine interest in people the way bartenders do in the movies. They're always portrayed as good listeners filled with sage advice. The only thing Carson ever asked people at the Oyster-catcher was if they wanted to cash out or start a tab. She's interested in making drinks, in providing quick, accurate service, and she's interested in cash on the barrelhead. But she isn't interested in people. She has too many problems of her own to take on someone else's, even for twenty minutes. But Marshall's plate seems pretty empty, so he can heap on servings of his customers' anxiety and stress.

"I got fired," Carson says. She holds his eyes. "I had a douchebag customer, big-money guy, who ordered kamikaze shots and asked that I do one with his group."

Marshall groans as he sets her Shirley Temple down in front of her. It's dark pink, nearly red; he had a heavy hand with the grenadine, but that's how Carson likes it, and he added three cherries. Bravo.

"That happened four times," Carson says, shaking her head. The situation with Brock Sheltingham is one that seems far worse now than it did in the moment. What had she been *thinking?*

"You did *four* shots with a customer?" Marshall says. He looks equal parts impressed and aghast. "Can you imagine if I did that here?"

"Then the guy asked me for a kiss," Carson says.

"You slapped him, I hope?"

"I was too angry to slap him. I kissed him good, trying to make a point, which was lost among all the people cheering us on and filming it."

"Oh, Carson."

"And that's not even why I got fired," Carson says. "I got fired because I insulted a barback who worked with me and she saw me doing coke in the ladies' room and told our boss."

Marshall is quiet. She has horrified him.

"My boss, George, the owner, had been clear about us never doing drugs on the job. So I got fired."

"I'm sorry," Marshall says.

"Don't be," Carson says. She stirs her Shirley Temple and watches the grenadine swirl through the ginger ale like watercolor paint. "I deserved it. George was way cooler than he had to be. He said he'll give me a glowing reference when I get my act cleaned up." She looks up at Marshall, who is staring at her, bar towel draped over the shoulder of his pink oxford shirt. He's wearing a madras tie. He's absolutely darling. "Which is what I'm trying to do now."

"You're doing pretty well," Marshall says. "You made it through dinner with your family."

"And I am not unproud of that," Carson says. "But after my mom died, I went off the deep end. I was smoking too much, drinking too much, doing coke, taking pills." She pauses. "I was abusing *caffeine*. I didn't want to *feel* anything. Also, I was in a bad relationship that just ended, so I thought, *What if I give up every-thing that's hurting me and see if I feel better?*" She takes a sip of her Shirley Temple. "I haven't given up drinking forever. I haven't given up weed forever. But I'm going to live clean until I feel strong enough to let those things back into my life."

"Well, when you're ready to date again, I'd love to take you out," Marshall says.

"What about your little Lilly Pulitzer chickie?" Carson says. "The girl I saw you with at the Box."

"That was my buddy's girlfriend. I asked her to help me make you jealous."

"Whaaaaa?" Carson says. "Are you serious?"

"I saw you dancing and I asked Peyton to pretend to be my date in front of you." Marshall grins. "Did it work? Were you jealous?"

Carson laughs. She can't believe sweet, adorable, fresh-as-pine-scented-air-off-a-deep-Oregon-lake Marshall would dream up such a long-game caper to get her attention. "Actually," she says, "I was a little jealous."

After Leo and Marissa leave the Field and Oar, Marissa wants to go to a party at Miacomet Beach—a bunch of summer kids from Connecticut they both know will be there—but Leo says he's not up for it.

"Do you want me to drop you at the party?" he asks.

"I'm not going without you," Marissa says.

"So I should take you home, then?"

"What is *wrong* with you?" Marissa says. "You didn't stick up for me at all during dinner. Your entire family was making fun of our wedding plans, insinuating they won't even happen—"

"Marissa," he says. He swallows. He should just tell her: *The wedding won't happen. I'm not marrying you. I'm not in love with you.* But he's too tired for drama tonight. He's too tired for drama anytime. He wishes Marissa would go to the party in her low-cut, extremely short dress and find someone else to sink her claws into. He wishes she and Peter Bridgeman had hooked up at the bonfire the night before his mother died.

This thought comes out of nowhere. Did he make it up? No, he thinks. He remembers seeing Marissa and Peter Bridgeman sitting together in the dunes—this was when Leo sneaked away from the bonfire with half a bottle of vodka that he'd snatched from some-one's cooler. Peter had his arm around Marissa; she was crying. This was before she drove her Jeep into the Bathtub and hitchhiked home (a story Leo still doesn't quite believe; she would never, ever hitch a ride home with "some rando"). Did Peter Bridgeman take her home, then? He'd taken that picture...

Leo can't ask Marissa to clarify the details. He doesn't want to know the details. All he wants is Marissa out of his car.

"I'll take you home," he says.

## The Chief

The Chief checks in with Lisa Hitt on her first day back from vacation. She says there were no good prints on the shoes—though there was some mustard.

"I need the clothes, Ed," she says. But her tone conveys what they both know is true: The clothes are gone. They've been tossed or destroyed.

The Chief calls the Greek and asks him to subpoena Peter Bridgeman's phone records. They won't be able to obtain the actual photograph, but they'll at least be able to see if Peter sent the picture to anyone other than Cruz and Leo on Friday night.

And...the Chief can talk to Jasmine Kelly. He finds out from Rocky Moore that the lifeguards meet every morning at a quarter past seven on Nobadeer Beach for a mile-long beach run and calisthenics. They usually finish up around quarter past eight and don't have to be in the chairs until nine.

"You asking for any special reason?" Rocky says.

"I need to speak to Jasmine Kelly," the Chief says.

"I hope she's not in any trouble," Rocky says. "She's my top guard. Top everything—she's smart, she's strong, she's a great kid. One of the greatest kids I've seen in thirty years of doing this job."

"I just need her help," the Chief says. *Bad,* he thinks.

He's standing at the entrance to Nobadeer Beach at quarter past eight the next morning, sand filling up his shoes. Nobadeer is wide and golden, a stretch of paradise, especially at this time of day. The sky is pink and there are a few high, gauzy clouds. The waves form neat rolls as the group of lifeguards—thirty of them, all in red shorts and white T-shirts—finish their jumping jacks and collect their things. They stroll off the beach in groups of three or four.

How long has it been since Ed enjoyed a day at the beach? Feels like forever. He used to take Sundays off when Kacy and Erik were small and then again when he and Andrea became legal guardians for Finn and Chloe. But it's been six or seven years since the twins needed or wanted a parent at the beach. Every once in a while, Andrea will pack a picnic, and she and Ed will drive onto Fortieth Pole to watch the sunset. Mostly Ed works so that the rest of Nantucket can safely enjoy the beach.

The Chief sees Jasmine Kelly. She's talking to two boys, and when the Chief hears her say, "Breakfast sandwiches at the Nickel," his stomach grumbles. He wants a bacon, double egg, and sharp cheddar sandwich with tomato and avocado on a griddled English muffin from the Nickel more than just about anything at that moment. That's another reason he has to solve this case. He needs to make things right for Joe's sake.

All of the guards seem to notice the Chief at the same time. He sees their backs straighten, their shoulders and jaws tense. Their eyes land on him in full uniform—and then they look away. Ed knows he makes kids uncomfortable. *Am I in trouble?* Sometimes, Ed enjoys this—but not today.

He smiles at the kids, waves, says good morning. He wants to assure them he's not here because of their unpaid parking tickets or a party at Gibbs Pond that they may or may not have attended.

When Jasmine is close enough to speak to, he says, "Miss Kelly? May I have a minute?"

Jasmine Kelly recoils. "Me?"

The two boys remain at her side, sentries. The Chief likes this; she has loyal friends.

"It's nothing bad," he says. "I just have a few questions."

She regards him frankly. Why her out of all the guards? she must be wondering. Why her and no one else? "Is something wrong?"

"No," he says, holding up his palms. "I could just use some help, and someone gave me your name."

"Who was that?" she asks. She's not being rude, but she's certainly not eager to help. The Chief can tell, even from this brief exchange, that she's a straight shooter and will give him the truth.

"Joe DeSantis," he says.

"Big Joe!" one of the boys says, then clamps his mouth shut.

"It'll take only a few minutes," the Chief says. "I won't keep you."

Jasmine sighs. "Wait for me, you guys, please," she says, and she trails the Chief over to his car.

Ed says, "I'm investigating Vivian Howe's death."

"Are you, though?" Jasmine asks.

*Whoa,* Ed thinks. *She's tough.* Well, she's Cruz's girlfriend, so he probably deserves her suspicion.

"Do you remember the night before Vivian Howe died?" he asks. "There was a bonfire at Fortieth Pole?"

"Yes," Jasmine says. "It was mostly seniors, my class, local kids."

"Do you know anything about a photo from that night being sent around by Peter Bridgeman?"

Jasmine frowns, shakes her head. "Peter? No. But I did see him hanging out with Marissa that night, after she and Leo broke up."

"Leo Quinboro?"

"Yes. Really, the only thing that happened at that party was that Leo broke up with Marissa. And later, Leo disappeared and I saw Marissa sitting in the dunes with Peter. But I don't know anything about a photo, sorry."

The Chief needs to think for a moment. Leo broke up with his girlfriend? Neither Cruz nor Leo mentioned this. And then the girlfriend was seen with the Bridgeman kid? The Bridgeman kid then sent Leo and Cruz a picture—of him and Marissa, maybe? Was *that* what had them so upset? Or maybe it was a photo of only Marissa, a nude or whatever, which would have been upsetting coming from Peter Bridgeman.

Peter Bridgeman is at camp for the summer in Maine. He must have left pretty soon after Vivian Howe's death. Peter Bridgeman's mother is Pamela Bonham of the Bonham Insurance Agency. Did Peter Bridgeman head over to the Howes' early on Saturday to see Leo? Did he want to confront Leo—or apologize?

Did Peter Bridgeman hit Vivian Howe? Cruz told the Chief that he was coming from the Bridgemans' house, that he went to see Peter but Peter didn't answer the door. He also said he didn't see Peter's truck. Maybe Peter had just left; maybe Cruz had missed him by a matter of minutes and knew he was heading over to the Howes, so he chased him, which would explain running the stop sign and speeding.

The Chief will find a way to talk to Peter Bridgeman. But before he does that, he needs all the information he can get.

"This Marissa," Ed says, pulling out his notepad. "What's her last name?"

"Lopresti," Jasmine says.

The Chief stops, looks up. *Lopresti,* he thinks.

# Willa

Pamela needs to talk to Willa, but she wants to do it when neither Zach nor Rip is around, which is tricky. Then a day comes when Zach is flying himself over to the Vineyard to see his "buddy Buddy," who heads air traffic control at MVY. They get together once a year. Zach is leaving early and will be gone all day.

"Can you come to my house at nine?" Pamela asks Willa.

"I have work."

"Can you come at noon?"

"I'm having lunch with Rip at the club," Willa says—though this isn't true. She has an OB appointment at the hospital.

"Cancel it."

"I can't," Willa says.

"The two of you are freakish in your devotion," Pamela says. "Do you hear me? Freakish."

Willa is proud of being freakish in her devotion. At least she's not monitoring her husband's every move trying to figure out who he's sleeping with.

"I know," Willa says with some smugness.

"Can you come now?" Pamela asks. "Stop by on your way to work?"

"I was planning to ride my bike to work today," Willa says.

"Drive instead, you'll have extra time that way," Pamela says. "There's something I have to show you."

Willa doesn't *want* to drive; she wants to ride her bike. And she's pretty sure she doesn't want to see whatever Pamela has to show her.

She's already in too deep, so deep that she had to confide in Carson, which was risky. Telling Carson *did* lighten Willa's emotional load a little, and when Carson said she had no friends to tell, she wasn't lying. Carson is a lone wolf. Willa is sure she has friends at the Oystercatcher and guys she meets at the Box, but she isn't going to tell any of them about Pamela and Zach Bridgeman's marital discord.

Everyone is so self-absorbed that it's nearly impossible to find someone who can be fully invested in your problems. That has been Willa's experience with the miscarriages. After the first one, people were sympathetic—but everyone wanted to hurry Willa along to "You can just try again," rather than sit with her in the pain and the loss.

Except Rip.

And Vivi.

"Willa?" Pamela says.

"What?" Willa says. She yanks herself up out of the rabbit hole. "Um...okay, yeah."

"You'll come? Right now?"

"Yes," Willa says. She will be invested in Pamela, she decides. She will go, right now.


Willa doesn't have time to waste, however. She walks into the Bridgeman house on Gray Avenue and expects to see Pamela waiting, but the first floor is deserted.

"I'm here!" Willa calls out. "And I need to be back in my car in ten minutes!"

There's no answer, and Willa is tempted to leave. This is *so* like her sister-in-law—impose on another person's schedule, then make her wait. Willa knows that Pamela is this inconsiderate (and worse!) with Zach.

"Pamela!" Willa calls out. She hears footsteps upstairs; she thinks they're moving toward the stairs—but no, they're moving away. "Okay, I'm going to work, then. Call me later!" Willa manages to keep the annoyance out of her voice, but she's miffed. She thinks longingly of pedaling past the turtle pond where Vivi used to take Willa and Carson and Leo when they were little kids. Vivi would patiently tie string around pieces of raw chicken and help them cast the lines across the surface of the water.

"Willa?" Pamela says. "Is that you?"

"Yes!"

"Be right down!" Pamela draws out the word *right,* letting Willa know that she *won't* be right down. Willa hears a clock ticking in her head as she studies the family portraits on the server under the stairs. There are four years represented, photos taken by Laurie Richards at Steps Beach. Pamela, Zach, Peter. They look happy, is the thing. Pamela is actually smiling. Pamela and Zach are holding hands in a photo of just the two of them. Looking at these pictures makes Willa think of family dinners, weekly game nights, driving lessons in school parking lots, and Christmas mornings, not of a troubled kid at school and a husband who's sleeping around.

Pamela finally descends the stairs. Her feet are bare, her hair is wet, she's wearing a turquoise linen shift with a statement necklace (oversize wooden beads on a string that looks like a bigger version of something Peter might have made at the Children's House), and she's clutching something red in her hand.

She holds it out to Willa. "I found this in the laundry."

"This" is a red lace thong. Willa has to fight to keep her morning tea down. She was right—she doesn't want to see this, some other woman's skanky underwear. At least they've been through the wash, Willa thinks.

"I take it those aren't yours?" Willa asks.

"Uh, no. Does this look like something I'd wear?"

*Definitely not,* Willa wants to say—but that might be insulting. And the truth is, no one can tell what kind of underwear a person wears, just like no one can tell what's lurking beneath a seemingly happy family portrait.

"They're Hanky Panky," Willa says without thinking. Despite her revulsion, she lifts the thong from Pamela's palm.

"How can you tell? There's no tag. Do *you* wear underwear like this?" Her voice sounds accusatory and also incredulous.

"No," Willa says. She nearly adds, *My sister does*, but she stops herself. Pamela is right; the tag has been cut out, leaving a hole the size of a dime. A wave of nausea rolls over Willa; there's no avoiding it. She races for the powder room right there in the hall and vomits.

When she emerges, Pamela opens her arms for a hug. "You poor thing. I made myself forget you're pregnant so I don't slip and tell someone."

"It's fine," Willa says. The thong is lying on the server at the base of the most recent family portrait. What a juxtaposition.

Willa says, "Have you asked Zach about it?"

"Not yet. I'm going to wait. I'm collecting evidence, building a case."

"And you're sure these aren't from a friend of Peter's?"

"Peter has been at camp all summer," Pamela says.

"I only ask because this is the kind of underwear that young people wear."

"Zach's lover is younger!" Pamela says. "She wears hooker panties!"

"Why was it in the laundry?" Willa asks. "Was the woman here, in the house?"

"No!" Pamela shrieks. "At least, I don't think so. I *hope* not. I found it stuffed deep in the pocket of Zach's khakis. I thought I would pull out a sock, you know how that happens in the wash sometimes, and it was this. She must have given it to him."

"Ew," Willa says.

Pamela shakes her head. "You have no idea what it's like getting older, Willa. I hope Rip doesn't ever do this to you."

The notion is outrageous. And mean-spirited. Willa is *pregnant.* Who says such a thing to a pregnant woman?

"Anyway, I have to get ready for work," Pamela says. Willa is being dismissed. "Thank you for coming over. I needed to share this with someone."

"You're welcome," Willa says. This whole encounter has been very distasteful and Willa is still smarting from the comment about Rip. As if!

But that's not what bothers Willa the most. What bothers her the most is...something she's too addled to admit even to herself.

Pamela heads to the kitchen, calling out, "Coffee, here I come!" and Willa heads for the front door, scooping the thong up as she leaves.

# Amy

Amy loves Sundays with Dennis because he knows how to relax. JP was always up at the crack of dawn, which arrives very, *very* early in the summer, because he liked to be waiting outside the Hub on Main Street when the guy arrived to deliver the *New York Times.* JP claimed this behavior had been ingrained in him from childhood in Manhattan—Sundays didn't begin for Lucinda or his grandparents until the *Times* was snapped open—but Amy suspects it has more to do with Vivi and the bestseller list. After he secured the paper, it was off to the Downyflake to get a box of doughnuts and then home to make a second pot of coffee.

Dennis, however, likes to sleep in. He has what Amy thinks of as a *talent* for sleep. He sleeps deep and hard and nothing can stir him or wake him until morning. He makes a soft growling noise like a snuggly woodland creature, a welcome change from

JP's snoring, which sounded like someone jackhammering asphalt. It was occasionally so bad that Amy would think, *No wonder Vivi didn't fight harder to reconcile.*

When Dennis wakes up, he heads to the bathroom to relieve himself and brush his teeth, then he returns to bed and makes love to Amy (skillfully; he's by far the best lover she's ever had) and falls back to sleep. Sundays are his only day off (same with Amy in the summer) and he doesn't feel the need to plan anything. Sunday is as God intended: a day of rest.

On the third Sunday in August—the summer is drawing to a close and Amy, for one, is relieved—she and Dennis are lying in bed. They're at the part of the morning when they have just made love and Dennis has fallen back to sleep. Amy curls up against Dennis's wide, warm back and kisses the tattoo of an American flag on his right shoulder blade. She can see bright sunshine trying to insinuate itself into the room around the edges of the room-darkening shades. Amy always wishes for a rainy Sunday, the gloomier the better, but she hasn't been granted one all summer. The Sundays have been painfully beautiful. They'll have to go to the beach later, she supposes. Or maybe she'll suggest a late lunch at the Galley. She has found Dennis to be lavish when it comes to spending money on fun, which is another thing she likes about him, in addition to the sex and the sleeping.

They're really very compatible, she thinks.

On this particular morning, Amy can't fall back to sleep, probably because of the espresso martini she enjoyed last night at the Pearl. She isn't quite ready to get out of bed—she spends so much time on her feet at work that it's a luxury to lie down—so she resorts to looking at her phone.

The only news she actually enjoys is entertainment news. When she clicks on the *People* magazine site, she sees the following headline: "'Golden Girl' and *Golden Girl* Claim Number-One Spots."

*Keep scrolling,* Amy tells herself. But she can't. She's lying in bed with Vivian Howe's ex-boyfriend after a bad breakup with Vivian Howe's ex-husband. Her adult life here on Nantucket has been shaped by Vivi, and even though Amy has vowed to change this, she clicks the link.

*Golden Girl,* the novel, is at number one. Amy saw the headline splashed across the front of the *Nantucket Standard* this past Thursday. Everyone on Nantucket was proud of Vivi because she had finally nabbed the top spot.

The article at People.com says that Brett Caspian, Vivi's "high-school beau," recorded the song "Golden Girl" with Apple Music shortly after his appearance on *Great Morning USA*. It shot straight up the iTunes chart to land at number one. It has twelve million downloads this week.

"Holy crow," Amy says. She taps Dennis on the shoulder. "Dude, guess what?"

He murmurs unintelligibly. He's asleep. She should let him be.

"Remember that guy I told you about on TV who wrote that song for Vivi in high school? The song 'Golden Girl'?" Lorna had been convinced that Dennis watched the segment and was only feigning indifference, but Amy knows he's given up on all Vivi-related things cold turkey in a way she can't seem to do. She doesn't want to bother him, but this is *cool.* This is rock-star stuff.

Dennis utters another soft mumble.

"The song 'Golden Girl' went to number one in iTunes," Amy says. She clicks on the iTunes chart and there it is! "I think this guy works at a Holiday Inn or something, and now he's famous. The song has a bajillion downloads this week."

Dennis rolls over, grabs Amy's phone, and sets it on the nightstand. He kisses her collarbone and nestles his face between her breasts. "Do you know who my golden girl is?" he asks. "Do you?"

"Me?" she says. She runs her fingers deep in his hair the way he likes her to.

"Yes, you," he says. "You and only you."

# Vivi

Vivi swoops down to check the screen of Amy's phone. (Quickly, quickly, the last place she wants to linger is Dennis's bedroom!) Sure enough: "Golden Girl" by Brett Caspian is the number-one song in the country—thirty-four years after it was written.

"Martha!" Vivi calls out. "Martha!" But she doesn't appear. She must be listening to the choir singing "Ruby Tuesday."

When Vivi checks on Brett, she finds him at a party in the lobby of the Holiday Inn in Knoxville. It's a farewell party. Vivi gathers from eavesdropping that Brett is moving to Nashville. He's going to write and record an album.

Brett Caspian has a hit song at the age of fifty-one. Vivi thinks of the boy sitting two rows ahead and one seat to the left of her in his detention turning around and winking at her and how she felt he'd *picked* her, like an apple from a tree. She thinks about the back seat of the Buick Skylark, him kissing her as Steve Perry wailed on the car stereo: *Stone in love!*

She's even more emotional now than she was when her book hit the top of the list. "Golden Girl" might have topped the charts long ago if only Vivi hadn't lied about being pregnant. If only she had been blessed with a stronger sense of self. If only her father hadn't killed himself. (Wasn't Vivi worth staying alive for?) If only she'd had the maturity to understand that she and Brett had different dreams and that was okay.

Vivi didn't lie about being pregnant because she was evil; she lied because she was young and she was still mourning her father. Vivi decides to cut her younger self some slack.

Martha appears. A red and gold scarf is tied around her midsection as a belt.

"Can I ask you a favor?" Vivi says.

Martha sighs. "Would you like me to use my powers of the Road Not Taken? Do you want me to tell you what would have happened if you *hadn't* told Brett you were pregnant? If he hadn't rushed back to Parma to be with you?"

"Yes, please," Vivi says. "If it isn't too much trouble."

"Define *too much trouble,*" Martha says. She chuckles. "Just kidding. But I have to concentrate."

Martha settles in one of the peach silk soufflé chairs, props her feet on the leather pouf ottoman, and closes her eyes. "Brett is in Los Angeles. He does a demo of 'Golden Girl'—"

"I know that already," Vivi says.

Martha opens one eye. "Would you like me to do this or not?"

"Sorry."

Martha resumes her concentrating. "Brett writes a second song called 'Miss My Baby,' and he records a cover of 'Carolina on My Mind,' and the record company grudgingly accepts 'Parmatown Blues.' But that isn't enough. Wayne gets arrested for buying cocaine on Sunset Boulevard. Roy's mother is diagnosed with brain cancer. The band breaks up. Brett keeps the rights to the two songs he wrote and finds a different record exec, one somewhat less reputable than John Zubow, who agrees to release 'Golden Girl' as a single with 'Miss My Baby' as a B-side. It has…modest success. 'Golden Girl' hits number thirty-seven on the top forty in February of 1988 for one week."

"That's it?" Vivi says. "Number thirty-seven for one week?"

"Kid Leo plays it on WMMS as a favor to his brother-in-law, who works with Brett's father. Brett's a local kid, Cleveland is a rock-and-roll town, Kid Leo genuinely likes the song, but even playing it as often as he does, the song doesn't gain much national traction, so it never gets any higher than thirty-seven."

"Then what happens?" Vivi asks.

"Brett moves to Las Vegas," Martha says. "He plays on the Strip, sings 'Golden Girl' and some cover tunes. He develops a gambling problem."

"Seriously?" Vivi says.

"He marries a blackjack dealer named Sonja. They have two kids, they get divorced, there's an ugly custody battle, Sonja takes the kids to New Jersey. Atlantic City. She's still a blackjack dealer." Martha opens her eyes. "And Brett stays in Vegas. If you hadn't told the lie about being pregnant, he would be living there still."

"Instead, he lives in Knoxville."

"Yes," Martha says. "And 'Golden Girl' is the number-one song on iTunes."

"So maybe my lying about being pregnant was a good thing for Brett!" Vivi says. "He had to wait three decades, but he made it to number one instead of stalling out at thirty-seven. Maybe this was the way things were *supposed* to work out."

Martha pushes herself up from the chair. "I think you're finally starting to get it, Vivian," she says.

# Willa

She keeps the red lace thong stuffed deep in her purse. It's the same brand of underwear that Carson wears and, more damning, it has that hole in the back where the tag is supposed to be. Carson's skin is sensitive (she can't handle even a thin bit of tag remaining along the seam) and Carson is careless, so to avoid irritation to her precious backside, she cuts a hole in a twenty-two-dollar lace thong. It's the kind of intimate detail you know only about your sister.

It's Carson's thong; Willa is sure of it.

But what was it doing in Zach's pants pocket? Are Zach and *Carson* having an affair? The thought is...outrageous, nearly laughable.

Or is it?

When Willa told Carson that Pamela thought Zach was having an affair, how had Carson reacted? What had she said?

*He doesn't seem like the cheating type, does he?*

Willa thinks about this. Was Carson trying to cast doubt on Pamela's suspicions? To downplay them, dismiss them?

Next Carson said, *Does she think she knows who it is?* Not, notably, *Does she know who it is?* Is this distinction telling?

Then Willa remembers that Rip told Willa a few weeks earlier that Pamela saw Carson's Jeep parked at the abandoned horse barn across the street from the Bridgemans' house. Pamela told Rip she thought Carson was there to meet her drug dealer.

Willa had been annoyed by Pamela's low opinion of Carson, even though she, too, thought it was likely Carson was there to meet her drug dealer.

Carson had *not* been there to meet her drug dealer, Willa thinks now. The red lace thong with the hole where the tag should be is Carson's, and the thong was in Zach's pants pocket, and Carson was lurking across the street from the Bridgemans' house because she and Zach are having an affair.

Willa shoots Carson a text: Are you working tonight?

Carson responds: No.

Willa says: Rip is golfing after work with Mr. B. Want to come to Smith's Point for dinner? I'll get Millie's takeout.

Carson says: Sure. Please order me the Caesar with grilled shrimp and chips with queso.

Willa says: Great. See you at 7.

\*    \*    \*

Carson shows up on time, which is very unlike her, and she seems serene, but in a natural way and not a stoned-out-of-her-mind way. She has brought Willa a bouquet of flowers from Bartlett's Farm—purple and white cosmos, Willa's favorite—and a thermos of iced tea.

"Mom still has all this mint growing in her herb garden," Carson says. "So I tried making her tea."

"I'll have some with dinner," Willa says. She has already been to Millie's to pick up the food. She doesn't want any distractions. "Would you like wine?"

"No, thanks," Carson says. "I'll have tea."

*Who are you and what have you done with my sister?* Willa thinks. A drunk or high or angry or condescending Carson is the only kind of Carson Willa knows how to deal with. Carson acting human, even gracious, isn't anything Willa was expecting.

"Come out to the back deck," Willa says. It's only four steps from the front door of Wee Bit to the back door.

"It cracks me up how small this place is," Carson says. "But, really, what else do you need?"

"I miss my dishwasher," Willa says. "And my Peloton. And reliable internet."

"Yeah, but look at this view." They step out to the deck. The eelgrass on top of the dunes is swaying in the breeze and they can both hear the pound and the rush of the surf. Willa has become used to the sights and sounds out here, is nearly immune to it, though there are still times when she walks down the deck steps wrapped in a towel on her way to the outdoor shower that she stops to marvel at the ocean or the gulls soaring overhead. Tonight, the sky is awash in golden light, and Willa nearly says something about heaven and her mother like *Do you think she can see us? Do you think she's watching us?* But she doesn't want to sound ridiculous. "I'm happy you have the night off—the sunset is going to be epic."

Willa pauses. "Although I suppose you see the sunset every night at work."

Carson takes a seat on one of the benches of the picnic table. "Will," she says. "I got fired."

Willa inhales. "You did? What happened? When was this?"

"End of July," Carson says. "I was inappropriate at work."

"*Inappropriate,* meaning..."

"I did shots with a customer. I French-kissed a customer. I did cocaine in the bathroom."

"Carson!" Willa says. "Tell me you're kidding. Please tell me you're kidding!"

Carson bows her head. When she looks up, her eyes are like two flashing emeralds. Willa remembers when they were little girls, their father would come into their room in the mornings and say to Carson, "Wake up and show us the jewels." He never said this to Willa; her eyes are brown.

"Not lying," Carson says. Her voice is taut and Willa relaxes. There's going to be a fight, which Willa is prepared for. "I suppose you're going to judge me now," Carson says. "Because you're perfect—by which I mean you're sheltered and unadventurous, and although you're three years older than me, I've lived a far more exciting life."

Willa wants to ask more questions about Carson getting fired— getting *fired,* how mortifying; what is she doing to the family name?—but instead, she cuts to the chase. She pulls the thong out of the pocket of her floor-length prairie skirt (she's surprised Carson hasn't yet made a crack about Laura Ingalls Wilder) and places it between them on the picnic table.

"That yours?" Willa asks. She eyes the thong with distaste. It's a scarlet scrap of lace with a hole in it. Tawdry.

Carson picks it up, pokes a finger through the hole. "What the hell, Will? Did you come home and raid the laundry? What's going on?"

"What's going on," Willa says, "is that Pamela found that in Zach's pants pocket."

Understanding sweeps across Carson's face like passing headlights through a dark house. "It's not mine."

"It is so. You just admitted it."

"I have underwear *like* that," Carson says. "But if they were in Zach's pants pocket, they obviously aren't mine." She brings her eyes up to challenge Willa. "Are they?"

"They are," Willa says. She turns to face the dunes, the ocean. The breeze lifts her hair, stirs the loose material of her skirt. "It's *you.* You're the one who's sleeping with Zach. The one person I chose to confide in, ironically. He's forty-two years old, Carson. He's my *sister-in-law's husband!*"

Carson stands and Willa is afraid she's going to walk out. That would be a very Carson thing to do—drive off without another word. "Don't run away, you coward!"

"*I'm* a coward?" Carson says. "You're the one who married your childhood sweetheart."

"Don't change the subject," Willa says. "I want to hear you admit it. You're having an affair with Zach."

Carson says nothing.

"You realize that's disgusting? And immoral?" Willa steps right up to her sister and lowers her voice. "Mom would be so disappointed in you. You're dishonoring her, you're disrespecting me, you're destroying the family that I'm trying to hold together."

Carson screams, "Not everything is about you, Willa!"

Willa slaps Carson hard, right across the face. Carson doesn't flinch. "You know nothing about what happened with Zach and me," Carson says, "and if I explained it to you, you still wouldn't understand. Because you aren't a human being. You're a...robot, a housewife robot, whatever those are called. You're miserable in your life because you can't grow a baby so you make yourself feel better by judging everyone else."

"I'm judging *you* because you're my sister and you've been screwing things up your entire life as a cry for attention and so people would look at you and tell you how pretty you are—"

"Ah," Carson says. "Now we're getting to the real issue. You're jealous of me."

Again, Willa slaps Carson hard, so hard her hand stings. She can't believe the fury that overtakes her. She's trembling; her ears clog, her eyes water. She pulls her hand back to hit Carson again, and Carson grabs Willa by the forearm and pushes her away.

Willa steps backward and her foot gets caught in the hem of her skirt. She tumbles down the deck stairs.

*Oh no,* she thinks. *No.*

# Vivi

"Go!" Martha says.

Vivi swoops down, both hands in front of her pushing through the membrane. She isn't able to catch Willa exactly, but she shifts her so that instead of landing hard on the flagstones in front of the outdoor shower, Willa lands in the sand.

Vivi senses a movement in Willa. It's the baby; he's jarred for a moment but then he settles back into his bubble.

*It's a he,* Vivi thinks, *and he's fine.*

Willa is crying, but she rises easily. "You *idiot!*" she says. "I'm pregnant!"

"Oh my God," Carson says. "Will!" She helps Willa up the steps to the deck and they sit side by side on the bench, hugging and crying. "I'm sorry, Willie, I'm so sorry. I had no idea." Willa tries to catch her breath. She hit her hip on the step; there will be a bruise. Thank God she landed in the sand. It could have been so much worse.

Carson says, "It's over between me and Zach. It ended the same night I got fired and I haven't contacted him since and I haven't had a drink or a toke or a bump or a pill since then either."

Willa excuses herself to go to the bathroom. She checks to make sure there's no bleeding. She looks in the mirror and says, "I'm okay. I'm okay." Her voice is filled with relief and gratitude and she casts her eyes upward.

Vivi, meanwhile, is a mess. She sobs into Martha's Hermès scarf, which Martha is generously offering as a handkerchief.

"That was so close," Vivi says.

"Yes," Martha says.

"I'm having a grandson."

"You are."

"But I failed as a mother," Vivi says. "My girls...*hate* each other." She peers down at Willa and Carson, both now sitting at the picnic table in silence, opening their takeout containers. Peace has been restored, but Vivi knows it's only temporary. "When Carson was born, I felt so happy that I had given Willa something she would have the rest of her life: a sister."

Martha sighs. "Being sisters doesn't mean being best friends for everyone, Vivian."

"Are you ever going to tell me what happened between you and Maribeth?" Vivi asks. "And how you happen to have all these scarves?"

Martha closes her eyes briefly. "I suppose August *is* drawing to a close," she says. "Which means our time together is almost over."

"No!" Vivi says.

"Yes," Martha says. She shakes the scarf out and methodically smooths it, then folds it. "Would you like to hear the story?"

*Yes,* Vivi thinks.

Martha sits on the velvet chaise, props her feet up on the coffee table, and pats the spot next to her. Vivi sits; out the open side of the room, they have a spectacular view of night settling over Nantucket, a navy-blue sky shot through with streaks of brilliant pink. "Maribeth was four years younger than I," Martha says. "She was, you might say, the Carson to my Willa—not exactly, of course, but close enough. My husband, Archie, was a boy Maribeth and I grew up with in Kalkaska, Michigan, so I am a bit like Willa because he was my first love, my only love. Archie and I both attended the University of Michigan. In my senior year, I received a job offer from FedEx, and after graduation I moved to Memphis. Meanwhile, Archie went to medical school at Michigan. We decided on a long-distance relationship. Well, the year I left for Memphis was the year Maribeth enrolled at U of M, and she and Archie started a secret relationship."

Vivi instantly perks up. "Oh my."

"I had no idea," Martha says. "It went on for four years, but it couldn't have been too serious because when Archie finished medical school, he took a residency at St. Jude's in Memphis. He was in pediatric oncology and St. Jude's is, of course, one of the top hospitals in the country for treating and researching childhood cancers. Archie proposed to me; we were married. Maribeth graduated with a degree in theater and moved to New York to become an actress, but she ended up marrying Richard Schumacher, a man who was much, much older than her and very rich. He owned a brownstone on East Seventy-Eighth Street, a house on Nantucket, and a sailboat named *Wind Castle*."

"Right," Vivi says. She remembers Maribeth talking about her home in Shawkemo Hills and her boat.

"Archie and I met Richard for the first time at their wedding," Martha says. "They got married at city hall and Archie and I flew in to be witnesses. We went to lunch afterward at Le Cirque—it was very chic, exorbitantly expensive—and it became clear at that lunch that Richard didn't care for Archie one bit. He was rude to

Archie throughout the meal." Martha clears her throat. "I have my suspicions now that Richard knew, as I did not, that Maribeth and Archie had had a love affair."

*It's interesting,* Vivi thinks, *that Martha calls it a love affair and not a fling.*

"Just wait, I'm getting there," Martha says. "Archie and I barely saw Maribeth after that. We were never invited to New York or Nantucket—though of course, Maribeth would send me your books, so I *felt* like I'd been there."

Vivi decides to take this as a compliment.

"And then one winter, Richard slipped on the ice on the sidewalk in New York, broke his hip, and died shortly thereafter. The following summer, Maribeth invited us to Nantucket." Martha rests her head back against the chaise and Vivi follows her gaze up to the lacy pattern of light on the ceiling. "We had a magical week. We drove onto the beach at Great Point with magnums of Veuve Clicquot— Maribeth made a joke about the merry widow—and we grilled lobster tails and littleneck clams on the hibachi. We walked through the moors, visited Bartlett's Farm, rode bikes out to Sconset during the first bloom of the cottage roses. We ate at the Boarding House and the Company of the Cauldron; we sang at the piano bar of the Club Car. We did all the things the people in your books do."

"Wow," Vivi says. All this time she had no idea that Martha was a...fan. She feels honored.

"We went for an all-day sail on *Wind Castle.* That boat had a captain and a mate and a chef who prepared lunch, but Maribeth liked to play bartender. She was making her signature cocktail, which she called the Bad Decision: vodka, St. Germain, and fresh-squeezed grapefruit juice with a champagne floater. Well, I had five or maybe six Bad Decisions over the course of the afternoon. As the boat rounded Abrams Point and we could see Maribeth's house in the distance, Maribeth said she was going to swim the rest of the way in, not to worry, she did it all the time, her captain would take care of the boat." Martha pauses. "I made my own bad decision to join her, and Archie wasn't about to be shown up by the two of us—we had all grown up together on Lake Michigan, don't forget. Those two dived in ahead of me and off they went. I almost didn't go after them, but in the end, I didn't want to be bested by Maribeth. I was much drunker than I realized and the water was choppy and I hadn't swum in open water in decades and it was much farther than I anticipated. I became exhausted and started swallowing water and I was dragged under for periods. I tried calling out and waving to *Wind Castle* but it was so far away that it was useless." Martha stops. Vivi is holding her breath. "Those two made it to shore and I drowned."

Vivi whispers, "I remember hearing that story as gossip, but it was never in the paper. And I had no idea it happened to Maribeth's sister. Though, come to think of it, I hadn't seen Maribeth in a while. When did this happen?"

"In 2019," Martha says. "Maribeth saw to it that it was kept quiet. And then six months later, she married Archie."

"You're kidding."

"I was brought up here to the Beyond, and my Person, Geri, gave me one nudge."

"Only one?" Vivi says.

"The policy changed back in January," Martha says. "Used to be one, now it's three. You got lucky."

"What did you nudge?" Vivi asks. "Didn't you want to stop Archie and Maribeth from getting married?"

"I tried but I couldn't," Martha says. "Turns out, they were in love. They'd been in love for...decades. And nudges can't change that."

"Ah," Vivi says. "So, instead?"

"Instead, I reached down and disappeared Maribeth's collection of Hermès scarves." Martha holds the silk square out, exhibit A. "She thought she was robbed."

"You were allowed to bring the scarves up here?" Vivi asks.

Martha shrugs. "Geri was a progressive."

Vivi marvels over this story. She thinks...well, what she thinks is that it would make one hell—oops, heck—of a novel, and it falls *right* in Vivi's wheelhouse. *The Swan Dive,* she would call it. But before Vivi can ask Martha what she thinks—could she write a novel and distribute it, maybe, to the angels in the choir?—she turns to find that Martha is gone.

# Leo

In one week, Leo's father and Savannah will drive him out to Boulder. They're taking the route Vivi mapped out and they're stopping at all the places Vivi chose. Savannah found the itinerary in the Notes app of Vivi's phone.

"It'll be kind of like your mom is with us," Savannah says. "I have her playlists and everything."

*Kind of like* is just another way of saying *nothing like,* in Leo's opinion. He has lost so much this summer, and although a part of him is ready to move on—get off the island, start a life somewhere new—he knows he has unfinished business.

Marissa has a list of things she wants to do before they both leave for college, and sleeping out on the beach at Madequecham is the only thing left. Marissa has some romantic vision of a bottle of wine, a couple of sleeping bags, and a sky filled with stars, and although Leo goes through the motions of preparing for this outing, he has no intention of sleeping on the beach.

He's going to live his truth.

When he picks Marissa up, she's subdued, and when he asks

what's wrong, she says that she had an unpleasant phone conversation with Rip Bonham about her claim.

"He thinks I'm lying about the timing of my accident," she says.

"Technically, it wasn't an accident," Leo says. "You drove into the Bathtub on purpose."

"Shut up, Leo!" Marissa says.

Leo's anxiety is rising like the water level in a *Titanic* stateroom. It's going to drown him. He fights for a clear breath. He promises himself it will be fine. It's no big deal. He just needs to get to the beach and talk to Marissa calmly and rationally.

The road to Madequecham turns to dirt; they rumble along. Marissa suddenly starts to cry, but Leo can't engage, he can't get distracted. He realizes the song on the radio is "Falling," by Harry Styles, which was the theme song for their senior banquet. Is that why she's crying?

It's an emotional time, the transition between one period of their lives and the next, leaving the cradle of this island, venturing into the wider world. For him the Rocky Mountains, for her the mansions and glamour of Newport. He wants to assure Marissa that she'll thrive without him; she's a smart and beautiful girl, she'll meet people, make friends, find someone who genuinely adores her. Leo has been pretending for years. That ends tonight. That ends now.

He pulls up to the lip of Madequecham Beach. It's the wild, windswept southeast coast, nearly always deserted at night. There are a few homes on the bluff, all completely dark. The owners have probably left for the season. Summer is ending.

The waves crash under a nearly full moon, which makes the water look dense and metallic, like mercury.

"Marissa."

"You don't want to sleep here, do you?" she says. "You look like I've brought you to the proctologist's office."

He wants to smile, but it's beyond him. "We need to break up." He turns to face her. "I'm not in love with you, Marissa."

Her face looks ghostly pale in the moonlight, like an image on black-and-white film. She isn't wearing any of the orangish foundation she favors, and Leo thinks she looks prettier without it. He watches her absorb his words. A flicker of recognition ignites in her expression.

"I know," she says.

"You do?"

She pulls out her phone and with a few finger-swipes brings up the photograph. It's of Leo and Cruz kissing. Leo pretends not to remember the moment, but he does, vividly. Cruz was trying to load Leo into the car; Leo was drunk, protesting. When Leo twisted away from the open passenger-side door, Cruz's face was right there, and an instinct, so long and so deeply sublimated, surfaced. Leo had grabbed Cruz's head and started kissing him. Almost immediately, there had been a flash. Cruz pulled back and Leo made out the shadowy figure of Peter Bridgeman, gawking at the image he'd captured on his phone.

Leo had socked Cruz right in the eye. "Get off me!" Leo screamed.

"What the heck, man?" Cruz said. He pulled off his glasses; one of the lenses was cracked.

"Get off me!" Leo said again, louder, in case Peter Bridgeman was still listening.

"*Me* get off *you?*" Cruz said. "Are you kidding me right now? Man, you're my brother and I love you, but not..."

*But not that way.* Which Leo knew, which Leo had always somehow known. Cruz was the Frick to Leo's Frack, Cruz was his best friend, his ride-or-die—but Cruz was straight.

"Get *off* of me!" Leo said. He stumbled away thinking Cruz would persuade him to get back in the Jeep, but Cruz didn't. Cruz drove off, leaving Leo in the parking lot. Leo somehow made his way out to Eel Point Road, where Christopher, who was heading home, picked him up.

Leo takes the phone from Marissa. "Peter sent this to you?"

"He did."

"So you knew? You knew all along?"

"I'd always suspected," Marissa says. "Because your friendship with Cruz... your devotion to him was weird, Leo. It was *unnatural.* But even so, seeing this was a shock. All I could think was that you lied to me... for years. A *profound* lie, Leo." She clears her throat. "I tried to convince myself that I was overreacting, that you two were probably just kidding around. I mean, Cruz isn't even kissing you back."

Leo nods and hands the phone back to Marissa. "I know he's not. But we weren't kidding around. Or I wasn't." His eyes are glossy. "I love him. I've always loved him. My whole entire life, I've loved him. But it was one-sided."

"It's disgusting," Marissa says.

Leo sits with this for a second. He's not sure if she means it's disgusting that he loves Cruz when he pretended to love Marissa or that it's disgusting because it's two men kissing. It doesn't matter. Marissa has revealed herself either way. She has no feelings, no empathy, no ability to sense anyone's pain but her own.

"I'm taking you home," he says. He throws the car in reverse and fights the desire to leave her on the side of the road. He is *not* disgusting. He has, finally, spoken his truth: He loves Cruz De-Santis. After he drops Marissa off, he'll call Cruz, figure out where he is, and apologize in person. He will get it all out—his love, his denial, his shame, his rage, his sadness, his grief. And then, once he's an empty vessel, he can accept his heartbreak, accept *himself,* and start to heal.

When Leo pulls onto Marissa's road, they see red and blue flashing lights. The police are waiting in her driveway.

# The Chief

He had nothing for weeks, then everything at once. No sooner did Jasmine Kelly say the name Lopresti than the Chief knew it was Marissa's sister, Alexis, who worked dispatch and her new boyfriend, Officer Pitcher, who tampered with the evidence. They destroyed Vivian Howe's clothes; they paid Justin to plant the running shoes.

Alexis wants to take all the blame. It was *her* fault, *her* plan. She had been able to persuade Pitcher because she had something Pitcher wanted. (This is an old story, Ed thinks.) Alexis was trying to protect her sister, Marissa.

Marissa Lopresti is the one who hit Vivian Howe. The Chief brings Marissa into the station and she spews forth the whole story. She and Leo Quinboro broke up at a bonfire at Fortieth Pole the night before the accident. Marissa then got cozy with Peter Bridgeman. It was easy, she said, because Peter had had a crush on her since fourth grade. Marissa thought Leo would get jealous seeing her with Peter, but Leo disappeared; no one had seen him. Marissa blew Peter off and left the party but Peter Bridgeman lurked around, eventually catching Leo and Cruz DeSantis kissing by the side of Cruz's Jeep.

The photograph, which the Chief had suspected was of two people in a compromising position, was of Cruz and Leo.

*Okay, okay,* the Chief thinks. He's a lot more "woke" (as Chloe and Finn would say) than he was twenty or even ten years ago, but *this* possibility hadn't even crossed his mind. Clearly, he still has some evolving to do.

Peter sent the photograph to Leo and Cruz in the middle of the night, but he didn't send it to Marissa until the next morning, right after Cruz woke Peter up by pounding on his door. (Peter hadn't answered, not wanting a confrontation that his parents might hear.) Peter Bridgeman's phone records, which the Greek managed to subpoena, showed a text with an attachment sent to Marissa's phone at 7:14 a.m.

Marissa says she was driving over to the Howe residence to see Leo and "make up" when she got a text alert on her phone. Because it was so early, she assumed it could only be Leo. She checked her phone and clicked on the photo as she was turning onto Kingsley Road. She had only glimpsed the photo—she said she wasn't even sure what she was looking at—when she heard a sickening thud. She slammed on the brakes and realized she had hit a person. She had hit Vivi.

She panicked, she said. There was no one on Kingsley and no cars on the Madaket Road. She backed up and drove west. She took the turn onto Eel Point Road.

"I had every intention of going back to Kingsley," Marissa said. "But I just…*didn't*. Alexis texted to say Vivi was dead and then…she told me another officer had seen Cruz running a stop sign and speeding and that Cruz had probably killed Vivi, and I felt *relieved* by that. I was angry at Cruz. By then, I had seen the photograph. So I drove my Jeep into the Bathtub and I told Rip Bonham at my insurance company that I'd done it on Friday night."

When the Chief called Rip Bonham, Rip said he'd had doubts about Marissa's story all summer; according to the mechanic, the Jeep hadn't been submerged for as long as Marissa said it had been. He thought she'd been lying as a way to angle for insurance money, not to cover up a crime.

Rip Bonham put Lisa Hitt in touch with the garage that was holding Marissa's Jeep. Luminol turned up Vivi's blood on the fender.

\*   \*   \*

"Every contact leaves a trace," Lisa Hitt says mournfully to Ed over the phone. "I can't believe how this turned out. It's like a..."

"Vivian Howe novel?" Ed says. As relieved as he is to close the case, his heart is heavy for all involved. He has joked many times about having job security—people will never stop making mistakes—but this isn't funny.

Ed doesn't get home until noon the next day; he stayed up all night questioning people and filling out paperwork. "Phones," he says to Andrea. "They'll be the death of civilization."

Andrea pulls Ed's phone out of his shirt pocket. "Leave yours right here," she says, plugging it in at the kitchen counter. "I got you the pastrami special from the Nickel, then you're going to bed."

# Vivi

Vivi doesn't have to call for Martha; she's right there, the same red and gold scarf from the other day serving as a pocket square.

"Marissa hit me?" Vivi says. "Marissa *killed* me?"

"I'm surprised you didn't figure that out," Martha says. "She checked her phone as she was turning and was just looking at the photograph of Leo and Cruz when she hit you." Martha pauses. "I'm surprised you didn't figure out about Leo and Cruz either."

Since Vivi has been dead, her children have surprised her, it's true, but she is *not* surprised to learn that her son has romantic feelings for his best friend. The whole Howe-Quinboro clan fell in love with Cruz at least in part because of the sterling quality of Leo's devotion for Cruz. When Leo was in preschool, he once drew a picture of himself and Cruz living in a house together, with smaller figures that were meant to be their children. The teachers at the school had chuckled about this, Vivi remembers, but at least they were open-minded enough not to tell him the picture was wrong—and Vivi, for her part, had taped it to the refrigerator.

Vivi watches Leo's conversation with Cruz from a greater distance than she normally does—she wants to afford them some privacy. The conversation takes place on the back deck of Cruz's house the very same afternoon that Marissa speaks to the police. Vivi can't hear a word, but she can observe their body language—Leo contrite and Cruz, initially defiant, then softening into forgiveness. The boys end up in silence, sitting side by side, both bent over their knees with their heads in their hands. When Leo stands to go, it's unclear if they can still be friends.

Leo heads for the side yard—it looks like he's leaving—and Cruz says something that makes him turn. Cruz opens his arms and Leo walks back to him. The two boys hug for a moment. When they separate, they do a complicated handshake that they'd once tried, unsuccessfully, to teach Vivi. "You two are Frick and Frack," she had said at the time. "I'm just the mom."

Vivi listens in on Willa and Carson later that day when they meet in Vivi's kitchen over glasses of iced tea. They seem to share the same opinion for once: they're both furious. Marissa Lopresti had been her usual *careless, thoughtless, irresponsible, entitled, needy self* and had picked up her *phone* instead of watching the *road*. She had become so absorbed in her own *drama* that she had hit Vivi. *Killed* her. *Murdered* her. It's absolutely *reprehensible*. She will *never* be forgiven.

Vivi takes a deep breath. A part of her agrees that Marissa deserves little in the way of mercy. She robbed Vivi of the chance to watch her children grow up, meet her grandchildren, write more books, swim in the ocean, eat a tomato sandwich on perfectly toasted Portuguese bread, to meet a new man, make love to that man, maybe break up, maybe get married again. Vivi would never again clink her wineglass against Savannah's at the end of a long week, she would never again fall asleep while reading or take an outdoor shower or laugh at a commercial during the Super Bowl or marvel at a sunset.

"And as if that weren't egregious enough!" Willa says. "She drove off! She plowed her Jeep into the Bathtub and lied to my husband in an attempt to cover her tracks. Then she tried to pin it on Cruz!"

"She hung out at our house all summer long as though nothing was wrong," Carson says. "She made a Bakewell tart like she was Mary freaking Berry come to the rescue! She's…a complete *sociopath!*"

"She sat with us at Grammy's birthday dinner and none of us were any the wiser," Willa says. "The murderer was *at our table.*"

"It was also Peter Bridgeman's fault," Carson says. "Sending out that picture of Leo and Cruz. Girl, who does that? Who *cares?* It's 2021!"

"I'm going to choose to believe that Marissa hadn't seen the photograph when she hit Mom. She was driving too fast because she wanted to get to the house to talk to Leo and she checked the text because she thought it was from Leo. It could have been from her mother or her sister or Verizon. I don't think we can pin this on Peter."

"But what if Peter knew about me and Zach?" Carson says. "What if that's why he was trying to gotcha Leo? Because he held a grudge against me. Against our family."

"Marissa said Peter has had a crush on her since elementary school," Willa says. "I'm sure he wanted to show Marissa the picture because he wanted her for himself. It didn't have anything to do with you."

Carson gnaws her bottom lip. "I want her to go to prison."

"Oh, me too," Willa says. "But I can't help thinking…"

"What?"

"That after all is said and done, Mom would forgive her," Carson says.

They both sit quietly for a second.

"It *was* an accident," Willa says. "I mean, she didn't drive over to the house intending to kill Mom. And I've definitely checked my phone while driving."

"I've done worse," Carson says.

"I'm sure you have."

"It's by the grace of God I've never killed anyone," Carson says.

"Would you have run, though?" Willa asks. "Either one of us could have gotten distracted while driving and hit someone and killed her. But the test of our character, our morals, is whether we stay and admit to it or run away. Marissa ran away. And she pushed the theory that Cruz did it. She wagered that people would suspect Cruz before they'd suspect her. Which is heinous for *so many reasons.*"

Carson says, "I would have been tempted to run. I'm not saying that's what I would have done, but I do understand the instinct."

Willa sighs. "So...we don't press charges?"

"She's being charged by the state," Carson says.

"But we could offer a statement of mercy," Willa says. "It might help."

"I just feel like we aren't honoring Mom unless we ask for the maximum sentence," Carson says.

"As usual, you have things backward," Willa says. "We honor Mom by offering forgiveness. You know how she treats the characters in her books? She gives them flaws, she portrays them doing horrible things—but the reader loves them anyway. Because Mom loves them. Because they're human."

"Like Alison in *Golden Girl,*" Carson says.

Willa is resting her hand on her belly. She takes another look at Carson. "Wait—have you been reading Mom's books?"

"I've had a lot of time on my hands," Carson says.

*     *     *

Vivi rocks back and forth, hands brought prayer-like in front of her heart, tears streaming down her face. "I'm so proud of my girls," she says. "They came to that conclusion on their own. I didn't have to use a nudge."

"Which is a good thing," Martha says. "Because you're out of them."

# Nantucket

With the investigation closed, the body of Vivian Howe is returned to Nantucket. The family gathers on the Friday of Labor Day weekend to bury Vivi in the cemetery on Milk Street. At some point, we know, this will become a popular pilgrimage for Vivian Howe readers across the country. They'll lay bouquets and seashells and pillar candles by the headstone. They'll take selfies of themselves in their Lilly Pulitzer dresses and Mystique sandals standing at Vivian Howe's grave. But for now, it's just the family and close friends.

Rip and Willa Bonham have their arms wound around each other as they lead the way toward the gravesite. Willa has just had her seventeen-week prenatal appointment and ultrasound and everything looks great. She has finally been able to share the news: she's pregnant with a little boy and due on February 11.

The elder Bonhams are over the moon, especially Tink. When Tink asks Rip if it would be appropriate for her and Chas to come to the burial, Rip asks Willa her thoughts.

"Tell them we're keeping it small," Willa says. "And pass that on to your sister as well. She and Zach and Peter don't need to come."

Carson attends the burial with Marshall Sebring, the bartender from the Field and Oar Club. Carson and Marshall have become something of an item. A few of us saw them out to dinner at Lola and still others of us noticed them anchored off the second point of Coatue in a Boston Whaler.

When Dr. Flutie, a regular at the Field and Oar bar, asked Marshall what he planned to do when the season was over, Marshall told Dr. Flutie that he and his girlfriend were going back to Portland, Oregon, for a while. His girlfriend had never seen that part of the country. It might be just a visit, or, if they can both find restaurant jobs, it might become something more permanent.

Dr. Flutie says he's jealous. He may be old (and a bit of a drinker), but even he knows the restaurant scene in Portland is top-notch.

Leo attends the burial with Cruz DeSantis and Cruz's father, Joe. We're all happy to see that Leo and Cruz have made up and are back to planning Cruz's trip out to Colorado after his first quarter at Dartmouth.

"We're friends for life," Cruz said when he and Leo reconciled. "Nothing's going to change that, man."

Leo has a hard time shaking the feeling that the accident was his fault. When he went to his father and Savannah and told them everything, they assured him he had done the right thing in breaking up with Marissa. Her reaction to the news was beyond his control.

"I should have broken up with Marissa a long time ago," Leo said. "I should never have been dating her in the first place. If I had just been truthful about things."

Savannah gave him a squeeze. "You had nothing to do with it, Bear. Your dad and I are both proud of you and love you more than you will ever know. Your mom does too, I promise. The love doesn't go away. She's looking down on you every second of every day."

\*     \*     \*

Savannah is leaving for Manaus, Brazil, on Tuesday and JP realizes how much he's going to miss her. He's had dinner at her house once a week since Vivi passed and those are nights he looks forward to. More than a few times, he's found himself wanting to kiss Savannah, but he's held back because he's afraid of muddying the waters of their newly formed alliance and he doesn't want it to be confusing to the kids. He would love to go with her to Manaus and volunteer, but it's still too busy at the Cone for JP to travel. By the time Savannah gets back, summer will officially be over and JP will be getting ready to close the shop.

He'll make his move then, maybe. See what happens.

Lucinda is attending the burial with Penny Rosen. "Someday that will be us," Lucinda says, nodding at the coffin.

"Someday soon," Penny says. "I woke up this morning with the worst chest pain."

"Well, for goodness' sake, see a doctor!" Lucinda says. "If something happens to you, who will I beat at bridge?"

Penny smiles and decides not to tell Lucy that the tightness in her chest remains to this very minute or that she has been having vivid dreams about her late husband, Walter. She knows that beneath Lucy's joke about the bridge, there's genuine concern. Penny will try to hang on for Lucy's sake. Maybe she's just hungry. Rumor has it that Joe DeSantis is catering the lunch after the burial. Joe's chicken salad with pecans and dried apricots in mustardy dressing is as good a reason to stay alive as any.

Marshall Sebring, of Gaston, Oregon, grew up with a mom, a dad, a sister, and a dog—a regular, happy American family—and although he wouldn't change a second of it, there's something about Carson's family that is fascinating in a way that Marshall's family is not. Her father, JP, owns the Cone; her sister, Willa, works at the Nantucket Historical Association; and her brother, Leo, just graduated from Nantucket High School and is going to the University of Colorado, Boulder. Then there's Carson's grandmother and Mrs. Rosen; they're two tough but elegant ladies—Marshall has served them dozens of times this summer at the club. And there's Savannah Hamilton, who founded Rise and whose family has owned their house on Union Street for something like three hundred years. Marshall has just met Leo's friend Cruz and Cruz's father, Joe, who owns Marshall's favorite sandwich shop, the Nickel. Marshall feels like he's standing in a cluster of real Nantucketers, people whose attachments to this island run as deep as tree roots into the soil of the island.

The person Marshall really wishes he'd been able to meet, however, is Carson's mother, Vivian Howe.

"She was magic," Carson told him. "But she was my mom, so I took her for granted. I didn't understand how lucky I was to have her until she was gone."

Marshall decides when he gets home from the luncheon following the burial, he's going to call his parents and tell them he loves them.

Lorna O'Malley drives past the cemetery on her way from the hospital to her apartment. The biopsy has come back positive for a malignancy. Lorna has triple-negative intraductal carcinoma—a complicated way of saying breast cancer—at the age of thirty-one, and although the news could be worse (she's still stage one, they caught it early), it could also be better. Lorna notices JP walking with Vivi's daughters—they're all dressed in dark colors, so they must have just buried Vivi. Lorna thinks about calling Amy to let her know that Vivi has finally been laid to rest, but she can't bring herself to think about death and burial right now. She'll call Amy later, with her own news.

*Pigeon,* she'll say, *I'm about to lose me tits!*

Amy will cry about it, Lorna is certain. But she will shore up and become Lorna's person. She will go with Lorna to her appointments, share her Netflix password during Lorna's chemo, be in the waiting room during Lorna's surgery; she'll keep Lorna's mother, back in Wexford, calm, and she'll take Cupid for walks. After all the hours Lorna has listened to Amy chatter about JP, Dennis, and, most of all, Vivi, she'd better! Thinking this makes Lorna chuckle. At least she still has her sense of humor.

# Amy

On the Friday of Labor Day weekend, Amy and Dennis are enjoying the raw bar special at the Oystercatcher. Amy had been purposefully staying away from the Oystercatcher because she didn't want to face Carson at the bar—she couldn't imagine what Carson would think when she saw Amy and Dennis together— but then Amy heard from her client Nikki that Carson no longer worked at the Oystercatcher.

"You're kidding!" Amy said. "What happened?" She felt a twinge of regret (quickly followed by relief) that she was no longer a part of the Quinboro family dramas.

Nikki shrugged. "I'm not at liberty to say."

Something bad, then, Amy thinks. Carson got fired—or got fired up and quit in a huff. The upside is that Amy and Dennis can return to the Oystercatcher without feeling awkward.

It's a festive scene—everyone is out celebrating the unofficial last weekend of summer. Amy and Dennis order two rum punches and a dozen Island Creeks from a new cute young bartender with a pierced nose. Dennis lifts his rum punch and says, "I'm taking you on vacation this winter. To the Caribbean. Maybe the Virgin Islands. What do you say?"

"I say yes!" Amy takes a sip of her drink and can already see the palm trees. "If we were the subject of a Vivian Howe novel, what would the title be?" she asks. "*The Leftovers?*"

"I think that's already a book," Dennis says.

"*The Cast-Asides?*" Amy says.

Dennis shakes his head with that look on his face that tells her he thinks she's crazy but in the best possible way. "How about we just call it *Love Story?*" he says.

"I think that's already a book," Amy says.


# Vivi


"They should call it *The Rebound,*" Vivi says.

"What Amy and Dennis have is more than just a rebound," Martha says.

"It is?" Vivi says. "Seriously?" She smiles. She finds she feels happy about this.

There's only one more chance for Vivi to travel back.

She chooses Willa's wedding.

It's June 13 of the year before. The weather is spectacular. It is, as Vivi's mother used to say, one of "God's days."

Vivi has abandoned her suspicions that Rip is "not enough" for Willa, and she now wholeheartedly embraces the union. Today, Willa is getting what she has wanted since she was twelve years old and attended the Valentine's Day dance with Rip at the Boys and

Girls Club. She's marrying the only man she's ever loved. Vivi has written about all kinds of love stories in her twelve novels, but she has never written about two people meeting in high school and making it work.

Why not? she wonders. She thinks about Brett Caspian and the roller-coaster ride of their romance. She has kept that story tucked safely inside of her for decades, but what if she brought it to the surface and used it? *What if she wrote a novel about her and Brett?*

She decides to think about it later. Right now, she wants to focus on her daughter.

Willa, Carson, and Vivi get ready together at Money Pit. Vivi has made a spectacular fruit salad (she went to the trouble of peeling six kiwis, even though nobody ever eats them), and right after her run, she picked up cheddar scones from Born and Bread.

Only Carson eats. Willa is too nervous, Vivi too excited.

Vivi opens a bottle of vintage Veuve Clicquot and makes mimosas with fresh-squeezed juice. Willa is in her slip, her hair damp. Carson is giving Willa a chignon with braid (they all looked through thousands of pictures online and picked this style) and there's a gentleman named Rafe coming from Darya's salon to do all of their makeup. Laurie Richards, the photographer, is due to show up any minute to take "getting ready" pictures. But right now, it's just Vivi and her two daughters. They're in Vivi's bedroom, which resembles a college dorm—her mattress and box spring are on the floor, her running clothes spill out of a jute basket by the side of a dresser she got at the Take-It-or-Leave-It at the town dump. The top of the dresser is littered with candles that Vivi lights for atmosphere; there are also receipts, pens, safety pins, a brush, half a dozen red lipsticks, and a pack of matches from 21 Federal, where she and JP went on their first dinner date. In other words, the room is a disaster. Vivi can't have Laurie take pictures in here—or can she? So many things in Vivi's life are works in progress (she will renovate this room eventually; she wants a round bed, some kind of cool light fixture, a boho-chic vibe), but this moment is plucked straight from Vivi's dreams. Shawn Mendes is singing "Treat You Better" over the wireless speaker. (Willa is an unapologetic top-forty fan and always has been.)

"My beautiful girls," Vivi says. She knows they'll both protest if she gets overly "emo," but how can she help herself? Her oldest child is getting married, her younger daughter is the maid of honor. Would someone please tell Vivi where the years went? It feels like she just brought Willa home from the hospital, just burst into tears because Lucinda said she "loathed" the name and JP had to explain that they (Vivi) had decided to name the baby after Willa Cather, the writer. ("First children are to be named after family," Lucinda said. "Is Willa Cather family?")

What about the eternity Vivi lived through when Willa was a toddler, going to the Children's House half a day, and Carson was a baby? Then it felt like a second eternity when they were both small, Willa six and Carson three, and Leo entered the world. The girls started battling for Vivi's remaining attention; there was name-calling and hair-pulling. Willa threw the remote control during an episode of *Caillou* and hit Carson above the eye (stitches). Carson bit Willa during bath time and broke the skin. (JP had joked about a rabies test and Vivi, delirious with lack of sleep, had laughed.)

Vivi raises her glass and the girls do as well. Through her tears, Vivi sees their three flutes come together; Shawn Mendes gives way to Lady Gaga. Vivi grants herself a moment of congratulations. She got her girls this far. Willa and Carson have always loved each other. And today, they like each other.

"To you, Willie," Carson says.

Willa smiles. She looks as beautiful as Vivi has ever seen her— without her hair done, without makeup, without wearing the ivory silk dress that hangs on the back of Vivi's closet door—because she is illuminated from within. Lit by love.

\*　　\*　　\*

The florist has outdone herself with pink roses, pink lilies, and ivy. The bridesmaids are in blush, the groomsmen in navy blazers, Nantucket Reds, and matching blush bow ties. There's a string quartet playing Pachelbel's Canon in D. As mother of the bride, Vivi is the last person to be shown to her seat before the procession. She's on the arm of Zach Bridgeman, with Dennis following a pace behind in his too-tight gray suit pants. Zach seats Vivi and Dennis in a pew with Amy, who was escorted down just before Tink Bonham. Amy pretends to be absorbed in the program.

When the bridesmaids come walking in, Vivi beams at the girls and winks at Carson, but she—and everyone else in the church—is waiting to see Willa.

Jeremiah Burke's Trumpet Voluntary begins. Everyone stands and Vivi turns. Willa and JP appear in the entryway; there's a collective intake of breath throughout the church.

Vivi quickly checks on Rip and sees his eyes shining with tears. He looks exactly as he should—as though there is no other woman in the world. There never has been, Vivi thinks with confidence. And never will be.

After the ceremony, Willa and Rip climb into a horse-drawn carriage that will take them to the Field and Oar Club. All the guests are walking over except for Lucinda and Penny Rosen, who are being driven by JP and Amy.

Dennis is busy chatting with Joe DeSantis, so Vivi links her arm through Savannah's. She has strolled the streets of town thousands of times but today is the day of her daughter's wedding, so it feels *distinctive*.

"So far, so good," Savannah says. "Everyone's being civil." She means Amy. She means Dennis.

"Of course," Vivi says. "We're all adults."

Vivi sounds a little more confident than she feels. The ceremony was the easy part; Vivi has reservations about the reception. She resents that JP insisted that Willa hold it at the Field and Oar, a club that didn't readmit Vivi after the divorce. JP and Amy will seem like the hosts when, in fact, Vivi is the one footing the bill.

*High road,* she reminds herself. She prefers life on the high road! The Field and Oar throws a beautiful wedding. Vivi got married there herself.

The family and the wedding party take pictures on the lawn. Vivi is wearing a peach silk slip dress which is maybe a touch sexy for a fifty-year-old mother of the bride, but it's nowhere near as attention-grabbing as what Amy has on. She's in an amethyst column dress with a neckline that plunges nearly to the navel and shows an eye-popping amount of skin. Amy seems to regret her choice of dress; she tugs and adjusts, smiles awkwardly, then tugs and adjusts some more. Eventually, she disappears, and when she returns, the neckline has been clumsily secured with a safety pin.

Cocktails and hors d'oeuvres. Vivi takes mental snapshots: Savannah leaning forward as she slurps an oyster out of its shell so she doesn't drip on her dress; Leo, Cruz, Marissa, and Jasmine posing for a picture while Peter Bridgeman lifts his mother's sea breeze off a table and takes a surreptitious sip, Tink Bonham laughing with Gordy and Amelia Hastings and saying, "I bet Willa will be pregnant by the end of the month!"

Dinner. The prime rib and Duchess potatoes are served with three spears of white asparagus and caramelized brussels sprouts; the plate is garnished with nasturtium blossoms. Vivi nibbles on one; it's peppery. This wedding has taken a year to plan and is costing...yeah, a lot. Vivi leaves the dinner table to visit with people and make a pit stop at the bar. They're serving only wine with dinner, and Vivi wants tequila, specifically Casa Dragones. The club doesn't carry it, so Vivi dropped off a bottle earlier that morning.

She has just received her glass when someone joins her at the bar: Zach Bridgeman.

"Maker's Mark on the rocks, please," he says to the bartender. To Vivi, he says, "First of all, gorgeous wedding. Thank you."

"You're very welcome," Vivi says.

"Second, I have a book recommendation for you. Have you read *Hamnet,* by Maggie O'Farrell?"

"It's on my pile!" Vivi says. "I have one for you too." Vivi sips her tequila and—ahhhhhh—instantly feels better. "*Sea Wife,* by Amity Gaige. It's told in split points of view, the wife and the journal entries of the husband—"

They're interrupted by Pamela, who is looking a bit severe in a high-concept black dress with an asymmetrical neckline and hemline. Frankly, it looks like a kindergartner took scissors to her dress.

"Trying to steal my date?" Pamela says. "You'd better keep your eye on your own."

"Wait," Vivi says. "What?" She peers into the ballroom to see Dennis standing with his wineglass aloft. He's giving a toast. Vivi can't quite hear him but his wild arm gestures are alarming. Vivi sees Gordy Hastings, who is sitting at Lucinda's table, bow his head and frown at the napkin in his lap. Gordy Hastings, Vivi knows, is the person responsible for not letting Vivi back into the club after her divorce.

She supposes he is now congratulating himself on that decision.

*Dennis, sit down!* she thinks. She hurries up the back stairs to the secret second-floor bathroom. Vivi had instructed Dennis to relax and have fun. There was nothing to be gained from going head to head with JP in the father-figure department. What would make him think it was remotely appropriate to give a toast? She notices he waited until Vivi was away from the table. That can hardly be accidental.

Vivi feels tears gather and she tries to calm herself—today is Willa's day, not hers, and Willa might have been touched by Dennis's toast; who knows? Vivi plucks a tissue from the box by the sinks and is carefully dabbing at the corners of her eyes—her makeup!—when Marissa emerges from one of the stalls. Marissa is wearing a white lace dress that is vaguely bridal-looking.

"Are you okay, Vivi?" she asks. She gives Vivi a concerned look in the mirror.

"Overcome," Vivi says. "I'm just so happy."

It's time for the first dances. Willa and Rip dance to Ed Sheeran's "Castle on the Hill," and then the bandleader invites "the parents of the bride and groom" to join the happy couple. Vivi knew this was coming but she still finds she's unprepared. She has been giving Dennis the cold shoulder since getting back from the ladies' room and she has no idea where he is now. She supposes she'll have to go find him; Tink and Chas Bonham are already rising from their seats.

Before Vivi can turn around to search the room for Dennis, JP approaches her with his arm outstretched.

*Plot twist!* Vivi thinks. She had assumed JP would dance with Amy and that she would dance with Dennis. But this is better. This is...correct. She and JP are Willa's parents.

Vivi takes JP's hand, and once the two of them are on the floor, the band segues into "Stay Together," by Al Green—which is oh so ironic—and Vivi and JP fall into the familiar rhythm of their married dancing past.

"Thank you, Vivi," JP says. "This wedding is top-notch, everyone has been commenting, and I couldn't have done it without you."

*Or at all,* Vivi thinks. But she just says, "You're welcome. I'm happy for Willie and Rip."

"Do you remember when we picked them up from the Boys and Girls Club after they went to the Valentine's Day dance together?"

"They were holding hands," Vivi says. "I thought you were going to drop-kick Rip out to the street."

"Before he got out of the car that night, he kissed her," JP says. "Their first kiss, and we were sitting right up front."

"Do you remember what she said on the way home?" Vivi asks.

"She said she wanted to marry him," JP says. He takes a breath. "And here we are—what, twelve years later? At their wedding."

"We've been through a lot in those twelve years," Vivi says.

"You wrote six more books," JP says. "And I blew through two businesses before the Cone."

Yes, first the yacht-concierge business failed, then the wineshop—exactly as Vivi had warned him they would. Who had suggested an ice cream shop? Vivi. There were so many times Vivi felt she was the only engine moving the family forward. She dealt with the girls fighting, she took Leo off-island to lacrosse camp and fielded the call when he was homesick, she attended the parent-teacher conferences and read all the books the kids had been assigned for English class. When the family hamster, Mr. Busy, died, JP had been on a wine-buying trip, sipping cabernets in Napa. *And then you fell in love with your employee and you broke up our family,* Vivi thinks. But she won't mention any of this because she prefers life on the high road.

Al Green croons, *Loving you whether, whether, times are good or bad, happy or sad...*

Better memories swirl around Vivi then. JP sitting on the side of the bathtub holding out the ring box. JP in scrubs and a shower cap while Willa was being born. And then Carson. And then Leo. JP standing on a ladder outside the house in Surfside, stringing up the Christmas lights. JP and Vivi fretting when Leo spiked a 104 degree fever from a double ear infection. JP and Vivi sitting at the bar at 21 Federal the night that Savannah insisted on having all three kids to the house on Union Street for a sleepover (she only made that mistake once) and then getting so drunk that they stumbled over to the Rose and Crown to sing karaoke. JP and Vivi watching the Patriots and high-fiving every time Danny Woodhead scored a touchdown. Sailing on *Arabesque*, watching fireworks from Lucinda's front yard, grilling on the beach at Fortieth Pole, attending God knows how many cocktail parties where they would spiral away from each other to socialize then spiral back to check in until one of them whispered, "Beat feet," their code for *Let's get out of here.* They would always stop at Stubby's on the way home for fried chicken sliders and waffle fries; whatever dress Vivi was wearing would inevitably get stuffed into the dry-cleaning bag stained with ketchup.

Speaking of the dry cleaner's, Vivi thinks of the first moment she ever laid eyes on this man and how excited she'd felt. Finally, a cute guy her own age, there at the dry cleaner's! Jackie Paper.

JP notices Vivi gazing up at him and he holds her a little tighter and bends down to whisper in her ear. "Vivi," he says. "I'm sorry."

Ever so briefly, Vivi rests her head against his chest. The song is almost over. "It's okay," she says. "I forgive you."

Martha shows up as the sun is setting on Monday afternoon. It's Labor Day, a day Vivi has always thought of as the saddest of the year. There are plenty of people on Nantucket who relish the sight of SUVs packed to within inches of the roof with luggage and trunks, surfboards strapped to the top and bicycles hanging off the back, lining up to drive onto the ferry. But it fills Vivi with melancholy. These people are headed back to their real lives— haircuts and school shoes, leaves to rake and burn, football games to attend. Kids are going back to college; summer romances are breaking up.

"Vivian," Martha says. She's once again in administrative mode, holding her clipboard, wearing her drugstore reading glasses. "It's time."

"You told me I could watch for the summer," Vivian says. "September is still summer."

"I said Labor Day, Vivian."

Did she? Vivi can't remember, to be honest.

"I don't want to go," Vivi says. "I want to stay where I can see my kids. I want to know they're going to be okay."

"You've given them everything they need," Martha says. "It's time for them to learn to live without you."

"But there are so many things left unresolved," Vivi says. "I want to know if Carson and Marshall stay together. I want to make sure Leo gets settled at college. I want to see if Savannah and JP hook up. Is Lorna going to be okay? And what about Penny Rosen? That chest pain didn't sound good." Vivi swallows. "I want to meet my grandchild, Martha. Just let me stay until he's born, and then I'll go without complaint."

"I'm not negotiating with you, Vivian."

"I just need a few more chapters. Please, Martha." How can Vivi possibly leave the greenroom with its Parsley Snips paint and fun striped wallpaper, a place that has been, if not heaven, then a haven where Vivi could still be a part of things? She can tell from Martha's expression that there won't be an extension—and so Vivi will have to draw on her faith. Martha has been both an angel and a shepherd; she has guided and advised Vivi well. She's an extraordinary Person; Vivi couldn't have asked for better.

Vivi thinks about how she likes to end her own books. She sets her characters down safely and walks away. She doesn't like to tie up every loose end neat and pretty with a bow.

Even so, she's hesitant.

"There are people in the choir you'll want to see," Martha says.

Vivi highly doubts this. "Oh yeah? Who?"

"Your father."

Vivi sucks in her breath. "My father is in the choir?"

"He is." She smiles. "Apparently, he has quite the baritone."

Vivi's eyes blur with tears. "Did he ever watch me?"

"He did," Martha says. "He even used a nudge."

"My father used a nudge with me?" Vivi says. She would assume that Martha is kidding, but of course, Martha doesn't kid. Vivi racks her brain. Her father didn't keep her from lying to Brett about being pregnant. Her father didn't make her first novel an overnight, runaway success, which could have happened back in 2000 if he'd nudged Oprah to take *The Dune Daughters* with her when she went to Hawaii. "What was it?"

Martha checks her clipboard. "He made sure you went to college without any shampoo," she says.

*"What?"* Vivi says. Then...she gets it. Vivi had to ask Savannah for shampoo; she and Savannah became friends; Savannah took Vivi to Nantucket—*where she met JP, got married, had three children, and wrote thirteen novels!*

"Yes," Martha says. "That's what we call a Rube Goldberg nudge."

"What about my mother?" Vivi asks. "Will I see her?"

"She does what I do," Martha says. "She's a Person—in the Devout Catholic division."

*Ha!* Vivi thinks. Of course she is.

"You'll see her coming and going," Martha says.

"All right," Vivi says. "I'm ready." She turns back to the open wall for one last look. Carson, Willa, and Savannah are sitting around the island at the Union Street house, designing Vivi's headstone.

*Vivian Rose Howe 1969–2021*
*Mother—Writer—Friend*

Underneath, they have chosen a Camus quote:

*In the midst of winter, I found there was, within me, an*
*invincible summer.*

"Do you think it's too long?" Willa asks.

"It's perfect, Angel Bear," Savannah says. "Trust me. This quote defines Vivi."

*Yes,* Vivi thinks. *Yes.*

"Is there any way I could come back from time to time?" Vivi asks. "Maybe check in on them?"

"What have I told you, Vivian?" Martha says. "Never say never."

*Never say never!* Vivi thinks. This feels close to a yes.

"Come along," Martha says, offering a hand. "I'll walk you down."

Vivi clasps Martha's hand and they head through the green door into a tunnel made of clouds. It's not so bad, Vivi thinks. It's pretty. Peaceful. She's looking forward to the Heavenly Banquet.

"I wish I could write a book about all of this," Vivi says. "You, me, the Beyond, the greenroom, the choir, the nudges, the Hermès scarves..."

Martha shakes her head.

"What about an Instagram post, then?" Vivi says. "It can mysteriously appear on my feed. A picture of you and me with the caption *It's all going to be okay*."

Martha laughs. "Oh, Vivian," she says.

# Acknowledgments

The idea for this novel came from four people, and I'd like to start by acknowledging them.

As some of you know, my father, Robert H. Hilderbrand Jr., was killed in a plane crash in 1985 when I was sixteen, which was the event that cleaved my life in two. I have long suspected that my dad has been watching over me all these many years and has been instrumental not only in nudging me along in this incredible career but also in keeping me safe during my breast cancer journey.

I was diagnosed with breast cancer in 2014 and in October of that year I faced a life-threatening infection that required me to be flown by helicopter from Nantucket Cottage Hospital to Boston Medical Center. Before I left, a nurse suggested I have someone pull my children out of school and bring them to the hospital so I could say goodbye to them. That, my friends, was a sobering moment. I told my kids that no matter what happened, I would always be with them.

If you've read the novel, you can probably understand how these two experiences led me to this book.

By way of thanks, I must start with the brilliant woman who edited this novel, the great Judy Clain. Judy brought out the book's very best elements and cut all that distracted. I am grateful for and in awe of her sharp eye, her attention to detail, and her deep reservoir of emotional intelligence.

Thank you to my agents, Michael Carlisle and David Forrer, who are my steadfast champions and my safe place in publishing. They are my family and I will never leave them either!

Thank you to everyone at Little, Brown, including (but not limited to) Miya Kumangai, Gabriella Leopardi, Ashley Marudas, Lauren Hesse, Brandon Kelly, my incredible publicist Katharine Myers, Tracy Roe, Jayne Yaffe Kemp, Terry Adams, Craig Young, Karen Torres, Bruce Nichols, Michael Pietsch, and the incomparable Mario Pulice, who designs all my covers. All I do is write the books. The rest of the magic happens in these capable hands.

Thank you to the Facebook Group "The Memories of Growing Up in Parma, Ohio." I found all of your reminiscences from the 1980s so helpful. Any Parma-related errors are mine alone.

Thank you to my work husband, Tim Ehrenberg, who sat with me in the basement at Mitchell's Book Corner for endless hours. Tim took photos and videos, came up with giveaways and promotions; he personally labeled mailers and dealt with the remarkable (and remarkably overworked) people at the USPS. In the era of COVID-19, a writer's best friend is her local independent bookstore, and I want to thank not only Tim but Cristina, Suzanne, Sue, and their fearless leader, Wendy Hudson. Nantucket Book Partners is my home.

Thank you to my family, especially my sister, Heather Osteen Thorpe, who is—quite simply—my Person. I owe her an Hermès scarf because she's in charge!

To the people who make my world go round: Chuck and Margie Marino, Rebecca Bartlett, Debbie Briggs, Wendy Hudson, Wendy Rouillard, Elizabeth Almodobar, Mark and Gwenn Snider, Evelyn and Matthew MacEachern, Katie Norton, Sue Decoste, Linda Holliday, Jane Deery, Deb Gfeller, Deb Ramsdell, Jeannie Esti, Melissa Long, Manda Riggs, David Rattner and Andrew Law, West Riggs (always my sailing consultant), Michelle Birmingham, Aleks Orbison, Christina Schwefel, my Peloton Moms Book Group, and the greatest Peloton instructor of them all, Jenn Sherman (thank you for getting me through the long months of quarantine in good shape). Thank you to Alex Small for allowing me to be his second mom. Thank you to Timothy Field—you rise for me in the east, set in the west, and shine for me every darn day.

Last, I want to thank my children: Maxwell, Dawson, and Shelby Cunningham. My love for you is wondrous and eternal. I will never leave you. I'll be up above, watching you from the boho-chic greenroom of my dreams. Trust.

## About the Author

Elin Hilderbrand is the proud mother of three, a dedicated Peloton rider, an aspiring book influencer, and an enthusiastic cook (follow her on Instagram to watch the Cringe Cooking Show). She's also a grateful seven-year breast cancer survivor. *Golden Girl* is her twenty-seventh novel.